ECHO CYCLE

Also available from Patrick Ewards and Titan Books

Ruin's Wake

ECHO CYCLE

PATRICK EDWARDS

TITAN BOOKS

Echo Cycle
Print edition ISBN: 9781785658815
E-book edition ISBN: 9781785658822

Published by Titan Books
A division of Titan Publishing Group Ltd
144 Southwark Street, London SE1 0UP
www.titanbooks.com

First edition: March 2020
10 9 8 7 6 5 4 3 2 1

A CIP catalogue record for this title is available from the British Library.

Printed and bound by CPI Group (UK) Ltd, Croydon CR0 4YY.

For Aurelia

Before

The day I went missing. That's where I'll start. Keep up.

Remember that flight into Rome? I do. It stank of peanuts and old farts. I was relieved when we touched down at Ciampino that I was the first off. Easter was his predictable self, yelling 'Monk's going to puke!', his idiot coterie guffawing along. I wasn't sick from the flight (I was just pale back then) but I had a dry mouth and Italy was outside. The terminal was dusty in the corners where no one had bothered to sweep it up and the ceiling tiles were browned and cracked. Every one of the dozen automatic gates was out of order, so we were stuck with the resentful eyes of a bored border guard, contemptuous as he flicked his eyes from my passport to me, then back again. Stupid hat like a gabled roof, but I kept my opinions out of my face because I didn't want my first day in the Eternal City to be in an immigration holding room. He looked to be the touchy kind.

Did your father ever question why a rich school spent so little on its boys? Mine would have put it down to making us strong. He was full of shit. We didn't even get the good flights that went to the new airport where things worked. No wonder the guard looked so pissed off.

The baggage carousel sat still for what felt like an hour

underneath a faded poster declaring *Benvenuti a Roma*, the Divine Augustus looking like he'd rather be standing anywhere else; two thousand years of majesty and gravitas undone by a half-arsed tourist-board committee from before the Confederacy.

It's not there anymore, Ciampino Airport. A relic of the old times, the whole lot of it from terminal to airstrip went the way of the bulldozer. But you already know that, don't you?

The carousel started up like it was being tortured. Bags were birthed through the flapping rubber strips in flurries, the baggage handlers no doubt going for a smoke between each load. Mine was almost the last which, of course, Easter and his crew found hilarious; it caught on some stray edge as I tried to haul it off, just as I stepped in a puddle of Coke or orange juice or piss, and before I knew it I was on my backside with my case half on top of me. The morons hooted like they'd blow the tops off their heads and I wished, lusted, for a magic red button that would make them cease to be.

The coach sped us from the airport at breakneck pace, the driver (bald on top, forearms of a gorilla) carving in and out of traffic, impervious to honks from other vehicles. He gave as good as he got, Italian swearing drifting over the musty seatbacks with their gum-crusted ex-ashtrays. The jerks and veers had my stomach roiling and I just wished I could get out and walk.

Not even a view, I thought, a wonderland of antiquity hidden behind flyover-underpass concrete sides. I could have been on any highway, anywhere in the world. I resolved to play a game, fixing my gaze on the outside and not allowing my eyes to budge, prohibiting them from following anything as we sped along. The concrete and metal became a monochrome blur.

A flash of brightness, like a gap in dentures. Another. Openness.

The city stretched out and I saw vaulted roofs, higgledy-piggledy tower blocks crushed together in clumps, dotted in between soaring facades, encolumned and engraved. Beyond, in the far distance, the skeletons of huge towers and the cranes building them stood in silhouette against a sky of dull, weak gold that illuminated but seemed to touch nothing. The vista was a postcard, a scale model, but I was electrified. This was where the great men of the world walked.

Something hit me on the back of the head.

Scrunched-up paper from a magazine, its glossed surface scarred by creases. In the back row, Easter and his fellow twats had adopted a thick silence, doing a terrible job of not gurning; a piggy one, Baden-Moncrief, I think, let out a snort.

Easter caught my eye. 'Wh*at*?' he cried, all mock outrage on the inflection.

On cue the others dissolved into fits. I had a flash of a fantasy: me, a claw hammer and the balls to use it. It passed; I was an angry boy but worrying about my future made me meek.

I knew the dance well: the charade was what he wanted, the play-act of it all that would get me flustered and wrong-footed. *Not today*, I thought, not here. Before the *no-I-didn't*s and the *shut-up-you-fucking-nerd*s could even get warmed up, I moved several rows forwards, hopefully out of range. On the way I passed Miliband Best – short, dull of eye and cursed with the only Lefty parents in the whole school. Another outcast (not that it was a club or anything – it was every man for themselves) and an unfortunate creature: bad at Games, didn't play an instrument and, to boot, thick as pig shit. He'd been the only one in the year to take a paper that covered all three sciences in one and barely scraped that; Daddy was an Old Boy with a chequebook, so Quintus made it back in to the Lower Sixth but I bet he wished he hadn't.

I remember thinking: *At least I know I'm clever; what does that poor fucker have?* I know. We're all wankers when we're young, and me more than most.

The vacant seat next to him was emptiness given mass. I mean, calling a child *Miliband* in that day and age, when things were already turning sour and lonely for anyone without an Albion Party membership. Not a snowball's chance.

The unlucky Millie was, by my forward move, made next in line to bear the brunt of the back row's 'games' – you remember that the law of our jungle was that someone had to occupy the last rung on the shitty pyramid. I earned a look that said *Thanks, dick* and I tried to look apologetic, but I think my face just came out looking shifty.

I dumped myself into an empty pair of seats and pressed my nose against the glass. Outside, the city had fled again.

True to form, the boarding house was a rickety, vertical refuse pile – I think you said something about it being little better than our dorms back at school. That narrow trench of street, where the sky was a pale slit; we were ushered through a set of gates, up a cracked driveway almost entirely plugged by an ancient van, then through a set of double doors. The round-shouldered woman with a wild nest of hair and triangular glasses perched atop her hook nose cast baleful looks at us as we trooped past.

My room, it was announced, was on the second floor. I was to share it with five others. *Like we're back in the third-form dorms for fuck's sake*, I remember thinking.

By the time I reached the landing my breath burned in my chest and my bag was pulling my shoulder out of joint – I wasn't sound of body in those days. Through a slit window

I gazed down through the empty well of space at the core of the building; each floor was its own stratum, concrete and brick mixed with not even an eye on continuity. Before I could consider it, I was shoved in the back, my name tossed at me like a swearword.

In the dorm room a single window looked out on grey concrete. My bed was creaky and lumpy. Even as I dropped my bag, from behind me came a sound of pure, manifest revulsion. Easter had a look on his face that said he'd been dealt the most monstrous injustice, being put in with us losers: me, Fatty Lamb, Quintus Best, your good self and one of the Thai Bobs. I was just glad that I wasn't the outnumbered one for once.

'This is a bloody outrage,' he said, all nostrils. 'You'd better keep your hands to yourself, Monk.' He made a limp wrist at me, then shooed Fatty off the bed the furthest away from me. When he hesitated, the poor lad received a thump on his fleshy arm for good measure and he went to claim another bed, mumbling threats we all knew he'd never carry out.

I slid my suitcase under the bed, avoiding Easter's eye, remembering the fifth form when we got our own rooms and his had been next door. Waking in the dark, early one morning, seeing the outline of him next to my bed, his dick in his hand. I never told you, and I never bothered to tell the Chaplain; the dead look on his face scared the shit out of me and he was alone – this wasn't some prank. I threw a lamp at him, and we all know what happened next. I was the one who'd snuck into his room. I was the mucky little bender. It had always been bad, but it got worse after that.

As the room went quiet save for the sound of boys unpacking, I knew the others were worried about stray hands in the night, and they weren't thinking about mine.

* * *

Rome. I wanted nothing more than to throw myself headlong into it: oldest of places, nexus of life and learning and war and death and art. I'd *dreamed* of it for years and years at the back of dusty classrooms as dullards and cretins with an eye on nothing but Daddy's business leaned back in their chairs, while equally bored masters droned out the life and times of the Gracchi or the bleating of M.T. Cicero. I'd been somewhere else. I'd been *here*. I soaked up every story I could, every book in the library. Soldiers, butchers, emperors and slaves; I'd breathed in Rome and exhaled Rome, carving its streets and palaces and theatres into my mind, building its topography from pictures in worn textbooks, sculpting the contours from the words of Ovid and Catullus. History was not *history* here, at least it wasn't for me. It was – is – the living, beating heart of pasts that refused to die. And here I was.

Well, not exactly. We were on the road again before long.

Doing their level best to cram as much into the time we had, our caretaker teachers had booked the trip to Pompeii that very day, with the smell of the airline barely gone from our nostrils. We were a hungry and truculent bunch by now (though I recall you'd managed to snaffle a chocolate bar from somewhere, which you shared) and Mr Oswald and Miss Boniface had given up on trying to sell the trip to us; I could see them dreading the long drive as much as we were. Two hundred and forty minutes on winding roads that all led away from the city instead of towards it.

Oswald, who had me for Latin, had been confused by my sour expression when I got back on the coach. Likely, he'd expected me to be champing to get to a few ruins but I had other things on my mind, like being tired and pissed off by Easter who'd already started holding court in our room and making it unbearable. I hadn't wanted to bring it up because, as Father always said, 'No one likes a moaner,' so I didn't.

'Why so glum, Monk?' he'd asked. He'd just had a cigarette and was chipper. 'Thought you'd be made up.'

'I am, sir.' Flat.

'Well, you don't look it. Best-preserved site in the country, Monk! All sorts, just lying around as they went. You'll see, it'll be great!'

'Yes, sir,' I intoned and he lost patience with me, waving me on.

I was being a sour little fucker, I can't deny. There was plenty to look forward to on the other side of that long drive. What's not to like about a town that got swallowed by a volcano? Women clutching babies, houses with intact plumbing, all of that shit. If I put my mind to it, I decided after the first hour, the bones of this provincial town could give me a flavour of life in Caesar's Rome, though it could never – in my adolescent mind – live up to the big shebang. Rome, you see, still had a beating heart and it was that I longed to see.

Gods, the bliss of ignorance.

I managed to get some shut-eye and came to when I felt the vibration of the coach change underneath me. We'd pulled into a wide parking lot where we disembarked, most of the others showing the bleary eyes of sleep barely snatched. A little café crowded one end of the open area with white plastic tables and faded blue Orangina umbrellas. A squat, marbled building was at the other end. Above the entryway, a sign greeted us in Italian, English, German, Japanese and – a sign of the change that was already happening in Europe – Latin. It proclaimed the entrance to the ancient city of Pompeii just through the automatic glass doors. A few other tourists mooched about under spindly trees and the sun beat down, wringing sweat from our pores. I was still dressed for England in worsted trousers and though I'd left my blazer back in Rome my back felt moist all the way down to the crack of my arse.

Oswald and Boniface marshalled us. I saw shelves of trinkets and glass-topped counters through the doors and heard the thrum of air con. To enter this wondrous jewel of the ancient world, we had first to pass through the gift shop.

We had ten minutes to ourselves when the coach dropped us back in Rome before dinner. Most of the boys filtered into the boarding house to crash on beds and unpack, but I went searching for coffee. My feet were sore and my neck was burnt – I always thought I could get away with it until the continental sun reminded my Anglo-Saxon skin otherwise.

I'd seen the 'bodies', of course, in their death poses, put on show for us tourists. They looked just like people who lay down for a sleep, but I couldn't feel sorrow or revulsion or shock. No matter how much I stared at them – just a pane of glass between my face and the lumpy ruin of theirs – knowing this was the very pose of a person who died in fear, I couldn't attach humanity to it: they were the sediment deposits in a chunk of cooled lava where a life had been. The life itself was nothing now. Easter and his idiots went in for selfies, loving the transgression, but it only made them look bigger idiots: geology had had its fun and these humanoid shapes were beyond mockery now. They might as well have taken the piss out of a mountain.

Ahh, but the other stuff got me, though. Little things, real signs of life like a restored mosaic floor or segments of wall still ochre with paint that had lasted the long, buried centuries. Stepping stones across deep-set roads. At one point I found what could only have been a tavern, with an actual bar and slots for amphorae and I think I got a little choked up. I didn't show it, old boy, but I did have a soul.

Most of the city was reserved for academics, leaving juicy titbits to get the tourists in – the odd temple, a bathhouse, assorted courtyards where the columns had been levered upright, Corinthian leaf still standing proud. The whorehouse was a hotspot, because everyone enjoys a good leer. A narrow passage with tiny cubicles leading off, each 'room' fitted with a concrete shelf and a nude fresco painted over the door. I'd seen a young couple in one of the rooms making those bunny-ears with their hands and grinning, probably on the precise spot where girls and boys were roughly fucked by dozens of men in the course of a single night. I didn't spend much time there – it had the flavour of walking over graves.

Boniface had been looking thoroughly scorched by the time she shepherded us towards the exit. I'd tried to snatch a few winks on the coach, but anyone who's ever done that will know it only leaves you feeling irritable, drool-flecked and more tired than when you started.

Coffee. We were in Italy, after all!

All I found was a minimart with one of those self-dispensing, automatic machines. I didn't even get to try out my smattering of Italian on the pretty boy behind the till. Smooth chest, thick lips.

It might have been from a machine, but the coffee was dark and sweet and damned good – nothing like the watered-down dregs from home. A few minutes of sipping it in the open air and I felt some life dripping back into me. It was quiet here in the late afternoon, fresh and clear despite the narrowness of the street and nearby traffic murmured, a reminder of the timeless metropolis within arm's reach. Tomorrow, I told myself, tomorrow I would dive in. Get through dinner, share a room with the nemesis, then the city would be mine. I'd place my feet on the same stones as those walked on by Caesars. Oswald had hinted there might be a free evening towards the end of the trip – off-the-record-not-to-be-mentioned-to-parents-if-you-know-what-I-mean. Freedom, for one evening. Who knew what might happen?

Then, home, said my mind, planning the future. A few exams, then an uncle had promised me a paltry wage in his bookshop. Then it would be time to pack up and off to George's College. I'd only been to Cambridge once, for the interviews, but I'd decided it was my sort of town: lush vines framing arched windows, a hundred courtyards and tiny wooden doors polished by history. Immaculate quads, deep leather armchairs and those wide lawns dropping down to the Cam. That single day of interviews had stuck with me. Less traffic than Oxford and less fumes, the spaces seeming more open. Maybe it was just the prospect of somewhere new that tantalised, but to me Cambridge seemed ancient and beautiful and yet alive.

Dinner wasn't bad, as it turned out. The bespectacled woman who ran the place cared about food in the way all Italians should, because the baskets that dotted the long table were filled with fresh, warm bread, and the pasta and ragù was meaty, wholesome. I didn't know if it was beef or pork and I didn't care. After the day we'd had, all were ravenous and even the worst of the idiots kept quiet as they shovelled the stuff into their mouths.

I mopped up my plate and said 'No, *grazie mille*' to the woman as she offered up seconds from an enormous, steaming serving dish. She was big and her hair could have been wound into a fence to keep out intruders, but the look on her face feeding all those boys was one of quiet contentment. For a moment I wondered how many kids of her own she had, if she missed cooking for them. When she smiled at me it was warm. I earned a throaty *'Prego'*.

Easter shot from his seat, struck a pose, and in a cod opera voice sang a drawn-out *'Nograzymillyeeeee!'*

Our hostess's face resumed its glower.

Easter caught my viperish look and did his usual *'Wha*t?'*

'Stop being a wanker,' I told him.

'Says the one sucking up to the locals.' He did a shitty Marlon Brando, thumb pressed to forefinger and cheeks blown out. *'Iyaaa lika de pasda, sinyora.'*

'I'm being polite.'

'You're being a fucking geek.' His boyband guffawed to his satisfaction and I knew from the smirk on his face that he didn't need to be reasonable to win.

My chest felt tight and my fingers clenched and I heard Father telling me Not To Take Any Rubbish, but Easter was bigger than me, had backup, and besides I knew that if I threw a punch now I'd be hauled up in front of the headmaster when we got back; what if that got back to George's College? Would they take a dim view of prospective students who brawled over pasta? I swallowed hard and looked down at my bowl, drowned by the gleeful triumph emanating from the other side of the table, feeling every titter and snort like a knife in the ribs and hating, *hating* myself for not just socking him one right there and despising my logical, sensible, coward brain.

A presence behind me, and I was sure it was the hostess back for more and I felt myself turning to lash out at her even though it wasn't her fault. The sight of brown corduroys and brogues stopped me.

'Eat up, Easter,' said Oswald, his brow furrowed. 'Save the theatrics for the football pitch, eh?'

Easter became sullen, firing a poison look down the table at Fatty Lamb, who'd let out an explosive snort of laughter.

'Monk,' he says to me, 'would you come please?' He saw my expression, then followed up with, 'You're not in trouble, I just have some news. Come on, you look like you've finished.'

I stepped out from the bench, feeling eyes on my back and followed Oswald out of the room, past a separate table for two where Boniface sat alone, scanning her phone with a look of pure boredom.

Oswald led me to what might enthusiastically be called a 'lobby', a corner by the reception desk big enough for two moth-eaten chairs and a glass table that might once have been clear. There was a fold-scarred copy of *Time* magazine, the cover a torn Union Jack drowning in heavy seas. '*La caduta finale dell'impero britannico*', read the headline; remember those days just after the second vote – the world was still reeling from our determination to become hermits? The drawbridge wasn't up yet, but the chains were being oiled even then. Oswald regained my attention with his cough-splutter and I took the seat his proffered hand suggested.

'I had some mail from home. From the school, that is,' he begins. His eyes don't settle on anything. The two yellowed fingers of his left hand skittered over his brown corduroy knee, absently brushing away imaginary flecks.

'Sir.' A fine catch-all of a word for dealing with teachers. An exclamation-confirmation-interrogative and more besides. It seemed to do the trick because he continued.

'Cambridge have come back with an answer. I have it here, but I haven't opened the attachment. I thought you might.' He handed me his phone.

The black screen reflected my eager face. In one corner a minute spider-web crack blossomed, showing the thing's age.

A brown leather cover (what else?) folded underneath. I'd seen a girl in Pompeii earlier that day, twirling her fingers in the air as if casting spells, though likely checking her media feed or calling a friend – the imbed models hadn't made it to Britain, leaving us a dwindling stock of ancient hand-helds such as this one.

I touched the screen and it whitened. The mail was from the school's second master, but the text whirled past in a haze of unimportance as I sought the attachment at the bottom and jabbed at it.

Document loading. *This is it.*

Document loading. *They have to admit me. I've done the work.*

One hurdle down, on to the next. The plan I'd coveted, shaped, polished was like a path stretching in front of me, the first cobble inscribed with the name of George's College, Cambridge. Study, research, deep archives where I'd rarely see the sun and wouldn't care. Loud girls in crowded, wooden pubs and quiet smiles from other quiet boys that cut through the noise like black thread on a white cloth. Hiding it, illegal and so exquisite, pretending to the whole world that we're the closest of chums until we're alone and lips meet lips and skin brushes skin. Always back to the work, though, whatever subject I'm led to because at the end of it is the star in the crown – the Cambridge Postgraduate Exchange, the only remaining cross-border research programme between Europe and Britain: maligned by the establishment, a politically acid thing that teetered on the brink of extinction every time Parliament drew a breath from riots in the North. A five-year transition period had been announced the day after the results came in, lessons learned after the last debacle, just enough time for me to earn my place, get out from under the eye of what home was becoming. Residency after a few years, followed by citizenship. Goodbye, Old Blighty, and all who sail in you.

Document loaded.

Dear Mr Monk, it read.

The Admissions Committee, together with the Master of Prince George's College, have convened to review your application to read for a BA in Anglo-Saxon, Latin and Greek.

My fingers sweated and my brow ached and my eyes didn't dare blink.

There were a large number of excellent candidates this year, and unfortunately this means that we are unable to offer you a place in the upcoming 2051 semester.

In that instant, I weighed thirty-five stone. I hovered over the mouth of a black hole, the bottom some sickening distance away. My eyes were raw, my hands clenched. Something clattered nearby but I didn't see it, didn't care.

'Here, here, Monk. Careful with that,' said a voice from a million miles away. I realised I'd dropped his precious phone and he'd scooped it up, running his thumbs over the screen to check for cracks. 'Well, what did it say, boy?'

'It...' my voice barely crawled from under its disgraced rock. 'It was a no, sir.'

Oswald huffed, still cross about the phone. 'Well... unlucky.' He must have seen my face then, bloodless, because his tone mellowed. 'Lots more places for you to try, good student like you. Exeter, Bristol, my old school, Durham—'

'I don't *want* fucking Durham!' The words fired out, petulant, the whiny child inside of me taking the opportunity to have charge of my brain while the rest is busy kicking itself to death in a corner.

Oswald's dry lips made a sort of 'W' shape of disgust. 'Language, Monk, if you please!'

'Sir,' I muttered, the rejection searing through my eyes, down every nerve. 'Sir, I think I'd like to get an early bedtime, if it's alright with you.'

'Well, you'll miss the Neapolitan, but I suppose...' He waved his hand at the stairs, permitting.

I mumbled a 'Thank you, sir' as I stumbled on legs of meringue. He patted me on the arm as I passed, a clumsy conciliation.

'Chin up, Monk. These things are sent to try us, eh?'

I refrained from picking up the over-flowing, heavy glass ashtray by his side and braining him with it, turning murder into a nod.

Every upwards step was lumpen, a struggle against gravity. Upstairs, I wanted to curl up under my thin blanket and sleep. I wished I was back in the womb, a mass of cells without thought, ambition, or expectations. Instead I just lay there, staring at the wall, Father's voice telling me to pull myself together, Be A Man About It. I imagined his face when I'd tell him that his only son, already effete and spindly for his liking, a drop-out from the Cadets and terrible at rugger, doesn't even have the wherewithal to secure a place at his old college. I hated myself for feeling guilty about disappointing him, loathed the base need in me to please a man who had only ever sneered at my achievements. Mother would be a wafting, conciliatory shade who breezed in and said something trite before leaving; she did so hate confrontation.

How had this happened?

I cracked open the single dormitory window, letting in a waft of heated evening Roman air that smelled of cigarettes and gasoline. Through a narrow gap between two pitched roofs I could see just a slither of the Eternal City – I'd visit tomorrow at the tail end of some dull tour party, but now would never call home. The intoxicating flash of tomorrows were twisted beyond recognition; a mockery of a life laid out before me: a second-rate college in a second-rate town where they Don't Like Your Kind Round Here, watched like a hawk by the local police because people talk. Maybe get a girl pregnant just to fit in and then meaningless, daily toil in some unimportant, vapid job that carried me on its back to retirement, pension, old age and death.

How could they do this to me? Those ancient *cunts*.

The door banged open. Easter and his goons came bustling in halfway through a joke, their eyes wide and mouths half sneering. They clocked me at once, and that look came to their eyes – the same they'd had that time I woke up with Easter egging one of them on to slap his balls on my chin. I was their prey, struggling with one leg caught in the trap.

'Jesus, Monk, don't kill yourself,' burped one of them.

'Doesn't have the stones,' said Easter.

I moved away from the window and went to my bed. I felt something terrible bubbling under my skin – I needed a book and a quiet place for a few hours. Not here, not now.

'Don't ignore me, pansy. What's wrong with you anyway?'

Leave it, my inner voice pleaded. This feeling inside me was frightening me. I could feel the bonds of control snapping one by one. 'Piss off, Easter,' I said to an answering chorus of *Ooooooooh*.

'That's not very nice is it? What's got you so testy?'

I rummaged in my bag, looking for something to distract me. My brow felt hot and my skin tighter than a drum. Behind, I felt the jackals gather for more blood.

'You need to relax, you'll do yourself a mischief,' said Easter. His voice was vulpine.

This feeling: I knew its cousin well, the anger that sits and smoulders when they taunted and called me *bender* and *geek* and *loser.* It was like that, but wilder and boundless and hungry. I didn't know what it would do if it got out and for the first time in my life I prayed, a wordless, directionless entreaty to the universe just to make it stop, make them go away just long enough for me to catch my breath.

'Maybe *this* will help you unwind!' said Easter, and whipped the blanket off my bed with a flourish.

The universe turned, looked me in the eye and gave me the finger.

It was an old magazine, torn at the spine and curling. A smooth man with bronzed skin and sculpted shoulders stared out with glassy eyes. The bulge in his white shorts was enormous. The text was Italian; they must have found it on the top shelf of a news kiosk or something.

'Well, look what we have here!' chimed in one of the chorus, playing his part.

'Nice literature you have there, Monk...'

'Need any help turning the pages? Not sure your wrists'll be up to it...'

'I'd stay clear; you might catch something from him...'

Somewhere in my head was the usual me, the one who could ignore them, but he was buried too deep; I couldn't move my mouth to speak, my jaw locked tight as I stared down at the man candy on the magazine. Easter hadn't said a thing (didn't need to), content to watch his followers pick chunks off me. I looked at him. He looked back. He knew I was beaten and moved in for the kill.

'Come on, Monky-boy,' he said, grabbing my wrist and trying to stick it down my trousers. 'You're so tense, maybe a little wank will mellow you out.'

I pushed him away but it was weak; he cupped me, stopping me from pulling away with a forearm around the back of my neck. 'C'mon now. Nice slick bumboy like that. Get you hard, does it? They're all like you here, you know?'

I pushed again but he was the captain of the 2nd XV and so much stronger. Gods, the smell of his hot breath. They were cheering him on, chanting and hooting like they were watching a show.

'Shame you won't make it back, eh?' he whispered in my ear, giving my cock a squeeze.

I don't know how he knew. Maybe he overheard, maybe one of his bitches.

It was too much.

I smashed my forehead into his nose. He didn't let go so I did it again, hearing it crunch, and felt wetness. He coiled to retaliate but something had snapped and I was out of control, hitting him with everything I had, teeth bared, screaming at the top of my lungs. He might still have had me but he tripped on something and fell backwards, his head smacking a side table. I followed with my full weight behind knees, elbows, fists. He tried to ball but I hammered him again and again and again. It was so sudden that none of them tried to stop me.

He was wet-wheezing when I came to myself. Blood on him, blood on my hands. The others had stepped back, appalled and the silence was an iron weight. It could only have lasted a few seconds but I'd shattered something, reversed some fundamental law of their universe. Easter's breath was a rattle, choked with fluid, and bruises were already flowering all over his face and neck. One eye was nothing more than a bloody ruin, the other stared at me, white with primal terror. Gods, there was so much red.

I've killed him.

I sprinted for the door through molasses-thick silence. In

my haste I slammed into someone, hard; it was you and you were hurt, more blood on me and streaming from your poor nose. Gods, the look of fear in your eyes almost stopped me, almost, but I was already moving fast, out onto the landing, down the stairs. The woman with the wild hair was behind the reception desk and I think she said something to me as I came rushing past. I was already out of the front door and down the side alley by the time I heard Boniface's reedy call.

Outside, the street was quiet and littered with parked scooters and vans. I looked one way, then the other. From my left I felt the call of the city, heard its traffic moan and its lungs exhale. The raw flesh of my bloodied knuckles screamed at me and I was off, not knowing where I'd go or what I'd do, wanting Rome to swallow me whole.

For a while, the walls and streets were blurred nothings, a labyrinth without boundary or form. At one point a car beeped at me and I jumped out of the way, clattering into a cluster of chained bicycles, leaving me with oil stains on the bottoms of my trousers. The car – a taxi that barely fit down this little side street – roared past with a *cazzo!* thrown in my direction and something about that insult, combined with the harsh exhaust fumes, brought me to my senses. I fished my cigarettes from my pocket and lit one, feeling the welcome scrape of the smoke across my throat, scouring my insides.

Did I kill him?

I think I killed him.

My hands shook, making the tip of the cigarette dance. For the first time I realised how dark it was here – no stars above, just a warm glow where the dome of the city's light blanketed the sky. I took another drag.

I needed somewhere to think. I was on the run, and I could do anything I wanted, go anywhere. An odd-won kind of freedom. The butt hissed in a puddle before dying and I was on my way again. The dark street became a wider dark street, which joined on to another even larger. There were signs of life now, and pavement. Passers-by ambled: couples, families, friends out to enjoy the mild night air.

A restaurant had sprouted an awning that straddled the pavement. As I walked through the warm tunnel, diners either side of me going about their lives, a waiter gave me an eyebrow and I was swamped with herbs, butter and garlic, then the sweetness of cooked meat flooded my mouth with saliva. On any other night I would have taken a table and stayed there until dawn if they'd let me, soaking it all up, but I needed something else, somewhere quiet. I left that temple of noise and company behind.

There was something big ahead – I could feel it all around me, an expectation of mass that drew me onwards. The street split like a fork around an island of parked bicycles and scooters, so tightly packed they could have been a sculpture. On the second floor of a purple neon-lit building a club thumped with a deep bass heartbeat; two slender boys stood outside and laughed. One took a drag on a silver cylinder and puffed great gouts of vapour like a storybook dragon, his eyes alive with the light of the streetlamps. Above their heads the rainbow flag, illuminated, colours stark against the night. Back home I'd only seen it on television, being waved at the heart of a milling sea of angry-sad faces just before the horses charged and the tear gas popped and the shield-walls went *boom-boom-boom*, heavy boots and visored faces kettling the protesters closer together so the ones in the middle dropped to their knees, unable to breathe. 'Victory over the perverts', said one paper the next day. I remembered how sick I'd felt then, bile sitting like a stone under my heart, wondering if that would happen to me.

The two boys joked and fired rapid Italian, heedless. One brushed a hand against the other's arm, a touch of easy friendship; a girl with a nose ring joined them and there were kisses, then I had to stop watching because then it would *look* like I was watching.

When I turned my face away, there it was. The sight hit me in the face: a mass of stone, concrete, marble, pillar upon pillar upon pillar that curved away from me, up-lights dotting the ground and stretching their warm glow upwards, other lights inside making the whole structure look like a giant's oven. Thousands had died in this place but it beckoned like a beacon. The Colosseum – being restored at titanic expense – through a trick of ancient engineering managed to both squat and soar all at once.

The in-flight magazine had had an article about this, the efforts of the dying European Union to centralise by moving its capital to Rome, spending hundreds of millions on restoring this totemic symbol of Empire, drafting in legions of archaeologists, historians, stonemasons and engineers. They were cladding ancient stone and brick in super-hard transparent film while constructing a delicate but strong inner framework – hidden from view – that supported the ultra-modern interior. It was some months from opening but already it shone into the night, fences and gates carefully placed so as not to obscure the structure. You remember how our press was all over this extravagance, comparing it to the last gasp of a hypothermic body drawing heat to its core, leaving its limbs to die. They knew, though, those Euros, even as they struggled to hold their heads up, how powerful this symbol could be – a place of death that now hosted the theatre of life.

I stood for a while, soaking it in. A few construction vehicles were parked around the exterior but it looked almost finished. I wasn't the only one watching – I caught flashes of implant cameras – the clunky, early ones, not like what they have today – and a few doors down a couple with a young child in a pushchair licked precarious ice creams under streetlamps like it was the middle of the day; the man pointed out something to the woman, who nodded and leaned in close with a smile the evening couldn't mask.

That ugly fucking gash cut through the ancient heart of the city by Mussolini, without regard for aesthetics or what was buried beneath, had lately been dug up. The asphalt and concrete was gone and the teams of a dozen universities had swarmed, ravenous for fresh finds; their dig sites were neat rows of tents and awnings covering the excavations from any rogue showers. Thirty feet above it all, arched and glassed and chromed, a skybridge followed the path of the former avenue, linking the Colosseum to that enduringly absurd pile, the Vittorio Emanuele monument. I took one of the four covered escalators up to the bridge and the travellators that ran day and night carried me, new rubber squeaking, towards the bustle of town on new, barely marked steel plates.

I didn't have a map, but I'd studied these streets enough to have a rough idea of where I was. I was drawn towards the place Keats had whimpered his last, but broke off before I hit the tourist traps. There were endless warrens of streets here, punctuated by piazzas where the tables of cafés and restaurants spread out like extensions of the creepers that criss-crossed the walls. When I thought I was far enough from the chatter I dropped into a chair and nodded at a waiter, giving him my best *grazie* as he offered a laminated menu. It's a wonder the chair didn't buckle under me.

My feet had led me to a kind of womb within the city. The buzz of a legion of tourists, performers, shopkeepers, thieves and motorists pulsed just out of reach, a noise-cocoon that reassured rather than overwhelmed.

Wine wouldn't be a problem, though I looked my age: this was Europe where it was a right, not a privilege. The waiter frowned when I asked for a carafe – a trick I'd read about – and asked in better English than I expected whether I'd prefer a bottle.

'No,' I tell him. 'A carafe. *Rosso.*'

He scowled, but went to get it. Fuck him, he'd no idea of the day I'd had.

The wine went down easy. I'd snuck a bit from Father's cellar in the past but he was into his oaked French – this was dark cherry on my tongue. I wanted to sort through my mind, to find some kind of order in the chaos, form a plan, but I couldn't. Every time I started formulating some kind of pathway, some way of dragging myself out of the mire of a future I had before me, all I got was a screaming chorus of harpies.

Failure. Loser. Queer.

An ancient column skewered the piazza. It was styled like Trajan's, though I couldn't remember the name of this one. Bands of soldiers and merchants and magistrates and royalty tramped up the spiral that wound from base to tip, always facing forwards. What I wouldn't have given to be one of them, with just a single path to follow.

I finished the carafe. He brought me another. I gave him a look that told him I was there for the duration.

The column was engraved on the base but I couldn't make it out from my table. Carafe in hand, not bothering with the glass, I walked over to it. My cheeks were flushed and my eyes couldn't settle on the neat ranks of bars that some chisel had put there two millennia ago. I knew I was pissed because I'd been deciphering worse engravings without breaking a mental sweat since the fourth form.

'Hey! You, come back!' It was the waiter, shouting at me from under the awning. A couple mid-dinner gave me a shitty look. I wandered back to my table and chugged the carafe, not caring when a rivulet meandered down my chin and plopped onto my lap.

A hand slapped the table, and under it a piece of paper.

'Didn't ask for the bill,' I said, finding it harder than I should. They'd always said I was a lightweight. The harpies returned.

'You have finished, I think,' said the waiter. He had dark locks and stubble that joined a patch of darker, curlier hair at the 'V' of his shirt. He looked pissed off.

'One more, then I'm gone.'

'Pay and go.'

'More fucking *wine*!'

I was pulled to my feet before I knew what had happened. He had manifested a partner from nowhere and I was already halfway across the piazza, too surprised to lash them with anything.

'Please,' I choked, unable to hold tears back. The harpies laughed and called me a baby, poor little baby queerboy, crying in public. They took the money I threw at them and in return dumped me in a side street. I called them wankers, received a *vaffanculo, pezzo di merda inglese.*

Have you noticed how many still speak Italian in the restaurants? Even though the menus are all in Latin and even with all those translators they gave out, the old ways stick around.

The wine was pumping up the veins beneath my skin and my feet were moving. I thought of columns, Trajan's Column, and I saw plastered walls and cobbles pass by, heard the tinny *meep* of scooters, and incense and old dust crawled up my nose. I passed a shop filled with wooden toys but one of them, a Guignol with a razor smile, grinned at me in a way that was far too personal.

Then I was there, standing in front of Trajan's Column. I'd gone back on myself, returning to where the skybridge dropped me. I stared up at the floodlit stone, feeling the weight of it as it thrust into the night sky. I was drunk and I was lost and I needed to lash out.

'It looks like a fucking cock,' I heard myself say, though my voice sounded like someone else's. 'Who's is it, Trajan?' I shouted, not caring about the looks coming my way. 'Yours? Huh? Is it Antinous'? Or is it yours? Was that what you were going for, planting a massive dong in plain view, just to piss them off?'

No, you idiot, I remembered. That was Hadrian. Hadrian and Antinous, the famous lovers, not Trajan. You can't even get that right.

Suddenly, I was laughing. It started low, small and delicate, then built into a roar that had me hunched double, my eyes streaming. It hurt my scalp, hurt my lungs. After a minute or two, it went away and I felt like I'd been washed in by the tide, leaning and breathing deep against the railings.

'Fuck off,' I whispered, to no one in particular.

There was too much light, too much noise, even here. On the other side of the railings I smelled open earth and concrete still wet from yesterday's rain. Before anyone could stop me, I was over the railings and down into the excavations.

It smelled old here, and I fancied I could hear earthworms move in the walls of sod that towered over me. It was a labyrinth, drawing me onwards under canvas roofs. I avoided the pits where the archaeologists worked by day with brush and trowel because a part of me still felt for them, valued what they were doing, knowing that some kid somewhere who'd had the same dream as I had got his wish and was now perhaps working here, living here, and why should I ruin his dig out of spite? I was drained of everything: anger, hatred, sadness, guilt, all of it poured into the drains.

I rested my back against a column half-buried in a wall of earth, feeling its fluting press into my spine like the fingers of a lover. How many men had lived and died since a craftsman placed chisel to this marble, I wondered? Did it get lonely under the earth as popes and fascists marched above, or was it all just the beat of a heart for an old stone?

I had to get a grip.

I stretched, fingers to the sky and I felt something like myself. Perhaps it was the trenches and the smell of posterity doing it – I've seen full colour three-dimensional pictures of the Somme, and where I was standing, barring the Roman junk sticking out of the walls and floor, wasn't that dissimilar. It was the differences that sobered me, however – namely the fact that I was an English schoolboy with a rich father, standing in a trench in the world's oldest city, not a poor East-End Tommy about to have his brains blown out.

Oh, goddess Perspective, I thought, *there you are with your sensible shoes and disapproving eyebrow.*

Easter. There'd been a lot of blood, but the head does that. There'd been that rugby match last year, the inter-house game where Robin McMurter and Sheepy Davis met each other head-on coming out of the back of a ruck. Sheepy's already pale face had looked ashen as the claret pissed down it in a torrent, not helped by the rain, and he hadn't even broken it. A lot of blood in the head, in the nose, around the eyes. Lots of capillaries.

That eye, little more than a pit. He must have hit the corner of something. The sound that his head made when it smacked the wood. And I'd just kept on hitting. I'd *wanted* to kill him, in that moment, but my rational mind was coming back bit by bit. I'd got lucky (or unlucky, depending on how you look at it) and knocked a few shades out of him but the skull is a dense thing; he'd been breathing, even if it was halting. The more I thought about it the more likely it seemed that he'd be alright – they must have been down those stairs on my heels to fetch Oswald and Boniface.

My heartbeat slowed to normal. I stopped my nervous playing with loose skin on my lip. He might think twice about coming for me again, or it would get even worse – either way, Nick Easter would live another day.

I leaned back, this time onto the soft earth of the wall. A few more moments here with the comfort of old earth around me, then back to face the music. Just a little while. I closed my eyes, inhaling deep.

There was a shift. A scrape. Then the dirt at my back just wasn't there anymore.

Ohshitwhatnow, went my brain.

I tumbled, feeling nothingness beneath and the bitch gravity pressing me down, falling fast, air whipping past. Dirt in my mouth and in my eyes, grainy coarseness that tasted of the bones of cities and men and there was something golden in front of my eyes, just a flash.

Then I hit my head and galaxies flew out of my eyes.

1

Trade used to drive the world, a boundless, intangible marketplace encompassing every nation and every individual. Everything bowed to it: tradition, culture, even self-preservation. In the days when a factory in Guangzhou supplied small businesses in Antwerp that sold tableware to the housewives of Cusco, the power brokers leaned into their drinks and delighted in how things were shrinking. 'Foreign' had become a fringe construct and everything was local.

Well, for whatever reason – fear, or perhaps just indolence – it turned out the world wasn't any smaller and was in fact too big for most. That's when the doors began to close and now there is barely one open.

I hear Orkney's phantom laugh, as I think these things. I'm sucking at the system's teat, he'd say, drinking their negativity and reverting to my natural, gloomy self. In the book-lined, mould-encrusted study of the corner tower of my mind, he creaks back in his ancient swivel chair and shakes his head, grey hair spilling over his shoulders and sprinkled with the light of a washed-out afternoon. His words come crisp over the gap of years: *If there's one thing I'll accomplish before you leave, Banks, it's to put a smile on that face of yours. Philosophy might make you want to kill yourself, but life shouldn't.* Well, you didn't have my life, professor. The adult me can answer back while the me-at-university could only bob an embarrassed head and burrow his chin into an old scarf. You missed the worst of globalisation's messy death. Your optimism had the momentum of a lifetime.

He's right, though. I am being gloomy. I'm in Rome and I should be enjoying myself. I blame the sea.

Dover to Calais was rough enough that I was sure the Minister would call the whole thing off. The Channel – as if getting its own back for twenty years of neglect – tossed the ferry like a toy, the atrocious weather keeping the delegation off the decks and firmly attached to the bars where rough gin dripped in double measures. I tried to snatch a look at that once-mighty shipping lane from a misted window only to be met with low cloud and spray. The boat was a relic, barely held together and missing one of its stabilisers – well, what use do we have for ferries anymore, after all? Not a craft for these seas, though I'm not sure many are: something to do with Atlantic currents switching, the melting of polar ice. The sea between us and Europe is now a gauntlet of white caps with murderous intent, far wider than it used to be; we were bounced, peak to trough, peak to trough, where once we would have glided, massive and imperturbable.

We docked at Calais after eight hours; shaken, sickened, mostly drunk. The vehicles that met us were like something out of a fiction, the kind of sleek, low-slung ovoids that littered Hollywood offerings thirty years ago. Sliding doors whispered open and the inside was plush and dark, curves everywhere. When they moved, they were so quiet! Nothing like the spluttering foul-smelling machines that crowd London's streets – in fact, to climb into any vehicle at all that wasn't laced with the odour of burnt dung-fuel felt wrong somehow, an absence that hinted at something worse hiding under the shining bodywork.

But there was no such thing. The electric motors hummed as the convoy whisked us away, the senior staff in cars, the support and juniors following in a no-less-impressive coach.

The Minister was already furious and none of us were surprised, least of all me; as his private secretary and old schoolmate, I'd known the curl of his lip and reddening of his face at the slightest provocation ever since our boyhood. Sir Tobias Easter, KCMG, PC, BA (third class, later elevated to a first) and His Majesty's Minister of the Interior, did not enjoy this stark reminder of the qualities (or 'excesses', as he is fond of saying) of the world outside Britain.

'They're trying to show us up,' he bristled. '"Hey, Jonny Brit, look what you've been missing." Just like the bloody Euros, damned degenerates.'

That triggered a flash of memory: a young Toby Easter walking from the boarding house showers with a smirk, mist and the sound of quiet sobbing behind him. I quashed the memory before it could show on my face, and he didn't notice anything, trying as he was to avoid letting his gaze rest on any aspect of the plush vehicle and betray the covetousness that gripped us all.

God, it all looked so fine, every inch of it. Soft leather smell. Our transports carried us along a four-lane highway, the way cleared by outriders on black, hollow-wheeled motorbikes.

Easter tapped the glass and said: 'It's a damn swarm out there.'

It took me a moment to catch on. I'd wondered why there was no police escort other than the bikers out front (who didn't look armed), but now I saw why: drones. Sleeker and smaller than anything I could remember; at least six buzzing around our car, keeping up with us as we sliced through the air of

Northern France. A glance: the other cars and the coach were also accompanied by precise formations. These machines were our keepers then; I wondered what they could do if things went wrong.

Easter's sour mood didn't improve over the miles and carried over to our first sighting of Paris. We skirted the rim of the city, seeing little more than the skyscrapers that had mushroomed out to encircle it – a sign of things to come, though I didn't know it – and I felt a little sad not to be able to take a glance at that place that clings limpet-like to our British imaginations.

The convoy brought us around to the great artifice of steel and glass that was the Gare de L'Unité, our first stop on our way to Rome. The station was a latticework of balconies and walkways packed with crowds drawn by the promise of a glimpse of strange folk from across the sea. A few looked disappointed – perhaps they were hoping for horns or cloven feet not men in old-fashioned grey suits.

I noticed a child's hand pressed against a glass barrier that overlooked the promenade, leaving a smudge on the otherwise-pristine surface, a mother hovering at her side. The girl looked around five or six – I remembered Sara at that age, never without grubby hands or a runny nose. I gave her a wink and her little head drew back, shocked at being noticed, but it didn't stop a gappy smile from forming.

Then, the train, a humming monstrosity of well-ventilated and comfortable interiors. With much to do (speeches to append and check, not to mention going through the schedules handed to us by our hosts) I managed to excuse myself and find a quiet compartment. All four long, gleaming carriages were at our disposal; such waste, they'd say back home. I suppose I should have agreed but I liked the warmth and the wood on the walls and the thickness of the carpets, the peace, the quiet of so much room. Outside, the countryside whispered by, dappled by the autumn sun; in the distance, stark as a needle, a church spire etched itself against the bright cold sky.

I settled into my work and saw little of the rest of France save for a rushing of fields and trees and hedges occasionally broken by urban areas that flashed past too fast to see. After the superscrapers of the Paris skyline it was an odd delight to see countryside untouched by time like this. The fields were wide and gold-green hatched, with not a plume of a steam tractor or canvas shanty town anywhere in sight.

We didn't pass through any cities – this line had been laid decades ago for just this purpose, when Europe got serious about centralisation and air travel went the way of the oil. 'Executive' rail channels snaked out from Rome to every old capital so that diplomats and ministers and senators could be whisked to the centre of all things, unhindered. This was Paris's own line, I read in the comprehensive binder our hosts had passed on for the Minister to read (which he never would); Britain's would have joined this one and run alongside it all the way down the spine of France and over the Alps but once we were gone the money went elsewhere. The rails that run up to the coast are from the days when the Tunnel was open, not made for these sleek beasts that blast along at over three hundred miles per hour.

God, we hadn't cared. We'd thought they were falling apart when we shut the borders, the heart of them sucked dry by the extremities: Greece, the Balkans, the bonfire that Portugal had turned into. When things were tough, at least it wasn't as bad as Europe, went the mantra.

Well, look at us now, screamed every perfect joint, every wall-screen, the endless variety of drones. Easter's irritation was understandable, even if I didn't share it. It was, and is, miraculous.

If they knew I think these things they'd have me up against the wall for treason.

This isn't the Rome I remember from that brief trip in my youth, when my friend, that skinny boy with bright eyes, bloodied my nose as he fled into the night. It was night when we came in and all I saw for an hour beforehand was the glow on the horizon; it resolved itself into a fire of artificial light, then I made out the thorn bush of skyscrapers. Rome is an ancient head with a sparkling, modern crown. In truth, the city is not the one we remember – which is kept preserved in the centre of this ring of hyper-modern, vertigo-inducing megastructures. The arcologies are twice anything I've ever seen in height, many of them joined by slender bridges that you could drive a mountain under. The sheer *blaze* of the place, almost as if shadows are an affront, to be chased away; as we got closer the glow coruscated from a flat white into reds, purples, blues – advertising, signposts. Everywhere I looked were those little flying things – the drones that are their delivery mechanisms, their taxis, their pets.

Cars just like the ones we'd left behind in Paris carried us to our final destination. Inside the ring of skyscrapers is the old city, and like an invisible wall had been erected, everything slowed down. Nothing flew here and the riot of billboards was left behind; what we entered was the city as it could have been a hundred years ago. Ground cars. Pedestrians taking the evening air. Only the absence of traffic (the swarms of scooters that took the side streets and pavements as their just domain) breaks the illusion that I am seventeen again, that Monk and I have just stepped off the coach.

The historical centre is a sacrosanct bubble in time, the

architecture of millennia unchanged in its repose. This new breed of Euros don't allow themselves to be held back by posterity, though they retain their symbolic respect for it.

The one exception to this demarcation of future and past is the EuroPar complex: the Colosseum of the Caesars, symbol of the bloodiest excesses of Empire, reborn as a parliament house, its ancient brick buttressed with modern composites to give it rigidity, the delicate antiquity sealed behind invisible polymers that keep it from decaying while still showing off the venerable skin. Rank upon rank, floor upon floor of arched windows – three inches thick and everything-proof – stare out at the city, creating a space that seems wide open from the outside; the interior is cocoon-like, reassuring and warm and smelling like new furniture. The message is clear: we have no secrets in here; we are transparent. And you will feel safe.

I remember them working on it when I was a boy and the stink of old, churned earth from the building sites that littered the area. The work was to undo the great projects of Mussolini, to rip up the hideous swath that was the *Via dei Fori Imperiali*, a crass parade route draped over at least three ancient fora by a small man looking to appear magisterial. Where there was asphalt and concrete and the stink of hydrocarbons there is now parkland and carefully preserved ruins, and trees to provide tourists with pockets of shelter from sun or shower. The ancient complex is enormous, the jewel in the crown. Next to it is the apron surrounding the EuroPar complex, linked by raised moving walkways to the rest of the city.

The modern heart of Europe beats around the remains of old Rome in a careful balancing act. The mood of the delegation was suppressed, almost sombre – every inch of vertiginous concrete weighed down on their sense of self, their assurance that we'd *Made the Right Choice*. Collars up, they hurried from the cars up the steps to the palazzo that will be our main base, Easter leading the way as if it were a charge into battle; a few juniors are being housed in another, more modest house some streets away.

I found myself stopping and taking the air. Pine and stone, fresh and raw.

Our second evening here and the cultural attaché, Mariko Albenge, is late for our meeting.

I've been waiting in the lobby of the Hotel Adrienne for over an hour, at first stunned into watchful silence by the opulence of copper and glass and the soft whisper of feet on marble, but now I'm bored, still tired from the journey south and worried about Sara. Lately she won't talk about school and I wonder if she's arrived at the age when children discover cruelty. I remember it so well and know it's a stage everyone has to pass through, but a big part of me wants to hide her from all harm forever. It can't be easy for her, especially without her mother around.

Back to work, for all the distraction it will provide. The attaché and I are to go over the opening address for tomorrow, proxies of our respective governments; word and nuance must be picked over by the other side and agreed. Too much bad water has flowed between us for there to be such a thing as trust; at least, not yet. Through some stilted initial exchanges over the phone yesterday, Ms Albenge – who still shows no signs of arriving – and I agreed to meet here rather than at the Residence. I was assured of more comfort, a more relaxing atmosphere. I've been eying up the wine behind the bar but deferring out of courtesy. That courtesy is pretty thin now.

The wall opposite has a chair mounted on it. A red leather,

button-back armchair of the old style with dark mahogany legs polished to a high sheen has been hung six feet up and rests there as if levitating, and it bothers me. Are we meant to sit in the damn thing? Is there a stepladder nearby I can't see?

'Mr Banks?' My name floats over in a lilt. It's a soft, woman's note, with just a hint of extra continental vowels and a smooth, French roll of the 'r'.

A slender woman with dark, shoulder-length hair has appeared at my table. Her face is chalice-shaped, cheekbones leading down from large, dark eyes to a small, plush mouth. A hint of epicanthic fold, something barely seen nowadays at home. Her hair is straight and serious but a few ebony strands have escaped to caress her cheeks. Her suit is a good cut, dark grey that follows her lines but proclaims business above all.

She's watching me, assessing, gauging, even as I do. What must I look like to her? A tired, middle-aged man who used to walk hills but doesn't anymore, red-faced from a lunchtime beer. I realise that I'm the curiosity here: that exotic, spiny creature from across the Channel, barely seen and barely heard for three decades. I must seem like a relic.

The edges of her mouth curve into a reflexive smile. Then her training takes over and the shutters of polite diplomatic discourse come down.

'Mr Banks,' she says again. 'Is now a good time?'

'Of course, please.' I'm a good public schoolboy, of course, so I let resentment at her lateness bleed into excessive courtesy. I indicate the other chair.

She sits. 'You are rested?' she asks, the question posing another, or perhaps making a statement. *You look terrible*, most likely.

'Thank you, yes. The Residence is quite comfortable.'

Straight into it then, after the initial foray. I use her large, wafer-thin tablet to go over papers and papers and papers, a dry and dull dance that nevertheless is the pro forma of two countries with closed borders talking to each other. When we get to the speeches for our respective delegates I realise my mouth is moving and making sounds but it's as if someone else is governing it. The real me sits behind the glass of my eyes and watches her quick white hands move over the screen, slender fingers deft and precise except for those tiny, almost-not-there moments when the shadow of girlish indecision makes her hesitate for a breath before the experienced adult takes over.

We're there for a couple of hours and it's getting late. She doesn't apologise for her tardiness but gives me a look that says as much. We agree on a second meeting the following morning, agree to share our files and shake hands. Her palm is soft as wool but I feel calluses there as well and her grip is firm. I realise two things in the moment she leaves. The first is that I'm watching her too closely – enough for it to be embarrassing if anyone caught me doing it. The second is that I'm not thinking about Elanor.

68 CE

I remember light stabbing me awake and all I could think about was the pain in my skull. It was insistent and deep, a real bastard behind the eyes. It was like that time at the start of Upper Sixth when Mr O.B. had us all over to celebrate our accession to the upper echelons of the school, or some such shit. We got stuck into his stock of Burgundy that night and no mistake, dizzy with being treated like *real people* – you more than most, if memory serves. I was a mess and didn't make it to Chapel the next day. That rumour about James Ridge waking up in O.B.'s bed with more than a sore head really gained traction (I found out later that he'd been fully clothed, alone and un-interfered-with, a thoughtful blanket thrown over him in his paralytic state) and by the end of the week the story had the poor boy waking up with apple sauce on his bare arse and a lemon wedged in his mouth. Such is the enduring power and greasy swiftness of the rumour mill.

Anyway, I was suffering, with only the dim memory of an earthy tumble and angry Italian waiters ringing through the bell of my head. I'd likely smacked it on the way down and the remainder was accounted for by cheap and dirty house red. After I prised my eyes open I found the floor to be white, veined marble and bloody uncomfortable. Nearby was a mosaic (which I've always thought were more trouble than they were worth, artistically speaking) showing grapes or satyrs or some other such muck, and I was certain there was a busted light because of how the shadows flickered and moved across the giant earthenware pots that were my only companions. When I had enough energy to raise my head and properly have a look about, I saw that it was good, old-fashioned torchlight – not the battery-powered kind but the Hollywood wrap-your-shirt-around-a-stick-and-set-it-alight kind.

The room was tall-ceilinged, though narrow, with a slot window high on the back wall. The walls were plastered, with delicate moulding running around head-height. Despite this kind of polish (straight from the African Despot section of the catalogue), it was clear it was nothing more than a storeroom, crammed as it was with the aforementioned pots – amphorae, a little voice insisted – and crates, old and blackened straw strewn across the rich marble. A particular funk in the air led me to one of the amphorae and had me lifting the lid, only to recoil as if struck in the face with the powerful stink of fish sauce.

I was in a larder.

The studded door of metal and dark wood was impassive and looked weighty, but a small tug on the rope loop had it swinging inwards on oiled hinges. Not a secure larder then. Outside was a corridor like the nave of a cathedral, quiet and ornamented and painted in flickering torchlight, one side open to the air. Beyond the colonnade the night sky was ink-black and there was a kind of perfume on the air – incense, adding to the ecclesiastic atmosphere. My mind went a-whirring. Had I been kidnapped by a senior churchman? I'd seen pictures of the corridors of the Apostolic Palace and they'd looked very much like this, barring the open-air bit. I also knew you can't trust the clergy. I was certainly, as yet, un-interfered-with, but to keep me in the food store like meat – those kinky shits. I spotted an ornate bust on a nearby plinth and considered kicking it over.

My initial impression had been bang-on: this place really was far too much. All gilt and lustre and marble gleaming. The corridor stretched for what seemed like miles, arrow-straight and lined with door after massive door like the one from which I'd emerged. As I walked the smell of incense was blown away in the breeze coming through the columns, a hint of cypress and horses just at the edge of sensation. When the colonnade came to an end the place became musty, like a thousand cats had lived here – unsettling in such a cavernous place, the reek of dust and inattention. Only about one in three of the torches was lit and most of the floor urns I passed were filled with the dry stalks of dead plants. The priests, I thought, should fire their cleaning staff if they hadn't already. Despite the pall of neglect, the paint on the walls and the gold leaf on the surrounds was clear and bright – new, even. Beneath the dust the floor was barely marked. Brand new, then abandoned – such opulence left to wither! I was musing on the contradiction (and precisely what the fuck was happening to me) when I heard the music.

It tinkled, funnelled by the marble. I wondered if it was wind chimes at first, but it was deeper, more sonorous. I followed it, the sound dropping in and out like a buzzing insect, leading me through a portico and into another long colonnade open to the air. Moonlight bounced from a large body of water, flat as glass. A still lake filled the entirety of the courtyard – so large I could barely see the torches flickering on the other side – and in its very centre floated a ship. At this point, I actually slapped myself to check if I was dreaming. Emerging from the middle of the ship – a trireme, I was sure of it – was what looked like a temple pediment.

Why wasn't I screaming and clawing at the walls, you might ask? Well, at this point all the Overlook Hotel-grade emptiness had put me in a kind of shutdown. Many would have lost it, but my brain's never worked like that – it just narrows the inputs until things become manageable again. In that moment of intense dislocation, all I knew was that I had one objective: finding out where I was. The temple on the water was where the music was coming from, and with it the hope of answers.

I thought about wading over – the water that lapped the feet of the columns was only about half a metre deep. I hoped it didn't get much deeper, that the boat was an ornamental feature built into the lake rather than an actual vessel with a draught. Then, thoughts of what might be swimming in it popped into my head – people who own enormous ornamental lakes, as I'd seen it, have an appalling tendency to fill them with things that clump and slip and slither and, more importantly, bite. I remembered a story about a Roman nobleman who owned a villa on the coast near Naples who'd regularly fling slaves and, on the odd occasion, enemies to his trained eels. I elected to stay away from the water and look for a rowboat.

No need, as it turned out, because there was a trapdoor. A huge metal thing about a foot thick, hinged in its upward position and leaning against a column. Steps led down under the lake to a tunnel that was well lit. The walls were even more splendid and looked to have been cleaned. My feet, which at this point were running the show, made soft pad-pad sounds and the draught was cool on my face. I recognised the frescos of Ceres, Minerva and Jupiter and they all watched me pass with their stony eyes; Neptune the Earth-Shaker looked ready to leap out of the wall with his trident. The only reminder of the tons of water above my head were the small bronzed drains set at regular intervals into the floor.

At the end of the tunnel was another set of stairs. I emerged into torchlight.

I was inside the boat, which was not a boat (just as I'd surmised). It was set out like a theatre, shallow banks of stone running in an arc around a stage, cushioned with what looked like thick cloth. There were banners hung about the place, mostly of eagles and wolves, though my attention was drawn to the half-dozen or so people sat facing the stage and the man that was on it. They were a cloud of gossamer and gold, their clothes seeming to barely be there at all. The performer was all in purple and his thick neck was hung with ropes of gold, his arms bulging between thick torcs and bracelets. He was a chubby sort, the kind of man that fat comes to very easily. If you'd stripped him of his robe and put him in a polo shirt he could very well have passed as a darts player. His pudgy fingers plucked at the strings of a harp and his eyes were closed, his body swaying gently back and forth. The audience was enraptured, though it seemed to me to be a lot of plinky-plonky stuff with little melody. Then he started to sing.

I had an inkling something had stung the man, or someone had stepped on his foot, but no. His fleshy mouth gave forth a kind of scratchy caterwauling, a tune that seemed to have no relation to the one he was playing, nor to any musical style I'd heard. A couple of times I heard hesitation in his fingers, as if they'd lost the thread of the music, and saw the piggy eyes crack the mask of reverie for an instant, looking at what his hands were doing.

An amateur, a beginner, he was bound to be laughed off the stage. But he wasn't. They went wild for him; I saw two grown men hold their hands in the air and weep. I heard the first words in a long while then, and they were Latin – proper schoolboy Latin of the Ciceronian mould:

49

Pulcherrima! Tales res mirabilis! and that sort of thing.

Priests, I wondered? They looked doughy enough, though, from what they were wearing – and knowing how many of the clergy like to spend their free time, a lissom young lad like myself had little business hanging around if they were. Then, standing to take the ovation, the fat man stood and opened his eyes fully. His profile was unexpectedly noble – the only word for it – I could see him on the face of a coin if only I squinted. Then he saw me and the place went still.

'Hi, I'm...' I garbled. 'Look, any chance you could tell me where—'

The fat man screamed like a girl.

Fuck me, but those priests moved fast.

You'll remember how, at school, we were all made to do Games whether we liked it or not – at least until we got older and better at coming up with excuses. I know from rugby what it is to be manhandled. These priests, or whatever they were, seemed fervent and loyal but they were not hard men. Their hands were plump and soft, and they were sweating under their gossamer as they held me down by sheer mass of numbers and then I had a bag over my head. There was some quick-fire discussion before I found myself lifted, carried over the marble floor, all the while hearing the fat one crying out breathy orders. With time to think (what else is there to do when you have a bag over your head) and time to listen, I took stock of the evidence. First, I'm in a palace (a proper one) that for all its mustiness has a familiar undercurrent of pine on the air. Second, I am surrounded by native Latin speakers who, on reflection, don't seem much like priests at all and more like some kind of sex club. The last item on my list is more bewildering – no one likes to be surprised, but their reaction seemed a little strong. The sods had pounced on me like I was the devil himself rather than a bewildered youth, and not in the way one would imagine perverts pouncing on a boy of my age. No, there was fear in their eyes to accompany the sheer terror in the fat man's screech. The look on his face before the bag was pulled over mine had been of a man who has seen a ghost.

I wondered if I was about to be killed like the poor sods that cropped up on the Internet (in the days when YouTube was a thing) in front of a black flag with a knife to their throats. There were so many things running around the inside of my head that I don't remember feeling scared. It was closer to morbid curiosity: I wanted to see this charade through to its logical conclusion.

I could see under the lip of the bag if I kept my head down. Marble gave way to stone flag, then the air changed as we went from the wide corridors to smaller, older ones. We went down several flights of steps and the temperature dropped even as the smell of wet earth bloomed in my nose. The party was quiet around me save for the slap of their sandals on the floor. There was a whoosh from nearby and a tickle of heat. Brightness intruded through the weave of the bag over my eyes as someone lit an actual, honest-to-goodness torch. A while later I heard the creak of a heavy door being swung on reluctant hinges and then we were outside and there was the smell of grass and hay and horseshit in my nose. The bag was removed and I saw we'd emerged onto a country road. A man slipped into a wooden building beside the door from which we'd emerged and, after some obscure thumping about in the dark, emerged leading a horse-drawn cart. I was veritably lobbed onto the back of it by the lummox carrying me (biceps like air balloons, and oiled up like a pole dancer) and made to sit in place while the rest of them clambered up to join me. The fat one took a seat next to the driver and wrapped himself in a cloak, hiding his face; the rest followed suit.

A delicate hand with painted nails reached out and passed me a rough-woven blanket. Not wanting to make things worse by resisting, I took it and wrapped myself up. It seems absurd to think of it, but this mass-mummification was meant to be some sort of disguise, though how the sight of a cartload of people wrapped up on a warm night wouldn't arouse more suspicion was beyond me. I turned to thank the person and found myself looking at a strong-boned face and eyes that had been stained dark and full, dusky lips. Her smile was lush and knowing even in that split second; a girl had never had this effect on me before, which was confusing and pleasant all at once. It was over in an instant and her face was veiled in sackcloth. The horse took the strain and soon we were bumping along the road.

It seemed like hours in the back of that jarring, creaking vehicle. Though open to the air, the proximity to so many other warm bodies pressed together made it sweaty and close, not helped by the thick blanket around my neck. I must have drifted off to sleep at some stage because I was awoken by the cart creaking to a stop. Either side of us were fields of corn and in front, a high wall. I looked at those tall stalks swaying in the night breeze and wondered if I was fast enough to make it to them before they caught me, but even as the thought occurred I felt a slab-like hand on my knee. The oaf with the biceps made eye contact and shook his head once. His hands were ringed and he was as perfumed as the rest, but those hands were rough and his eyes were dangerous so I let the corn sway at my back. *Later*, I thought. *There will be other chances.*

There was an exchange from atop the gate. The fat man stood tall from the driver's bench and whipped off his shawl in what I thought was a rather dramatic motion. There followed a scramble inside and before long the gates were swinging inwards and we passed through into a courtyard lit by torches. A single-storey house, daubed white, filled most of the compound and the air was thick with the smell of horses.

I was beginning to make out a few words here and there now, my ear tuning to those around me. My schoolboy Latin – practised in quiet corners of the library – found words and latched onto them, drawing them into phrases. The accents were smoother, less jagged: this wasn't Tacitus on his soap box, nor Catullus complaining about his neighbours – these were people. The language had all the lisps, faults and pauses of a natural tongue, and that was the hardest part to get over. A small voice in the very rear of my skull started to niggle at me: fluent Latin, horses, no sign of electricity anywhere. I pushed it down because I was still running on logic and what that voice was saying went against all reason.

I began to understand that the fat one was very important, that we'd fled to the countryside, and something about it was to do with me. I also heard a name cropping up every so often, whispered as if it carried a curse with it – *Galba*. I knew a Galba. Well, my history books did: successor to the matricide who burned half of Rome. The sound in my head was a roar now, a single word repeated: *Nero, Nero, Nero.* That was when logic cracked.

Impossible. I had to be hallucinating; I was drugged. A palace that any despot would die for, a fat man with golden hair who played the harp for a captive audience. Galba. Fucking *Galba*! Then, just as I was about to hyperventilate, the kicker arrived in the form of twelve big bastards in segmented, lamellar armour straight from the pages of an encyclopaedia. Roman bloody soldiers in *lorica* that clanked and stank of oil, clomping through the gate on nailed sandals. I think I lost it for a bit; one of them came over and punched me. It got a little hazy, after that.

The woman stepped in, the one with the eyes who'd smiled at me. She advanced with a lash of words and the man who'd knocked me down shrank away from her as if stung. He even apologised, if I'm any judge of tone. The woman glared until the soldiers found better things to do with themselves.

She wore gossamer and was festooned – no other word for it – in gold and jewels. Her long dark hair was tied back with gold wire. Her nose was pierced, and a gold chain linked it to an ornate pendant on her left ear. Despite this, she stood solid, feet apart and shoulders – wide shoulders, for a woman – square. It was more the stance of a battlefield commander than a courtesan; looking at her like that, I started to wonder if she was what I thought she was. Under the gossamer she was flat-chested, and though her long legs were smooth they were well muscled. She caught me looking then, and her eyes flashed annoyance, then she softened again. It was like seeing an after-image – her face seemed instantly rounder, her mouth thicker. I didn't know how I'd missed the shape of her breasts and her hips because they were there, flirting with the fabric of her clothes.

'You must come with me,' she said.

I think I did something dumb like nod. She took my hand and led me into the house. In a room with a white-painted trough at one end, she left me with clothes to change into and told me to wash. I had dirt on my knees and elbows, and my reflection in the trough had blood trickling from its nose.

'Thank you,' I told her as she was about to walk out the door. 'Your name?'

She paused, her elegant fingers draped over the doorframe. 'I am Sporus.' She gave me that smile again and was gone before I could stumble out a reply.

I stank of sweat and old wine from what felt like a lifetime ago. The dream of waiters throwing me into the street, Easter's blood on my knuckles, all of it so far away. Had I gone mad? I splashed water on my face and it was icy, snapping me back into some kind of focus and my mind whirred. The evidence all around me supported a conclusion that I didn't want to acknowledge, but there was no antithesis to come to the rescue. The penny well and truly dropped.

I'm in ancient fucking Rome.

I threw up on myself. It was very dark vomit from the wine.

I left my stained clothes on the floor – more bloody mosaics – and washed myself again, rinsing my mouth. I was still groggy, still walking through a haze of hows and whys and what-the-fucks but some deep habit had me pulling on a white cotton tunic and belting it around my waist. A man with a shaved head came and took my old clothes away, wrinkling his nose at the smell but saying nothing. It was only after I'd splashed my face a third time that I noticed he'd taken my shoes as well. *Oh well, barefoot like a beggar I'll go*, I thought.

The same man returned and gestured me out of the room.

'I don't have any shoes,' I said, pointing at my feet.

He blinked with comical slowness.

Caligae? I tried.

He shook his head, then shrugged. Must have been an idiot. He gestured me forwards again. The villa – I suppose that fits the description, and my brain was starting to fill in the gaps as if it had accepted the impossible reality I found myself in – was nothing like the opulence of the palace but was, nevertheless, expensive. The walls were clean white and tapestried, the floor cool marble. The whole place flickered orange in the torchlight. Then the night air hit me with its background of crickets and horses and a susurration of wind in the branches of the single tree planted in the middle of the central courtyard. This was different to the one we'd come into, which had been a dusty, utilitarian thing. This place was wrapped in the arms of the house on all four sides and surrounded by colonnades. Grass grew in a border but around the tree there was fine sand. A dais with an awning had been set up at the foot of the tree, and on it was the fat man with the golden hair. By his side was an oiled brute – perhaps the one who'd carried me – and Sporus, her of the large eyes. Both looked worried, but the fat man had his eyes closed and appeared calm. Beatific, I think they call it, like those Buddhas that sit or kneel or lie on their sides – a kind of detached contentment.

Sporus gestured and I was brought over; she waved the servant away. The fat man opened his eyes and looked me up and down. There was no fear there anymore.

He spoke in a high, musical voice. I barely understood it, something about life and song and some such. I noticed the wine on his breath, as close as we were. He was drunk. The big one by his side was uncomfortable, shifting from foot to foot and shooting me warning looks; I was closer to his master than he would have liked, I realised. If only he knew, I thought, how far I was from being able to kill anyone. Then I remembered Easter and his bloody pit of an eye socket, and I wondered if maybe he was right. Maybe I looked like the sort of person who hurt people now.

I struggled out some Latin, something like 'Don't know why here. Stranger. Help, please.'

The fat one responded by reaching out and caressing my face. His hands hadn't seen a day's work (not that mine had, back then, either) as he brushed my cheek. He smelled of herbs and honey. Then, he said a single word:

Nemesis.

A troubling thing to hear from a man standing that close to you, upon whose word several nearby soldiers were clearly waiting.

He could have me skewered, right here, the mad bastard, I thought.

Don't panic, pull yourself together. You can talk your way out of this. I looked over at the girl, thinking she might help.

'Please, help. Stranger. No Nemesis. Scholar.' The only word I could summon up at that point.

The girl looked at me and smiled the saddest smile I'd ever seen. She'd changed again, no longer voluptuous or commanding – just a skinny, tired-looking girl in robes that had seen several hours of dusty travel.

'First Man thanks you for showing him truth,' she said.

That annoyed the fat one a little, I think, because it was obviously the gist of his words and he must have prided himself of flowery delivery over being succinct. He flicked his hand and I was taken from the dais, the soldiers' hands rough on my arms.

I was made to sit a few paces away in the circle of onlookers. All of them had their robes pulled over their heads, and I noticed most of them were quietly crying. There was a tension, an anticipation in the air, now that I'd been presented and taken away. Something big was about to happen. Both the oiled hunk and Sporus kissed the fat man – long, deep kisses that went on a little too long, then they left the dais as well. They sat beside me and bowed their heads.

Pudgy fingers reached for a side table. The sword he picked up was as long as my forearm, gold and silver intertwined on a tooled leather sheath. He wrapped his fingers around the grip and drew the blade. It flashed red in the torchlight, and the men and women around me gasped. I saw him then, his features cast in the light by the length of that blade. Under the fat was a strong chin and a high brow. His nose drew an aquiline wedge from his forehead to his lower lip and his mouth was drawn in a grim line. He looked like the statues in the halls of the Ashmolean Museum. They'd called him *Princeps* – First Man – and they'd bowed to him. He'd played his harp on a boat of stone in a private lake and called me *nemesis*. He'd seemed unmanned then, soft and fragile, but not now. He'd made a decision and was going through with it.

He placed the sword against a white, bare wrist, blade running along his forearm, and cut. He drew in a sharp breath but that was it. Quick as a cat, he did the same to his other arm. A man in the crowd sobbed aloud. The sword clattered onto the decking and I watched as blood welled, then spewed from the wounds, splashing the white tunic and soaking into the rich carpets spread around the dying man. He didn't say a word, didn't close his eyes. The hulk next to me melted into a wailing mass and set off the rest of them, but I was drawn by the stillness on the other side of me. Turning, I saw Sporus' face fixed like granite while all around her everyone turned to mud. She kept her eyes on the dying man, then almost at the edge of perception, a nod.

There was a soft whump as the body toppled to the grass.

A door banged open. Shouts of alarm. Heavy sandals on marble, skittering. A soldier in a plumed helmet and sweat on his brow exploded into the courtyard. He froze as he saw the dead man, now ashen-skinned where the blood hadn't splashed. It carried on pumping, an incredible amount of liquid coming forth until I worried it might get on my toes. Call me insensitive, but I'd never seen a man die and I'd already had plenty to get through my head that evening.

The soldier swore, breaking the mood. I didn't recognise the word he used, but the sentiment of 'Fuck!' breaks all barriers of culture and language. He rubbed his eyes, any solemnity lost on him – he looked pissed off. He gestured to the soldiers who had, until now, stood back. His authority was clear.

'Take them,' he said, and I understood he meant us, me and the two companions.

As I was hauled away through a door, I fixed the image in my mind of the Emperor Nero lying on the gravel band around the wide-limbed tree, his blood seeping down to its very roots.

2

Outside the chromed sleekness of the train – quieter, smoother and faster than anything from home – Italy slips into Southern France, silvered by the morning sun. Lemon groves give way to pasture; further away are ridges cross-hatched with the latticework of vineyards, like something from the kind of postcard Orkney used to hang on the back of his pitted office door between the picture of the King (complete with dart holes) and some ancient High German I never took the time to understand. I wonder how the real Orkney – that is the man who taught me for three brief years at university rather than the construct my mind has surprised me with, this unexpected face of my conscience – would feel about this view. My mind is in raptures so I take his lead, pressing my shoulder blades into the plush envelopment of the dark-grey seat, taking in every dip and secret of the land sinuating past the enormous plate glass window.

We're off to France, following a track that runs along the one that brought us here scant days ago, though this train is newer and even swifter. A few hours in comfort and we'll be in the walled city of Carcassonne, a trip that would have taken a day and an evening in old money. This is the programme our hosts have laid out for us, breaking from a week heavy with opening salvoes of work for a series of guided trips to show us better how the Confederacy has changed. They're proud of what they've achieved, and I can't fault them for it, but it does feel like looking in a mirror, the reflection staring back that of what we could have been. This had a predictable effect on Easter until he was mollified by his destination – Venice. Some are shooting north to the mountains, others crossing the Adriatic on hydrofoil craft to see Dubrovnik's red-roofed panorama.

It's still early and beautiful. Above the hills the sky is lacerated by golden filaments of cloud, like something from another world has clawed the veil, letting golden ichor flow into ours.

You're as wistful as I am, whether you like it or not, boy, Orkney intones with a ghostly chuckle.

He's right, though I'd never confess it to anyone but the dark between my own eyes. Elanor would have loved it; her hair would catch the milky light *just so* and all of a sudden, I feel my chest tighten, breath hesitate. Before I allow myself a look at the memory of her green-flecked grey eyes, I turn back to my pile of papers to break the spell. It's no good, though – she's there with her little half-smile, like she's misbehaved and doesn't care. I get up, not really knowing where I'm going except that it needs to be away from the inside of my head. Perhaps there's a bar.

In the vestibule at the end of a car a young man in a waistcoat smiles and enquires. I want to talk to Sara – the need is a weight around my neck. International calls are a thing of memory now except for the most urgent of government communiqués, so I try to keep the surprise from my face when he nods and says in accented but clear English: 'Of course, sir, the phone is right this way.' He shepherds me towards a booth with a screen on the wall and a headset, then leaves me alone. Is it really that simple? To call home from a train hundreds of miles away from Oxford? Personal phones are something the middle-aged among us remember but it's just another thing these Euros take for granted.

My fingers brush the ingrained digits of the telephone in Sara's boarding house into a smooth touchpad, the numbers making little electronic clicks as I touch them. The headset hums at me as the call bounces from the train to one relay station to another, then to the Confederacy vessel moored semi-permanently at the edge of British waters for just such a purpose (though it has been a lonely, quiet watch for the last couple of decades), and on to England and its failing, rusting cables – I fancy I can hear the signal crackle as it burrows through concrete and earth and across decaying, bird-shat spans. Then, the ring tone.

The housemistress picks up, her normal disdain is absent for once – perhaps my posting to the delegation has made its way to her ears – and she goes to fetch Sara. The minutes tick by.

'Umm, hi? Dad?' She sounds tired and bored.

'Hello, Mouse.'

Silence. When she speaks, she sounds irritated. Her voice is echoey and I realise we're on speakerphone and the housemistress is, doubtless, present. 'How's the trip?'

'Oh, alright. A little strange. How's school?'

'It's OK.'

'Are you working hard?'

'… yes.' Definitely irritated.

'Well, that's good. It's really very beautif—'

'Actually, Dad, I need to go. I've got hockey.'

'I didn't know you did hockey.'

'Yeah, I do now. I have to go get changed.'

'Well, alright then.' I can feel her edging away. 'Be good then. Miss you.'

'Umm, yeah. You too.'

'Alright then, darling. Be good.'

'OK. I'll write.' The line dies, the screen blinking the disconnection at me. Sara is eight hundred miles away and getting further with every year. My God, fourteen years old. She's all I have left of Elanor now and the same tide that pulled me from my parents is taking her; sometimes, the fear of it unmans me. When I exit the booth and find my way to my seat, I'm in an even darker mood than when I left.

We disembark at Carcassonne after two and a half hours. The air is absurdly clear and bright with the sun riding high. Each of us has about our necks a silver pendant which, when pressed, will translate what it picks up into English – a basic version of what most citizens have embedded under their skin (along with other things, like communicators). A quick search on the tablet left for my use (and my God, didn't it come back to me fast!) revealed they're the same models favoured by older citizens, the ones most reluctant to adapt away from their mother tongues.

There's been gossip for years about what the 'morally bankrupt' on the other side of the Channel use their technology for, none of it substantiated and always salacious. Devices to change your gender at will, others to prolong sex – it always returns to sex, saying more about the person whispering the rumour. I don't see evidence of people winking out of view under invisibility fields (another favourite among the more paranoid) or anyone flying on rocket boots. Just then, a girl of about seventeen squints into the glare, taps her wrist and mirror lenses slide out of her brow, covering her eye sockets. She does it like it's the least interesting thing in the world – which it likely is, for her – but I'm transfixed. It's only when her friends start giggling that I think to gather myself.

The attaché speaks good, barely accented English to us, so a couple of our lot have already pocketed theirs out of disinterest, but I key mine and the earbud I have in to pick up the background chatter from around the concourse. A lot of French, of course, but Latin from the group of teenagers that passes us by with sideways glances. They think we're odd, and they're probably right: matching chinos and pale blue shirts with sports jackets – Orkney would call it *mufti*. We've ended up in uniform, despite ourselves, a strange, standout gaggle. Charteris the under-minister, two of his minions, a nameless bald man from Trade and myself. Ms Albenge takes the lead and we wend our way through the onlookers like baby ducklings; Charteris emits his typical snort of displeasure at the insolence of these 'Euro degenerates' whose world we've entered.

On the hill above the modern city sits a castle, bigger than it seems possible. A fairy tale made adamant: high towers, crenellations, a moat, guardhouses, the works. The stone, cut hundreds of years back by serfs from the surrounding hills, is a dusty orange and the roofs gleam with clean, new slate.

'The *Cité* is one of my favourite places to visit,' says Mariko – Ms Albenge, cultural attaché, I correct myself, knowing some damage is already done by that slip into informality. She has left her suit behind in favour of a yellow silk blouse and a long cream skirt that floats on the breeze. Her sunglasses cover half her face.

Charteris huffs again. 'Well, it's no Windsor, that's for sure.'

We're on the same side and I should agree, but I'm having a hard time with this comparison: Windsor is far behind barbed wire and dog patrols nowadays because the Crown loves the

People but it's evident it doesn't trust the People; the fortress before us is alive with streams of people bustling in and out of the many great gates, not a dead thing of searchlights and gun towers. At home most carry on with their lives, fed what they need to be fed by media, but not one of us at the Ministry hasn't heard the rumours of riots as far south as Birmingham after last winter, which was a bad one. I wonder at times how thin the veneer is, that oft-repeated refrain of royalty stepping into the breach where politicians so utterly failed – does the Prince of Wales sit in his stone halls and wonder if the tipping point of national forbearance is approaching? No wonder the papers are so bland.

As usual, I choose not to share this with the group.

Inside the curtain walls the town is a laced maze of cobble and stone, full of shops, bars and restaurants whose second and third storeys lean into each other across the empty space, creating tunnels. Crossroads and open spaces arrive suddenly, leaving us blinking in the light while tourists eat ice cream. Squares bustle around burbling fountains, carved from stone to look like fat little cherubs carrying bowls. Despite the sun that sweats our backs and burns our Albion necks it's cool in here by some trick of ancient masonry – the warren funnelling the breezes to fan our brows. The others tramp on, glowering at the locals who stop and stare in a manner that is fast fading into ubiquity; I pause at a stall and swipe the charge card they issued all of us over the sensor a grey-flecked woman presents me and accept in return an iced drink that smells of lemons but tastes of something quite different. Grenadine, says Mariko, who's doubled back to pick me up. She buys one for herself with a cheerful *Merci!* When we catch up the rest of them glare at me with one part scorn, two parts envy for the drink that is beading condensation in my hand.

My lot aren't seeing what I see. For them the keep is pathetically small, the gates too wide – a lot of this comes from Charteris, who must think it's expected of him (though I have more than a suspicion he's impressed: for all his formulaic bluster, he's no Easter). Mariko accepts the unflattering comparisons with great British fortifications with good grace, content to let the soaring walls do the talking. On the way up towards the crown of the hill and the heart of the citadel, the bailey, we pass squares full of vines suspended on trellises. People are drinking, eating, smiling, arguing. Two women entwine their fingers over a carafe of deep red wine, then lean in for a small, unfussy kiss that speaks of years.

'Perverts!' blurts one of the minions, louder than he meant to.

The couple glance around at the sound and Mariko moves us on before a scene can develop. With a mumbling and a nodding of heads, the delegation agrees that this is the very sign we all expected, that the Confederacy is, for all its technology and power, today's Sodom. I can't get away from the casual ease on the faces of the couple before we so crudely disturbed them – an everyday love without theatrics that I used to know.

Another half-hour of Charteris's charmless critique has me longing for the train's quiet interior, and I can hear work calling me back just as we come to a desultory halt.

'Now *this* looks worth seeing!' A couple of juniors bob their heads and make the appropriate noises. The brass plaque announces (in English and six other languages) the 'Museum of the 100 Years War'.

'Hmm, didn't realise we made it down this far. We can take it from here, ma'am,' ruffles Charteris, holding out his hand to stop Mariko from offering. He sweeps into the building with his entourage in his wake; Trade's head pops back out and asks if I'm coming. He looks suspicious, like a bulldog denied dinner.

'I'm a little light-headed,' I declare. 'Perhaps I'll find something to drink.'

Mariko nods. Trade takes this at face value and disappears.

'Are you unwell?' she asks and I'm surprised by how pleased her concern makes me.

'Oh, I'm fine really.' I wave at the plaque, the empty doorway that has swallowed my compatriots. She smiles and an eyebrow hints at arching.

'I know a place, come,' she says.

We leave the citadel, passing back into the modern city of Carcassonne. The buildings are more current here, none of the soaring glass edifices on the periphery of Rome but functional cubes in a neat grid pattern, jutted with the occasional high-rise. After a few minutes on an avenue then a hair-raising dash across a pedestrian crossing that appears to be just painted on for show, Mariko leads me into a side street. It is, apparently, a shortcut, a thin defile that narrows into a trench, framing a royal blue slice of sky. The hum of traffic is muted by concrete, the sounds of a living city taking over: somewhere above a woman shouts to a neighbour; cats squabble, then scatter; a huddle of rubbish bins gives off the rotten-sweet tang of old melons. Part of me is relieved to see ugliness – I was beginning to think of the Confederacy as a little sterile in its futurist glory. Here real people live and work and die, much as they always have, a humanising and habitual kind of squalor.

Mariko strides along, leading me through the back alleys with purpose and I follow, looking around at the dirt and flower-decked windowsills.

'We don't want to miss the others…' I say, immediately loathing the whiny edge of my words. 'When they come out.'

She smiles at me in a shaft of dusty yellow sunlight and makes a small gesture with the fingers of one hand that tells me not to worry, or care, or both. 'I know these streets. I grew up here.'

The young man that appears like smoke smells like roasted cloves in the press of the alley. He must have been waiting in the shadowed doorway which reeks of piss and the knife in his fist is rust-pitted, reddened with age – or something my mind doesn't want to consider – though it has a clean, sharp edge. His close-together eyes are hooded, and while my French isn't good enough to catch everything he says, the thrust of his words is clear enough. Mariko replies, rapid-fire, placating tones as he holds the knife up. I'm oddly glad of the half-dark of the buildings that hides the rush of blood that I can feel mottling my face. I'm a sorry thing of flared nostrils and wide eyes, breath and heart pounding, every blood vessel wide as an avenue. In the eternal binary choice of fight or flight, my body has elected to take the lesser-known third way, that is to take its hands off the wheel and take whatever comes.

The knife glints. My lungs freeze.

In a split second, the other two exchange broadsides of words. The knifeman shoves her, and in my heightened state I can see the embedded dirt under his fingernails and smell body odour under the spice of him. She hits the wall with a scrape of designer cloth on brick.

What is this now? My right hand is gripping his shoulder, feeling the bones under the worn pad of his jacket. My mind didn't order it there, yet there it is – the meat has taken action that the grey couldn't, the field commander screaming down the phone as a division of brave but foolish infantrymen charge onto enemy guns.

Orkney shakes his head, and I don't know if he is appalled or impressed. I shout something high-pitched, like 'Hey!'

The man looks at my confused, scared face with disdain and my world explodes into white, fire spearing up between my eyes as his elbow crunches into my nose. I reel back.

When the pain clears, she has already hit him several times. There's nothing flashy to what she does and she moves like a predator, controlled strikes to his face and neck. He steps back, has the blade reversed and goes to stab down on her but she jars the arm before it can move two inches, her other, balled, hand hitting him in the throat in synchrony. He gags and she has the knife somehow; she drops it and a knee flashes up, the hem of her skirt flutters, coiled power unleashed into a point that drives the air from him. He is bent double and she hammers once, twice on the exposed nape of his neck and he goes down hard, head clunking off the rough concrete. It happens so fast that I don't feel the first drops of blood running from my nose until it's all over. He's breathing, I think.

I don't remember getting up, but I'm on my feet and being led by the hand. It feels strong.

Sunlight hits me like another punch and we're clear of the warren. She looks alive, her face flushed and her eyes alight and I'm struck by embarrassment for my wretched attempt at being the saviour; the dull, bovine set of my features stale where hers is fresh. I feel so damn old although I'm no more than five years her senior, at most.

'Coffee?' she asks.

It's absurd. My face cracks with a tide of relief. Today is a day of firsts.

'You did not run,' she says.

'I couldn't leave a lady to be assaulted.' This is, of course, entirely bullshit.

'That is bullshit,' says she with a smirk. Her slim fingertips – elegant, with trimmed, practical nails – dip into the white sugar bowl and pick out two lumps (one brown, one white), which she places with care on the foam surface of her coffee. I watch them sink slowly, like stricken ships. When she ordered the coffee this way – its twin sits before me on the marbled top of the table – she told me that, though this is a breakfast drink, she likes to order it this way all the time. She seemed to find this amusing.

'And your nose?' she asks. She's being generous, giving me an opportunity to walk away with my pathetic pride intact. My ego breathes a sigh of relief.

My mouth says: 'I could barely move,' and my ego holds its head in its hands. Well, I owe her at least some honesty; it's more than just an obligation, but a compulsion.

'I've never been much good with my fists. The nose is much better, thank you.'

She reaches out and touches the livid skin under my eye with the expression of a carpenter inspecting a join. 'You're lucky. He wasn't a fighter. Only a little bruising.'

I should feel another dent to my pride but there's only the brush of her fingertips, robbing her words of any sting, intended or casual. Her hair falls back and I follow the curve of her neck from under her ear to her collar. It's the same barely caramel colour as the foam on my coffee. Was she pale as a girl but burned under the glare of the southern sun? She leans back and takes a sip of her drink and my face feels the absence of her touch.

'I thought all you English boxed at school.'

'We do, mostly. I wasn't much crack at it, though. Was small and a little fat. And I was scared.'

'But you are a brave man.'

The statement is odd. I wonder if she didn't understand me. I rub at my neck where the cord of my translator device snapped – she told me she'd get me another back in Rome. I already miss it. 'No, I was very afraid, always.'

She's fairer than the rest of the Euros I've seen in Rome, though the sun's left its mark on her, baking her golden. I wonder if she has to apply cream just to get by and I notice how her tan lightens as it disappears beneath the collar of her blouse, and for an instant I'm struck by the flash memory of a bare thigh beneath a flaring summer skirt as she spun in the air. Hot on its heels: guilt, of course.

You look like a guppy, says Orkney. *Change the subject, boy.*

'Where did you learn to do that? I mean… fight, like that.' It's the only thing I can think of to say. God, I hope my face isn't reddening again.

'That…' She rolls it around in her mouth, enjoying herself.

I don't mind indulging her. 'I've not seen anything like that before.'

'My father,' she replies, not before allowing another cube of sugar to be enveloped into the creamy depths. 'He taught my brothers and me some things when we were children, but I forgot most of it.'

'But what you did—'

'I took some courses. It was part of my diplomatic…' she thinks, feeling for the word, '… pathway? You know of Krav Maga?'

'I don't, no.'

An umber look flits across her face. 'My father said the world was difficult, unpredictable. He was right. In the beginning, people saw the Japanese part before they saw the French.'

Early thirties, I'm sure of it. Orkney, ever-present echo of my favourite university professor, performs the arithmetic of time on his walnut abacus and confirms my supposition with a nod. I doubt she remembers much from before Britain cut itself off when our Sceptred Isle was 'reborn' unto its own destiny and the rest of Europe woke to its own problems. She would barely have been a teenager when I took my first job, straight out of school, the most lowly of clerks at the Ministry of Agriculture. That tiny box of a flat in a mouldering high-rise, before I ever met my Elanor.

God, I wish I didn't have such clear memories of that time. Father was triumphant at the sight of scrolling news bars: failing economies and erupting tensions across the continent, news readers treading the ephemeral line between sympathy and satisfaction and, more often than not, over-stepping. *We got out just in time*, was the mood. *Look at them rioting, standing in bread lines.* We were comfortable with the sea surrounding us like a warm coat, oblivious to it turning into a straightjacket.

Or a noose, opines Orkney, lobbing another dart at the face of his Imperial Majesty.

'It was hard for you all, in those early days.' I say it because it feels like something should be.

She shrugs, then glances over at a pigeon taking its chances under a neighbouring table. 'My father came from Hiroshima. All Japanese know about survival, especially people from that city.'

The pigeon, disturbed by the approach of a waiter, takes flight in a flurry of dusty feathers and a sibilant coo. A dog barks in a nearby street. The hum of car horns and engines and the rest of the indefinable, ever-changing background of the city fills the silence I can't.

She's looking down at her coffee but she must, doubtless, hear the thoughts rampaging through my head. *How awful... I'm so sorry...* and also, the unspoken *thank God it wasn't us.*

God, Tokyo.

I try to shove away the memories of pictures of blasted skyscrapers and wooden temples on fire, dead carp filling the ornamental ponds. I can't. That horrid image that burned itself into all of our minds that day in November cannot be avoided: the twin spires of the *Tochō*, floor upon floor of modern Gothic, slowly toppling like a punch-drunk fighter going to the canvas as Chinese bombs lit up the sky. Millions dead, again; a cruel joke. In that moment, I wish I'd never heard her say the words and I loathe my own cowardice.

She's looking right at me, adamant. I wonder how long it is since I spoke. Her eyes are the mouths of cannons.

'He got out just before Tokyo. He made a life here; he met my mother. But he didn't forget.' She nods, a shadow of agreement with an unseen figure. Her face is set, and I see the shadows of a hard childhood. Then, without warning, she softens again, as if feeling sorry for raising the subject. 'You could have run, back there. You say you are not a brave man, but you could have left me even before you knew I could fight. You didn't.' She pats her shoulder, miming my lowly attempt at restraining our attacker. Then she sips her coffee, licks away the foam in one deft motion and smiles just with corners of her mouth.

Sunlight, jumping from windows somewhere above, turns the square a deep bronze.

'You were gallant, helping a damsel in distress.'

A playful barb, its edge blunted by a raised eyebrow. But I see something else there, underneath the armour of weariness and experience, maybe a fond memory of a girl's dreams. A vision from her childhood of the misted isle across the sea with its dragons and knights and castles and ladies, the storybook land of Albion.

'Englishmen aren't the knights we perhaps once were,' says my mouth before I can stop it. Her eyes widen, and I know that I'd guessed right. 'Not that chivalry would have got me very far against a rusty knife.'

The pigeon is back – or one like it, who knows one mangy bird from the next? He's a grafter, this one, unfazed by kicking feet. He pecks at crumbs – bread, cake, croissant, all manner of crust with the occasional gem of chocolate or crystallised fruit.

You were a gryphon once, now you peck around tables for the scraps that fall to you. The bird fixes me with its dull, black eye for a moment.

Mariko has noticed me staring and is also contemplating the sickly bird. There's a mutual understanding of the symbology at work here because in a quiet voice, like that of an old friend to another, she mouths: 'Why are you people really here?'

Shutters clank down and the diplomat replies: 'His Majesty and his ministers agreed that it is time Britain re-took its place at the heart of European affairs.'

She nods, unconscious of – or indifferent to – the change that's come over me. 'But so long with nothing. No ferries, no trains, not even a diplomatic line. You were ghosts. Then you are here, so many of you at once, and all this talk of coming back into Europe—'

'Merely a re-establishment of diplomatic ties,' I interrupt. She frowns at me and her unspoken meaning is clear: *Who are you kidding?* We both know what really sits behind the usual bluster and bluff of our leaders' speeches: we're here with our tails between our legs.

'What changed?'

Tell her about the way it is at home, says Orkney. *Tell her about the riots, the inner-city children dressed in rags picking at the landfills. Tell her how Manchester and Leeds are decaying husks where people have returned to the land, scratching a life from cold hills like the last three hundred years didn't happen.*

Tell her about that winter when the power stations couldn't cope and you and Sara huddled under blankets with ice on the inside of the windows, heating her bathwater in the kettle over the fire. Tell her we go to the allotments, that the poor make their own soap. Our vaunted cars, so-called exemplars of doughty British pluck, are rattling menaces that break down more often than not. Blitz spirit, even though no one knows what that even means anymore. Easter, a holder of one of the Great Offices of State, still comes into work smelling of wood smoke and dirty hair.

Tell her how we make do with hardship because we are Masters of Our Own Destiny and thank God and the King that we're not suffering worse, like they are on the other side of the Channel. Tell her how painful that lie has become, seeing all of this plenty laid out before us like a catalogue of our failures.

I resolve to ignore him and tell her none of this, but the truth is, all of us were caught off-guard by the announcement of this trip and were sworn to secrecy with a threat of official retribution hanging in the air.

Her eyes are bright and intent on me. A sliver of doubt creeps under the skin of my skull – has this been her aim, this whole long day? A soft smile and a dress on the breeze to soften a flabby, middle-aged diplomat. Was it possible she arranged for that man to assault us? A handout to a dirty, desperate man and an instruction to wait in an alleyway, to press hard but not too hard and take what came to him; make the foreigner feel brave, let his guard down in the lull that follows the run-off of adrenaline.

The diplomat plants his feet and sprouts roots. 'We should get back to the others,' I say, finishing my coffee too fast. I stand before she has a chance to respond and she looks disappointed – at what I can't be sure. She dabs at her lip with a napkin before leading me back towards the station.

* * *

On the return journey I sit apart from everyone, wanting the glass in front of my eyes to melt, wishing I could crush something with my hands or slam my fists into the walls.

She had no right, to make me feel that way;

It's been too long;

It's a betrayal;

She understands me;

She's playing me.

Back in that café, before things soured, I'd felt a moment of peace and – whisper it – contentment that I have no right to. My jaw is clenched so tight the skin of my face is a drumskin. Under a pall of blueish pipe smoke and from behind his battered and beloved, much-annotated copy of *Pantagruel*, Orkney shakes his head.

68 CE

A pair of soldiers had us fast by the wrists, dragging us back through the villa and to the front courtyard where horses waited. They'd ridden hard, judging from the white sheen on their mounts' coats and the spittle flecking their bridles. The man holding me was twice my size – I didn't have much meat on me back then, if you recall; that skinny boy could do nothing to stop the veteran who smelled like sweat and polish from hoisting me bodily over the back of the nearest animal and lashing me to the saddle. I could see nothing but the sawdust underfoot and the horse's flank and felt the rider mount up in front of me. Then, I heard Sporus' voice, too quick for me to follow, my ear barely tuned to the rhythms of a language we can only guess at from books and the droning of clergymen. My rider shot his companion an irritated exclamation, doubtless in the vein of 'Hurry the fuck up, Gaius' and wheeled the horse around to face the gate. I lifted my head and saw Sporus there, hands free of their bonds.

It had happened again. Some trick of the light, I told myself, but the boyish angularity of her shoulders had rounded and there were deep shadows leading from her collar bones and down the front of her flowing dress. She was Venus rising from the shell, curve and form, as fluid as wine over-brimming a cup. Her long hair shimmered in the torchlight and her hand rested with vapour lightness on the cheek of the soldier who'd, until moments before, been manhandling her. She was staring into his eyes and her lips were red and plump, glistening with moisture and invitation and I swear I saw that cut-and-sanded veteran – that killer – whimper like a boy. He was as captive as a spider under a glass.

I doubt either soldier, the one mounted in front of me or the one whose fingers twitched, ready to reach out and seize the ripe fruit that was being offered him, saw the change. I did, though – I was razor-cut alert from the strangeness of my long night – the dislocation of the fall, being kidnapped, seeing none other than a sodding *emperor* open his veins; perhaps it was nothing more than the innate terror of being bent over and bound to something, but I saw her change. Her jaw became taut, her body lithe as a whip and her eyes were pure, purple murder; her hand, raised behind her head in a parody of sensuality, plucked a golden pin some five inches long from her hair and stabbed it into the man's eye with a wet crunch.

The soldier howled; Sporus pulled him close and buried the withdrawn pin in his leg, just beneath the groin. Blood jetted like a garden hose, spattering her dress and staining the sand and chippings underfoot. I felt the horse under me start at the violence and its rider snap out of his trance. His knuckles banged my temple as he went for his blade.

Another wet *thunk*, deeper in tone, like a wet rag hitting the skin of a drum. Droplets of something moist and warm spattered me. A gurgle, then I felt the weight of the rider fall away and thump onto the ground. A thrown gladius, a heavy length of stabbing iron, had taken him in the chest, the weight of the throw pushing the blade deep. He squirmed a little, coughed. I was sure he'd scream for help, but his movements were weak; after a few seconds he stopped moving all together.

Before me, Sporus stripped and there was no eros to it, pure practicality: the dress was in the dust and the dead soldier's tunic replaced it, followed by his mail surcoat and sword-belt. The bodies were left in a darkened lean-to, then she mounted in front of me. I wasn't untied and not a word passed between us, but I was evidently to go along. Perhaps two minutes had passed since she'd been Aphrodite waiting for Mars to mount her, and now she was a common soldier carrying me off into the night.

As we cantered down the dusty trail between the fields the horse's rump tossed me about like a toy. I was too preoccupied to complain. I'd never seen a dead person before that night and in the last hour I'd seen three. I was numb, though I could feel the shadow of the shock that would hit me later, the water rushing away beneath my feet, gathering for the crash of the wave. Something else had caught my eye in the midst of all this action and death, something most unexpected. When that gossamer dress had hit the floor and Sporus had stood there naked in the torchlight, two things had stood out about her. Namely, a brace of milk-smooth balls and a hooded cock, proud as day.

The house that took us in and was our home for the next couple of months belonged to Pythagoras. No relation to the Greek triangle man but another former lover of Nero. A huge, gnarl-fingered brute but soft-spoken. I wondered if he was a eunuch, the must-have accessory of every certified ancient despot, though I wasn't about to ask. Sporus explained that Nero had actually married him: an ex-gladiator cast as the husband in a partnership meant to shock fuddy-duddy elder senators; the late Caesar was always on the lookout for scandal. The partnership had endured beyond the initial joke and Pythagoras had been in the Imperial bed night upon night until Sporus usurped him. Instead of the resentment you might expect from a spurned concubine there was instead a kind of kinship. They were both Greek, you see, and a Greek belonged to his island, then Greece, and only then to Rome. At first, I think I took them for actors playing a pantomime of grief, but I came to understand that their mutual sadness for Nero's passing was raw and real. For all the pomp and theatrics there had been real love between the three of them.

We hid in this house, which was rustic but no hovel, just outside the city walls and a gift from Nero on Pythagoras' 'retirement'. There was a vegetable patch and a few goats, some chickens. The herb patch near the kitchen was thick with growth and scented the air. I've always loved the smell of rosemary and I found it calming to bruise the leaves between my fingers.

I walked around as if in a daze, seeing myself from the outside like a character in a film. The shock had given way to fear and disbelief but I'd bypassed the other stages and gone straight to acceptance – I was in *the* Rome! I hadn't the faintest clue of how or why, but I was walking through my fantasy, having recently escaped death by soldier, and every day eating the food and drinking the water of people I'd studied and admired from the other side of two millennia. Through the wardrobe, through the looking glass – take your pick of Oxford Don analogies – I was sent to pump water from the well in the courtyard one day and the simple act had me laughing my arse off.

My reality was surreal and quite magnificent. I'd wanted out of a bad future, and somehow I'd got my wish and more. And then, of course, there was Sporus.

He became my teacher. As a foreigner his Latin had been hard-won, so he knew to start with the simple things: water, food, the nearest latrine. Not a cavorting Aeneas, nor a plucking Orpheus to be heard of – our lessons were of sand, earth, fire and the simple cloth of our clothes.

'They have name?' I asked him one day, indicating the hens clucking and pecking at some scattered corn.

'Why?' he answered. His smile was puzzled, as if I'd asked if the sky was made of cheese.

'Sometimes, at home, animals name give.'

'Wrong. Try again.'

'At home, we give animal name.'

'One animal?'

'Many animal. Animals.'

He drew a finger across his throat and made a quacking noise. 'They are for the market and the table. We don't become friends.' He reached behind his head to pull his hair tighter in its leather thong. His neck was long and smooth and his armpit, always entirely hairless, was a dark and musky hollow on the way down from his arm to under his tunic. Even with the animal smells and the ever-present aroma of hay, I could breathe in the perfume of him.

Gods, I was smitten even then. Embarrassing, when I think of it now.

I had to stay within the walls of the house for the first few days, then Sporus allowed me to use the little courtyard out the back. Rome, I learned much later, was in uproar, though not in flames. One Nymphidius Sabinus, Prefect of the Praetorians, had a ripe old go at taking the laurels for himself, setting himself up in Nero's house and issuing edicts to the Senate. Rumour had it (I tuned my ear to the dialect by listening to locals gossiping on the street outside from a small window) he'd been seen wearing purple, which was the limit as far as Romans were concerned. Be an absolute despot with every trapping of power, fine; flatten half the city for your private palace, fine; call yourself king, deck yourself in royal purple and slap on a crown and the mob would be at your door quicker than you could say Lucius Tarquinius Superbus. That plebeian mob, I later found out, had nothing to do with his demise: Sabinus was a soft patrician lad who soon fell out of favour with the crook-fingered murderers he commanded. The Praetorians ousted him and advanced another from within their ranks, who duly chucked in his lot with the new man, Galba, and before you knew it there were divisions of men baked hard by the Spanish sun clomping their way down the Appian Way. I don't know if Sabinus took the honourable way out or a gilded Praetorian sword found his back, but he was a corpse before Galba reached the steps of the Curia.

Ah, Galba. That homicidal piece of dried-out old shit.

Sporus had been calm, almost aloof, during those early weeks, playing word games with me in the sun. When he smiled he showed his age: only a couple of years older than me, though his worldliness was years beyond. His voice was pure music. As soon as Galba's troops entered the city, he changed: his eyes became guarded and he made me stay in the house for long stretches until I was begging for fresh air. He spent most evenings in hushed conversations with Pythagoras which were too fast for me to follow. I scratched at bites on my skin and the rough cloth of my tunic rubbed me raw, but I did as I was told.

It wasn't so bad, but I missed the garden. There was a warm spell and the nights in my attic room became an itchy, sweaty ordeal, one that I couldn't fully shake off the next day without the chance to feel the breeze. I felt cooped up and even my sense of wonder at where (and when) I was started to fray – you have to remember, Banks, that I had *nothing* to do in that house. Sporus eventually – perhaps seeing that I was morose – allowed me to use the courtyard but not the rear garden where I might be seen over the fence by a passer-by (who could possibly have recognised me was beyond me, but he was so cautious). He continued to teach me during the day when Pythagoras was out doing whatever Pythagoras did. He'd hold my hand and say *manus* and I would repeat, his touch firing shocks up my arm. The days like that made the nights easier to bear.

I lost track of time in isolation. One day, just like that, it was at an end.

Noon, with the sun high in the sky and the inside of the house seething, there came the *clop clop clop* of a shod horse on paving and then the *tramp tramp* of iron-nailed boots. There were a dozen of them and an officer on his horse, and we were out the front of the house and down on our knees, all three of us, before I knew what was happening. Sporus was firing rapid Latin at them while Pythagoras merely hung his head like an old bear. The officer listened to every word, even nodding at times as if captivated, then flicked his fingers in a dismissive sort of way. A soldier with a wooden rod the length of a cricket bat and shoulders like a wrestler clonked Sporus across the head, laying him out. Then – needlessly, he gave me some too.

The battering didn't knock us out but it kept us docile as we tramped along between the soldiers, bound with a single length of wound leather. The soldier – an *optio*, as I later learned to distinguish them, kept within batting distance as the walls of the city rose up either side of us. We headed towards the centre of the city. Back to the Golden House.

* * *

How do you talk to a relic? If you, Banks, were brought before
Queen Bess or Genghis Khan, how would you look them in
the eye, knowing what you do about the life that awaits them?

I was pulled through the streets of Rome, the upward-
sweeping majesty of its temples, cloisters and porticos lost on
me – I, you see, was down in the mud and the animal shit
that gathered in the high-kerbed streets. It stank of rotten fruit
and rotten people and horses. Every wall was a riot of graffiti,
most of it phallic of the kind that has graced the textbooks
of many a schoolboy; one, I remember, was a fat man with a
crown of leaves being buggered over a chair, ripe commentary
on the proclivities of the late Nero. That Caesar was cold and I
was being taken to meet his successor; just a little more mind-
fuckery to add to the pile.

Sporus was a close companion of the late emperor, so I
understood why they wanted him; Pythagoras as well, if it
was a show they were after – bringing the trophies out to
stamp all over them – but me? I wanted to live but I didn't
understand why one of the soldiers' swords hadn't ended up
through my chest.

We entered the Golden House through a side entrance.
Servants were sweeping a simple courtyard. The officer
dismounted and handed off his horse and we were led through
a wide door. I recognised the colonnades and the pattern on
the floor from my last visit to this great pile, the place where
I'd found myself on that first night. We even passed the stone
boat in the flat pond, though we turned away from it and went
deeper into the House. Servants were deployed in what seemed
like their dozens, scrubbing floors and sweeping piles of leaves
from the bases of columns; I smelled bonfires on the air where

they were burning them. I watched two women uproot a dead bush from a huge planter and throw it into a wooden barrow; a short way on a boy my age tottered on a wooden ladder, re-stocking a brazier. The palace was being renewed, flushed of the stagnant air I'd smelled when Nero had been its master. I wondered if we were being brought here only to meet the same fate as those piles of leaves.

We left the light of the colonnades and entered a series of darkened rooms. Most homes back then, grand and base, were cave-like. The function of atria, inner gardens and cloisters was to allow light into a house because they seemed to have some profound distrust of windows, leaving most rooms in shadow. There was something else here: blinds had been pulled over what narrow slits there were and even at the height of the day candles and braziers fugged the air with their oily scent. It reeked like old bandages and piss, the incense that burned giving the funk a sickly edge, like old people – it makes me smile to think of it now, though at the time I didn't dare.

In the innermost room, on a gilded campaign chair laid with hides and furs that rose on a high dais, sat the Emperor Galba. In armour fit for a Caesar – polished, moulded, like the washboard abs of Jupiter himself – he leaned on a bony elbow, one leg tucked back, the other stretched out before him. The man looked like a corpse, skin so pale and thin that in the firelight he appeared like some manner of albino cave fish, the kind that has never seen light and lost the use of its eyes, forever poking around in the dark on scent and touch alone. His head poked out from the breastplate on a scrawny neck with veins like ropes; a nose you could open a can with. If Rome was an eagle, here was its vulture lord.

Galba watched us approach with hooded eyes. He was breathing hard, even though he was seated. Even with the threat of death hanging over me I remembered my Suetonius: how Galba would meet his fate by a pond near the forum, too weak to walk and carried in a palanquin. I could believe it, looking at the old bastard.

If his body was broken, the voice that came from it was not. The note of command was powerful as he barked at the officer who'd brought us, who snapped a hasty chest thump and batted the three of us prisoners forwards, towards the dais. The vulture eyes watched us like morsels while only the scratch of the pens of two scribes off to one side disturbed the quiet of the thick room. After what felt like an hour, but was likely a couple of minutes, he indicated Sporus with a nod of his chin.

'You were Nero's boy, yes? His...' I didn't catch the word he used with my nascent Latin. From the smirk on the faces of the soldiers that flanked the foot of the dais, I could tell it wasn't a compliment.

Sporus bowed his head like a dancer, ignoring the insult. 'First Man, I was His companion. I saw him die like a Roman, with dignity.'

Galba scoffed, the sound like dry leaves. 'A pig died; you saw it. Dignity was lacking.'

The calm on Sporus' face was unnatural, as if a half-dozen swords weren't primed to plunge into our necks and instead he was engaged in pleasant chat about the weather. Later, I learned that this was not the first time he'd bargained for his life.

'Rome is safe again, under your strong hand,' he said, bowing again. He was the consummate courtier – graceful and flattering, never pushing too far and saying anything that might set off a cranky old psychopath. His voice was a fraction lower than his natural pitch, a pleasant tone that wove its way like the bends of a slow river, soothing. I could tell that Galba was a mean old bastard, but whatever murder

I assumed he had planned was held at bay by that soft voice.

That said, he lost none of his directness. 'And what am I to do with the great Nero's playthings? I don't favour the arses of boys.'

Sporus smiled as if he'd been complimented. 'I submit my fate to your keeping, First of Men, Power-Holder. But I know my manners: I bring you a gift. I hope it will bring friendship between us.'

'Oh?' Galba didn't bother looking around at the splendour that surrounded him, but his meaning was clear. What gift could Sporus give this man that sat at the pinnacle of the Western world? Was there a diamond horse hidden in a stable somewhere?

Sporus turned to me and for the first time the smile on his lips was thin enough to scare me. 'I bring you the boy who killed the Emperor Nero.'

Galba hesitated, then scowled. 'Nero opened his veins, surrounded by his lickspittles. I spoke to the officers who saw it. What horseshit is this you're trying to sell me?' He looked me up and down and I felt like a side of salmon being haggled over. 'This puny thing? He'll go to the mines, you two with him.'

Pythagoras, who'd not said a word since we'd been taken from his house, emitted a low groan that reeked of despair. I remembered one chilly afternoon Latin lesson reading about the horrors of living and dying in the tight embrace of a wormhole bored into the mountains, hands and feet scraped raw by rock and stinging with salt; the sound he made brought the hideousness of it to the fore. Here was a fighter, who'd killed in the arena, unmanned by just the mention of this fate.

Sporus didn't flinch. 'If I may beg indulgence. The late emperor took auguries often, and one such man – a Thracian seer of some renown – foresaw that a harbinger would come on the eve of Caesar's death.'

'I am Caesar,' intoned Galba, in a tone that showed his frailty. What was meant to sound grand came across as petulant; I say this now, with the benefit of hindsight – it scared the wax out of me at the time.

Sporus continued. 'The seer told him to look for a boy who spoke with the tongue of the gods.'

Galba licked his lips. He was a superstitious man. 'But what of it?'

'One night, as we watched the emperor play, this youth appeared before us. He was dressed in odd clothes and spoke a tongue none of us understood. In that moment, my lord knew his fate had come to meet him.'

I was torn between shock at being tossed up as a sacrifice and outrage that this utter drivel was being passed off as an excuse. Sporus didn't look at me, the smile on his face placatory and humble. The betrayal hurt more than it should – I think I'd already be shaken by the first tremors of what I came to feel for him; the sting of it, the feeling that every word of kindness had been a preparation, grooming me to be his trump card. I didn't expect for a minute that Galba would swallow it and that made it worse – to be sold out for such a lacklustre piece of theatre!

Swallow it he did. Galba was a slave to soothsayery in his old age. He leaned back in his furs like a bag of dry bones and stared at me. 'From whom, I wonder?' he muttered, to no one in particular.

From the corner of the room a hooded figure stepped into the torchlight, a priest in yellowed robes. 'Lord, many is the Divine that sends messengers of doom. Mars speaks on the eve of battle and Artemis calls to the hunt. Even Dis speaks through his messengers.'

'Dis, has to be,' said Galba, sitting straight. 'The omen of death. Yes. Well, I won't have that filth in my house. You,' he flicked a skeletal hand at one of the guards by the dais, 'cut his fucking throat.'

The sound of the sword being drawn was that of butchers' shops, Father sharpening the carving knife for the roast. A cavalry blade, a longer edge meant to be swung at necks. The man was thick-set, his polished armour ornamented with a motif of prancing horses, and there was gold edging his cloak. Despite his finery, his eyes were those of a killer – I didn't know much about death back then but one look was to know how a lamb feels before the wolf rips out its throat. As the soldier advanced on me, Galba's face was blank, as though watching a spider die.

How odd that in that last moment what flashed before my eyes was my fifth-form exams, a passage of Plutarch to be translated. The life of this very emperor, the man who'd casually ordered my murder: he'd been indolent in exile, content to sit out his days in Spain until Nero, spooked by rumour, had ordered his assassination. Once stirred the old man was ruthless: he executed the Praetorians who met him at the gates of Rome, demanding payment for the support that had won him the purple.

Plutarch had mentioned how much stock this man put in talk of gods. The number of priests in the room matched the guards. I was desperate, I was terrified, and I tried my luck.

I threw myself on the floor and rolled my eyes like a madman, arching my back. I picked a groan straight out of a Japanese horror film and made claws of my hands. If melodrama was what they wanted, I'd give it to them.

'Dread Apollo speaks, to the Spaniard of Terracina.' I put in the place of his birth, just to crank it up a notch. 'Beware the—' I garbled here, because although I'd committed to this chicanery, I still couldn't recall the place where he'd been murdered. I writhed and flecked my lips with spit, trying to win a few moments. What was the place called?

'Shall I do it, sir?' I heard the guard say.

'Wait,' said Galba. I saw him lean forwards, his face for the first time breaking its aloof façade.

The memory came like a breaking wave.

'Beware the Lake of Curtius!' I shouted the last bit, giving it that Hammer Horror wobble for extra spook. Then I collapsed, as if a spirit had passed through me and left me exhausted.

As I lay there, the cool marble numbing my cheek, I wondered what the hell I'd been thinking. Why didn't I just try to run, or beg like a normal person? Did I really think those secondary-school-level dramatics would convince a man that led legions to spare me, to take me as some messenger of the gods? I wondered if I would even feel the sword as it ended me.

The silence stretched, and still no steel came.

The emperor spoke. His voice was a dusty rattle. 'He is touched with prophecy. I'll not harm Apollo's messenger.'

I opened my eyes and felt them begin to water. I think I sobbed, just once, with relief. Perhaps they didn't notice, or perhaps they took it for the exhaustion of one used by the Divine.

Galba sat back, his eyes wide. His skin may have been even paler, if it were possible. When he waved a hand, I think it shook a little. He didn't speak, but I felt hands gather me up under the armpits and lift me to my feet, then guide me, not harshly, out of the room.

As I left, I saw Sporus' face. I expected anger, or fear that his plan had been usurped at the last minute by my play-acting. He made eye contact, and what I saw surprised me: the deep blues pleaded forgiveness even as the set of his features was one of relief.

3

It's already dark outside, and work to be done isn't getting any smaller. Easter is going into the negotiating room tomorrow and I have to precis thirty years of Euro history and trade for him so he can look like he's on top of the detail. My notes look pathetic and my head hurts and still there's a mountain of economic and social milestones to study and contextualise so a man with no interest can pull them out of thin air when he needs to look good. I miss my Sara, though Orkney's quick to point out that she's not the child I want to pick up and swing around anymore. Her school releases her most weekends, and I'm still bothered I missed the last one before I left, when the organisation of this hurried expedition reached fever pitch.

I feel like I'm getting nowhere. This is futile.

So much has happened here in the time since we cast off the anchors – I've read up on their early years on the brink of collapse, the riots, followed by the tendril of hope of a new trade deal with Argentina first, Brazil the following year. The core European Nations banded together, shedding the existing bureaucracy in favour of direct collaboration – the fact that the world was falling apart around them must have been a powerful motivator: America was a pile of cinders, its northern and southern borders choked with refugees, straining the Mexican and Canadian economies to the point of ruin and China's social implosion had spilled over into the surrounding region as one faction fought another. Other nations paid the price, Japan the heaviest, though no one really understands why.

The loose European alliance hunkered down and took the austerity, working with method and patience as the ligaments of trans-Atlantic trade that once went north-west gradually thickened south, and the fledgling Confederacy, rising from the EU's pyre and the Mercosur bloc, fattened on mutual gain. As the old Anglo-centric world faded the Latin one quietly got on with business.

Rome as a capital made sense: it came down to language. With the history of aggressive intervention by the USA and Britain even the idea of using English as a common language was unpalatable – besides, the former superpower had its own problems after Yellowstone, rarely seen at the international table anymore. It was more than getting away from one language, though – they wanted a common tongue that was not proprietary to any individual member-state.

Mercosur once again lent its partner a hand, this time in the form of a left-field suggestion from the classics-professor-turned-Peruvian-president: revive Latin as Europe's common tongue and double its use as a trade language. The common ancestor of the lion's share of European languages and with enough loan words spread about in the others, its structure was familiar and it brought a healthy portion of gravitas to high-level diplomacy – there was an elegant logic to it. It didn't go smoothly, but that's to be expected. One of the last news reports I remember about Europe was about how the new-old language was awkwardly making its way through schools and state-sponsored web portals into common use, struggling against hundreds of years of torpor.

Just because it made sense to the politicians didn't mean the everyday citizen wanted their children to come home speaking another language. Our press lashed out with glee at another example of the 'Euro yoke', compounding how sensible we'd been in withdrawing.

It was important to them, though, as intrinsic to the fabric of the new super-nation they were building as the dissolution of their own national executives in favour of the new Confederate one. The amount they spent on translation devices like the ones I've been using was eye-watering, but they did it anyway because it was a symbol as potent as a common currency. The older generations resisted but before long road signs had been replaced with bilingual ones. The old tongues hung on, of course – Parisians still buy their bread in French and *piwo poproszę* will get you served in Warsaw, but the new generations used it more and more as it permeated television, the Internet, music and books.

It's a lot to condense, though my biggest obstacle is Easter's ingrained distaste of all things Euro – his desire is to appear in command of the detail but he becomes bored so quickly, as if learning about them sullies him. He was never much for study at school, more interested in rugby and the junior common room and, to my knowledge, never set foot in the library. The only thing that has changed is his temper is worse and his sense of entitlement rendered boundless by his rise.

The last memorandum I come to is about an English-speaker turning up in a halfway house on the outskirts of Rome. It's a photograph of a hand-scrawled note, inserted seemingly at random with the rest of the files. For some reason, the strangeness of the content – and its very inclusion in the pack – irritates me and I realise I've been at this for too long. Even I have my limits. I'm going for a drink.

I'm drawn back to the quiet bar of the Hotel Adrienne. There's no one there save for a bartender, all white shirt and slick hair. My Latin's getting better but I still feel a bit of a fool as I stutter out an order – making an effort seems important. He does something with the glowing patch on the inside of his wrist and as he replies I get clear English in my earbud. He tells me to take a seat and he'll bring it over.

From a plush corner couch I wait until I'm delivered a crystal goblet the size of a toddler's head, its lower third filled with something cherry-dark. It's languorous, swirling like velvet, the legs dripping back with infinite slowness. On the nose it's plums and dark earth, on the tongue it smacks me sideways with darkest chocolate, bitter and full. Acrid at the edges but never enough to overpower, it finishes like a breeze across the wheat fields, a perfume that hints at lilac but never imposes enough to be definite.

Always brings the lyric out in you, says Orkney, sardonic.

I had enough practice after Elanor. Though that wasn't about flavour.

It was blackberry wine back home. I made my own and bartered with my allotment neighbours for more. It was crude stuff, liable to leave you with a smashing head the next day: not for me the secret caches of Old World wines enjoyed by Easter and his set. My solution, after she passed and when Sara was in bed, had been to head the rampaging armies in my skull off at the pass with more and more of the simple, sour stuff until I couldn't think straight. That had been a bad year.

'I can see you're enjoying that,' says a voice, bringing me back. Mariko Albenge in a long coat belted at the waist, a light scarf hugging her neck. I nod to invite her to join me, but she remains standing, still cautious after my outburst the other day. She's here, in the flesh, though that may just be her sense of professionalism at work. I shrug at her refusal, wishing I felt as casual as I'm trying to appear. Her scent reaches me, pushing the wine aside. Spices, laundry, coffee. My resolve crumbles.

'Please, join me for a glass. I owe you an apology.'

She sits, nodding at the barman to bring her a mate for my glass. She makes me wait until she has it in her hand before replying. Her eyebrow arches as she sips, savours, swallows. 'Apologise. For what?'

She's dragging it out of me and I suppose I deserve it. 'At the café. I was impolite, and after you… helped me. I'm sorry.'

Her smile turns impish. 'It's OK.'

'We British are a mistrustful lot. It's bred in I'm afraid.'

'You are different to them, though.' She swigs, a deep pull that has nothing dainty about it.

'I'm delighted you think so.' Ugh, get it back, you fool. 'I'd like to make it up to you.'

The turn of phrase confuses her. She frowns. 'Make it…?'

'Let me buy you dinner?' God, why is this so difficult? My insides twist. I never was any good at this.

'Do you think that is appropriate?'

My gut sinks, my hands go clammy. 'Of course…'

'You are busy, getting ready for tomorrow's meeting?' She nods at the book on the table, its pages marked with place-holders. 'Learning history?'

I nod.

'I can help you, if you like.'

A glimmer of hope flutters.

'I can help, and perhaps we will eat at the same time?' Her smile is back.

'Gladly. I'm famished.'

'I know a place.' She sweeps me along with her into the cool night.

* * *

The main streets are thronged with electric vehicles. Streetlights pool in the narrow byways. At one point we have to step back and press into a row of parked bicycles to let a taxi whisper past – I almost lose my balance, threatening to send the bikes domino-like onto the cobbles. Mariko smirks at me as I extricate myself. In the distance the metropolis hums with night-time traffic but here the night is chilly and deep and quiet.

We pass through restaurants that have annexed the pavement outside, making tunnels with their awnings where waiters wait to usher us inside. Mariko says no with a smile, in Latin and Italian, switching between the two with ease. I scurry along behind, the wine from the hotel hot under my skin. It's late but people are still arriving for dinner; one group erupts into laughter as we pass, bubbled in their own private enclosure even as their mirth spills out onto the yellowed streets. I can't remember the last time I ate out back at home, not that there's much to pick from. There are carafes and bottles on every table, waiters ferry baskets of endless bread and steam rises skywards from the dishes that make their way from the kitchen to be devoured. I pass a table with a family of four, two kids climbing over their parents, a half-eaten sharing plate of pasta sitting between them. My earbud picks up the borders of their conversation and all they're doing is talking about the day they've had. This isn't anything special to them, just another evening.

Mariko leads and I feel like my feet are carrying me away from the sure path; I'll be lost forever at a quiet corner table of some busy restaurant, watching as life buzzes around me. A group of guests rising from dinner and saying their goodbyes intersects with us and we become entangled in their warmth; Mariko smiles and jokes and apologises and reaches, taking my hand to guide me. It's like I've been plugged into the mains.

Our destination is an old-fashioned place with an archway over its door. It doesn't have a name, just a yellow sign that's even older than I am proclaiming it as a 'Trattoria'. Inside, the ceilings are low and the furniture is from the last century, worn smooth by time. It's packed tight, guests shoulder to shoulder, the buzz of conversation bouncing from the low vault. Every inch of spare wall has been painted, a riot of colour. Here, St Peter's dome rises over the Needle; over by the phone – an ancient and disconnected landline in a nest of dusty cables – the Forum is picked out in cartoon blues and greys; statues of various emperors pop their heads over piles of books and framed black and white photographs of people from another age. The place is unashamed and simple: the thick-set man who looks too old and possessive of the place to be just a waiter waves us to a vacant table by the wall without a word. He squeezes his bulk through the gaps between guests with a grace that speaks of decades of experience.

'There's no room here to work,' I say.

'Ah yes. This was absent-minded of me,' Mariko replies.

The table wobbles, but before I know it the old man is shoving a wedge under one of the legs.

'*Vuoi del cibo?*' he asks.

'*Si,*' says Mariko. '*E anche vino.*'

'*Rosso o bianco?*'

'*Si.*' Her face is puckish.

The old man likes that. He pats me on the shoulder and rumbles something amused before disappearing through the beaded doorway at the back.

'It's alright,' says Mariko, brushing some crumbs onto the floor. 'We can find time tomorrow for work, I think. Also, "*la cena è la cena*", as they say.'

'Do they say that?'

'It might be the kind of thing they would say.'

I'm cut off by bruschetta on little white plates that descend on our table. Chunked tomato drips with olive oil, flecks of garlic hide in the green folds of aubergine. Each piece of bread is just slightly too big to eat in one mouthful and both of us have to make use of the plentiful paper napkins provided as the juice runs down our chins. She sniggers like a girl as a fleck of tomato lodges on her upper lip and her tongue darts, quick as a rabbit, to retrieve it and I realise that the size of the portions is entirely intentional. Work is a thousand miles away.

We never actually order anything – food just arrives in waves. We don't have much time for conversation even, as bruschetta gives way to mozzarella and olives and cured meats, then to steaming plates of pasta with a cheese and pepper sauce; platters of herbed lamb chops; spinach with garlic, so dark it's almost black and glistening on the plate. Throughout, there's wine. Two little carafes – one of red and another of white – never empty as our host replaces them with diligence. By some unspoken agreement, Mariko drinks the white and I the red – it's uncomplicated and fruity and lets the food do its business without interfering, and is therefore perfect. We communicate through gesture and eyebrows and at one point I realise I must be drunk, and it's not the lonely, bitter kind I'm used to. The drink is an exact match for the bustle of the restaurant and the fullness of the simple food and the hint of woodsmoke wafting from the kitchen.

Mariko drains her glass and nibbles on the end of a lamb chop with asymmetric white teeth. She drops it, wipes her hand on her napkin, then reaches over, past the white, takes the handle of the carafe of red wine – that has been marked by all the gods, the laws of man and our unspoken agreement as *mine* – in her thin, strong hand and pours herself a glass. She takes a deep, transgressive gulp, her eyes daring me to say something and I feel like my head is buried in cotton wool. We shouldn't be looking at each other like this; I shouldn't be feeling like this but I don't want it to stop and I have an inkling that this instant will be etched inside me for as long as I draw breath.

I pay the bill, because of my stubborn, bred-in sense of duty but also because I enjoyed myself so damn much I want to give the old man anything he wants for such a superb time. As the night air hits us with a perfume of old stone and the river that is somewhere nearby, I feel my cheeks flush as my lungs suck in a breath, savouring it.

'Thank you,' I tell her, and in any sane universe I would bring her close and kiss her, but I'm still British and I'm still Lindon Banks so I smile and nod instead.

'I can call a taxi to take you back to your hotel.'

'And you?' says the wine.

'My apartment is only a few streets away.'

Italy when I was a boy: I remember its urgent pull even then, when my slice of the world was shallow. Despite all the years and silences that have gone since then, I've never forgotten it: I'm not closed off like the others (though I must pretend I am for the sake of form and the sake of employment) but beyond the narrow, uncrossable sea the crushing weight of an entire nation's suspicion has not left me unmarked. I know I'm drunk; I know there's a woman I find beautiful standing before me, telling me in a way that seems casual (but – and I know this with every fibre of my being – is *not*) that her place isn't far away. Suspicion winds its sickly way into my good mood.

Oh, for the love of God, what are you protecting, boy? says Orkney.

He has a point. This evening, unexpected and warm and full of life, seems worth any treason. When I look at her hair following the line of her cheek, the brightness of her eyes, the line of her mouth, I wonder if I might knowingly, willingly, follow her into the trap when the teeth of it are so sweet.

Currents and counter-currents. What shall I do?

You're on your own on this one, my lad.

Over her shoulder are trees bending their heads low towards the river, a living tunnel of leaf. A lit bridge, lined with gorgeous statuary, stretches over the Tiber towards the great pile of Hadrian's tomb. On top of the structure they built a palace and called it *Castel Sant'Angelo* – the angel extends its sword into the night hundreds of feet above our heads. Popes hid there when plagues whipped through the city and men died there, tortured by the Holy Inquisition, traitors to the faith. Were those men like me, on a precipice, knowing that the darkness beyond the crumbling lip would be fatal but that its velvet embrace is worth the fall?

She's not looking at me as I make my decision, but I know every ounce of her is waiting for the first sign of my acquiescence. My defection.

The vagrant stinks of grease and unwashed hair and old cheese and his breath is rank. Neither of us noticed him approach through the patches of streetlight, stumbling. He totters, slipping off the kerb and into me and we both go flying into a tangle of mopeds. He grunts as he hits the cobbles and I feel my earbud fall out. Plastic bodywork scrapes on the ground and glass smashes. Mariko gasps. She says something sharp at the vagrant who knocked me over and I hope she doesn't have to fight someone for me again. '*Per Mars, tibi non opus ultra hanc,*' he replies. '*Tace!*' His voice is clear and his Latin fluid as water. Then, out of nowhere, in English: 'For fuck's sake, woman, give it a rest!' It's rough but there's some Home Counties lilt to it. Coming from the filthy, ragged man on the floor next to me, it is an absurdity.

'You're British? What are you doing here?' I manage. This can't be – the threat of revocation of citizenship brought the diaspora back home twenty years ago, when we cut loose, and I'd heard of only a few individuals who'd not answered the call – the ones rich enough to buy themselves a new life. This man's clothes are street-dirty, his hair unkempt. Unless he's a former millionaire fallen on hard times (which I seriously doubt), this is the first I've heard of a common man outside of our barbed wire and checkpoints and beyond the angry Channel.

'Wouldn't you like to know?' He hesitates. 'Wait, you're English? Hang on, you...'

Recognition hits me like a truck. 'My God.'

The vagrant looks like he might cry or scream. For an instant I saw behind the dirty beard and grimy cheeks and there was the impossible staring back at me: a face I knew a lifetime ago. A ghost. He's looking at me the same way, his mouth working without sound.

'Tell me your name,' I ask, barely able to breathe, ignoring the puddle of something I'm lying in because my mind is telling me I've snapped under the pressure of contemplating treason but my eyes and every other sense that lives in the spine of me tells me different, that this is *him*, a man grown from the boy I'd called friend.

'*Monarchus sum*,' he answers, then shakes his head as if clearing it. 'Monk. My name is Winston Monk.'

68 CE

Three months in the house of the Emperor Galba. They took everything I had, including my freedom. What a thing that is, freedom.

You've told me about things at home, how bad it's become. I can believe it, because I saw the start of it before I went away – why do you think I tried so hard to find a way out? But for all the shit and chicanery of home, most are free. I know people go without back in the Old Country, I know the authorities move with little regard for rights that used to be cherished, but people are *people*. In Rome, in that house of gold and marble, I was just an object.

In dark corners of every nation – yes, even this wondrous Confederacy of yours, I have little doubt – there are those who keep men and women chained. It's a wretched existence, but they have at least the glimmer that, even with how far the world has changed, the prevailing attitude is that people have worth. In that time, in my new reality, once freedom was taken there was no going back because the entire *world* flicked a switch in its mind and you were worth no more than the dog, the vase on the table, the couch they rested on at night. There was no hope of rescue because the people who owned you were doing nothing wrong – no one really gives a shit if a cup falls out of the cupboard, because it's just a cup.

Do you see this, here, on my shoulder blade? We all had one – the Aquila of the Imperial household – branded into our flesh. I'll never forget the feeling of that hot iron burning through skin and fat which took weeks to heal. From then on I wasn't a man: I was a slave. You see, that old world had the most astounding capacity or compartmentalisation: a general who massacred tribes right down to women and children could be hailed as a good provider on his return, a paragon of virtue and nobility. A woman who wept at the tragedy of an unkind death on stage would, the very next day, be baying for the blood of men hacking each other to pieces on a sandy circle. Fuck me, but they could put up walls, those Romans.

This was no adventure anymore, no Narnia where I was the chosen hero in my own fantasy. I'd been branded, beaten and almost murdered in short order, and all I had to do was be less than useful and I'd be thrown out with the refuse.

It wasn't the mines, where they sent poor Pythagoras – I heard he slashed his wrists with a rusty pick after a few days – but it was a hard life. When I wasn't up to my elbows cleaning fish guts and rank meat offcuts from the concrete pits that served as refuse bins for the palace kitchens, I was moving nightsoil from under the barracks' latrines. There was no real plumbing in that part of the building so we had to crawl into the tight space below the benches with a wooden scraper and pull the stuff out, bit by sodden bit, lest it clog. The orange and brown shit was mixed with my own vomit the first few times, until I became tolerant (or a little part of my mind went out, like an overloaded fuse). There was a particular Praetorian bastard who delighted in timing his visits just as two of us were about to start our work: he'd wait until we were on our hands and knees in the coffin-like space before popping his fat arse on one of the circular openings and letting go with a volley. The first time it made me retch dry. I soon learned the importance of listening and how to time my dodges but sometimes it was all I could do to curl into a ball. Better to let shit roll off your back.

The worst jailers are those who are themselves prisoners, and so it was with that grotesque cunt we only knew as Perfume. Whatever name he'd once answered to had been lost – slaves didn't last long in the Imperial household, at least not the ones like me that were at the very bottom of the pile, so no one remembered him from before he was the king of the lowlifes. Slaves had their own hierarchies, you see, informal but more byzantine. We rarely saw the body slaves, those pretty boys and girls who waited on Galba's table and all the way into the bedchamber; they might as well have been in the stratosphere. The gardeners weren't much better than us, but they still shooed us away if we swept too close to their flowerbeds. We were the lowest of the low and Perfume had risen by cruelty and a pinch of guile to be the floating scum at the top of our rancid bucket. He enforced us, kept us going into those foul tunnels, made us heave pails of kitchen offal until our shoulders burned and our throats were dry. He was a mountain of fat sloping down from a bald head that shone, as if polished, over a multitude of chins. A single earring of brass denoted his status and he worked us all, men and women, without a scrap of mercy.

I remember my first day in that life, when I had my clothes torn from me, replaced by a piece of rough cloth with a belt around the waist. My first task was to heave buckets of piss from the latrine, and I refused – I'd learned enough Latin for that.

'What's the matter?' said Perfume, sidling over to me with his rolling gait. For all his size, he spoke with a sing-song voice.

'This is disgusting, I won't do it,' I think I said, because I was stupid and didn't yet know how far I'd fallen.

'This? This is not for you? You'd prefer something else?'

'Yes. I write, I read. Not this.'

Perfume took my left hand in his. His slab of a palm dwarfed mine and I remember it feeling like cold ham. 'Yes, I see, you have fine fingers. A scribe's hands. You want to work for the palace scribes?'

'Yes, I can do that. I know... the world. History.'

Perfume smiled at me with teeth that were, by a bottom-feeder slave's standards, intact. He wrapped his whole hand around my little finger as fast as a striking snake and snapped it.

I screamed, and as my mouth gaped wide to howl he grabbed the back of my head and dunked it into the bucket. My body reacted to the shock and tried to take a breath, so I inhaled some of the yellow, nutty liquid. There I was, drowning in piss, held under by Jabba the fucking Hutt's less-attractive cousin. It felt like forever: I saw purple spots before my eyes as I squirmed, then I was out and lying on my back, cradling my poor, throbbing hand to my chest and coughing piss onto the floor. Perfume's little smile never wavered as he looked down on me; he nodded and despite the pain I picked up that piss bucket and did as I was told from then on. After the first few weeks, I stopped fantasising about throttling the fat fuck: such is the power of captivity. The finger healed but it still won't bend like it used to.

I'd fallen far, so far that even being hounded for who I might choose to sleep with back in dear old Britain seemed like a memory of happy days. There had been a lot of humiliations down the years (more than I told even you about) and you've told me how bad it's become since but this was daily torment without hope of reprieve. The beatings came often and without warning – Perfume was a master of the ambush and knew the byways of the palace like a tiger knew its territory. Most of the time we were so miserable we barely spoke unless it was about the work: *pass me that brush*, or, *you missed a patch*.

Esprit de corps, it was not.

One day I found myself in a part of the palace that felt very familiar. The door I was polishing with a rag was large and heavy, and I knew with the intuition seared into me on that first night that this was the very storeroom where I'd fetched up. Perfume was just down the corridor, his voice low but carrying as he browbeat a girl my age – I didn't dare go in with him that close. The prospect of a way out on the other side of that wood made my fingers tingle but I didn't dare, not yet.

And I know what you're thinking – I did think about the *other* way out. Oswald had once told us the story of a man so terrified of having to fight in the arena that he'd stuffed a toilet sponge down his throat and choked to death. I might not have considered that, but there were always sharp things about and dark corners. I had something else, though, a private act of rebellion that carried the weight for me; my pressure valve. Because of this one small act of defiance, I could act the mute, servile youth all day and not snap.

Here's what it was: I stole little scraps of cooked meat, stray pieces of fruit or bread that slipped from the baskets in the kitchen and hid them under my tunic, stooping so at once to appear a good, cowed slave as well as to hide the bulge of my bounty. There was a little courtyard at the side of the house, a service entrance for one of the many kitchens – Galba liked his food simple, this one wasn't in use. At the far end of the dusty yard, where creepers had been allowed to grow wild, the bricks of its throat only a foot above the sandy apron, there was an old, dry cistern with a broken trap door. As often as I could, when my bird shit cleaning and sweeping duties took me to that part of the palace, and when Perfume was nowhere near, that's where I'd go to sit by the lip of that dark hole and talk to Sporus.

He'd been there since that day with the emperor. Lacking much in the way of sadistic imagination, for all his bone-deep cruelty, Galba had told his men to throw Sporus away, so they'd stripped him naked and cast him down this forgotten hole in the ground. The bottom had been dried by the summer but there was enough earth to break his fall with only some bruises (though he'd screamed about a broken leg because that's what they wanted to hear). I don't think they ever came to see if he was still alive, content to let him starve a stone's throw from the gilded hallways where he'd once lived as Nero's favourite.

'How is the sky today, Monarchus?' he'd always ask when I sat there, close enough to hear his voice echoing from the hole. I'd tell him about the larks flocking in the trees. To think of the heat of the days, making that dark prison unbearable, but he always managed to speak to me. The emperor stayed wrapped up in his musty wing of the palace and so did his entourage, though we still cleaned the whole place from end to end, unceasing as poor fucked old Sisyphus. That little kitchen stayed unmanned and I bargained and traded and cajoled to make sure I was the one sweeping it. I had to be careful, but I'd got better at hearing Perfume when he was on the hunt for violence and managed to look busy when I needed.

Sporus and I talked, mostly of plants, in little snatches, his voice barely a murmur. If anyone had seen, it made for a curious scene: a young man in a dirty tunic speaking to the mouth of the old cistern. I was careful none did.

It went on for weeks this way. I began to notice a change in his voice, a grating that betrayed his growing fear that the scraps I brought him would not keep him from death. I told him I'd try to bring more but he refused.

'I'd not have you risk it, Monarchus. It's enough. I'll be fine.'

He was proud, even though death must have felt as if it was stalking ever closer. I knew that if I was caught I'd be lucky to join him, but likely the punishment would be worse; and yet still I did it. Why? As I said, the rebellion sustained me, but more than that: I was drawn to him in a way I'd never felt before, even though he'd tried to sell me for his own freedom. Perhaps, in a little way, it was also revenge by kindness. The longer it went on, the more I put off trying to break into that storeroom, to find a way back to my own time.

As I mentioned, my rounds were during the times I was unlikely to be seen and I was kept away from the grander apartments. Every night, as I went to sleep in the tiny cell with a single straw pallet, there was that nugget of knowledge that this couldn't last: Galba's days, as the autumn set in and came around to the cold fringes of winter, were numbered by history. Though I waited for time to do what it does best with men of power, a little bud of fear blossomed in my belly as the nights got colder: I'd told him where he was going to die, and the fact that I still breathed told me that he'd believed me. Was it possible that I, speck as I was, had somehow perverted history? What if Galba circumvented his fate? What would that mean for me – years more of this, until I forgot I was ever free? That thought blossomed and grew into a creeper – even during the day, the terror gnawed at me. Perhaps I should have died then and there and have had done with it, I told Sporus once.

'No, boy.' For that's what he called me now, in the quiet moments. 'Fate is the best of wrestlers. You can slip and dodge, even gain a hold, but it will always get you in the end. My people know a lot about fate.' He was maddeningly cryptic, even in that hole.

'What people?' I asked.

'They call it Thera now. To these Romans it would be just Greece, but they oversimplify everything. It's less work for their map-makers to round everything up into big parcels, but not for me and not for my people. We were great before them, greater than they'll ever understand. They are to my people as kittens playing with the tassels of a carpet.'

'Then why are you down a well and they're getting drunk from silver cups?'

'My point exactly, boy. Fate can't be evaded. The gods play a longer game than the mind of man can contemplate. We thought we were special too, and then the sea and the angered earth reminded us that we are just flesh. Rome will learn that in its own way.'

I thought of all the centuries to come, when the heavy permanence of the Golden House around me would be reduced to nothing, barely enough left to show off to tourists. He was right, but it didn't change anything for me.

'Thank you for the food, boy.' He always thanked me, even as his voice became weaker.

Rome got cold as winter flowed in, earnest as a wound. Even us bottom-feeders were given extra blankets, because a dead slave is worth even less than a live one, though it didn't stop the biting wind from sliding through the colonnades and our meagre tunics like we were naked. I hadn't known true, life-sapping exposure like this: even a bleak rugby afternoon, shivering on a muddy pitch was better. One or two of us tried wrapping our blankets under our tunics but Perfume put a stop to that. We stuttered, cack-handed through our duties, scurrying from brazier to brazier. Even the latrines were better than the gardens because at least they were warm. It was in this cold, when a simple graze of the hand against a rough stone wall is agony, that the palace went mad.

The talk was that a rival for the throne was approaching Rome. I heard soldiers talking about it as they sat for their morning shits – an old friend of Nero come to claim the throne.

'He's sour that Galba left him out of his will,' said one. 'He's another soft one, I heard. Couldn't keep his woman from going to another man.'

'The other man was emperor, remember. Not so easy.'

'Still.'

'Still nothing. I'd rather a cuckold and a fop who pays than a half-dead miser who's a slave to augury. I had better pay with my old Legion on the Rhine.'

'Can't argue there. Hey, you! Dozy fucking slave. Stop gawping and hand me that sponge.'

Perfume was in a worse mood than usual, lashing out at anyone who came within reach. A Syrian boy had his arm broken for allowing a leaf to blow onto the surface of an ornamental pond. The horrible big bastard was rattled by the news of another master coming in; no Imperial household looks forward to change, especially those within who've scratched a semblance of status for themselves. Perfume had the look of a man waiting for the cards to be re-dealt and didn't fancy his odds. He wasn't the only one – the old men who trooped through the corridors to meetings with the emperor, hauling ungainly bundles of purple-lined toga after them, were to a man drawn and wide-eyed. The air was thick with brazier smoke and worry.

Other than the shortening of the days telling me we were moving into the tail end of the year, I had no idea what date it was. I chanced asking one of the cook slaves one morning, risking a clip around the ear.

'Hey, Florus, what day is it?' I pitched my tone as bullish as I dared, hoping a show of strength would stop him from hitting me.

'Why the fuck do you want to know?' His beard was a bushy mess of old food and dirt.

'Because I just do. What month are we in?'

He regarded me like he would a yapping dog. 'It's January. Five days past the Calends, if you have to know. Now piss off, I'm busy.'

'What's this about Otho?'

He lowered his voice and it became dangerous. I was very aware of the cleaver sticking up from the wooden bench. 'Say that name again and you'll be out for the crows.'

I ran from the kitchen. The tone of his voice had told me everything I needed to know: Otho was coming. The second of the four, the next in line. The man who would kill Galba – I hoped.

I told Sporus a day or so later, when I managed to sneak him some scraps. I'd begun to worry, with each visit, if he'd still be alive to answer me. With the weather turning, I'd brought a blanket and thrown it into the hole for him; he kept out of the pale circle of light so I had no idea how bad he'd got, but his voice had become frayed.

'Otho must be coming. It's the right time of year.'

'So you really are an oracle, after all.' Even the mockery in his voice had grown weak. 'What good is that to me?'

'He won't leave you in there.'

'Why won't he? A slave's a slave to them. They think me dead, if they think of me at all. One emperor is as bad for me as the last.'

111

'Otho was close to Nero. He must know how much you meant to each other. He won't just leave you to... be like this.' I managed to avoid the word 'die' at the last moment.

'You're soft, boy. He's just like the rest: ambitious, likes to screw and drink and write terrible poetry. He kept Poppaea warm until Nero wanted her, then offered her up without a fight. We barely ever spoke, he just eyed me over the dinner table whenever he came to visit.'

I'd expected this, remembered it from my lessons. Nero had, Suetonius alleged, taken Otho's wife as his mistress and later married her. The trouble was, Otho was meant to have fallen for her as well, causing a rift between him and the emperor that saw him packed off to a province.

'He'll bring you out,' I insisted, desperate to give him some glimmer of hope.

Sporus was silent. I couldn't get another word out of him, though I could hear his shallow breathing at the bottom of the well. I left him, not knowing if I'd ever see him again.

The soldiers in the palace seemed to disappear, like the drawing back of the sea before a monster wave. Then, like the most maddening of Greek plays, the main event took place offstage.

All I saw, hidden behind a low hedge, was Galba and a contingent of guards mounting their horses. There was no palanquin, as history had said there would be, and the emperor looked drawn but spry as he stepped off the stable slave's back and onto his mare. I remember the mist from the horses' nostrils and the skittish way their hooves danced, until a signal had them clattering out into the streets of the city. Later that day, Perfume came into the room where we were washing the grime of the day from our backs and said: 'There's a new

Dominus. Nothing changes.' That was it. We were the property of a new man; Galba was no more and Rome had a new Caesar. I don't know if Galba avoided the Lake of Curtius and died elsewhere, or if that day in the throne room had slipped his mind in the rush to reclaim his soldiers before they swore loyalty to his rival. Either way, he was meat for the dogs and Otho was in charge.

Suetonius did get one thing right. Over the next couple of days, a cloying smell pervaded the chill air of the palace corridors. Curious, I followed my nose to the grand front entrance. There, on that sweeping flight of marble steps that I'd never dared approach before, a spear had been wedged between two of the slabs. At its tip, the flesh already black from decay, the severed head of the late master of the Western world greeted the rise of the sun over the rooftops of Rome. What a view Galba had to feast on with his dead, glassy eyes.

I saw our new master the next day. He was at the heart of a crowd of two dozen in the very kitchen courtyard where Sporus lay at the bottom of the cistern. I couldn't get close enough to get a good look, but my impression was of a plump man with little chin. For someone who'd just captured the hearts of the Roman army, he didn't look much like a soldier, more like a baker with his paunch and his thinning hair that had been curled in a frivolous attempt. I hid behind a rough column as the Emperor of Rome watched four slaves haul on the rope that had been lowered down the hole.

My gut churned as I watched them pull. What emaciated, frozen thing would emerge from it? I'd almost forgotten what Sporus looked like but he'd carved a place in my mind with his voice and his little laughs that I associated with warmth, and now I might be about to see his lifeless corpse.

Someone must have shimmied down and tied the rope around him. Sporus flopped onto the ground like a landed fish, and there was an agonising eternity of heartbeats where he was still. He looked tiny, sucked clean of life – the scraps I'd brought him had barely been enough. He was dead, had to be. I felt a chill that was nothing to do with the weather.

Then he raised his head and I saw his sunken eyes and I let out the breath I didn't realise I'd been holding. He looked like death, but hadn't been taken by it. The next thing was a greater surprise. Otho pushed his way past the slaves and lifted Sporus in his arms. One hand stroked the matted hair, and he murmured something I couldn't catch. Then, like young lovers reunited, they kissed.

4

Monk defines famished. At an outside table of the first place we come to, he sits and devours everything the waiters bring. I see their mixture of confusion and revulsion at this oddest of scenes – a man and a woman, dressed professionally, feeding a vagrant – but they keep the food coming. He only drinks water as he gorges himself. He smells of the street, though I don't smell booze. Mariko keeps throwing me looks like I've grown a second head, though she's at least sitting back in her chair, stirring her herbal tea instead of running for the hills.

He goes through a plate of pork and two heaped bowls of pasta before even drawing breath. He pulls on his glass of water as if emerging from the desert.

'That's good,' he says. 'Oh, so good. Been a long old road.'

'How are you here?' I ask, barely knowing how to frame the question.

He tears bread, dips it in the remainders of the tomato sauce in his bowl and chews on it. For a while, he says nothing. Then, 'You'll not believe me.'

'You're sure this is him?' Mariko asks.

I watch the man in front of me. Was it a trick of the light, I wonder, making this man look like a ghost from decades ago?

Wishful thinking, the wine, the headiness of the evening? Still, the face under the beard and the greasy locks is the one I remember, a face of edges and a mouth that looks primed to barb at any moment.

'You're staring, Banks,' he says, just like he used to.

I resolve to apply a little test. Orkney nods his approval. *Empiricism, my boy.*

'The fourth form.'

He screws his eyes up. 'What?'

'At school. There was a toilet on the fourth floor of Ezekiel.' To Mariko, I explain: 'Our boarding house.'

'I don't see where you're headed with this line, Banks. Any chance of some hard cheese? I'd murder cheese.'

'The fourth-floor toilet in Ezekiel. You found something, showed me and only me. Do you remember what it was?'

He stares straight at me. It is a familiar stare, one that is half-amused and half-annoyed that anyone would even attempt to test wills against him. At a young age he'd become accustomed to being the cleverest in the room. 'Alright,' he says. 'I get it, it's been a sudden encounter, a long time. Longer for me, I can assure you. I'll play.'

'Well?'

'It was porn, Banks. An old magazine, crusted pages and full of women with pendulous tits and plenty of bush. Behind the radiator. Been there for years, by the looks of it.'

Mariko scoffs, looks away as she takes another sip of tea.

A lucky guess?

'Oh,' he adds, 'and it was on the third floor. The fourth floor of Ezekiel was attic and even I never made it up there.'

Shit.

Mariko sees the realisation dawn on me. 'You are serious. This man is a *schoolfriend* of yours?'

'His only friend, my dear,' says Monk, leaning back and picking at his teeth.

I can't quite bring myself to say the words, but my mind's made up. Of all the impossible things I could have expected to encounter here I'd never have put money on Winston Monk growing to manhood here on the continent when all thought him dead. I'm ready to believe it, but I can already feel the host of questions jostling for position. I make do with: 'What happened to you?'

'Fell down and hit my head. Woke up somewhere strange.'

'You've been living on the streets? Your family think you're dead, you know. We all did. There was a funeral.'

He holds his glass of water up to the light and plays with the liquid, sloshing it against the sides. 'I've known filth that you wouldn't believe and splendour you can't imagine.'

'A poet, this friend of yours,' says Mariko.

'I like her, Banks, she's spiky.'

'Tell me what happened,' I say, needing to keep him on track.

'I think I'm ready for a little wine now,' says Monk. 'Then I'll tell you.'

It's dramatic, to say the least, but I indulge him. When three glasses of ruby Chianti are poured, he takes a sip, considers for a moment, then begins.

'Remember that flight into Rome that stank of peanuts and farts?'

A bottle becomes two. I drink little because my head is already swimming and Mariko nurses hers. Monk takes occasional but deep draughts of the dark, fruity red. He talks like a man brimming with words, desperate to get them out. He starts with the school trip we shared and the detail is exact down to the dilapidated accommodation and our vacant teaching staff, the way Easter and his band crowed at anyone else, the feel of the city which was only just shedding its old skin. The fight in the dorm, the prank, his flight where he knocked me to the floor and I felt like, for all that he was a wisp of a sixth-former, I'd been hit by a truck. God, the way he tells it I feel the panic of those hours as Easter was rushed to hospital where they wired his jaw but couldn't save the eye. We were all on a flight home the next day while the teachers stayed behind, working with the police to comb every alleyway for any sign of Monk. It was as if he vanished, which is exactly what he's claiming.

His story turns then, becoming something else, and I start to feel uneasy. Long hallways and musicians on daises, soldiers dressed like ancient Romans and suicide under a spreading tree. I have a leaden feeling in the pit of my stomach when he says he can't speak anymore tonight.

He's addled, just look at him, says Orkney.

I can see Mariko thinking the same thing. Something has broken in his mind and perhaps that's the reason we are where we are. I've seen the effects of trauma on the mind, how it can warp and twist and eventually tear reality without the sufferer understanding what is happening to them. When Elanor died I felt those shadowy tendrils myself. Post-traumatic stress disorder, they used to call it; mental breakdown, the crazies to the less medically minded. Madness from grief: a fissure that gives way to pressure, flooding the soul with its own version of events just to allow the body to go on functioning.

This man has invented a past for himself after it diverged from mine rather than accept the reality of what has doubtless happened to him: poverty, a life on rough streets, fear and cold and unforgiving bleakness.

It doesn't matter, I tell myself. Beyond reasonable doubt this is Monk, my schoolfriend, changed but alive. Sick in the head or not, I owe it to him and his family to bring him home; the diplomat at work.

'I'll bring you back to the Residence,' I say. 'I'll make enquiries in Britain, see who we can put you in touch with. You can go home.'

He looks down at this, and his voice catches. 'I... don't know where I belong anymore.'

'My office can help as well,' Mariko says, professional despite the hour. I can see her cataloguing it already, thinking which part of the bureaucracy to bring in first: a lost citizen is a matter of international relations as much as a personal story.

As I look at her, I'm back in that moment when we seemed to be heading towards some fundamental transgression. Relations with the 'other side' are anathema – a diplomatic rule that goes a long way back but there's something else now, a species of doubt that casts every moment of our evening together in a sour light. Why did she ask me to dinner, was the intimacy of the setting an accident? Can I say, in complete sincerity, that I'd expect what almost happened tonight to happen to a man like me?

It's those doubts that make me shut the door on her.

'You'll need to leave this with me, Ms Albenge. This is an internal matter.'

She frowns, but she's good enough not to be flustered at my sudden change of mood. 'This man has been living illegally on European soil. It's unfortunate how it happened, but there are processes.'

'We'll notify your administration in good time. Until then I have to insist you leave this with me. Report it if you must but we'll be looking after Mr Monk.'

Her eyes are dangerous enough to make my heart beat faster and for an instant I almost apologise. She doesn't give me the chance, rising from her chair and grabbing her coat in one fluid motion. She drains the last of her wine and gives us both a hard look. I expect her to snap something, but instead she turns on her heel. I watch her leave with my hands clenched hard enough to make my knuckles ache.

'You've become a cold fish, old boy,' says Monk.

'We don't know anything about these people. We have to be cautious.'

'Gods, is it that bad in the Old Country? You were always the optimistic one.'

'Come on, let's get back to the Residence and get you a room.'

'Alright,' Monk says, looking tired. 'It's been a long time since I slept in a decent bed.'

In the gleaming metropolis that spikes the air outside of our little bubble of sedimentary history is the place the locals call *Il Portafoglio* – the wallet. It's an unofficial district taking up part of the rim of superscrapers that looks down on the Old City and it's where business is done, business and politics. Trade missions are based there as well as offices for the thousands of corporations that sprung up after the Euro-Mercosur pact was laid into law, making it a hub of commerce that both imitates and eclipses what the City of London used to be. The only transport line allowed to breach the wall of Rome's historic centre is the tendril-thin monorail line that links the district to the EuroPar complex and it ferries the thousands of functionaries that keep daily life running – the former Colosseum is where the speeches are made but the hard graft takes place in the anthills of those vertiginous towers.

None of that for us, though. In a show of quite startling perception, the Euros have put us smack bang in the Old City where the reality of the new, successful world they built without us cannot overly alarm or antagonise us.

What skittish things we've become.

The Residence is in an old palazzo, vacated for our use for the duration of the trip. There were tentative mentions of using it for an embassy, but that was quickly shut down by Easter – he refuses to commit beyond the bare minimum and, in fact, resents being here at all. Only a direct order from the Crown – the Prince of Wales himself – brought about this breach of our cherished and self-imposed isolation. For all that he rants, raves and lashes out at anyone who comes close enough, Easter has always been a good servant and does as he's told.

Monk seems stronger for the food and walks up the steps to the Residence by my side. The soldiers at the gate are set to throw him back down before I produce my pass and explain the situation in broad strokes: he is an Englishman who was believed lost, now recovered and in need of repatriation. They look uncertain, but as private secretary to the Minister my word carries some weight and they let us through. Inside, a chamberlain roused from his bed looks at me as if I'm mad when I ask him to arrange a room for Monk.

'There's nothing I can do, sir. All the rooms are taken and it's too late to move anyone out into the other residence.'

I can't blame the man for being foggy from his bed – and he has a point about the hour. Instead I take Monk to my room and pull an extra blanket from a cupboard and give him one of my pillows. I leave him to get settled and head for the comms room on the second floor, ignoring the headache creeping past my temples and the faint nausea of having been awake for too long.

Our radios are old and rely on two-man relay stations that we have deployed along our route down from Calais to bounce signals along. Easter refused point-blank to use the technology offered by the Euros, though it would allow us to beam messages in a fraction of the time. An unacceptable security risk, he insisted. The message I write out for the operators is short and to the point because I want it to get there fast so a family who thought their son dead can start the process of stitching him back into their world.

I don't know where I belong, he said.

MSGCOMM..
WINSTON.MONK.BRITCIT.
BELIEVED.DEAD.C2050..ALIVE&WELL..
CONTACT.RELATIVES&ARRANGE.DOCUMENTS..
AUTH.L.BANKS.MININT..
MSGTERM..

The operator, as she's trained to, taps the message into the system and dispatches it without any sign of interest. I take a spare desk and compose a longer memorandum for the Minister, knowing with every word what Easter's response will be.

Sir,
We have, through happy chance, encountered a person reported missing and heretofore declared deceased. Winston Monk, lately of St Jude & the Martyrs School, Oxford, was lost on a trip to Rome in 2050. Mr Monk's identity has yet to be officially confirmed, but I have vouched for him as an ex-classmate. I have extended the courtesy of His Majesty's diplomatic mission to him while he recovers from his ordeal

and have made arrangements for his family to be notified.
I am sure that you will be pleased to welcome a lost sheep
back into the fold.

I stop, consider, then cross out the last line, knowing my Minister and remembering the boy he grew out of. Easter's answer is anger as a first strategy, always – little need to invite more of it by putting words in his mouth. I sign off with a *Your obedient servant* and my name and type the whole thing up on Ministry-headed paper before having it sent upstairs. The senior staff will be in bed, so no need to do anything further until later in the morning.

I can feel the night's events pressing me down into the floor and I know I have to sleep, to prepare for the next day's work. Bed calls me. I find mine like an old friend and when I dream it's of arches and statues; clouds over Pen y Fan and Elanor's hair.

When the banging starts, I think for a second that I'm back on National Service and I've slept through reveille. After a confused minute, I get a look at the clock display built into my bedside table and see it's 4.25 a.m. The hammering continues, harder now so I pull on a shirt and a pair of trousers and pad barefoot to the door, wishing I had time to splash some water on my face and tame my disordered, receding hair.

I take a quick glance through the peephole and see the thundery face of the Minister staring at the floor, his eyepatch askew, the strap pushing his hair into a crest.

So, he's read the note already, says Orkney, smug behind his copy of *Birds of Paradise, A Guide. This should be interesting.*

There are men with him but their faces are out of view. Before he can boil over, I crack the door.

'Minister, is something the matter?'

'I should bloody say so. What the hell is going on, Banks? What have you brought into my residence?'

'My note, sir—'

'I read the damned note. That's why I'm here with these gentlemen.' He indicates the soldiers flanking him. Both are armed with sidearms, still holstered. 'I'm coming in there now to see this fantastical apparition of yours, then we'll sling him out on his arse when you realise you've been duped while half-cut.'

I think about contesting but abandon the notion. As they push past me, I have a moment of panic that it might be true and the man I've taken in is in fact an impostor, that I was caught out in a stressful moment.

You saw his face, boy, says Orkney, *you heard him tell the story.*

I expect Monk to be asleep, as I was, but instead he's up and waiting for us at the small table as if he knew we were coming. Perhaps he heard us speaking at the door? No, he is dressed in his threadbare old clothes – I'm embarrassed for a moment that I didn't get him anything clean to wear. He's sitting with a glass of water in front of him and has been awake some time, by the looks of it. Seeing him like this, the resemblance to the boy that I knew is unmistakeable, though at the same time it makes his transformation all the more apparent. Monk is a fit and lean man in his forties and his browned face is lined, his eyes marked by deep crow's feet. His arms, where they emerge from his t-shirt, are toned. For a man that has been homeless for years he looks pretty strong.

Easter goes to talk, but Monk gets there first. 'A glass of water. The dullest thing we can think to drink, the fall-back option when nothing else is available. But *look* at it: it's clean, nothing floating, no colour in the water or the glass.' He takes a long drink, finishing the whole thing in one go. 'A marvel, when you don't have it. Hello, Easter.'

Easter's features darken. 'It's "Minister", to you. Who are you and what are you doing here?'

'You don't remember me? Well, I suppose it's been a while. I remember you, though. You may find it hard to believe, but I'm quite glad you're alive.'

'Banks here has swallowed your story, but I'm not so gullible. Do you have anything that can prove who you claim you are? You could be a charlatan for all we know.'

Why are you here, Easter? I wonder. *This is hardly worth your time.*

Because he's curious, Orkney says. *He remembers that night and he wonders.*

'Sir,' I interject. 'I've vouched for him, but even if he's not Monk he's still His Majesty's Subject.'

'Don't be so damned naïve, Banks,' Easter snaps. 'He could be a Euro spy trained to mimic our dialect, an infiltrator. This Monk thing is a little convenient, don't you think?'

'Oh, it's convenient,' says Monk. 'Especially for me. Twice in one lifetime I fall down a fucking hole and wake up when I didn't expect to. Bumping into old Banks here makes me think there might be forces at work.' He points upwards. 'You know, up there.'

'You have one minute to convince me,' says Easter, 'or you'll be locked in the cellar until we arrange for the Euros to sling you in jail.' He turns to one of the soldiers. 'Go and see if this place has a cellar. Double-time, man.'

Monk sighs as if inconvenienced. I envy him being so immune to Easter's bark.

'I'm Winston Monk, though I've not used that name for many, many years. I'm not sure why I'm here, but I know damn well who I am. I came to Rome on a school trip; I got some bad news from George's College and I got upset. We,' he flicks a finger back and forth between himself and Easter, 'fell out. I ran away, got drunk. Got lost. Banks knows the rest.'

Easter ignores me, his eyes intent on Monk. 'I'm willing to countenance that you're who you say you are. But tell me,' he gives him a little, sour smile, 'why did we "fall out"?'

'You were a bully and you and your little cronies tormented me for years. You know the things you, personally, did when the lights were out, you fucking hypocrite. Then, when you saw I was at my lowest, you waved pictures of cocks under my nose and ridiculed me. That didn't end well for you, in fact...' Monk cranes his neck, as if trying to stare around Easter's eyepatch. 'I suppose I gave you that.'

The Minister colours, heading in the direction of puce. 'This was a wound earned fighting for His Majesty's possessions in Wales against the damned separatists. You think a little nancy boy like you could have done this to me?' Easter glances at the remaining soldier, a forced grin on his face. 'The thought of it! I had my school Colours, and he was nothing but a disgusting little boy-lover.' Just for a split second, his eye burns into me.

There it is. The fiction none of us who were in the room that night ever dared question. Easter, when he recovered, took little time constructing his own truth – he had a new, frightening gleam in his eye that spoke of retribution more terrible than a schoolboy could understand – it was an adult's rage we saw in him. A year's commission in the Guards trudging through Wales was enough to cement his fiction – if anyone wondered why his eye was already gone beforehand they had enough sense to keep it to themselves. He got older, entered politics and rose fast; I – for one – put what had really happened to the back of my mind. When you spend so long repeating a falsehood, it looks just like the truth.

The soldier, ever-dutiful, snorts.

Monk is calm but there is an edge to his voice. 'The boys I've loved were twice the man you are.'

Easter bristles. 'Watch your tone.' He takes a step forwards, his shoulders bunched. There's violence on the air like a miasma.

Monk stands, and something in his eyes stops Easter in his tracks. The soldier tenses, his hand dipping to his unclipped holster. The room goes still.

'Easter. I'm in your house. I'm on your generosity. But come at me again like you used to, and I'll take the other eye.'

Easter steps back. 'I could have you shot on the spot for threatening me.'

There is no explicit order but the soldier draws his sidearm and thumbs back the hammer. Everything about Easter's poise screams that he has done this before, with impunity. I've not been his private secretary long enough to know for sure, but there are rumours – people who'd got in his way vanishing overnight. I know enough of his character to believe them.

This is our chance to make things right, my mind screams even as I wish I were anywhere else. *I can't let this whole mission fall apart now, not over this.* Before I know what I'm doing I'm in front of the pistol, staring down the barrel, catching the glint of the bullet that will tear a hole in me if a finger so much as twitches.

'Sir, you can't shoot him.'

'Out of the way, Banks.'

'Sir.' My hands are up, placating, defending. 'We're on a diplomatic mission on foreign soil. The Prince of Wales himself ordered it, you know that.'

'Stand aside, sir,' says the soldier, his gun steady.

'For pity's sake, man,' I say, unable to keep the tremor out. 'They've already started unbricking the Tunnel! There is too much at stake here to waste on revenged slights.'

'Watch your tone, Banks,' snaps Easter. 'Remember who you're talking to.'

I gamble. 'If you gun down this man, a lost subject, the mission will collapse before it begins. The Crown will see it as a failure, and you'll be held accountable.' A stain on his reputation with his masters is the one thing that will make him think twice.

God, I hope I'm right.

Easter's breath hisses. He's looking over my shoulder at Monk, vein at his temple throbbing. His hands clench once, then he tips a finger and the soldier lowers his weapon.

'I'll not forget this,' says Easter. I'm not sure at whom the barely veiled threat is directed. 'He's your problem, Banks. On your head be it.'

Before I can speak, the Minister sweeps out of the room with the soldier in his wake. Monk watches him go, eyes like stone.

'Still the highest grade of prick, then, our Easter,' he says.

No *Thank you for stepping in* or *Thank you for not leaving me in the gutter*. Not even a *How've you been, old chap?* I'm tired and I'm hungry and I'm out of patience with him.

'Go to bed,' I snap. 'I'll see you later.'

Then I'm in my bedroom without bothering to close the door, to salvage any sleep there is to find.

69 CE

Otho was the new Nero, hailed by the people. He knew how to act the part – after all, they were the best of chums before a woman came between them. He hadn't the profile of the Caesars, that's for sure – it takes a certain ratio of nose and chin to face to suit the side of a coin, and Otho was lacking in both. What he did have was steel – plump and pampered he may have appeared, but his voice was a whip-crack and men followed his orders with no hesitation.

His arrival was a fresh breeze through the palace, clearing the corridors of the stale funk that, for all the cleaning and repairs, Galba had brought to the place. The hangings were ripped down from the windows in the state rooms and the fires burned plain wood and coal without incense. The priests that had cluttered the place disappeared. The only ones who seemed to dislike the transition were the kitchen slaves, because Otho demanded more than his predecessor's meagre fare. This new Nero wanted the Golden House to shine again.

This was so much background noise. With that embrace, Sporus was lost to me and so was my one lifeline. I felt true loneliness in those first few days, the world around me fogged and distant as I went about my tasks. They'd taken him to be bathed and fed and healed, on Otho's orders, and he'd disappeared into the finer parts of the palace where I couldn't go – what reason did I have to think he'd return for me. As much as he'd grown on me I knew he was a survivor above all things.

I had one thing left, a solitary sliver of outlandish hope and that's what brought me back, in the dead of night, to the great storeroom door while the other slaves slept. It was harder – Otho had more guards about the palace, but I had the anonymity of a rag-slave as I didn't look suspicious. I pressed my hand against the heavy wood and lifted the latch. No one had locked it. My heart quickened as I held my lantern and pushed the door open.

There was fuck all. The place was empty, not even the great storage jars were there that might have given me a sliver of hope that the portal I sought was in a blocked-off corner. The oblong room was swept clean save for a few clay shards in one corner where someone had dropped a small amphora and missed a few pieces. The light from my lantern bounced from the marble, taunting me. I pressed the walls, kicked the skirting – nothing. It was a storeroom ready for new stores and my last escape was ashes.

Gods, but that was the lowest point, when even my delusions were flayed from me, leaving me raw and exposed to the truth: I was stuck here and doomed to be property for the rest of my life. Sporus, who'd been my unsaid reason for hanging on even as I was beaten and forced to shovel human shit, was off being wined and dined by the most powerful man in the world; I was another broken thing left behind. I sat there in the corner of that echoing room for some time and I could do nothing but stare at the ceiling, my chest heaving and face soaked.

After a while, my head a singing mayhem, my eye was drawn to a broken pot shard about a hand's length. I picked it up and pressed my thumb to the edge; it was sharp enough to draw a little blood.

I really thought about it. I could feel the skin of my wrists itching at the prospect of it. A very Roman way to go, but for a nice, hot bath. A gentle spreading of the waters, then no more.

I could have done it. But I realised then that I didn't want to. I wanted to see the next day more than I wanted the pain to stop, so I dropped the shard and left. On my way back to the slave quarters, I narrowly avoided Perfume rolling back from wherever he'd been, stinking of wine and candles. I slipped by when he'd passed and made it back to my cell. That was a miserable night, the thoughts colliding in my head endlessly, leaving me groggy with fatigue the next day.

That's when it got better.

He came to me just a week after being pulled from the well, clothed in fine gossamer. His walk had its old confidence and his frame had, against all reason, filled out again. I remember him sashaying through that door like an empress, his hair bound in silk knots and with gold at his wrists and neck. It was only the eyes that gave him away – that note of caution that speaks of recent pain and perhaps the faintest darkening under them where the makeup hadn't quite masked it.

If he was offended by the look of me and my squalid surroundings in that filthy common room, he showed none of it. His chin was high and imperious; a sinuous flick of the wrist dismissed the others, including the guards. Only Perfume dallied, but an eyebrow arched and he was gone as fast as his fat legs could take him. Then, when the room cleared, the architecture of his face fractured into a smile that warmed me down to my fingertips and toes. He took me in his arms and held me. Gods, he smelled so good.

'You'll get dirty,' I said, all of a sudden mortified by myself.

'I don't think I'll feel clean again, boy. But I'm alive.' He lifted my chin and his eyes made my heart pound like every drummer who has ever lived was performing a solo inside my chest. 'Thanks to you.'

'I couldn't watch you die,' I said, meaning so much more. He understood.

'Who would teach you if I died?' Without warning, he crushed me to him again.

This was the crux of Sporus' art. What greeted me under those diaphanous folds was not the body of the man I'd seen when we escaped the villa. Sporus was a fine physical actor, knowing everything from the sway of the harlot to the upright totter of the aristocrat, but his body also *changed*. There were real breasts pressing into ovals against my chest, not large but definitely there. His cock was a discreet bulge that I only felt because I was so tightly drawn to him, our legs almost interlocking. He'd explain his particular magic to me – because that's what it seemed and that was what it was – but only later. At that time, I was cloaked and bathed in the scent and feel of him and felt safe for the first time in months.

The feeling didn't last long. I knew Perfume was lurking outside the door. I was a slave, a latrine emptier, a floor scrubber. I could see by the clothes he wore, the effort the emperor had gone to pull him from the well (the kiss that had, even then, given me a stab of jealousy) that he was favoured. I knew I'd be pulled back into my foetid world soon enough, leaving him to his soft life.

Perhaps he saw all this in my face as I pulled back. He stroked my face with a finger and said, 'You need a bath.'

'Not much chance of that,' I said. There was a little anger but mostly sadness that I was losing him again.

'I'm still a slave, as you are,' he said, not looking unhappy about it. 'But it doesn't have to be like this. There need not be any more shit-raking for you, boy. You read, yes?'

It had been a hard graft deciphering the few scrolls I'd laid eyes on in Pythagoras' house, but I nodded. 'I do.'

'Perhaps a scribe's assistant? Would you like that?'

My breath shallowed as the prospect of a degree of freedom fluttered before me.

'... unless you like cleaning gutters, of course?' He grinned, for a fraction of a moment bereft of grace and looking almost gawky.

'You can do this? Really? Take me out of here?'

'Caesar and I have an understanding. I have certain privileges, though not my freedom. I owe you my life, boy, which you had every right to let wither.'

I didn't know what to say. My threadbare, filthy tunic seemed to scratch at me with a thousand bristles and I felt I might tear it off and scratch myself bloody. I closed my eyes and breathed deep.

'Will you come then? Will you shovel words instead of fish guts?'

'Please, now. Right now.'

He kissed me on the cheek, but the corner of his lips grazed the corner of mine, and there was a new heat in me.

He wrinkled his nose. 'A bath, before all else.'

I bathed alright. Once, twice, three times, scouring the stink of months from me. I shed my skin that afternoon, letting the scalding heat and icy cold of the water strip it away. The slave that oiled and scraped me then trimmed my hair and shaved my face. I teared up a little from the relief of it all and he was good enough not to say anything. My teeth were loose from the poor food so I ate carefully the first few times, choosing soft breads and softer fruits. My new accommodation was no cell, rather a real room without a lock on the door; a small table, a chair, a carpet over the marble and a real bed with thick covers. I had candles, three fresh tunics and new leather sandals that hurt my feet until I broke them in walking between the shelves of the cavernous library. But more of that later. I was still another man's property, but I was valued now – a fine goblet or a sharp quill rather than a toilet brush. I felt almost human again.

Sporus was the emperor's favourite, and he'd managed to lift me from the mire with his newfound influence. Otho had no interest in me, not being a slave to omens like his predecessor: he was content to do something to please his lover. I never found out if he knew Sporus and I were involved – I like to think a man with so much doesn't feel jealousy, at least not for possessions shared.

'It's not so bad,' Sporus told me one night, as the sweat cooled on our flanks, the smell of sex mixing with that of the low-burning candles. 'He makes me call him husband and I make myself womanly for him. He fucks quickly and doesn't feel the need to beat or bite. I've known worse.'

'He wants you to be his wife? Doesn't *this* break the illusion?'

'Your hands are cold! Even now, after all of that, you feel like ice. I must get you some fur mittens to wear or you'll freeze the damn thing off.'

'You didn't complain before.'

He hadn't, and he didn't when I kissed him and took him in my hand and stroked him the way he liked. This was the way it was now, between us.

He'd come to me on the second night of my freedom and we'd talked. He said he was sorry for what he'd done; I told him I didn't care. I was the first to kiss him and the instant before he kissed me back was terrifying. We tried to make love until he stopped, not wanting to hurt me; for all that I'd wanted to, I'd never fucked before. Sporus knew these things well and he held me and I held him back and we felt the heat from each other's skin for a while until I couldn't stand it anymore. He used his hands and his mouth on me and told me not to worry when I, of course, came far too soon. We tried again a little later and I told him I wanted him, wanted to cross the barrier, and he was slow and used sweet oils and after that first agony the feeling of him inside me, with his hands on me, was beyond beauty so that I didn't care anymore. I felt loved, and that's worth a little pain.

He didn't come to me every night but when he did he stayed until the early hours and I had to make him leave me so I could get some sleep and be able to attend to the scribes at daybreak; they worked me long, copying scrolls in between the stacks. There was often sex because we wanted it – we gloried in each other's flesh like all new lovers – but as often we sat and talked: sometimes in bed, sometimes at the little table when he brought offerings of wine and bread with him. I told him of my childhood, the world I came from; I even taught him a little English, a secret few words we could share which no one alive could understand. He never once hinted that he didn't believe me.

'How could I not believe, boy? The gods sent you to me. I change my face and my body, I come from a people who breathe magic. Greeks never took our gods for granted like these Romans. They're not allegories to us – they breathe and they heal and they kill. The people of my island were holders of great power before Neptune grew jealous and drowned our great cities.'

My first thought, despite the fog of infatuation that covered me, everything that had happened to me, was to think that he was talking utter nonsense, not so much hinting but stating outright that he was from fucking Atlantis. But before the thought could go much further, my own experience stepped in and told me to pay attention: hadn't I fallen through some sort of hole in time? Was I not, at this very moment, a young Englishman of the twenty-first century living as a slave in Ancient Rome? Try as I might, the evidence was stacking up and what is the scientific method but conformity to empirical weight? Having lived the impossible, how could I not at least grant him the courtesy of belief?

'Are there many of you now, your people?' I asked him.

'Not many, mostly farmers growing little tomatoes on dry hills. Thera is a husk now, but once we were kings of the sea. The sadness is that few of the survivors of the cataclysm were of the upper castes, and because of this most remember nothing of our history.'

'I suppose you're not from a lower caste then?'

'Ah, you shouldn't tease me. Well, of course I'm not. Do you think I would know all of this history, teach you about the unseen world, if I were a fisherman?' He ran his fingers through my hair. 'My family was of the few who remembered the old ways, the magics that gave us dominion over all others. Face changers, mimics, descendants of the holiest of castes.'

'Then what are you still doing here? Can't you use these... gifts to run away?'

'To what, boy? A hut in the hills, watching goats? For such a little price I can have wealth and the First Man of Rome asks my advice. It's power, of a kind, and I had it before. It's not so easy to walk away from.'

He went quiet then, and I knew he was thinking about

Nero. It was a wound that wouldn't close for him. I hated seeing him sad.

'Did you ever manage to flip over a bull then? That must have been something.'

'I told you not to tease me,' he said. 'Just for that, I'm going to do it again.'

My heart became the heart of a man in those nights with him. He taught me pleasures of body and mind and he continued to help me with my Latin. If there was a word I'd struggled with during the day, he'd give me its meaning and its root and make me repeat the lesson until I understood it properly.

'Why am I here?' I asked him one evening. He was stretched out naked on his front, his chin resting on his crossed arms. I just sat there on my stool, gazing at him.

'I told you, the gods. I felt them in the air that night, the place was thick with power. They knew what he was going to do. I prayed to them to be saved and I thought they might spare him. My salvation came in another shape.'

'You called me?'

'You're not listening. I prayed and there was an answer; the gods are not so specific. Nero was a special man, his shadow weighed down the world. Who knows?' He yawned and scratched his flank. 'Maybe something about that night weakened a gap in the universe, let you through. Maybe you were just meant to be here.'

By day I'd move quietly between the huge honeycombed stacks, each cubby filled with rolled parchment, carrying volumes for my masters, assisting them more often as the weeks went on with the copying as I grew in skill. It was hard to preserve the written word back then: if a text was showing its age or had a touch of the mildew it would need to be painstakingly transcribed or the contents would be lost. This was the true leech of ancient knowledge: not the great library fires the histories like to mention because, after all, what's more dramatic than a conflagration! Inattention and a lack of staff coupled with wet autumns plagued the libraries of the ancient world and my fellow scribes and I had the unending task of trying to counter it.

If there was life beyond the thick walls of the Golden House, I didn't care to see it. Though I was still a slave I was kept like a cat, everything I wanted there before me as long as I never overreached. Wasn't this what I'd wanted, after all, to be a scholar living and working in the Eternal City? Instead of studying these people over a gulf of millennia I was instead here, eating their bread and smelling their incense. My mind was fogged with it, never seeing beyond the immediate for fear that it all might waft away, or that I'd go mad. I fell more in love every day and it wasn't just the fucking. I lived for him. The sounds of distant songs or passing carts sometimes crept in through the little window high on the wall of my room on a breeze of fresh pine, but I paid them little mind.

'You look half-asleep,' he said to me one evening. 'This palace, it's leeching you.'

'I'm happy,' was all I could say. It sounded gauche even then.

'We should get out. You should see the city you claim to lust after.'

'Slaves don't leave the palace,' I said, meaning *I don't want to leave.*

'No. This is Rome and you're missing it in this gilded temple to tyrants. I go where I want. I choose you as my escort.'

'What good am I as an escort? You think I can stop a thief?'
I realised I was smiling, though. Perhaps the deep parts of me
understood.

He didn't reply, only stood and held out my cloak.

We walked out through a side door, bold as spears into the
crepuscule. The guards knew him, nodded, barely glanced
at me. Once we were a few streets away he ducked into a
doorway and emerged without his fine silk gown, revealing a
plain brown tunic. A knife was strapped to his wide belt and
he tied his hair back with a leather thong even as the last of
his womanhood fell away from him. We were just two young
men out in the streets now, moving quietly over the flagstones
and hopping between crossing stones.

There was marble, but it was flecked with the filth of an ancient
city's life and most walls had lean-tos where traders and priests
sold their stock deep into the night. Within dashing distance
of the palace every street was a tunnel of sound and torchlight.
Gongs and cymbals. Wine spilling. Water flowing, or maybe piss,
maybe both. We climbed a hill under the watch of the same stone
pines you'll find ten minutes' walk from here and he pointed
out the very rock from which the ancient Republicans used to
hurl their traitors, but soon we were back in the maze. On some
corners the sound died and there were gangs of men watching.
Sporus led with a straight back and his dagger showing and I
followed his lead, the instinct to hide weakness hardly new to
me after the school I went to. Sorry, that we went to.

'Where the hell are we going?' I asked him just once, as we
walked through a gate in the old walls. He smiled and pointed
at the river that curved its way at the foot of the fortifications
– we were just below the island in the middle of the Tiber and
I could hear the roar of the waters parting. A stone bridge led
to the other side.

It was dark out there, in the middle of the span, and we were alone. The city proper hunched at our backs and the river rushed white and loud against the piers far below our sandals. It was like the night paused mid-breath, waiting. You'd have to go far out to sea to see the stars we were seeing.

We kissed for a long time, and it was like we were free men.

He refused to let me draw breath, pulling me onwards over the bridge into another warren. The houses were cheaper and more close-packed here, mostly wood and daub, a mad tangle of alleyways shooting off at angles. Ivy was everywhere, lacing one house to the next in a natural tapestry. There was none of the press or threat of the city here: the streets were warm, welcoming with the orange glow of torches. People drank in bars like they still drink in bars – every true Roman knows you have to cross the Tiber to have a good time. We drank too, standing by a fountain with white wine dripping down our chins from heavy wood cups. Jesters and jugglers played for *denarii* and not a punch was thrown, and before long we were off again, tearing meat from skewers with our teeth, looking for the next place.

I danced, Banks. Me, I danced. I was pissed as a first-timer, buzzing with it all. The smoke from braziers stung my nostrils and I felt their heat as the sweat soaked my tunic, drums and pipes playing a deep rhythm. There were tradesmen there and whores but also some in rich tunics. Sporus was always there beside me, clasping me, spinning me, holding me and his eyes were wide, his smile unending and I couldn't stop laughing like a crazy bastard. I threw up, I think, but then I was back in the mix.

Just before dawn we made our way back to the Golden House, the wine coursing through our veins, ignoring the stern faces of the guards. I hit my bed alone – I don't remember saying goodnight, and the room spun in jerks over my head. The next day was cold; thumping hell but by all that's holy, it was worth it.

Then, one night a few weeks later, Sporus came to my room and though he kissed me in greeting there was something in his stance and his eyes that put me on guard. I'd developed a keen nose for this sort of thing – the life of a slave is always at risk of tumult – but I'd also come to know him. Something wasn't right.

'You must take this,' he said, unwrapping a bundle from his pannier, hidden beneath the bread. A sword, a foot-long and double-bladed with a wooden handle bound in leather. A simple tool, a thing for stabbing in a close press. It felt heavy in my hand but not unnatural.

'What's this about?' I asked, but I knew better than to refuse. Sporus, for all his capacity for acting, was not prone to dramatics.

'Maybe nothing. Maybe something. Just keep it and hide it under your bed. If it comes to it, use the point and don't stop stabbing until you're sure.'

'You'll have to give me more than that.' I was rattled by the cold in him, and he saw it. He touched my cheek and ran his fingers along my jaw. 'It's a difficult time. Caesar is not secure in his rule, in fact he's never been the only one claiming it. There's a man on the Rhine; word is, several legions have declared for him and he's leading a horde through Italy.'

'Vitellius.'

He gave me a look, the one for when I said something that to him must have seemed like prophecy. 'Him. Galba sent him out to freeze but he's made a name for himself. He's a brute

141

and that appeals to men who've spent years facing the savages of the dark forests. Now he wants it all.'

If I'd learned anything from my fumbled attempt to steer history it was that I was nothing more than a leaf on the current. This would come to pass; all I could do was to remain alert to it, be ready as much as possible. 'He's no friend of yours, then,' I said.

'I know him to be without mercy. He knows who I am, though we've not met. He had no love for Nero and breaking Otho's toys will come as second nature to him.'

'How soon can we get away?'

He smiled, but it was a bleak one. 'Not so easy for a slave to leave Rome, even one who shares the bed of the First Man. And with a scribe's assistant? Impossible.'

'You're good at impossible. Tell Otho you're feeling unwell, that you need sea air or something.'

'Sea air?'

'Well, I don't know! Something that can get us beyond his reach so we can slip away for true.'

He paused for thought. Gods, he was beautiful when the light caught him like that. 'I have a few ideas.'

5

I've become, by default, Monk's minder as well as his room-mate. Easter has been distracted by the business of State and I've barely seen him, though his messages are perhaps a little curter than usual. The early, high-profile meetings between us and the Euro bloc are out of the way and, other than the odd recorded speech for the news channels at home (the cassettes relayed by courier train), he leaves the diplomacy to the functionaries that we have brought with us and me with the rote administration. For all that he professes to loathe the decadence of it all he is content to attend an endless string of lunches and dinners and receptions. He did always enjoy a formal.

Still no word from Monk's family. I sat him down for the rest of the story he's insisting on, this ancient fantasy, but he hesitated. His English has survived well, in my estimation, for man who's not spoken it for two decades, but he says the missing pieces bother him.

'I know what I want to say but the words are under lock and key in my brain. It's frustrating, Banks. I feel like an idiot.'

I offered him one of the translators the Euros had given us so he could speak in the Latin he's grown so used to.

'That seems a little absurd, doesn't it? Speaking to you through a... gizmo. Just give me something to write on.'

We settled on a tablet device in the end, something the Euros would look on as antique but that he can use – I'd been using a similar one to consult with Mariko on matters of Euro policy.

I feel like a fool for speaking to her the way I did.

I've only seen Mariko once since the night we found Monk, on the other side of the room at a gala. Her dress was black and cut high at the front, low at the back and silver sparkled at her neck. She seemed to waft more than move. My three-piece evening suit felt ridiculous and stuffy, heavy sash and thick jacket more suited to British weather, not the clement autumn nights of Italy. She made eye contact and she looked – ambivalent? That was worse, somehow, than if she'd looked outraged. I tried to go over to her and make some small conversation but I was waylaid by one of our negotiators and a swirl of waiters passed between us; when the path cleared she was gone as if she'd never been there. There was food later and I scanned the length of the long table, looking for her in vain. The diplomat at my elbow asked me something but I didn't catch it.

'I asked if you had ever come to Europe before the separation?'

I gave him an apologetic look. 'I'm so sorry, yes. I was fortunate enough to come here as a boy.' Then I realised that the accented but precise English is not coming at me from my translator earbud (which I much prefer to carrying a speaker around my neck), but from the man himself. I remarked on this.

'Yes, well, English is a little project of mine. Outmoded for a long while, but I always liked those American films about men driving cars very fast.' He spread his hands in mock embarrassment and shrugs.

'I didn't catch where you said you were from,' I said.

'I'm from Oporto. I'm a EuroPar delegate from Portugal. Gabriel.'

We shook hands.

The Sump, our press had called it in those last years. The country had been another in a line of mismanaged economies, with spiralling national debt and a tax system on its knees. With America out of the picture – this was before the Mercosur brought their trade up the Atlantic – Portugal was a mortal wound in the new Confederacy's side. 'How are things at home?' I asked him.

'Excellent, very good. The ships from Brazil come to us first, so…' He raised his eyebrows and I could tell he knew what I was thinking. 'We do alright these days. We put our past where it belongs and look forwards. Our politics has become a little boring, but that is a very good sign, I think.'

We toasted. The champagne was crisp and excellent. At the end of the night Gabriel from Oporto shook my hand and went on his way, leaving me to ponder the small miracle of what had happened in his home. Portugal had been just another reason to get out of Europe as soon as we could, lest we have to bear some of the cost. It seems they coped just fine without us.

As I went to leave, I quite literally bumped into Mariko. A little sotto *'Merde'* slipped out as she dropped her bag. I picked it up and gave it back to her.

'I'm sorry, Ms Albenge.'

She nodded, watching me for an instant. 'Not a problem, Mr Banks. Accidents happen.' Her mouth didn't move, but her eyes softened a little bit – or was it just my imagination? She nodded again and we said goodnight.

We'd said nothing to each other, really, but I felt relieved.

Monk's day is orderly, regular, not that of a man swept away by penury. He rises before dawn – I'm myself an early riser but he's always up before me – and does some kind of exercise, stretches of the legs and arms, push-ups, sit-ups. He planks his body and holds it there for long minutes, unmoving, then relaxes before repeating the whole thing again. A light lunch which we usually share, then he reads – all of it modern history, as if the last thirty years have escaped him, like he's been living in a cave. I wonder if this is some part of the delusion and how deep it really goes. I'm beyond believing that he is playacting – Monk is caught up in this fantasy to the point where it is his whole reality. I've no training in the ways of the mind but sense dictates he not be wrenched out of it for fear of tearing anything.

Either way, he is a quiet roommate and is content for me to get on with my work. Sometimes, I find him at the window, staring for long periods out at the city beyond. I don't know what he's looking for, and he never tells. We're sharing a salad with a vinaigrette and some crumbling white cheese that sits salty on my tongue, softened by sweet figs coated in honey. It's light and it's refreshing and I have a tall glass of carbonated water that bubbles contentment beside my spoon. Monk is eating with his fingers, tearing bread between them and popping little mixtures of the stuff into his mouth with his eyes downcast, intent on his meal.

'I'd like to go for a run,' he says.

'Really?'

'Yes.'

The Monk I knew saved the worst of his scorn for the physical. A few days of clean living have scrubbed the street from him and it's clear he's grown used to exercise. He's healthy and doing a much better job at holding off time than me; I am reminded that time sculpts us into shapes that bear no relation to what we aspired to as children. I wanted to climb mountains, the bigger the better. I walked every peak in the British Isles by the age of eighteen and I wanted more. I wanted Mont Blanc, the Eiger, Everest even (because the mind at that age doesn't have room set aside for caution). At no point had I anticipated becoming this: a widowed, unfit functionary in the great mechanism of government.

'So,' he asks. 'Would that be alright?'

'I suppose so.' This is the first he's talked of leaving the Residence, and I have to wonder why. I want to believe him, to help him, but there's too much oddness about this situation for me to be deaf to all suspicion. 'Perhaps I could come with you? I could do with some exercise.'

He smiles. 'I could slow down, a little, if you like.'

'I could help you plan a route. I've studied the city.'

'I know this city better than I know any other,' he says, and gets that faraway look in his eyes. I choose not to pursue it – if he chooses to elaborate further, he will. He's still writing down parts of his story and I read it when I can. If I handle him with care, he'll get to the end of it. Perhaps that will do his absent mind some good.

'How are things at home?' he asks. He picks up a fig and rips it in half with his fingers, popping one half into his mouth, followed by the other.

'It's not without its challenges, but it's Britain,' I vacillate, too much training in me to give him the whole truth. In my mind's eye, I see a car on fire, upended, in the middle of Victoria Square in Birmingham as the mob surge around it, an ocean of discontent. Horses charging, flares, blood on the cobbles.

'You can tell me, you know,' he says, perhaps catching something in my expression. 'It was a long time ago, but I remember how things were headed. I already knew, as a young man, that I'd have to hide what I was just to get by.'

'I think,' I say, looking down at my food, 'that you'd need to be very careful about what you say about that.'

'That bad?'

I nod, still not making eye contact.

'Fortunately, I've learned a lot about hiding. You don't survive in a culture of absolute rule by blurting out the first thing that comes out. Living under four Caesars taught me that much.'

There it is, as sensible and level as if he were relating the cricket scores. Too soon to push for the truth then. If he catches my hesitation, he lets it slide and returns to his food.

I felt like a fool the moment I bought the book, more so when I wrapped it in crepe paper, and yet here it is in my jacket pocket as I sit down to another formal dinner. Proust, for God's sake – why do I even think she'd like Proust just because she's French? Something made me bring it, though, instead of leaving it in my room and I can feel the ridge of its spine as I push the quail around my plate. I'm so distracted by everything that I can't even appreciate the food.

No Gabriel from Oporto tonight – my neighbour is a taciturn older woman from Belgium who hasn't said a word since the vichyssoise. The room is grand and there's string music behind the hubbub of conversation but I'm an island within it. Easter is opposite and a little further down the long table, cheeks flushed with wine and chatting to the Confederacy's head of finance, who wears a look of polite forbearance that goes unnoticed by the Minister. At one point Easter spots me and nods and I wonder if the tantrum over Monk has passed. Unlikely, given his track record with grudges.

What am I doing, hoping to see Mariko again? Why do I have this book – am I really going to give her a damn book? I know I need to turn away from this but somehow I keep finding my way back, like a damned teenager with a crush.

The quail is taken away and dessert comes, then cognac which I barely touch. There's no sign of her and I should be relieved but instead feel heavy in my seat.

Enough of this. I'm tired and I have work to do. I make my excuses as the decanters come around for a second pass and make for the door. I look to see if Easter has noticed but he's deep in conversation, so I take my chance and call for a car to take me back to the Residence. Even Rome's streets have no appeal tonight. Sara and I spoke again, this time even more stilted. I wonder how much of it is the age she is, the natural reluctance to talk to a parent and how much is the Housemistress, who doubtless sits opposite her as she talks to me over the phone, listening in. Neither of us was satisfied by the exchange, though there was a glimmer of hope: she said she'd write. If she can get me a letter without going through the school there is at least half a chance of hearing my girl's voice for real, not the stilted sentences and long silences of our recent exchanges. I know her face, know how she looks when she's annoyed or sullen as well as I know her smiles. Even when I was angry with her, I've been unable to do anything but adore every expression that crosses her face.

I miss my little girl.

The place is almost deserted when I get back, security on the door managing the feat of looking bored and alert all at the same time. My footsteps echo around the cavernous lobby and up the stairs as I pass the portraits of some Renaissance Romans I don't know but were rich enough to commission themselves into the future via oil and canvas. God I'm tired and I want to rip this bow tie off my neck and sink into my bed. I hope Monk isn't up and I feel a little guilty about it. I just want my own company. Proust jabs me in the ribs, mocking.

I open the door to my rooms as quietly as I can, trying not to wake him. The living area is down a small corridor, further from the door than the bedroom and I think I can make it, though Monk's sleeping habits are erratic at best – I'm yet to rise before him and I leave him reading most nights. The door, though old, is well kept and doesn't make a sound as I push it shut.

The bathroom is halfway along the corridor, which is a checkerboard of light and shadow. I'm thirsty enough to risk it; in the bathroom a sliver of silver mirror presents two glasses, one containing my toothbrush. I swill water around my mouth and spit before filling it again.

A thud. It's from the living room.

It sounded like Monk knocked into something in the dark. I step into the corridor but there's nothing else – no light goes on. Odd. Then I hear something else, a rasp of canvas on canvas and just the hint of a ragged breath, muffled by cloth. From the direction of the lounge I catch low voices, more than one.

My heart drums in my chest as I take the few steps. The voices again, urgent. Rustling, the sound of someone breathing through their nose. I freeze. Whoever they are they could be a hair's breadth from me in the darkness. The night is tattered by the light of the city, and I dare, millimetre by millimetre, a look around the corner.

A masked man has his back to me, just two feet away. Another has Monk on the floor, holding him down by the chest while a pistol presses his temple. I can't see Monk's face but I know he's conscious from his raised hands, though he still doesn't utter a sound. The man holding him holsters the pistol – compact, with an unmistakeable cylinder attached to the barrel – and draws a large knife, the blade blackened. Monk exhales.

This happened before, in the alley with Mariko; my body takes over before my brain has time to run through the implications. I swing the glass in an overhand arc, smashing it, open end first, into the head of the man with his back to me; it shatters and I feel the sting of it on my palm, then, an instant later, the dull ache of a deeper cut. He pitches sideways with a grunt of pain and bumps into a sideboard, but he's only off balance for a second, already turning and I spot the tell-tale bulk of a protective vest, and he's armed.

He's going to shoot me, stab me, taser me until I shit myself and enter cardiac arrest. Again, my hand obeys its own whim without waiting for the slow brain and stabs the shattered remains of the glass at the nearest point: the balaclavaed face. He screams as the jagged edge grinds home. I don't know what I've hit, only that he's hurt and he steps back, properly this time, reeling, swearing at me in garbled words. *English* words. I'm fixated on him, numb to the fact that I've just maimed another human being, floating in a hazy dream state: a moment ago I was looking for water and now there is blood on my floor.

Monk has used the time well. His assailant must have looked up, distracted, giving him a chance to kick him to the floor; I see Monk with his legs hooked over the black-clad chest and neck, then he heaves, arching his back and the arm still holding the serrated knife pops.

'Ah, you *cunt*! The masked man yells.

Monk sweeps up the fallen knife faster than a fish swimming downstream and he's on top of his attacker; the blade slides sideways with a noise like cardboard being ripped; a wet gurgle.

The man I hit with the glass is fumbling at his leg – his holster contains his pistol. Not knowing what else to do, I run at him, screaming like a terrified boy in his first rugby game. He hammers a punch into my face and I smack my head on the floor; my mouth is full of coppery blood. He frees his pistol and I know I'm going to die, as clear as moonlight.

He takes aim and I shout 'No!' or something else suitably brave. He hesitates, his head cocked sideways as if in recognition.

'What the fuck are you, *ugh*—'

The thrown knife catches him under the ear, butt-first, and he lurches sideways.

I crawl backwards out of the way. Monk is already there, throwing punches at him; there's nothing panicked about it – each blow is fast and accurate. The masked man takes one, two hits, then blocks a third and counters with a kick that takes Monk in the stomach, pushing him back. He raises the pistol, but Monk dips sideways and forwards like a snake and grabs the arm. The two of them are locked together in the struggle to bring the pistol to bear on the other, a mad dance that sees them push each other against walls and furniture. There is a cough – some part of my mind that has divorced itself from proceedings tells me it is like that of a big jungle cat I saw on a documentary almost ten years ago. Monk gasps, and I think he'll go down but instead he whips his head forwards in a savage butt that connects with a hollow thud. He grabs the man behind the neck with one hand and smashes a flurry of four hard elbows into his face, then kicks his legs out from under him. Monk has the pistol in his hands, and just as I cry 'Wait!' he fires a single shot. The assailant lies still.

The silence rushes in like floodwater. Only our breath disturbs the room. There is a stink of death here, bowels and blood and acrid sweat. Then Monk sags to his knees.

I ignore my own pain. 'Are you hurt?' I ask as I go to him. He nods. 'You could say that.'

In the pale light I see his hand come away from his side where he has been clutching it, the whole thing black with blood.

'We have to get you help. I'll call the medics.'

'No, not here.'

'See sense, man! You'll bleed out on the floor.'

Another shake of the head. 'I know my body. I can make it a little further. I won't stay here to be murdered.'

'They're dead, Monk.'

He hisses at me through clenched teeth. 'Didn't you *hear* them? One of them sounded fucking *Welsh*!'

My God, is this possible? Could Easter really be this rash, this idiotic? This night is upside down.

'Get me out of here, Banks,' he says, lurching to his feet. 'Before they send any more.'

69 CE

I didn't see Sporus for a few nights after he gave me the sword, though I caught glimpses of him sliding through the corridors. I trusted that he was concocting something so I kept the nagging voices away. I'd been miserable under Galba but what Sporus had told me of this Vitellius frightened me – perhaps I'd recovered some measure of my old self through the relative comfort of my life as a scribe, or perhaps my knowledge of the next emperor in line was hazy compared with the other three. I didn't know what to expect of this man, but I'd seen something of the brutality of this time and I didn't want to be anywhere near a man hailed as a hero by those whose daily grind was hacking bearded German tribesmen to pieces in the mud.

Four nights, and I counted every one. By the fifth day, I was frantic, and that's how he found me.

'I'm going to Ostia tomorrow night. It took persuasion but he's agreed.'

'How?'

'I told him of herbs, sold by an old woman I know, that only she knows how to obtain. It'll keep a prick standing for hours and make coming feel like an earthquake.'

'And this actually exists?'

'Probably, but I've never found it. In truth, he's preoccupied. I have to do most of the work.'

It's a strange feeling, a slave being jealous of an emperor. There's no powerlessness like it, no imbalance of status greater. I gritted my teeth and he saw me and smiled for the first time that evening. 'It's just a show, boy. Let me show you what I can do when my heart's in it.'

After, when I held him, I asked him why Otho had such a fire for him.

'I look like his wife,' he said, as if it was the most natural of things. 'I make myself look more like her, of course, but he says there's a cast to my eyes that is just like Poppaea. His is a sad story, in truth.'

I knew the outlines of it but I let him continue, enjoying the vibration of his back against my chest as he spoke.

'I remember her from when I was a body slave, invisible to the masters. A classic beauty, all eyes and curves, but also a sweet woman. She was cursed with the narrow view of a girl brought up in a rich house whose sole purpose was good marriage; she never had the wits to survive at court. Nero saw her and wanted her and that was it, she was trapped.

'I've no doubt she enjoyed it, the flattery of the great Caesar wanting you, and she divorced her husband in quick order. Otho was as close as cousins with Nero – some say they shared more than wine and girls. It was he that agreed to marry Poppaea, to keep any other men from snapping her up: Nero was wary of scandal, after that business with his mother – baser than that, he only wanted her body and wasn't looking for another empress.

'Otho did a fine job as a stand-in, delivering his wife to the palace on request. The problem was that he also shared his home with her the rest of the time and somewhere in the quiet moments between visits to the Golden House something grew between them. As I said, she really was a very sweet, attractive girl.

'Then the time came when Nero changed his mind, as he often did. He decided Poppaea was wifely material after all and took her from Otho. Things soured fast, because Otho was dispatched to Spain before the month was out where, as fate would have it, he neighboured our dear friend Galba for many years. He used the time well, making connections, building wealth and securing the loyalty of his troops. The court fop made an effective commander, and I doubt any were more surprised than him.

'He told me of the day his last tie to the emperor broke. This was before I became close to Nero, so all I saw was the tremor that ran through the palace that something awful had happened. Later, the stories jumped from person to person, each adding his or her own embellishments; we all knew Poppaea had just given birth, and the word was that the child was a misshapen stillborn. This was the second time she'd lost a child by him and she shut herself away. By the time the tale came to me, the Empress had declared her husband cursed by Artemis, which did not go well for her.

'You see, though Nero was first an artist there was a line of madness in his family, the kind that had some of his predecessors tearing the balls off their playthings at Capri, or killing their sisters in their beds. The sour streak came out in him that day and he broke down her door with the axe of one of his German guards. The story was much changed from its first telling to the time it reached me but I heard he'd found her, still bleeding and exhausted from the birth, and kicked her to death.

'I never found out what really happened, but Poppaea died that day one way or another – perhaps it was natural, perhaps he really did kill her. Nero kept little from me, especially near his end, but if that subject arose he'd grow dangerously quiet. I think the only way he could deal with the blackness was to put high walls around it.

'Life went on and there were no repercussions because he was the First Man, the August One, Caesar in all his might. I saw the loss in his eyes, and little by little I changed myself to look like her – my nose one day, my forehead another. I grew my hair longer. I didn't affect any of her womanly charms because that would have attracted the wrong sort of attention, but I pushed those things I remembered best about the late Empress to the fore, and one day, Nero looked at me directly; from then on my life was quite different.

'Otho, out in his provincial capital, had heard the stories of Poppaea's passing – if the story had changed so much in a single household I can only imagine the tale of butchery and debauchery that reached his ears. On a rare court visit I saw a look of unfiltered murder in his eyes, though he took care to hide it from Nero himself. It only went away when he saw me watching him, and it was as if he'd seen a ghost; I suppose, like Nero, he was seeing half of what he wanted to see, the other half was what I'd allowed.

'So, there you have it. Otho fawns on me because I bear a passing resemblance to the woman that was stolen from him, and I have art enough to make it convincing. And now, I need to go, and you need to sleep. Be ready to go tomorrow morning before breakfast; I've arranged for the door by the kitchen to be unattended and left unlocked. Bring a cloak and don't forget the sword I gave you.'

He left then, pulling his dress about himself. In a moment before he turned for the door, as he ran his fingers through his curls, I saw him as they must see him – a woman of rare and regal beauty, dark eyes and soft lips. But there was no placidity in those eyes, instead viper sharpness. It was as he'd explained: his mastery was allowing the powerful to see what they wanted, not what existed. He was beautiful, though in that moment it wasn't *my* Sporus that stood there: he'd already retreated to the quiet place inside him.

I didn't sleep much that night, the few stretches I managed were flecked with dreams of unending corridors that melded into honeycomb scroll cases that held giant, pulsating pupa and golden honey dripped everywhere, slowing my steps as I tried to run after a man in the distance that I knew, without seeing, was Sporus. It was the kind of dream that you wake from for a few minutes before falling back in just as deep, again and again; the kind that takes hold like a fever and leaves you feeling unwashed and tired, the opposite of sleep. I didn't even wait for the dawn – as I saw the sky through the hatched slit of a window high on the wall begin to rose over, I gathered my things and wrapped them in a blanket, not forgetting the blade. I kept the hooded cloak over my arm, in case I was approached, and I made for the kitchens.

There was that feeling in the air, the one from the very first night I'd come here. The breathlessness, a kind of emptiness that weighs heavy with the expectation of something momentous. There was no one about, not even the torch lighters who roamed the halls at night, tending the flames. It was as quiet as a tomb.

Through the kitchens was a heavy side door to a small courtyard where the butchers' carts delivered the meat. The door was open, like he said it'd be, but as I placed my hand on the leather thong to pull it open two things stopped me in my tracks. The first was a tinkle of metal on metal, a creak of well-tanned leather. The second was the smell of horses.

Tradesmen in Rome used oxen for their carts, and their meaty, dungy scent is a long way from that of a horse. I took the door's weight and hoped it wouldn't squeak, and I pulled it a fraction ajar.

Four horses whickered and stamped in the morning dew, vapour coming from their nostrils. By one of them stood the unmistakeable form of a legionary, a squat man wearing a cape over his infantry armour and blowing warmth into his hands. Beyond the horses, sat against the far wall, were two of the cook slaves. Their throats had been cut.

I retreated from that door with my breath bursting from my lungs – at any moment I expected the door to come flying open and soldiers to come in with their swords raised, but I made it to the corridor. I ran, not caring about the slap of my sandals on the marble, towards the only place where I thought I might find Sporus – the private apartments of the emperor.

There were no guards flanking the door – I should have seen this as another warning. My possessions weighed me down so I left the bundle resting on a couch of rich velvet, speckled with spots of wine. I took the sword, still in its sheath, though I'd no idea what to do with it. Perhaps, I fancied, I'd use it as a club.

Past a mosaic-floored atrium of unusually restrained splendour, two African ferns in man-high pots of earthenware flanked the doorway to the bedrooms. I'd only been here once to deliver some obscure legal texts to a senior scribe, but those ferns had stuck in my mind as had the thick red curtain that hid the interior from view like I was the spectator in a theatre. The curtain was ripped plumb down the centre and there was torchlight coming from beyond. I heard voices, one of them I recognised. With goosebumps on my skin, I crept forwards.

It's odd to me now, years later, that I can remember things like the fact that the couch I'd left my belongings on was wine-stained, or the fact that one of the tiles bordering the pond was cracked in half, but I cannot, for all I try, remember what the room beyond the curtain looked like, barring a general impression of plush earth tones. What is stark like a blade is the discarded fruit peel of Otho's headless body by the side of a large bed and a bearded legionary trying to push his head onto the end of a pike. The blood had made the man's thick fingers slippery and every time the skull skidded off the point he grunted with the irritation of a man trying and failing to mount a picture on a wall. On the bed, a hound-jowled, middle-aged man squeezed into a sculpted bronze breastplate watched, an expression of intense boredom on his face. And there was Sporus on the floor, curled into a tight ball and whimpering like a child. I saw blood pooled between his legs and my breath ran out of the room.

Fuck, Banks. My mouth was so dry my tongue stuck to the palate; my hands itched and there was an icy throbbing in my head. Rough hands grabbed me by the shoulder and leg and I was lifted bodily, the lights tipped and I was upended. I came down with a slap on the marble floor that knocked stars into my eyes.

'There you go, Dominus, a little bird for you,' said the rasping, broken voice of Perfume. 'This one's another favourite of the usurper.'

The man on the bed, who I took to be Vitellius, looked at me and ran his fingers through his thinning hair. He didn't say a word and his expression never wavered. He was like a man watching ants scurry.

There were more people in the room, all of them soldiers. The space was close with the smell of sweat and iron and the stink of the palace's underbelly coming from Perfume.

'You want to keep your eyes on this one, Dominus, the

slippery one. Has something going on with the woman-man there. Though maybe just a woman now, eh?'

'What does it want?' said Vitellius, his voice as dull as a spoon, addressing the soldier who'd now managed to fix the head of Otho to the end of his spear.

The soldier handed the spear to Vitellius – who examined it with a detached curiosity – and turned to face Perfume. 'Slave,' he said, 'you let us in, like we paid you to. It's good you caught this one, but you've no business in the presence of Caesar. Name your reward, and be quick about it.'

'Could a slave hope for his freedom?'

'No, he couldn't.'

'Then perhaps a more comfortable life in the service of Caesar would be even greater reward?' His voice was grease on water. Sporus let out a little moan.

Vitellius, not taking his eyes off the severed head, gave a nod that was barely perceptible.

'You can run the kitchens,' said the soldier. 'You'll have your stipend increased and we'll give you a bigger room. That will suffice.'

Perfume bowed like an actor, then fixed me with a sickly grin. 'You'll be lucky if they send you to be torn apart by beasts, shit-raker. Enjoy the rest of your short, terrible life.'

'Keep your mouth shut, slave,' said the bearded soldier, but I barely heard him for the pounding in my ears. My blood was hot as I scrambled to my feet, ignoring the sound of armed men tensing; the animal that lived in me, that had been silent ever since that night in the dormitory, was awake and pacing.

I'd dropped my sword in the fall and someone had kicked it away from me – it had come to rest against Sporus' back and the blood from his wound had spread to engulf it, turning it into an island in a rich dark sea.

'What's this, child?' said Perfume. 'What the fuck are you going to do now?'

My rage was an intoxicating sweetness.

'Slave, I'll not tell you again to shut your—'

The beast erupted.

I only recall patches. I know I hit Perfume in the balls and throat before he realised I'd even moved and he went down. I was on his chest, my knees barely able to straddle his girth, and then I was raining down fists, splitting his lip and hearing his nose crunch as it splattered across his face. I'd no reason to stop this time, and I know I would have carried on until he was a pulp, but soldiers pulled me off him. I remember pulling a tooth out of the meat of my palm, then one of them kicked me in the mouth and I saw black.

I was only out for a moment, but when I came to they were dragging Perfume out by his armpits and Vitellius was watching me with something bordering on interest.

'It fights,' he said. 'We'll have it in the games. It might amuse.' Then he stood and walked out without a backward glance.

The bearded soldier nodded and I was lifted off my feet. He looked at me up and down and shook his head. 'I'd have sworn a strong breeze would have pushed you over, but there you are. It'll cost us to find a *ludus* that'll take a strip like you, but Caesar wants what Caesar wants.'

'What about the other one, sir?' asked a legionary.

'Dress the wound and find a brothel. Someone is bound to want to fuck it, knowing this city.'

I tried to reach for Sporus as they dragged me away, just to touch the hem of his robe or feel his palm on mine, even gather some of his blood on my finger but he was too far away.

6

Monk is stretched on the floor of Mariko's apartment, a thick woollen blanket under him, his head cradled by red silk pillows. I hope that he won't stain them with sweat or blood, then Orkney chastises me for being so entirely, inappropriately fussy.

He almost died, boy. If it weren't for her...

He's munching on olives now, but only hours ago he was as pallid as the departed. The bullet had bounced off a rib, snapping it: how he didn't lose a lung is enough to make one believe in divine favouritism.

'Stop staring, Banks,' he says. 'It's a nasty habit you've picked up there.'

'You should be in a hospital,' says Mariko, leaning over the balcony. She catches my eye. 'Antoni can only do so much on my couch.' The friend who checked Monk's wounds was efficient, bordering on brusque, but whatever the blinking device he adhered to his ribs had brought a man on the brink round to consciousness, another reminder of where we are: a gunshot wound back in Britain would likely be fatal, especially with the price of antibiotics since the labs had to close. We'd been ordered to feed him and keep him from moving around for a couple of days, though, like Mariko, the opinion had been that we were mad to keep him from a proper facility. Monk, though, had been adamant about staying away. I suppose being attacked in the dead of night is enough to stoke paranoia – I can feel the fringe of it myself. Mariko's head retracts into her sanctum on the mezzanine, leaving a gap against the panelled ceiling.

The man on the back door of the Residence saw us leave, of course, but either he thought us a couple of drunk old chums off to sow mischief or Easter has spread the idea that the higher-ups are to be left alone to do whatever it is they choose. Either way, we were down the steps into the little cobbled street, the bulk of the palazzo looming over us. I was going to take him to the second residence a few streets away, just until I could sort this mess out, but he refused.

'I'd be safer in the gutter,' he said, the hyperbole forgivable.

I called Mariko from my tablet as we sheltered in a double doorway, the she-wolf and her suckling twins carved into the lintel. It was late and she took a while to answer. I didn't know where else to turn and I panicked, but she gave me directions and when we got there she was waiting with her friend the medic. She smelled like sleep and her hair was mussed.

She only said one thing before helping Monk up the stairs (no elevator in this old building): 'This could be trouble for me. He can't stay long. You have to be careful, Lindon.'

God, to hear her use my name, even as she turned away from me.

She was right, though. Even now, a room at the second, smaller residence is set aside for Monk's use. That he hasn't been yet does not appear to have attracted attention: it's a busy little place, which I'm counting on.

As for me, I can't visit Mariko's place for too long but while I do, I take it all in.

It's split-level, down below a living area and kitchenette,

two wide sofas at right angles around a low table spread with magazines. One wall is mostly taken up by a multi-paned window with lead strips that looks down into one of Rome's typical courtyards; currently the rolling news cycle flits across it, the image spread across several feet of what was ordinary glass before Mariko activated the television. Monk has been glued to it for hours, alternating between current affairs and the inexhaustible library of documentaries Mariko can access. The rest of the room is clothed in books, every spare inch stuffed with shelves that overflow. She loves Picasso, Dalí, even our own Turner, big volumes with shimmering pages that smell of varnish. The rest are a jumbled mixture of novels, poetry, history books. A slim volume from a middle shelf catches my eye with its hatched green spine. Heaney's *Death of a Naturalist* – I'd swear it's the same matte paperback edition I had at school. I think I read it to Elanor once.

One corner of the room is unadorned – Mariko has created an alcove by the omission of a bookcase and within stands a slim vase, a sparse collection of long-stemmed flowers jutting out. A scroll with Japanese script hangs on the wall, black characters sinuating downwards in lines that thicken, then narrow, then intertwine. When I asked, she told me this is called a *tokonoma*, and her father had made space for one in every home they'd had, no matter how small. The *kanji* means 'harmony'. A reminder of half of her heritage, small enough not to impose but seeping into the room, making it a place of comfort. Here, she could be quiet and alone with her books.

I wish I could stay, just sit and read in the light that falls through the windows. Mariko's presence is everywhere, the smell of her. The mezzanine, with its balcony that looks out over the lounge, it a tantalising unknown. But I have to go back, to make some sense of this mess.

'You've made arrangements,' she says, appearing at the foot of the little staircase.

I nod. 'Enough for now. I have to see what's happened back at the Residence since last night. There's a lot of questions.'

'You must be careful.'

'They weren't after me,' I say, wishing I felt the confidence I'm trying to project.

Monk lets out a little groan.

'I have to give him another drug capsule. Come back soon, Lindon. But be careful, this is...'

'I know, it's irregular. I'll wear a hat or something.'

She smiles a little and turns away; I watch her for just a moment. I leave Proust on the little table by the door.

I expect Euro police, our security men bustling. Instead, the Residence is quiet as I approach. I walk through the main doors. Jarvis, also from Interior, crosses my path in the lobby.

'How's your vagrant friend, Banks? Got him cleaned up yet?'

I give him a closed smile and a nod. He goes on his way without pause. I don't see anything in his face, no alarm, no confusion, nothing more than the ordinary detachment. It's not enough to settle me, though – just because Jarvis doesn't think anything's amiss doesn't mean I'm in the clear. For all I know, there are police waiting in my rooms to arrest me.

The corridor is quiet at the rear of the palazzo. My door swings open on silent hinges.

What will you do with the bodies? asks Orkney. *You're not one for the sight of blood.*

Maybe I should come clean. I have my suspicions about who ordered this attack, but not everyone in the delegation can be complicit. I'm the innocent party here, after all.

166

And your old chum? What of him?

Monk will have to stay where I've hidden him. I have to hope the cover of the other residence holds for a little longer.

There is something in the air, something odd. As my feet carry me past the bedroom to the lounge, I realise what it is – the place smells clean, fresh even. No blood, no death, just the undercurrent of flowers and dust from the old chairs. Where the struggle took place is nothing, no stain, no scuffs, just a bare floor. There is even fruit in a bowl. It's been hours only, but it looks like nothing happened here.

Did I pick an identical room that isn't mine, by accident? Am I going mad? No, I recognise that patch of mould on the ceiling of the kitchenette that looks like a mouse. There has to be something. I move furniture, flip carpets, but there is no sign of the scuffle. It's only when I shift the heavy cabinet by the wall a few inches and catch a glint that I know I really lived it: a piece of glass wedged in a gap between floor and wall. I pull it out, examine it; there's still blood here, a fleck from when I smashed this shard into a man's face in a blind panic.

Someone has come in here, removed two bodies and cleaned it in just such a way as to make it appear that nothing has happened. Two English-speaking men with guns have been removed by someone else within the delegation, with diligence and skill that speaks of complicity and authority. Someone senior knew about this – who else could order a damned hit in the middle of a foreign city, in our own accommodation? I wasn't meant to be there. Monk is only alive because I felt sorry for myself.

My blood is as cold as a high tarn, but it's not fear but anger. I saw the way Easter looked at Monk, the hint dropped with the subtlety of a lead pipe that he could and would have retribution. Could even he be this *idiotic*? To chance this whole enterprise on a petty piece of point-scoring?

You know him, how he gets, says Orkney. *Especially when he drinks. He's been drinking a lot, trying to impress. They flatter him. Monk didn't flatter him.*

No one is kicking down the door, to accuse me or finish me off, though I've been seen entering the Residence by a dozen people. I'm prominent enough that I can't just disappear. So be it then, I have to play the game.

I'll move out to the other residence – a little distance will be good. I'll have enough to be getting on with as in two days' time a fresh round of talks begins and I will take my place behind Easter's chair with a stack of notes, ready to feed him the information he needs to at least appear cognisant of the facts. And when things are quiet, I'll ask my questions.

'Banks.'

I almost jump across the room.

Jarvis holds his hands up. 'Steady on, old boy. Only me.'

'I'm sorry, you just startled me.'

'The door was open, I hope you don't mind, only...'

'No, no, it's fine. Was there some reason you—'

'Yes, you've a phone call. From home. In your office.'

'Oh, right. I see. Who's it from?'

'Your daughter, I believe.'

The line is scratchy for a moment, then clears. My voice sounds steadier than I feel.

'Sara? Can you hear me?'

'Hi, Dad.'

'Is everything alright?'

'I—' She cuts off. I can hear her breathing.

'Sara, what's wrong?' There's something in her hesitation, a tremor in those few words that spooks me. She's upset about something.

'They took Miss Sampson and Miss James, Dad. The police came in the night and kicked the doors in. There were flashlights everywhere.'

Sampson and James. The Deputy Housemistress and... the House Nurse? 'Are you alright? Did anyone hurt you?' My mind is reeling. Did they send people after her as well? What is all of this madness?

'No, not me. I'm fine. I was just scared. They shouted at us to stay in our rooms.' Her words start to tumble over each other. 'We saw out the windows, though. We saw them drag them out of the House and across the quad in their pyjamas. Miss James was crying and shouting, and she tried to hold her hand, but Miss Sampson just *let* them. There was a big black van and the police had riot gear on and some of them even had guns, Dad. I thought one of them looked up at me and I thought they were going to shoot. I was *scared*.' Her voice cracks.

I feel like a giant spoon has scooped up my insides and dashed them against the wall. She's growing older and every eye roll tells me she needs me less and less, but suddenly she's a little girl again and I want to slam down the phone and charge off to the train station. I take a deep breath. I need to be the collected one here. 'Where are you?'

'I broke into the D&T studio. I'm on the phone in Mr Stephens' office.'

'You broke in?'

'I don't want *her* listening to me!'

'Alright. Now listen to me, you're alright. You don't need to be scared, you've done nothing wrong.' I leave the breaking and entering part out – sometimes you need to be selective. 'Are the police still there now?'

'No, they've gone.'

'Alright then, see? You don't need to be afraid.'

'But they just came in and *took* them! Just like that.'

I could guess why. The Crown had been cracking down on 'Subversives and Abnormals' for several months now. But still… a girls' school in the dead of night.

'I hate it here, Dad. It's all bullshit and I've no one to talk to, nowhere to go. I can't even call you without that bitch listening in on me.'

'Mouse…'

'Don't call me that,' she says, but there's no bite to it.

I let her be quiet for a moment, to let the dust settle. No one teaches you how to do this and I've got it wrong more times than I've got it right. 'I'm sorry you feel you can't talk to anyone.'

'I don't go back to the flat anymore at weekends. It's empty and it makes me feel sad.'

I lease a two-bedroom in the centre of town, a couple of miles from the school. Somewhere to spend time with her on exeats and long weekends. Somewhere for her to go on a Saturday if she wants to get away from it all. Now I can see it, in my mind's eye. She's sat there at the kitchen table and she's alone with four bare walls and I feel like I've been stabbed through the chest.

'Listen,' I say, trying to hold it together. 'I'm going to make arrangements. You're going to stay with Aunt June down in Cornwall.'

'With all the dogs?'

A smile cracks its way through. 'Yes, with all the dogs. Would you like that, for a little while?'

170

I hear her wipe her nose. 'Yes.'

'I want you to hang up now and leave before anyone notices you. Just go back to your room and wait for someone to be in touch. It'll be alright.'

'Are you coming home soon?'

'I hope so, darling. Love you.'

'Love you, too.'

The line goes dead. I ignore the operator, who's already upset by this unsanctioned use of the relay line, and make two calls. The first is to June, and I hear the sound of her menagerie yapping in the background. I don't need to tell her the circumstances; she knows me well enough to know it's important.

'I'm sure the old Rover will make it that far,' she says. 'Are you doing alright over there? Meet any nice Italian women?' Always pushing, June. She's worried over me since Elanor passed; though it's heavy-handed, it's done with love. I'm sorry I don't see her more often.

The next call is to the Housemistress's office.

'Mr Banks, this is most irregular. Your daughter is already behind and going through a most disagreeable patch. An extemporaneous absence will do little to improve the situation.'

'I think she's a little upset, Housemistress, about the events of last night.'

I hear her drawing herself up. 'We respect the rule of law here, sir, and will not allow degenerates to pollute formative minds. If Sara cannot show a little moral fortitude in the face of justice, I fear for her future.'

I'm an apology man, the kind that goes out of his way to calm situations and turn as many cheeks as it takes, but her tone does something to me: I can feel the hairs stand up on my neck and my jaw tightening to a hard line.

'My daughter does not feel safe in your House or your school.'

'Mr Ba—'

'She is unhappy in your care. *Your* care. I'm out of the country, and I have trusted the school as my proxy. This is by far and away the most confusing time of her life and it is your job to guide her through it, not double down on stiff upper lip nonsense.' I hear her intake of breath but I'm away now and I don't allow her to cut in. 'You listen to me very closely: Sara is taking some time away. You will arrange for any term papers to be couriered to her so she doesn't fall too far behind. When I am back in Britain I will arrange a meeting with you and the Headmistress to discuss this further.'

She splutters a little after that, but she agrees. I've found a new edge to my formal ministry voice that works. I can tell she's afraid for her job and I feel a little bad about it. Perhaps it wasn't her fault the police acted the way they did – though that sort of thing is more and more common. If it wasn't for my suspicion that she'd called them in, I might have said something conciliatory. As it was, I let her say goodbye to a dead line.

69 CE

Before they replaced all the movies with that god-awful propaganda, I got to see a couple of the old ones from the height of Hollywood when the stories were big and unashamed. America had dropped its surface prudishness (though they still had some aversion to arse cracks) and there was blood, sex and language to make a granny keel over. One of them that stuck with me (about Rome, of course) was the one with the chap who goes from general to gladiator, a real riches-to-rags type thing with lots of stabbing and moody staring along the way. It was dumb and simple and fun as hell, and I adored it.

A real *ludus* was nothing like that, no robust camaraderie forged in the fires of battle; oiled Nubians and rakishly scarred Germans were thin on the ground and the training area was not a warm sandy courtyard: it was a death pit crammed with desperate men who knew they were there not only to die, but die for sport. Many pissed themselves with fear nightly in the small, mud-floored room we shared with the chickens. When I arrived it was raining and as I heard the iron gates slam shut behind me I saw rows of barbed, brutal weapons on racks and tables. My hands shook and my jaw was locked in a rictus, as if I was constantly on the verge of throwing up. I remember, clear as a nosebleed on linen, the *lanista* taking one look at me and backhanding me with a hand heavy with gold. I must have been limp because my jaw was unbroken but it was swollen for days after.

We were the dregs of Rome, lower than miners; at least they could be relied upon to complete a task, short and brutal though their lives were. We were fodder, nothing more, there to be meat targets for the real fighters. There were just five of those, and they lived in another low building on the other side of the courtyard.

I don't know if this was a particularly poor *ludus* but those trained men were not the colossi I'd imagined. Not a burnished thigh among them – most were plump running on fat, all the better to absorb impact and bleed just enough for the crowds if it came to a proper one-on-one match (which were rare in most games – crowds were less interested in the subtle flash of strike and parry than seeing living props slaughtered by the dozen). They were horribly strong bastards, though, with plenty of trained muscle under their outer layers of blubber. On my third day one of us worms backed into one as he trained with a padded dummy and he turned, picked the snivelling young man up by neck and groin and tossed him a full three metres onto a rack of weapons. His screams were terrible and the *lanista* had to cut his throat.

We were tired from the training, our fingers sore and sometimes broken from being hit by wooden swords, hastily splinted by one of the house slaves who looked down on us like we were animals (which no doubt we smelled like). We didn't speak – mealtimes were a snatched bowl of gruel, crammed in as fast as possible in a corner in case someone tried to take it. Even sleep was fitful, no one trusting anyone else. Those who died in training or were killed in 'sparring' with the fighters were replaced in short order by fresh arrivals; Rome had an inexhaustible supply of wretches.

I was quiet, I watched, I made no friends. I ate what little they gave me and I stayed out of the way of the fighters and the whips (though not always, as you can see by these scars). I hit other men with bits of wood and tried to stop them from hitting me and managed not to lose any teeth.

After a month, I was better at it, but I knew better than to show it and be dragged into the saw-toothed plank circle and be practised upon by those chubby, cold-eyed psychopaths. We weren't being trained, you see, only being shown the rudiments of how to swing and stab with a length of iron or how to hold a shield. There was some wrestling, just enough to get us back on our feet but it was rudimentary. Mobs haven't changed a tuppenny fuck in two millennia – Rome wanted the illusion that we were trained combatants to allow for their deepest, most primal desire which was to watch us being butchered. So I swung and I blocked and I punched until my shoulders were exhausted and the vibration of a battered shield left bruises all up my arm and welts where the leather cut into my skin.

Every single night, without fail, I breathed a goodnight to Sporus and tried to think of him during our beautiful nights together. I fought so damn hard, harder than I ever did in the practice yard, not to think about what was being done to him. After the bad days, when they ground me under their whips, I was too exhausted to stop the images of him being used by sick-grinned fuckers for a few bent coins; my imagination made a living hell for me. Sometimes I wished him dead so he'd not have to bear the hurt and the shame of it all, but I never let the cunts hear me cry. Weakness is as blood to sharks.

The sun rose and fell and scorched my shoulders, except when the clouds came in and washed the yard to mud that stained for days after, leaving us whitened like a troupe of ghosts. There were fewer coming in through the gates now and those of us who remained, around twenty, were given rough tunics to wear and a single blanket each. By now each one of us was an island, distant even as we stood shoulder to shoulder for morning inspection or when we tried to beat each other into the dust. I began to read tiny motions of shoulder and knee and eye and I used it to keep myself from harm but I didn't do anything showy, keeping the attention on others.

We were nothing like skilled fighters – those skills took years to hone – and not one of us had been tested by sharpened iron. I used to glance at the racks of pikes and tridents and barbed clubs in their chipped wooden racks and wonder what it would feel like to have one of them lacerate me, pulverise me, smash my brains from my skull. Which one would be quicker, I wondered? Which would hurt more, and for longer?

One day, practice was interrupted by a whip-crack from the *lanista* that wasn't followed by a cry of pain. We all turned to watch the small, balding man with thick arms stride into the middle of us.

'There will be games next week. The First Man wishes to thank Mars and Ceres for his victory over the usurpers, so he's putting on a show. We'll be playing against a *ludus* from Capua. There'll be a couple of team-of-two matches, some individual bouts and a melee. If you disgrace me and my place, I'll have you fed to the dogs.'

And then he left, and we carried on just as we had before but the strokes were slower and the bite of wood on wood not as pronounced, even from the other end of the yard where the fighters were training with net and spear and sword. Every man in that yard was thinking one thing: this might be how I die.

* * *

Of my time in Rome, the days that followed are the most clearly etched in my mind. That much death will mark a man for good.

The arena had been erected outside the walls, though I never worked out where except we crossed the river to get to it. I knew there would be no Colosseum for us poor wretches: the site of that was under the Golden House, still flooded by Nero's lake and stone boat. I wondered if we might go full Ben-Hur and fetch up at the Circus, but Vitellius, as the sponsor of this pageantry, had other ideas. He'd spared no expense on tall banks of wooden seating, festooned with red and gold banners bearing the Aquila or the Wolf-mother, or the glowering profile of the new Caesar himself. Beyond the arena a warren of stalls had sprung up, selling everything from food to toy horses, linen tunics to the thick, heady wine the Romans took with iced water. The air was filled with the smells of frying meat, body odour and incense, and snatches of lutes and pipes and drums wove between a thousand voices arguing, laughing, shouting at the poor bastards being driven through their midst in an iron cage on wheels. Someone threw an egg that smashed on the bars and showered me and the man next to me in slime; a chorus of laughs arose that had everyone thinking what a good idea this was and soon missiles of horseshit and half-eaten food were raining down on us from all sides. One of them hit the man driving the wagon and he swore; he kicked and someone went down with a shout. There were some more laughs, then the storm abated. The oxen pulling the cart lumbered on, unperturbed, and I envied their tiny bovine minds.

The holding areas were under the stands. No Flavian Amphitheatre, but it was still a big construction and a testament to the skills of Roman carpenters. There was room to house the stables of two *ludi* horses, equipment and more besides. On the first night I curled up in the straw next to a wooden partition and heard some large beast snuffling and scratching at the dirt on the other side. I didn't move away from it – my thinking was that if the lion or bear on the other side managed to break through it would be a better way to go anyway. In the darkened hours I became used to the smell of it and fancied I could feel its heat through the planks. You know, I felt closer to that animal than any of my fellow condemned; I spoke to it, softly, like I would a child.

'If you eat me,' I told it, 'at least I won't have gone to waste.'

The first matches were held around noon the next day, though it was hard to tell in the dusty darkness under the stands. I was not part of the first group, or the second, and I had to listen to the baying of the crowd, the high shrieks and the roar of beasts for several hours before a man in a leather tunic and missing an eye got me to my feet. With deft taps of his club, he had four of us line up on the upward-sloping ramp that led to the arena doors; the sun streaming through the gaps was blinding.

I wish I could say that I was beyond fear but the truth is, fear was all I had. Mortal terror manifests itself differently for everyone: some beg and cry and piss themselves, some go catatonic, others lash out like madmen at anyone close by. I found myself obsessed with little things, locked in a prison made of muddy fear, checking the straps of my greaves or bracers or the chin strap of the thin baked-leather helmet I'd been given. I was so occupied with this that I didn't notice the shield and sword being offered to me until the one doing it lost patience and rapped me on the head with his baton. All four of us were armed in this way; I must have adjusted my grip on the leather handle of the shield two dozen times before the man with the eyepatch returned with a bucket of blue paint which he splashed on each of us. When he was done, one of the fighters joined us, clad in a breastplate and full-faced helmet, a large square shield on his arm and a curved sword in his hand. He took his place at the head of our little column, then our *lanista* came to us and said, 'Kill the yellows, or die well.'

The doors were flung open.

The heat battered me like a fist.

The sound of the crowd thrummed in my guts.

The man behind me threw up, splashing my calf but I was already walking up the slope towards the noise and the heat and the stink of dead men.

The men from the other *ludus* were already there, the yellow paint on their faces making them look like the walking dead. They watched us enter with wide eyes and faces that mirrored our own terror; they had their own fighter, the only one taking the applause and cheers of the crowd. Our man raised his arms and bellowed, which was met with a fresh roar from the people of Rome who'd come to see death and were not yet satisfied.

The sun seared the back of my neck and the arena sand scratched between my sandalled toes. There were dark streaks where bodies had been dragged away and patches of it where blood had pooled. It stank of shit and copper. I hefted my shield and sword, and noticed the large box set aside for the Imperial household. Vitellius looked bored in his burnished armour and white tunic, his fat head surmounted by laurel leaves and a pinch-faced woman on his arm. He was surrounded by senators, old men with sour expressions. A peal of trumpets sounded and the voice of an announcer shouted something that was lost in the uproar. Vitellius raised a languid fist.

Then we fought.

7

The Spanish Steps recline like a drunk man snoozing off a heavy lunch and off to one side Keats-Shelley House squats, box-like. They've never changed the name, continuing to honour the young poet who died there even as the land of his birth pulled back beyond its moat. Perhaps they hoped we'd come back one day to pay homage, but this is likely whimsical. The verse, the romance, the death masks – it's a good story and tourists are still part of the fabric of this city.

The sweep of off-white marble terraces isn't what catches my eye, though. There's a little fountain – relatively little, given the generosity of proportion of everything else in this fold of the old city – and it tinkles in the early afternoon sun. Mariko leans against it, talking to an old woman who's selling roses. She's grey-haired but unbowed, though I can see the decades marked in the deep grooves of her cheeks. Mariko patters at her in a tongue I don't understand, replete with -*des* and -*ka* endings. I think it's Japanese.

Mariko buys a half-dozen roses and the old woman bows her head. Mariko does the same, and they part with a smile.

'She came here at the same time as my father, on the same ship, she says.'

'Really? That's quite a coincidence.'

'It is.' She nods, re-arranging the roses in their brown paper sheath. 'She sells more flowers this way, though. Not many made it out of Japan: it could be true.' She shrugs, a ripple of shoulder under her light blue shirt. 'Or not. It's a nice story.'

I take in the triangular space of paving around us, abutted by cafés and the wide, recumbent stairs. The *Piazza di Spagna*. There are so many people around, and I find myself watching the faces that pass by, searching for a knife, a gun, a fist. 'I'm not sure about this.'

'I am,' she replies. 'My apartment was not built for three people. We need to get out. You, for sure.'

'I'm sorry, I should have taken him somewhere else—'

She cuts me off by puffing her cheeks and blowing out the air. 'Enough apologising. Is this a British thing, or just you?'

'Both, I think.'

'Come, shopping now. And not just for old books,' she says, teasing. She thanked me for the gift but said she didn't really care for him. I think she liked the gesture, though – we're easy with each other again, though I'm careful to stay professional while we're outdoors. I still feel like the world is watching me.

Leading away is the *Via dei Condotti* and it glitters. I remember some of the names from when I was a boy, *Dior, Levi, Gucci*, joined by newer ones I don't. The formerly busy road is now pedestrianised and paved with a mica-flecked granite that sparkles like the bejewelled handbags and bevelled perfume bottles that make up tasteful, sparse window displays on both sides. The street is strewn with slow-moving browsers, not one of them badly dressed. I feel like a fool in my slacks and polo shirt, but Mariko is oblivious to my discomfort and draws me on, past doorways that assault me with complex perfumes, others that beckon with the sensual pull of real, plush leather. As I pass, it occurs to me that there is not a single price tag on display.

After about two hundred yards we turn off the main street and down a narrow alleyway, the walls painted a deep blue and the paving immaculate. At the end is a plain glass door etched with a single word in foot-high capitals: *Maschio*.

Inside, the air is cool and crisp with hints of lime and, though less powerful, that smell of leather again. Dark wood cases display men's dress suits, ranks and ranks of them, in every colour and cut conceivable. Some are displayed on mannequins. I own several suits back home – I live in them, as does the rest of the Civil Service – but they are to these garments as a bow-backed mule is to a thoroughbred.

'You'll find something here,' says Mariko, her hand alighting on my shoulder. My dinner suit was ruined in the fight at the Residence and I need a new one, though coming to this sumptuous place feels rather like cracking an egg with a hammer.

A slim young man rises from behind a counter and greets us in formal Latin that I'm happy to say I understand. I keep the earbud switched off most of the time now.

'You are welcome here. How can I help?'

Mariko answers. 'My friend needs a new formal suit.'

The young man smiles, and indicates a circular dais off to one side with an outstretched hand. 'Please.'

There's an ungainly moment when I have to remove my shoes and almost topple over in a mal-coordinated heap, catching myself at the last moment. I step up onto the dais, which glows with an inner luminescence and is warm through my socks. 'I really don't think this is necessary. I can just go off the peg.'

'Just try it,' she says. 'This is how we do things here.'

I hate clothes shopping. It's why I live in my work suits – easy to replace and as little fuss as possible. The assistant hands me a sort of thin visor. After a moment of incomprehension, he mimes for me to pull it over my eyes. The film is clear, barring a slight sheen. I feel a fuzzing at my temples, but otherwise the thing seems to have no effect.

'Name one thing you own that you find beautiful,' says Mariko, switching to English.

'Nothing,' I lie. A locket, buried deep in my travel case, with a strand of Sara's hair woven through another of Elanor's. I haven't opened it in years but I know they're undimmed by decay or entropy, my own personal capsule of time.

'Clothes are just... functional,' I add, a little curt but I feel exposed up here. 'They serve a purpose. They don't need to be beautiful.'

The assistant pulls a tablet from behind the counter and activates it with a swipe of his hand. The surface glows with symbols and text, and then the room around me fades away to nothing. Mariko and the assistant are still there beside me, but we are in a plain blue room whose edges blur in the distance, metres or miles away. Curious, I tip the visor up an inch and peek underneath. The room with the suit racks is still very much there – it's the visor projecting the image of the boundless space. Fluttering a hand at me and with a polite *pone reportavit*, the assistant has me re-seat the visor. Back in the simulation his image does something to the pad and I see a copy of myself take form a couple of metres away, facing me, three-dimensional and frozen mid-slouch. God, this portly form; I wonder when I started to lose my fight with gravity. My widow's peak is pronounced and my shoulders are rounded in a perpetual slump.

God, I look so old.

Tempus fugit, *dear boy*, chuckles Orkney.

I'm aware Mariko is looking on and the thought that this is what she sees every day is unsettling.

'Look, can we just get this over with? A dinner jacket's a dinner jacket.'

'Just wait,' she says, her voice pitched for reassurance. Not for the first time, I wonder how much of her is natural and how much is schooled.

The shop assistant does something else to the pad and the clothes on my doppelganger disappear. From the neck down, it's clad in a white bodysuit that, mercifully, obscures the outlines of things I'd rather not be on display. Before I can even mouth a complaint, underwear and a fitted white t-shirt appear, as well as a pair of black laced shoes. He says something I don't catch, so he repeats it: 'Do you have a preferred colour?'

'Look, black tie is just black tie.'

'Sir,' he says, activating my earbud so I can understand him. 'I'd like to try one thing on you before the dinner suit. It's to understand what fits you best. Will you trust me to do my job?'

'I... yes. Yes, if you must.'

'Colour?'

'Blue, I suppose.'

The assistant scratches his eyebrow, then does something else. In an instant my mannequin-double is wearing a white collared shirt and a pair of trousers the colour of an autumn afternoon sky in Cornwall, the kind where cold clouds have become so enmeshed they no longer have distinction, grey with just a hint of azure. The image is striking in as much as it is unexpected; I smelled cut, wet grass for a moment. A jacket in the same colour joins it.

'Do you wear waistcoats?' asks the assistant.

'Not usually, no.'

'I recommend one. Shall we see?' He doesn't wait for me to respond, and one appears on the model. 'You like the colour?'

'Yes, I do.'

'We can discuss fabrics later. We carry a large selection and can arrange for orders of more select materials.'

There's another twinge of satisfaction that I'm keeping up with his Latin. I'm sure he's slowing down for my benefit, but the city is rubbing off on me. I notice the clothes on the mannequin look several sizes too big – God, I hope this isn't some current Euro fashion trend and I'll be expected to walk around like a little boy in his older brother's hand-me-downs.

'It's a little... baggy?' I say.

He actually tuts.

'He's not cut it to you yet,' says Mariko. 'This is just a template.'

The assistant taps his pad a little more firmly, a minor protest at having his professional integrity questioned. He puts the pad down on a little side table and pulls on a pair of gloves from his back pocket. Then, like a conductor, he raises his hands and sets to work.

With a downward cut of his hand the left leg of the trousers pulls in as if shrinking in the wash, tightening to the model's leg. The gesture is repeated for the right. A diddle of fingers alters the bottom of the trousers to sit just on top of the shoes. Frowning, the assistant makes a gesture like the turning of a dial and the black shoes morph into light brown brogues. Then, a sharp downward flick of the fingers folds sharp creases down the centre of each trouser leg.

He begins to walk around the mannequin, his eyes intent, every gesture sure and confident. The waistcoat and jacket slim down until they follow the arc of my ribs, seeming to pull me in at the waist. The shoulders widen a little and the arms shorten to just above the wrist. Another flick of his hands has the shirt sleeves extend by a few centimetres so they protrude from underneath. As an afterthought, he adds silver cufflinks.

He slims the lapels and draws the 'V' of the suit downwards to sit just below my sternum, it and the waistcoat inverted chevrons that somehow make my jaw seem firmer. The shirt collar fastens of its own accord and a slim navy blue tie snakes its way around my neck and disappears under the waistcoat. The assistant steps back and admires his work.

Mariko makes a little noise in her throat like cooing.

I must admit the suit is magnificent, every line of it enhancing my shoulders and narrowing my waist. The damn thing even elongates my legs. It is a marvellous illusion, one that doesn't allow the eye to settle long enough on one thing and see through the façade, always distracting away with something else – a pocket square that matches the tie, which in turn is held down by a gleaming silver pin.

The assistant pulls a small stool behind me and steps onto it. He places one hand on the small of my back and the other on my chest and gently pushes. I allow it, and find myself standing taller, pulling my shoulders back, straightening my spine. He lifts my chin with a finger, and I stare at the mannequin which has mirrored my movements and now stands there, resplendent. I look younger; I look fitter. I'm taken aback at how the years and the sorrows have compacted me. I see the man I could be staring back at me and all it took was a fine suit.

'Wonderful,' I say, my mouth dry. I can't take my eyes off it.

'I am pleased you like it,' says Mariko. 'Though… they are just clothes.' I hear the smile in her voice.

What the hell am I doing here?

There are still a few tailors in London that do this kind of thing, albeit the old-fashioned way with more brandy. I could save for a year and never be able to afford them. In an instant, the suit is an anchor on my shoulders. Orkney is already saying something about her meaning well, that she's just showing me a good time but I want to be out of here, away from this opulence I can't hope to pay for on the money I earn. I feel like my nose is being rubbed in a world I can't attain.

'Look,' I stammer, 'I really can't stretch to this sort of thing...'

'Lindon, you really must—'

'I must *nothing*!' I snap, surprising myself. Mariko's eyes are wide. I step down from the dais and push the visor into the hands of the shocked assistant. 'I just... needed a simple suit for dinners. None of this...' I wave my hands at the artistry all around.

Jesus, I can feel the blood rushing to my cheeks. Mariko begins to say something but I grab my jacket from the counter and storm out through the etched glass door, embarrassment and disappointment hand in hand.

I lurch down the street, furious at myself, furious at her for putting me in this position. I saw an ideal; it tantalised me, reminded me of what I once was before everything was stolen away from me by a creeping horror that buried into Elanor's lungs and kidneys and liver, leaving her a hairless, racked thing. Did I really believe that I could just step from under the crushing mass I've carried ever since my daughter's eyes were red with tears at seeing her mother taken away, piece by piece?

Mariko. We keep going around in these circles.

You're angry because you want it to be something real, says Orkney.

'Oh, piss off,' I mutter, causing a young couple to look around at me as I bustle past.

I'm at the foot of the Spanish Steps before I realise that I don't have any shoes. Like a balloon with a knitting needle through it, I drop down onto the cool marble and put my head in my hands.

I feel her approach. As much as I'm frustrated, disappointed, angry, sad – some of it for her, some just for me – I am a pole sensing its opposite. I don't look up but I know she's slipping through the crowds, lithe as a breeze, and I know that when I look up her face will stun me to silence. I know this, and I know it despite the figure of Elanor floating on my brain, raw as a wound, and I wish I could not feel this way, think these thoughts. I want to tear my hair out.

'Here,' she says. 'You forgot your shoes.' She holds them out and I take them without a word. 'I thought you were enjoying yourself.'

There are not enough words in the libraries of all the countries in all the world, though a battalion of them rushes to the tip of my tongue, jostling for position so that not one gets out. I look at her, finally, and I see her eyes are worried for me. My God, if she's dissembling now then she's really, really good; she's breathing fast and I don't think it's from catching up to me – she even has a flush to her cheeks.

'You looked good in that suit. You looked happy for a moment.'

The diplomat tries to step to the fore, but this time he doesn't make it in time. 'It was wonderful. I like the way I looked. I liked the way you looked at me in it.'

That's going to hurt in the morning, son, Orkney winces.

'That's the problem, Mariko,' I continue, heedless as I tip over the cliff. 'You're beautiful to me and I like your company. But I can't help but ask what a woman like you is doing looking at a man like me? I'm not young or in shape. I'm not interesting.'

'*Oh, putain!* I'd have paid for the suit, it hardly costs—'

'What do you really want from me, Mariko? What is dinner and drinks and suits worth?'

She slaps me, hard. It stings all the way down to the bone.

'*Va te faire foutre, enfoiré! De quel droit tu me parles comme ca? Hein?*' Her anger is a Gallic storm surge that is all the more shocking coming from her fine-boned face. Her eyes are pools of ire. The cliff face hurtles past me at a thousand miles an hour and I can feel the rocks rushing up to meet me with a jagged embrace.

Her chest heaves, once, twice, three times, then she takes a deep, steadying inhalation, closing her eyes. People are staring at us now. When she looks at me again, the inferno has been banked back to a smoulder.

'I am proud of this Confederation. You might say I love it because it holds people together when they are determined to tear themselves apart. But hear me, Lindon Banks of Britain: for all that I would do for it, I am not a *whore* for my nation.' The last part slides into my gut like a knife and twists. She drops my shoes and turns to leave.

'Please,' I say. My anger has soured into a curdled panic. I feel cold; every fibre of me doesn't want her to leave because it might be the very last thread that snaps. 'I'm sorry. I'm... I don't know what to think.'

She hesitates, turns back. Her face is conflicted: anger and something else. Sadness? Don't let it be pity. 'I knew about you, before we met. If that's what you suspect, then it's true. I read about you. I know about what happened to your wife.'

'How?'

She shrugs and arches an eyebrow. 'We have files.' She won't say it aloud, in plain view like this, but I know then that the Channel is not an impenetrable barrier, that the eyes of Europe have not been completely shut out. I shouldn't be surprised.

She blows out her cheeks again in that contradictory way, continental mannerisms and eastern features melded. 'I read your file and you're right, I wanted to know more about you.

My department, the head of my department, wanted me to get close to you and see if anything slipped out but I said no, that I would work with you and nothing more. But I was curious. And then we ate, then we laughed, we got a little drunk.'

'I remember. It's been a long time since I enjoyed myself that much.'

'You're wrong, you know. You are interesting. Here.' She points at my eyes. 'I can see you, behind these walls you put up. I think you do what is *difficult*, and that is real courage.' A smile creeps up at the corners of her mouth. 'Sometimes, you can even be a little funny. Here...' she taps her wrist and my tablet chimes. I open it up and I see a price list for *Maschio* appear.

'Really? That can't be right.'

'Automated weaving, dyeing, cutting, sewing. It cuts the costs. Did you think I was rich, Lindon?'

I have found the ripcord of my parachute and am buoyed, though now I feel like a different kind of idiot, caught out in a tantrum. 'Look, I am truly sorry, and not just about the suit thing.' I find it hard to look at her when I say: 'Sometimes I feel like I'm betraying her. Elanor.' How long is it since I said her name out loud?

Mariko takes in a little, shuddering breath. She leans in close; I feel her lips, velvet on my cheek, just below my eye. When they're gone, they leave a ghost of moisture there along with the scent of her.

'Take your time, Lindon. But allow yourself some happiness.'

69 CE

Remember the night in the fifth form we snuck in some vodka, then got dragged along to the lower fields where, in the darkness, it seemed the whole of our year group had gathered to play Bulldogs? It was muddy, a quagmire after days of rain but we formed up, sprinting from touchline to touchline, avoiding the chasers who, fuzzy on drink and the rush of being out of their boarding houses after dark, went in hard with the tackles. Well, replace mud with sand, darkness with blinding sunlight and the motivation of drink and escapism with sheer terror. And add in heavy lumps of sharpened iron.

No, come to think of it. I suppose the two aren't that alike.

The first man's face was a blur of teeth and gums as he ran at me. I dipped my shoulder like I'd been taught and then pushed up with my shield, catching him in the chest and allowing his momentum to flip him over my head. As he hit the dust and the wind was driven from him I had a fraction of a second to look on in surprise that this had actually worked. With rote motion that had more of muscle memory than killer instinct to it, I stabbed him through the neck. That was the first poor sod I ever killed.

I'd not hit bone so I pulled my blade free only to be knocked forwards by the impact of a shield. I rolled to the side and heard something thud into the sand; I slashed blindly at the source and hit something, heard a scream. The yellow who'd charged my back was holding his ruined club of a hand to his chest and panting in thick, rapid gasps – I doubt he even saw our fighter's sword as it arced in the sun and then his gorge was a yawing red crescent. He looked at me, confused, and then toppled, though not before arterial spray hit me in the mouth.

The fighter on my team didn't acknowledge me, instead loping off to the other side of the arena where the rest of the fighting was going on. His opposite number, a huge black man clad (because the Romans were suckers for stereotypes) in leopard skin wielded an enormous hammer. I saw a man who'd slept in the next bed at the *ludus* whimpering in the sand, unable to even lift his sword. The crowd's boos turned to screams of delight as his head was pulped by a heavy swing.

I scanned the arena – sheer walls without handholds and doors studded with iron spikes. There was no way out of this place, save by being the victors. If I could just distract, divert, be quick on my feet, I could help the armoured man on my side to get us both out of here. I kicked up dust as I jogged towards the battle.

There was one blue left besides me and our fighter to two of theirs and the huge Nubian, whose hammer was whirring through the air like a pack of hornets. If they stuck as a pack, they'd bring our man down so I kicked sand at the nearest yellow and got his attention. This one was a little more seasoned, advancing with shield held high and sword ready to stab like a soldier. I knew what was coming from the long hours in the practice yard and the memory of dry school lessons on legionary tactics from another life; still, I was surprised at how *slow* he was as he barged with his shield, lifted slightly, then stabbed forwards into my belly.

My belly wasn't there – I'd allowed myself to slide off his shield to the side and backswung low, catching him in the crook of his bent knee, feeling the blade bite. I ripped it free and he went down with a grunt; it felt like I was barely rushing but I was able to slice his throat open before he could raise his shield in defence.

Our fighter was still held at bay by the swings of his opposite number, but the remaining blue was locked in a tangle of limbs with the last yellow on the ground. He managed to gain the top, then get his hands around the yellow's throat and held on until he stopped kicking. The blue bellowed pure hatred into his opponent's unconscious face, then retrieved a fallen helmet from the dust and pounded the recumbent face to a bloody mess, oblivious to the crowd that was climbing over itself with delight.

I watched the Nubian's swings. It was a metronome of pain and he knew what he was doing: our fighter couldn't get close enough to bring his blade to bear. His arms shone with sweat but there was no let up to his pace. I could see our man edging, looking for the gap he could surge through and stab at the bare chest of his enemy but I could also see that this was the Nubian's plan. All he needed to do was be patient and the helmeted blue – the only thing between me and that hammer – would over-extend himself.

I was surrounded by death and bone-tired of it. It was no life sleeping next to lions and shitting in a shared bucket, but better that than being brained by that hideous lump of metal. Thinking of the night Sporus had killed the soldiers and spirited me away, I drew my sword back and let fly.

I missed, of course.

The iron went spinning end over end and would have missed the Nubian even if he'd not seen a glint or heard a gasp in the crowd and ducked sideways. The sword clanged onto the ground behind him, and he flashed me a white smile as I stood there, unarmed but for my shield. His eyes were liquid death…

… until a moment later, when they went wide with pain. I'd interrupted his swings just long enough for our fighter to dart in and bury his blade up to the hilt in yellow-speckled flesh. With a roar, our man wrenched his blade upwards, slitting the stomach open, then ripped it free. The Nubian didn't even make a sound as he dropped like a stone.

The bellow of the crowd was animate, a concussion of sound like the battering of the sea on the shore. I was alive.

I was back in the underbelly of the arena when the daze abated and the nausea hit. I doubled over and left what little food was in my stomach in a pile in the corner. I'd ended life, snuffed out two men with stories of their own. I knew they would have killed me, sure as Tuesday, but it changed nothing. God, Banks, it was just so fucking intimate. I hadn't hit a button and levelled a city a thousand miles away or shot someone with a rifle: I'd been close enough to smell their fear that matched my own. It had been real wet work, the kind that leaves a stain on the soul, but that wasn't what made my hands shake like I had a palsy; it wasn't what I'd done, it was how I'd done it. It had been so damn easy. I was *good* at it.

As I stood there over a pool of my acrid sick, I could see every fight I'd ever had – you were there for at least one of the times I tussled with Easter, though his little band of goons got the better of me most of the time. I only hurt him the night I ran away because I was off the edge, not caring about getting into trouble anymore and, besides, half of his chums were in the other room. It had always been the same, though:

I'd watched them move in slow motion, expecting it to be some trick – surely no one could be so languid in the heat of the moment? It helped me get a few punches in at school but now, with some hard-won training and death staring me in the face it became a simple thing to find the angle, disrupt the balance. As those men in the arena had moved through honey I'd seen where shield and sword and helmet shifted, leaving a gap, and it had seemed so *obvious* where to slash and stab with my blade. I'd seen those men as an engineer sees the stresses and loads of a house, knowing without consciousness where to apply enough force to bring the edifice down.

I hadn't enjoyed it; I'm no cold killer. I just didn't find it as hard as I should have, as a civilised man should have, as a pampered boy of independent schooling should have. And what was worse was I knew I could do it again.

Someone slapped me on the shoulder. It was the fighter from the arena, his hair mussed with sweat now he'd doffed his helmet. He didn't smile, but he nodded and grunted in the closest thing I'd seen to words, then wandered over to a barrel of water and dunked his whole upper body, surfacing a few seconds later with a blow like a whale. My fellow *damnati* (I learned later this collective name for those destined to be cut to ribbons) were giving me looks ranging from confusion to outright fear; even the other man who'd survived watched me as if expecting me to bite.

I didn't say anything to them, nor they to me, and I knew in that moment that I was no longer one of them. I'd killed other men and done it easily. I was a fighter, and they were afraid of me.

The next day, we fought again. I was strapped into a boiled leather guard that covered my left arm from shoulder to wrist, given metal greaves for my shins, a better sword and shield. Just two of us blues faced a pair of yellows. My partner, carrying a sickle sword, went for the one in the breastplate and helmet, leaving me the net man with his trident. I watched him move for a few moments that could have been hours, the crowd nothing but a dull fug in the distance. He moved well but I saw fear in his eyes. There was tension in his shoulders as he coiled to whip the net and trip me or thrust with his weapon; it made him slow, gave me warnings of when the strike was coming.

After a few passes, I fainted a stumble and saw the net coming. I lifted my foot to let it swing past and, as he recovered from the swing, pushed off my toes with my shield held high. I batted his trident away with my sword then slammed the bronze rim of my shield into his mouth, sending teeth flying. He went down and I didn't perform any theatrics – one quick slash and he bubbled his life away into the sand.

The crowd bellowed like the thousand mouths of hell and in his box Caesar looked on, his chin resting on his knuckles. He was looking right at me, his eyes no longer vacant but interested. It made me feel cold despite the heat of combat in the weak spring sun. Another roar; I saw my partner holding his blade to the throat of his kneeling opponent, looking up at the box for a sign. Vitellius fluttered a disinterested hand and another yellow was sent to whatever afterlife he favoured.

On the third day, I fought in a team again. I killed three men and then I sat in a corner of the fighters' quarters – I'd been moved – and ate dry bread, watching the dust shiver in the beams of light peering through the gaps. It was cleaner in this part of the runs, though still bare and cold at night. I was allowed to wash myself and given better tunics, even sandals. The *lanista* himself presented me with a cuirass of hard leather and bracers with strips of iron sewn in, though I refused the full-faced helmet and took a hardened cap with a neck flap instead. If I was to be this horrid thing, this wind of murder, I'd do it without hiding behind a mask. Letting them look me in the eye was my one link to sanity and anything that remained of my old self.

The fourth day was cruel, when I walked up the ramp beside the man who'd fought beside me on the first day, the one who'd strangled his opponent. No paint was splashed on us, and he shot me a look of sadness and fear as the arena gates swung open. He put distance between us and soon two men from the other school joined us on the sand. One was a spearman with a conical helmet and thick padding all along his shield arm. The other was Perfume.

He looked like he'd not eaten for days and was wearing his palace tunic, filthy and ripped though it was. In the Imperial box Vitellius had genuine curiosity on his jowly face. I looked at Perfume, seeing nothing but a frightened man bound in flab, holding his sword like it was about to bite him, and I understood. This was for me. Perfume had been brought here to draw more fight out of me. Never had it been so explicit that I was a piece in the emperor's little game.

I should have enjoyed it, killing Perfume. I should have revelled in it, for what he did to me, for letting those men into the palace where they did what they did to my poor Sporus. When it came to it, though, he could hardly hold his sword and the snot ran down his face. He barely recognised me anyway and begged for his life through the raw gap I'd smashed in his teeth last time. He was a bully but no fighter; with no position or patron to cover him he was pathetic, mewling into the sand after I knocked his weapon away and punched him in the gut. I sliced his throat, almost tentative, seeing if it would give me some measure of satisfaction but all I saw was another man dead by my hand; all I could think about was another pool of blood on a marble floor, gossamer soaked in red. The crowd booed, robbed of a spectacle. *Fuck them*, I thought.

At least I was spared the unpleasant task of killing my stablemate – the spearman left his body hanging off the spikes of the arena door. The two of us then squared up, hefted our weapons, and joined. He kept me away with deft thrusts for a little while until I saw the angle at which he was weakest and charged, taking the point flush in the middle of my shield and driving him back, feeling the weight fall away as he stumbled. Once I was inside the arc of his weapon, it was all over.

That day ended with the air smelling like bonfires as they piled the dead, men and beasts, on pyres. An orange glow permeated the night, casting shadow plays on the walls of the enclosure. The next day was to be the last of the fighting. I didn't know what that meant for me, even if I survived: I never allowed myself the luxury of assumption. Just because I'd not met anyone to test me didn't mean I wouldn't, and tomorrow was the ultimate day of the contest. If there were monsters out there, this would be when I'd meet them.

I was about to lay down to sleep when the *lanista* came for me. A woman wanted to talk to me, had paid for the privilege. He leered at me like something from a pantomime and told me to be quick and not to be too rough, then left me in a room just off from the main gates. I waited for this woman whose idea of the erotic was to slide under a killer, not knowing quite what I would do or say.

That's when Sporus walked in.

I'd spent so long locked in pure physicality, barely addressing another human being, that I was unable to say a word and, for the span of a breath, wondered if I still could. Instead I went to him and held him in my arms, feeling the ridge of his spine and the sharp angles of his shoulder blades; he was gaunt and cheap scent hung about him like a sickly cloud, but underneath it all was the true smell of him, the one that I'd carried in a hidden corner of myself during all the numbing days and nights that had passed since I'd seen him. He'd always seemed taller than me but our roles had been reversed: the practice yard had filled me out, straightening my spine while he stooped as if carrying a heavy load. As I held him, he squirmed a little as if from discomfort and I remembered his terrible wound. Pulling back, terrified of hurting him, I saw his face up close.

He was painted like a cheap whore. The white lead paste was thick on his cheeks and forehead, his eyes darkened into kohl pits. His lips were an obscene, twisted mockery, daubed, slapdash, with red. Before he'd beguiled by using his arts to emanate the feminine; illusion so impenetrable it was impossible to split from reality, seduced through its very subtlety. This was mockery, pantomime, lowering him to just a skinny man with a painted face. He saw something in my eyes and must have read it as disgust (or its cousin, revulsion), and he pulled away, closing his eyes as if to ward off pain.

'I'm sorry,' I stumbled. 'You look... how are you?'

'Oh, I'm fine, better than ever, actually.' His tongue was bitter and I deserved it.

'I'm so glad you're alive. After, what happened.'

'Yes.' He looked off to one side, seeming to find fascination in the cracks of the plank walls. 'I'm not sure you'd call my days and nights "living".'

I took his hand and was relieved that he didn't snatch it away. 'I missed you.'

He looked at me as if he was making his mind up about something. 'I wanted to see you one last time before I go.

199

Because I owe you my life and because you might die tomorrow. In truth, it's remarkable you're standing here now. You have a following, you know?' He waved his hands at the world beyond the wooden walls of my prison.

'If I win, I go free. That's what Caesar said.'

'Caesar is a cold-hearted cunt to rival the greats. He'll do no such thing.'

'But what if I do? If you wait for me, we can leave together. Be together, without all of this.'

He smiled, but it wasn't a good smile. 'Do you think I'm free to walk the streets? I took a risk even coming here – by morning they'll find the bodies and they'll be searching for me. The people who kept me, they find what they look for.'

'What have you done?'

'It took every ounce of strength I had to keep me alive, from my... wound... becoming infected. There was no room for anything save survival, a slow healing. Why do you think I'm plastered like a harlot, when once I made lords fill my cup? Tonight, I finally had enough spare to trick two legionaries who'd paid to fuck a freak into looking away, long enough that I could grab a sword. I cut their throats and I'm not sorry. I'm leaving this putrid boil of a city to its foetid people; may they dissolve in their own ambition and filth.'

My heart hammered in my chest. 'Where can I reach you?'

'You won't,' he said, soft, not meeting my eyes. 'You won't see me again. I'm going where these animals can't find me, to draw my strength back. And then I'll break them all.' His voice was quiet, piercing and cold as hell.

The panic rose and I felt like I might puke. The idea of never seeing him again, now that I knew he was alive, scared me more than any of the brutality of the arena. 'You can't. I love—'

'Tsk,' he hissed, cutting me off. He looked away, but I saw

that frailty in his eyes first. He'd built a wall around himself and I didn't have the tools to climb it. When he looked back, I could see it was taking all of his nerve to do it. 'I hope you live. I hope you go on living, even that you find some happiness. Our time together was very special to me. Never—' His voice cracked and before he could say more he turned and pulled the door. His last words to me were with his back turned, and I could hear the catch in his throat. 'Get out of Rome the first chance you get and stay gone.'

His absence was a vacuum that pulled light and sound into it. I watched the space where he'd been for a long while. My eyes were wet but there were no histrionics, no dropping to the floor, weeping, clawing at the ground where he'd stood. That's the lie that's sold to us by fiction; I felt as if I'd been winded, the air stolen from my lungs by an impact, leaving me on the borders of panic, wondering if I'd ever be able to take a breath again. The capsule of warmth and light deep in my mind, that had sustained me all through my days at the *ludus*, flickered and went dark. I came out of that room without life, a walking shell of flesh with no guiding purpose. The stumpy *lanista*'s smirk died on his face as he saw mine. He saw something that terrified him in my eyes and took a step backwards in spite of himself.

I don't remember the night, though I expect I slept, rose, ate some gruel. I do remember that others had to fit my armour for me and someone forced my fingers closed around the hilt of my sword. I was daubed with gold paint, ankles to neck, then I was guided up the ramp to the doors that swung wide. It was a strange, hot day for that time of year, trumpets and screams and chants and cheers flooding in on a wave of heated air. All I remember was that, in the heat, I was cold and that in the middle of all that noise, I was a pool of deep silence.

8

Three days since that most fleeting of kisses and I can still feel the echo of it there, on my cheekbone in spite of everything that's going on. Sometimes, in the middle of revising a speech or reviewing another clause of the trade agreements, I find myself touching it, remembering. Everything else is muted, faded somehow, by that brief caress.

It makes me try again where I'd failed – a little bookshop a street away from the palazzo with close-packed shelves reaching into darkened rafters. A volume had stuck out at me, the muted gold of its Art Deco spine catching the light – a collected edition of Wodehouse. I think Messrs Wooster and Jeeves have a lot to do with how she sees me, so I bought it as a little joke. Unlike the time before, her eyes lit up as she opened it. Her hand on my arm was gossamer-light as she read the first page, eyes already engrossed.

'This English will be hard for me to read, how cruel,' she said smiling, her eyes warm. God, I love how she looks at me like that.

The guilt is still there – I doubt I'll ever be free of it – but the anticipation, the excitement of reciprocal attraction is stronger at least for now. Though I step outside myself and witness the signs of infatuation, I can't stop myself from giving in.

It's a complication, however pleasant. There is so much to do. Compromise between nations is closer than it's been for half a century; opening conferences and speeches are over and done with and the negotiating teams have been hard at it trading in advantages, pushing and pulling for the optimum deal for their side, though I can see from the papers (many from our side on actual, old-fashioned paper) that we have little to bring save a sense of need. This has been an extraordinary series of events just by its mere speed: we are fired by an overarching mandate of rapid rapprochement, but what we haggle for is a semblance of our old relationship – independent currency, token border controls. There is the thorny issue of monarchy – to be full members of the Confederacy our head of state would, like all members, be one of the co-Presidents, moving power away from the Crown and returning it to something like its previous, ceremonial incarnation. This will take a long time to address, but already the relays have been heavy with back-and-forth between Easter and the Palace back in London. The Euros, for their part, seem to feel some moral obligation to accommodate. In their primacy, they have the luxury of being magnanimous.

A paper from one of their departments sits on my tablet where I have just finished reading it. Translated into English, it is titled *Economic collapse in the Scottish territories and Northern England*. This is the truth of how they find us: an economic basket-case and – though I'd not say this aloud – I find little room to argue. They sketch out the early days of our long withdrawal in the early twenties, the resentment rising on both sides of our social divide as the process dragged on for years. Accusations flew across the despatch boxes and the Commons hardened into two wings as the compromise that made democracy work died. The Right forged ahead, hell-bent while the Left shed its old skin of equivocation and got militant; marches got ugly and burning cars in the capital became a common sight.

The turning point was The Speaker, Neil Dodds MP, a decent if unremarkable man who'd held the Chair for seven years – a man with the old European flag carved into his chest broke into his house one night and butchered him and his two children. That the murderer also had swastikas on his arms and a history of mental illness was left out by the press and the Right whipped up the popular storm; Europe (which by now had its own problems) had been tarnished, regardless of the facts.

Moderate voices on the Left began to find themselves outnumbered. Hardened cliques formed, and some of them took something else than horror from what had happened to Dodds – they saw weaponry. The report before me sketches in cold terms the major events that followed, the European Defence League cropping up again and again. A school held up that resulted in three dead teenagers, the bombing of the train lines outside Didcot Parkway. The one I remember, vivid as a scar, is when one of those damn fanatics drove a van full of concrete slabs through a Remembrance Day parade in Bristol. The sight of those twisted bodies, the blood speckling the European flag sprayed on the side of the van, is etched on me, as it was on the nation. It didn't take much for the National Party, the aggregate of the hardest separatists in Parliament, to ride into a majority government.

Liberal freedoms didn't disappear overnight, instead they dripped away gradually. Certain films and books dropped out of circulation; girls were encouraged (through social media, in a twist of irony) to tend to the home. The report doesn't mention when gay marriage was repealed but I remember the early protests, the condemnation in the press, the return of ugly words. Same-sex relationships were made illegal not long after we got back from Rome. I remember it, because the next day America exploded.

Everyone suffered from that economic and social implosion. The very thing that kept our economy propped up was gone, overnight. Our industry hadn't been up to the task for over a century, power stations were ageing and the roads weren't being maintained. Yellowstone set off a panic across the world and the whole apparatus of state buckled under the pressure. We went hungry as a nation and the politicians blamed each other. The public blamed them. There were some dark days – Elanor and I collected rainwater and barricaded our door for some weeks while London's streets rang with the clash of rioters and police.

When the King took control of the Army and brought some form of order, there were few that weren't glad, though that was the death knell of our old way of life. The change, coming almost unmitigated from a single figure, was swift. The borders were shut before what happened to Canada could happen to us. Self-reliance became our watchword and we left the world to deal with its own problems and enveloped ourselves in the cosy visions of the past when all that was needed was grit and spirit to thrive.

Seeing our descent summarised in succinct bullet points in the dispassionate language of economists makes the reality all the starker.

Barter Economy.

Extreme fuel poverty.

Life expectancy nearing pre-industrial levels in major population centres.

The report posits that Scotland is the greater problem – after the oil wells went dry a large proportion of the population drifted south. For the last ten years all we've done is push convicts through the gates and shut them behind the thirty-foot-high walls that run across the country from sea to sea. The entire country may well have turned feral.

The report is comprehensive, damningly so. They know everything about us, and I know Mariko wasn't exaggerating – there have been observers on our shores for some time. And yet they still want to take us in, giving concession after concession. From what I've seen of Rome, how it has blossomed into this ultra-modern metropolis, I can believe that they can afford us but I keep looking for some deeper motive for this willingness to take on the challenge of a broken state. Living here these few weeks has made me partial, I'll admit, but I can see some imperfections; despite this, it cannot be denied that their society has moved on to become one that thinks beyond knee-jerk suspicion. The Confederacy, fat on trade with the South American bloc, has the social and economic capital to allow compassion.

The longer I spend here, the longer I have to think on nationhood. An expanded tribe mentality, a necessary tool to guard against the dark and the wolves, then later the rapaciousness of other tribes. Perhaps, sometimes, to supplement ourselves, we had to be the raptors, creating a tit-for-tat that has lasted down the ages. As tribes grew into clans, which grew into kingdoms, which matured into nation-states, the ancient instinct of tribalism allowed us to suspend our empathy: I did not kill this man, I killed an enemy; I did not bomb this village, I burned out an enemy stronghold. The old judgement, that his face is not my face, his ways are not my ways. By clinging to whatever symbol it was – a crest, a flag, a skin colour – we insulated ourselves against the creeping notion that those we killed were just like us, only separated by geography.

I know that I'm so very tired by it all: losing my Elanor, seeing the land I live in crumble around me, at odds with the Great National Message. I also know I'm guilty of viewing the Confederacy through rose-tinted lenses. I look at their government, their laws, their towers of steel and glass that shimmer with a thousand colours in the darkness, and I see what I want to see. Mariko, born of two cultures and made whole by the super-nation she calls home. Even in my most cynical moments I see more around me to like than to dislike.

This report has affected me far more than a dry piece of analysis ever should. It has given a statistically verified face to what I'd already long suspected. I've already begun to wonder how I could bring Sara over here, perhaps to Rome itself; that lazy golden light on the French hills as we rushed past on the train. The possibility of escape is tantalising.

I don't think I want to go home.

You've lived in the shadows for too long, Banks, says Orkney, grinning. *You've left what little sense of humour you had to moulder in the dust. Get it out, shake the crumbs off it and start living your life, you miserable sod.*

All the more important to get back to work. If the mission falls through due to any amount of inattention, we will have failed millions back home. I shut my little fantasy away in a filing cabinet beside Orkney's desk and return to the present. Still, the dappling of the late afternoon sun on the rich panelling of my office wall leaves me feeling full up.

Monk's family has been contacted regarding his miraculous re-emergence, and by which I mean we traced a spinster aunt living near Cambridge who has not left her house in several years. The father and the mother, dead; the estate is held in the trust of lawyers, and they are demanding significant proof of identity before any further action be taken. There is a file of transcribed relay messages on my desk that grows by the day, forms from every department of government I've ever heard of and several I have not.

It is no small thing to bring a man back from the dead.

The Residence's entrance hall is busy as I descend the main staircase, carrying my briefcase and my jacket. I need to sleep – perhaps I'll actually use that other room I'm meant to be sharing with Monk. I'll check on him first, though, and Mariko, if the streets are quiet. I'm still furtive around this place after what happened, though not so much when it's busy. Easter has been avoiding me, though I caught a sidelong glance yesterday that raised my hackles. I'm torn between fear of what he can – and is willing – to do and how angry I am. His arrogance and his entitlement, his lack of vision. He should be leading the way to this agreement, not be its biggest risk.

You've always known what a damn fool the man is, says Orkney. *The boy who never grew up.*

But he's wrong, of course, this little figment in my mind. Easter did grow up, and apparently he grew very dangerous. I keep going down the stairs, eager to get out and avoid as many people as I can.

The staff are dressed in their finery – white tie for most, military No1s for anyone with even a sniff of Forces about them. There are medals to sink a passenger liner and the champagne is already flowing; this isn't even the event, merely the warm-up before another stop on the never-ending road of gatherings and boozy dinners. I hear my name barked from the sea of tailcoats. I shrink away, but I know it's too late. Charteris the under-minister emerges, clutching a brace of champagne flutes.

'You're not changed, Banks. Most improper, you know.'

With a sinking feeling, I realise I'm meant to be attending this one. A look at Charteris's red cheeks and I know I'd rather be anywhere else. Or, specifically, one other place. 'Apologies, sir, I'm just on my way to get changed.'

'Ah, dead man keeping you busy, eh?' He takes a slurp from one of his glasses and purses his lips. 'Continentals certainly can fizz. You should have one.' He makes no move to hand me the other glass however, so I smile.

'I'm on my way to the other residence to change, sir. I just have a few errands to run first.'

'Never understand you Civil Service types. All labour and no jollies. Bad for the constitution, having a stick up one's fundament, you know?'

I give him the awkward laugh he wants, but nothing more. 'I'll certainly be along for a glass or two when we move on to...'

His eyes look off to one side as if searching for some piece of information. 'No... don't have it.' He turns and gesticulates at a junior staffer. A droplet of champagne escapes the rim of the glass and splashes my trouser leg. I ignore it. 'Where is it we're going tonight? What? Speak up, man! The Vittorio Emanuele? That dreadful pile of meringue?' He waves the staffer away. 'Bloody eyesore. Decadent architecture. Still, the drink tends to be on par, so we shan't complain unduly. You met the newcomers?'

I'd drifted off, so the question catches me off-guard. 'Sir?'

'New arrivals from Blighty. Catering, or logistics, or some such. Came in a moment ago. Look like soldiers to me, but ours is not to question why, eh?' He actually winks, like we're out of bed after hours and stealing biscuits from Matron. I suppose, to Charteris's sort, life is one long adventure in the boarding house. I look over his shoulder and see three men in identical suits, each carrying a briefcase. One of them is talking to Easter, who looks mightily displeased at having been drawn away from whatever he was doing. The other two stand watching, the tide of the party flowing around them like rocks in a stream.

'Go on then, Banks, be about it, eh?' says Charteris, patting me on the shoulder. A little more champagne splashes me and there's an awkward moment where he tries to brush it away which only results in more spillage. I make my excuses, and I wind my way through the crowd.

I can't hear what Easter is saying, but I can hear the trumpeting of his voice over the clinking of glasses and the hubbub of trivial chatter. I dodge behind knots of my fellow diplomats, trying to avoid the eye of my boss; I'm already spent and I want to get out of here, and the sooner I do the sooner my absence will be clouded by the wine that continues to flow. I catch a glimpse of one of the new men standing off while their leader converses with the Minister, and I notice a sheen of sweat on his forehead. Odd. The evening has turned clear-skied and cool but these men look like they're standing under the glare of the sun. There's tension in their necks and shoulders.

As I push the heavy wood and glass door open, I take a last look back, my curiosity getting the better of me. What is it about these men that rings little alarms in the pit of my stomach? As I do, I see one of them watching me leave. He turns and says something to his companion. Some instinct makes me quicken my pace.

The street outside is filling with diplomatic vehicles and the usual throng of mopeds. Rome's night is full of the perfume of masonry and hints of garlic from a nearby restaurant. I take a deep breath and set my foot on the first step.

The earth heaves. Something massive slams into my back and sends me flailing through the air. The world is a white sheet full of noise and fury and I'm arcing over the steps, travelling onwards like a bird on the wing. The first time I feel the flames is just before I smash into the bonnet of a car.

Screams.

Smoke.

My briefcase is gone and there are flames licking up my arm. I feel like I've been hit by a rugby pack, rolled over by a bus, knocked down by a bare-knuckle fighter. There's blood in my mouth and everything smells singed.

I manage to roll off the car onto the ground. The flames carry on licking at my arm so I tear the sleeve off. Above me, at the top of the steps, a man howls in pure agony.

I can walk, though the world is at crazy angles and I can't catch my balance. Each step is a mountain and my back and sides are pulverised into a terrifying numbness. I follow the screams and I find Charteris; his hair is singed clean off and his left leg is gone. There is a trail of blood leading back to the front of the Residence. Every window has blown outwards. My eye catches on the ruin of twisted flesh and bone and rubble and fire that is the inside of the lobby before a cloud of black smoke swamps me and I have to drop to my hands and knees, and throw up.

Charteris is whimpering now. His leg dribbles blood but the blast seems to have cauterised it. It's the glass shard lodged in his neck that's the problem. Somehow, he's now cradled in my lap. I can't get my fingers around the dagger-like shard to staunch the flow; my hands are red and slicked with his arterial spray, red as death and smelling like copper and raw beef. I think about pulling the glass out but I can't get a grip on it and it would probably kill him faster, so I just rock him back and forth, back and forth, like a child. I'm sobbing, the pain in my back getting worse as the initial shock wears off. Around me, everything is Dante made real, a smouldering charnel house.

Charteris tries to reach up, but he's too weak now from the blood loss. His body is entering shock, massive fluid loss beginning to affect the brain. His mouth bubbles, his breath is wracked and spasmodic as I hold him and his eyes, grey rings in bloodshot whites, fix me as his life streams away.

The lights flash blue and red, and I'm not sure what belongs to the ambulances and the police as they swarm the scene and what is inside my own head. Everything is discordant, broken. The world around me reeks of death and ash. Hands grab me under the armpits and drag me away, away from Charteris's body with its pale, glazed eyes. I fight them a little, but there's not enough in me to do much and they know what to do, how to stop my limbs from flailing and hurting anyone, even myself. I wish I could get the taste out of my mouth, this rank palate of burnt bone and sulphur. Then the flickering of the flames is gone and I'm washed with neon strip lights so powerful I have to shut my eyes. They are doing things to me, jabbering at each other too fast for me to follow even if my ears weren't still ringing, ringing like St Paul's. Through the fog of it all I feel a sharp scratch on the back of my hand.

I want to know what happened. I have to know... what did... why am I here... too bright... no, no, no, no...

69 CE

I wasn't the first to face Geminus that day – that was the name of the arch bastard they'd sent me against. As the roar of the crowd broke through, I became aware of the arena pit around me. At least a half-dozen corpses littered the sand in various states of dismemberment or disembowelment. Four large wooden pillars had been installed, each with rows of spikes embedded – one wretch hung from them, the blood dripping from the points of the foot-long barbs and running down his legs, dripping in a pool on the floor from toes that dangled inches off the floor. A glorious slaughter had taken place here, a day's work by a man who'd whipped the crowd to new frenzies with greater and greater displays of cruelty. A net man had been strangled with a length of his own gut, a swordsman lay on his front with the hilt of his sword sticking from his cloven rectum. And in the middle of it all stood Geminus, waiting for me.

He was tall and his lean, sculpted arms were long, so much so that the tips of his twin cavalry swords almost touched the sand. His breastplate and greaves had been painted black and his face under its rounded helm was daubed with soot. A creature of the underworld, a vengeful shade, enough to unsettle some, always good enough to get the crowd going. He smiled at me, a broken-toothed thing of malice. His was the business of putting on a show and he was no blustering idiot with a sword. This was a killer of killers.

I'd been saved for last, or so the announcer said. Vitellius was in his box, staring down at me with the same pointed interest, the estranged cousin of the disregard he'd shown when he ordered me into this brutal life. Without taking his eyes off me, he flicked a hand at the announcer, who gestured at the buglers, who blew a long, discordant blast. And just like that, we fought.

It was like a dream, watching him walk towards me, swinging his swords in great arcs, limbering up his shoulders. The crowd, who'd intruded on my solitude, faded again as if beyond a high wall of fog until it was just the two of us there. As he came close, he swung both blades at me at a diagonal and the reflex of practice raised my shield. The impact jarred my arm and knocked me sideways, and I saw his left blade already arcing in at me. Perhaps by accident my own sword – a leaf-bladed Greek thing longer than my forearm – was in the way just enough to deflect the blow over my head. I didn't see the kick that took me in the stomach and landed me on my arse in the dust.

There was no rage in his face, none of the foaming, rabid distortion to which I'd become accustomed. As I lay on my back he studied me, a small smile leaving creases in the soot. I suppose it would be chilling to see a man so confident that he didn't need aggression to win but I was so cut off I still felt nothing. I waited for him to plunge one sword or the other into my chest, neck, face, but neither came. He was waiting for me to get up, to prolong the fight. He wanted to draw more sport from me for his slavering audience.

I rose, smelling rust. He came at me again, swinging at my

shield. I checked the blow, my muscles working where my mind had taken leave, but the block was sloppy: he grabbed the lip of my shield and used it to pull me onto a fast knee which drove the wind from me, followed by another and another. I couldn't breathe, only hunch under the onslaught. I could feel him standing over me, my neck itching, sensing him readying to strike, cleave, kill.

The blow, again, didn't fall. He spat in the dirt in front of me, called me a coward. The great Geminus hadn't expected this easy kill, unworthy of the final bout of the day. He'd waited and warmed himself for another true killer to match him but found a broken, listless man instead. With a grunt of frustration, he kicked me in the face.

The blast of pain was sharp and flipped me on my back, blood dripping down my cheek. I'd dropped my sword, so I wiped my face with my free hand. The sting of my broken nose snapped me out of my dream just for a moment and I happened to look at the Imperial box.

Vitellius didn't look disappointed that this last, grand spectacle wasn't living up to the hype. Neither was he angry; he rested his chin on his knuckles like a disinterested child, not even watching the fight but staring up instead at a flight of birds that had chosen that moment to swoop over the arena. His distant expression was the same it had been the night I first saw him, when they'd forced Otho's head onto a pike.

When Sporus was cut.

Like a distant drum, I felt my heartbeat;

Sporus, lying on the floor, mutilated agony;

Another beat, louder;

Whimpers. The cherry blood seeping;

The knocking of an army on the gates of a fortress;

Sporus, stripped of dignity and power, abandoning me here.

215

The cage shook, the bars bent. The animal surged out.

I took Geminus' legs with a sweeping kick. He almost dodged, but not quite; he stumbled, giving me time to rise. He regained his footing as I came at him and he knew the fight was on this time. Gods, that horrid fucker was fast, faster than anyone I'd seen before.

I was cold with anger and I was faster still.

I drove in between the killing arc of his blades before they could close on me and punched the rim of my shield into his face, hearing the crack of bone, then kicked straight up into his balls. His breath exploded out but he was good and managed to jump backwards.

The pain climbed him like a creeper of agony and I was impressed he stayed standing even though his blackened face morphed and shifted: he was Easter, leering at me, he was Perfume, he was the Praetorians that had kicked me and shat on me. He was a succession of Caesars who'd stolen my freedom.

He was Sporus, who'd stolen himself from me.

My rage was beautiful.

I threw my shield like a discus and came at him low as he was distracted; I pushed up with my knees and took him in the belly with my shoulder, wrapping my arms around him as I lifted. As he reached the top of his arc I pivoted and slammed him down, all the hours of training in the *ludus* abandoned in favour of a lesson learned on a cold afternoon on the lower fields, practising tackles against pads. The spiked club of a downed opponent was there to meet him and he grunted as it pierced his back.

I let the anger carry me; I was swimming in it, flowing around him as he tried to grab at me, not letting him, smashing elbows and fists into his face; red spattered, ran through the soot. I was close, intimate in my violence, too near for his swords to be of use; he tried to wrestle me off but I took his chance away with more blows, fast strikes, a piston of undying anger. One of his swords was in my hand and I beat him with its hilt, then stood just enough to chop at him, hacking, hacking: no art to it, no intricate cut and thrust, no shifting of balance, reading of eyes. This was bloody murder, plain and simple, cold frenzy with a blade. He carried on trying to fight me even as I ripped into his chest and belly, then he began to shake and his hands fell away, but still I clove the fucker. When I came to myself, some minutes later, there was no man left beneath me, only bone and meat.

I rose. His blood had drenched me, turning the gold sickly pink. I was an abattoir, a walking charnel house. The crowd was silent.

Vitellius had stopped watching the birds.

The sword slipped from my slicked fingers.

The roar that followed was like no noise I'd ever heard.

There was no ceremony, no acclaim from the mob. No wooden sword to signify my victory. I like to think that there was a look of mild alarm on Vitellius' jowled face, but I doubt it was anything like it: this was, after all, a man with the worries of the Western world's greatest sovereign territory on his shoulders. A wave of the arm brought another clarion of war trumpets and the doors to the pits swung open. I expected more death, more men to throw themselves at me until I too was nothing more than scraps for carrion birds – and I was too drained to care, in truth. Instead, two other men entered. One was a fighter from my *ludus*, carrying a pronounced limp and a leg bound in cloth. The other was bare-chested and the hairiest man I'd ever seen, any skin not covered in black, pelt-like body hair burned dark by the sun. His head was bound and blood had matted his hair on one side but his eyes were defiant. Neither acknowledged me as they stood beside me, facing the Imperial box. Vitellius stood and raised a hand to silence the crowd. Then he waved a hand and the word *manumittio* floated towards us, barely audible. Then the crowd went wild again.

We three were free men, by order of the First Man of Rome. I should have been elated. Instead, I stooped and took a handful of arena sand in my fingers and let it run through them, feeling the rasp of the particles on my skin.

Freedom. But freedom for what, with him gone.

Later, I was given my prizes. A document of my sale was ripped in two by the *lanista* in front of me and two witnesses. I was given clean, new tunics and sandals and a small dagger that I left behind. There was money, not a fortune but enough to see a man on his way in a new life. The other fighter from my school accepted his gifts and instantly pledged himself back to the *ludus* as a free man; the *lanista* clapped him on the shoulder and drew him into a hug of equals.

Both looked at me, one with fear, the other with avarice, but I shook my head. No more games for me.

The man with the thick body hair had pulled on a shirt and was heading for the doors, and I followed. As they were swung wide for us, to the grunts of approving guards, I took my first steps as a quasi-citizen of Rome. My fellow freedman looked at me a moment, assessing. I thought he was about to walk off when he held out a hand. We clasped forearms.

'Herakles,' he said.

In another time, I might have laughed. I told him my name.

'I'm going to drink and fuck everything. Coming?'

I shook my head.

He shrugged, then turned on his heel and walked off towards the warren of stalls that surrounded the arena. A breeze ruffled my thin tunic; I was suddenly aware of how clear the air was away from the fug of the pits, of how clean my clothes felt against my skin, though I was still the playground of lice. The air smelled, as always, faintly of horses, but also pine, river water and cooked meat. I looked up, but Herakles had gone.

I found lodging. The first day and night I didn't go out, unable to keep my eyes from the door that at any moment might burst open with collectors come to take me back to the sand. In the deepest part of the night, when only stray dogs troubled the narrow streets outside, I dreamed Sporus entered and took me in his arms like he had before and everything was right again. It didn't happen and he didn't come. With the dawn, I regained something of my old self.

Enough, I told myself. Enough of this.

There were baths nearby, big and public and cheap but with hot water, which is what I needed. I ordered the slaves (because I had also acquired that magic switch, though I never came to own any) to pump the bellows even harder until a couple of my fellow bathers swore at me and jumped out of the clay cauldron, retreating to the *tepidarium*. I let the water turn me red as a lobster, scalding the filth and the death from me. When I stepped out, my head was light and my skin felt raw. I had the masseurs shave every hair from my body, only in part because of the lice – I would have shed my outer layer in its entirety if I could have. The oil they rubbed into my muscles was thick and golden, then the bronze strigils were wielded in deft passes, scraping the dirt away.

I emerged onto the streets shorn of my old self, leaving it behind in filthy piles to be swept away at the end of the day – a hairless man that attracted a couple of glances from passers-by, but no more. Just another curio in a city of them. I went back to the tavern where I lodged and sat in the tap room. At the bottom of the second jug, the air cooled and the light thinned and the evening's clientele filled the other benches. They left me alone and I was happy just to watch from afar the knucklebones, jokes, little fights, laughter. I drank more than I ever had before but I didn't feel drunk (and Romans could make wine that knocked you on your arse). Instead, with every jug they brought me I felt the burning vessels under my skin, the tips of my fingers, every ounce of life that coursed through me. A girl asked, and I declined. A boy asked, and I declined. They smiled, there was no rancour. I was alive. It had taken me many hours to process it, but I was *alive*.

The thumping hangover reminded me that I was no god the next day. In the late afternoon the landlord hammered on my door and I rolled out of my blanket and pulled on my tunic. I gathered my few things into a bundle like Dick Whittington on his way to London and off I went.

The first drover told me to fuck off, as they tend to do, but the second accepted the *denarii* I held up and agreed to save me a space on his wagon. I used the couple of hours spare to buy a thicker blanket, a cloak, a hat and some fruit and bread for the journey. And a jug of wine, because if drovers prefer anything to money and cattle, it's wine. I shared it and some of the bread with him as we juddered out of the main gate. The city of Rome crawled away behind us and we headed to the coast.

I picked Ostia because I remembered it was Rome's nearest port, and I fancied I might go and see the world. A little voice at the back of my skull called me a fool, that it knew very well what I was up to: I had not, and would not, give up on the idea of finding him again. But Ostia was no tourist port

– what wasn't military was laden with grain, with little space for private passengers.

I found a tavern a few streets from the docks and I waited. I waited some more, a few days; I started to ask around, serving slaves, barmen, other patrons. I was looking for a man with dark hair and striking eyes, but that was the problem – Sporus had always been what he needed to be in the moment but was unremarkable in appearance otherwise (except to me), so I had a hard time describing him. One night a whore nodded and took me by the hand, leading me down the switchback alley maze by the quayside. In a wide-open space there was theatre, of a kind – male slaves dressed as women. They danced, sang, writhed with the oil on their skin catching the light of the guttering torches, their faces painted with thick white makeup that stank of sheep's milk and vinegar even over the smells of the street and the sweat of the onlookers. Everyone there was having a roaring good time, but my guide had misunderstood me. My Sporus was not here.

I started asking sea captains if they'd taken on passengers, but no one had taken on a passenger like the one I described. I knew, even weakened as he was, how good he was at playing a role and futility began to gnaw at me. I spent my evenings in the bar opposite my lodging, listening to the sailors gamble and the whores argue, and I started, little by little, to think of other things. I needed to pay my rent so I took work as a scribe at a merchant's warehouse – totting inventories and the like. I kept myself to myself. My hair grew back after a while and I let my beard grow out.

I gave up on travelling. But every time I saw a door open, I imagined him sweeping in on the sunlight.

9

Mariko tells me, on what I come to learn is her third visit, that I smashed my knee in the fall and that I had severe burns on my back and head. The ambulance crews applied a gel pack and I was put into a burns bath the moment I arrived. The surgery came later. Had I been back in Britain I would have died from fluid loss and the scars would never have healed. They grafted artificial fat to me and covered it over with vat-grown skin. They fixed my knee with some articulated, metal replacement joint. I am hooked to intravenous tubes; my hair has been shaved and I am medicated around the clock. I was lucky there was no nerve damage. I am alive.

The silence in my head is thick, massive.

'You'll be walking again in ten days,' she tells me. 'The surgeon says you'll be on immune suppressors for a month until the knee heals around the implant, then it will be back to normal.'

I don't think anything can be normal anymore. Not after that. 'What does it look like?' I ask her, and I mean my back; she understands without me having to spell it out. Despite what I've already been told, I can only imagine a pitted, suppurating horror.

'You will look like you've been tanning your front too much.'

222

She gives me a little smile and she takes my hand. 'It will be fine. Burns medicine has come a long way.'

I try to drop my head so she doesn't see the tears, but my body betrays me with great convulsions. Despite the risk, she holds me with a gossamer touch about the shoulders, not daring to encircle me, and presses her cheek to mine.

'It will be alright,' she says. 'You were lucky to be outside when the bomb went off.'

Her perception has its limits, and I'm in no position to explain to her. It's not disfigurement that's made me afraid. It's that old friend, guilt, back with a gleam in its sickly eye and stronger than ever. I was lucky; I was outside the main doors; the shock wave carried me clear of the worst of the heat blast.

And who the hell am I to still be lying here when all the rest of them are piles of ash?

It passes, though it takes some minutes. I'm too exhausted to be embarrassed, too hurt in body and mind to care anymore. Mariko shows no signs of wanting to leave and I'm glad for her presence, if only to hold my hand. I'm not the only one, I tell myself, there were others that survived – junior staff in the upper floors, the second residence, others out on errands around the city, like Jarvis. But the main delegation – Easter, Charteris, the senior negotiators and an assortment of colonels – were annihilated.

I roll that word around, turning it over. Annihilated. Reduced to nothing. Removed from the world, no mortal remains left behind, like some deity had simply reset reality without the need to include them. I'd seen Easter eating breakfast that morning and now he is *not here*, every selfish cell and every fleeting kindness he ever bestowed like a vapour on the wind. He will have an empty grave waiting for him

– with so many within the immediate blast radius, who could even begin to sort whose ashes from whose?

The horror of it threatens to roll over me and it feels like I'm falling from the top of a building, acceleration and vertigo all at once. I keep my eyes open and fixed on Mariko, who has fallen into an exhausted sleep in the chair. I push my buzzer for a nurse. She doesn't even question me when I ask for more drugs. A button-press and one of the tubes pumps something into me that makes the darkness recede, then the picture blurs around the edges, then I am gone.

I am alone for the first time in years. Every turn of the road has had its commentator, that soft voice that gently mocked while buoying me up at my worst times, the counterpoint to misery and the foil of pride. He's silent now and his study door is closed to me.

Orkney is gone. I've not heard him since the explosion. The days lying in my bed in the hospital, feeling the new flesh knitting into me, have been voids. Mariko comes and fills those gaps for a little while and I am glad of it – contact that warms me. She tells me that Monk almost came here to see me, but that she dissuaded him – I don't need to answer for him reappearing, not now.

When she leaves the silence falls again.

Where did he come from, this figment? I think that in the cavernous solitude after Elanor passed, I'd resurrected the bolder bits and pieces of a half-remembered figure of authority, someone I admired: Orkney, who took on new form and life inside my mind even though he's been in the ground long years – I never saw the real Orkney after graduation. He was my inner critic, sometimes unwelcome but always frank. Now he's gone and I miss him. How lonely a place the mind can be! I am a grounded church bell: all potential sound, muted.

Facts trickle in over the following few days. Jarvis, uninjured, has stepped into the breach in the absence of anyone more senior and re-established faltering contact with London. All but two of our relay engineers died from smoke inhalation after the firebomb (because that's what it was – a thing meant to burn, not concuss) and Jarvis fell back on the established protocols: that is, he flat-declined any offers of communication assistance from the Euros and insisted on dragging one of the pour souls out of his hospital bed to compose a message back to the Ministry. Mariko, on one of her visits, told me that the Confederacy's own report had been sitting on the Prime Minister's desk for three days by the time our own made it through. The response to both channels was brief and ambiguous: 'His Majesty's government is saddened by the tragedy to befall its servants about their duty. The implications of this failure will be assessed in due course.' Whose failure, is up for debate.

Jarvis has the missive in his hands as he paces – I don't know if I've actually ever seen anyone do this for real, though it's what books will always have you think people in crisis will do. It's unnerving and rather irritating watching someone walk backwards and forwards. The paper from the operator is crushed in his palms and he wrings it like a dishcloth.

'This will go to the top now, Banks. People at home are crying for blood, Euro blood. It's seen as an attack, by them on us.'

'Preposterous,' I say. The skin at my hip, where the new skin joins the old, itches like nothing I've ever known – it's all I can do not to tear it off.

Jarvis looks at me down his long nose, his round spectacles reducing his eyes down to tiny piggy points. 'Why would you say that, eh? We don't know who it was, but look at the facts: we're in a hostile city and we've been attacked. Smells Euro to me.'

This man is in charge. Jarvis shouldn't run an ice cream stand on the pier at Brighton, let alone the most important trade mission in a generation. 'Hostile hardly covers it. They've been throwing parties for us most nights, and the negotiations were going well. Until all this.'

The eyes get even smaller. Jarvis tends to lower his head, perhaps in an attempt to appear intimidating, in situations where he's contradicted or challenged; no one has ever had the heart to tell him it only removes what little chin he has, making his mouth part of his neck. 'You're pretty in with them, aren't you, Banks? That Chinese one that visits you, she's made you sweet on the Euro life, hasn't she? Ever thought she might be pulling the wool over your eyes?'

'Oh, do fuck off, Jarvis,' I snap, before I realise what I'm doing. This isn't like me, but I've been blown up and burned and left bedridden hundreds of miles away from my daughter and I've seen a man bleed out in front of me. Orkney isn't here to temper me anymore and I am too close to the surface to stop myself. 'If anyone here is blinded, it's you. It was all of us. The Euros have cars that drive themselves and all the money in the world. Why the hell would they bother blowing us up inside their own capital?'

'Because we're their enemy! They drew us in, weakened us, and then they took us out. You'd realise that if you weren't so blinded by the chance of a good fuck.'

I close my eyes to shut out the hammering. The thought flits across my mind of whether I could strangle him with the tubes that run out of the back of my hand. I take a breath. When I open my eyes, the light in the room is pale.

'We're not worth the effort, Jarvis. We're housecats to them. They survived the collapse of the world economy and prospered while we mouldered. If you can't see that, you're an even bigger fool than I thought.'

I've thought these things for a while but the impact of their articulation on him is stark. His cheeks flush with blood. 'I'm acting Minister, you can't—'

'You're the last bloody scrap left, Jarvis, don't kid yourself. You're acting nothing-at-all. They'll send someone out to take up the reins.'

His smile is venomous. 'That's where we agree. Someone else is coming alright, someone with the know-how to demand our rightful duty from these thieving Euro toads. I suppose your tart didn't tell you that, did she?'

'Get to the bloody point, Jarvis.'

'No one is being *sent*. The Prince of Wales himself is gracing us with his presence. We've communicated,' he actually licks his lips, 'and he appreciates my efforts. His Royal Highness will extract our due, then he'll clean house.'

The Prince of Wales, leaving Britain? Of all the unheard-ofs in the last few months, this is the greatest.

Jarvis drops the screwed-up paper in the waste-paper bin and shoots me a sickly smile. 'Your comments have been noted, Banks.' He looks like he's about to say something else, but instead leaves, neglecting to close the door.

70–96 CE

Things got commonplace for a long time, for the most part. I lived a life and I suppose it was a content one. I'm not given to belief in gods, but surrounded by the daily rituals and obeisance of the people of Rome and its Empire, these things have a tendency to start rubbing off on you; second-hand superstition isn't as good as the full-lunged thing but just as likely to kill you.

Anyway, the thought crept into my mind that perhaps some deity on its mountain had seen my year of trials, all the iniquities I'd suffered – being stolen from my own time, falling in love, losing it, being shaped into a murderer – and decided I was due some mundanity. I worked at my scribe's job and earned some measure of respect, even for an ex-slave.

I had the money from my win in the arena, though I hid it away like it was corrupted, but I always had it in my head that I'd use it to go sailing around the Mediterranean in search of Sporus. Especially after a few cups of wine I fancied I'd wake up the next morning and march down to the docks and find passage, but I never did. Common people didn't go on cruises – you'd need your own ship for that, and generous as my pay-out had been it would never buy me a sea-going vessel. The most I could hope for was passage to Greece, where I always thought he'd go, but once there I'd have to pay passage to one of the islands. What if I didn't find him in Thera, where then? Greece is full of islands. Once I'd sobered, I thought of myself begging for change on the streets of Corinth or Athens and I stayed where I was. Even later, when I had money, I stayed where I was.

I saved enough to rent a flat in a neighbourhood where stabbings were only occasional and none of the buildings had collapsed recently; I ate and drank what I wanted, though I had no taste for the high life. Back in Rome, history continued happening to others.

Vitellius didn't fare much better than his predecessors. All the while I was killing in the arena another general had been declared emperor by the legions in the provinces. In short order half the armies of the Empire declared themselves for this Vespasian; no wonder our man had seemed so distracted up in his box. As had been the eminent fashion ever since dear old Gaius of the Julii got the idea, a host of legions descended on Rome and set to it with the civilian supporters of the incumbent. We saw the flames on the horizon as the city burned, and many well-known merchants never returned to Ostia. They say thousands died on both sides in a dirty little melee on the tight-packed streets of the slums.

In the end, iron and discipline won over fervour. Vitellius was dragged by his heels from his hiding place and hauled to a high place in the centre of his erstwhile city. They cut his head off and threw his remains in the river. Vespasian was not best pleased others did this without his say-so, or so the story goes. For all I know he ordered it (or even swung the sword himself) and then only affected disdain for crass butchery for appearances, because this new breed of Caesar always had an eye on posterity. Who knows how much gossip starts life at the desk of a zealous secretary?

Ostia was not a place of politics: its concerns were keeping the city fed and the money flowing into and out of the Mediterranean. Little changed for us: night was still night; Caesar was still Caesar. After that last spasm of violence Vespasian settled things and the legions went back to hacking at tribesmen instead of their own citizens. I worked on and after some years a colleague who drank with me sometimes told me I should use my name to set myself up in business, earn some real keep.

'What about my name?' I asked him.

'Come off it, Monarchus. We all know you fought in Vitellius' games. People will trust an ex-fighter who survived. They'll think it'll bring them luck.'

After that, I pulled the pig hide sack with silver in its belly out of the hole in the wall where I'd hidden it. The bag still smelled of that last day and it was all I could do not to fetch mortar, seal it away. Sense kicked in and said, *Why not put it to use?* So I rented some offices and a section of a warehouse for supplies, hired two junior scribes from my old workplace and set myself up in the copying business.

It was a small enterprise and the first two years were hard going, but there was plenty of work to go around now that politics had stabilised back in the capital. What passed through our doors was the sinew of Roman life: local marriage certificates and bills of sale; legal records and trade agreements. Boring, rote paperwork that was the filigree on which daily life grew. A time came when I found I had enough trusted employees to spend most of my days not hunched over a parchment. I never bought slaves, as I might have mentioned, and I liked to give work to other freedmen. It was just as well, because that's when I met Herakles again.

He was in the tavern when I walked in one evening, a jug

and a cup in front of him, staring at the wall as if it had given him offence. His hair had grown even wilder, a great bush of a thing, though his face was shaved – his pelt-like chest hair ended in a straight line below his throat. He didn't look at me but when I approached he tapped the bench opposite with a thick finger. I sat and nodded at the serving boy for another cup.

'You live here,' he said.

'I do. You?' The curtness of his speech was contagious, refreshing.

'Been sailing. Alexandria, Athens. Now I'm back here.'

I saw the rope scars on his hands and arms, the corded muscle under the bronzed skin. His face was leathery from wind. The boy brought another cup and a jug of watered wine. We drank and listened to the sound of the bar room for a while.

'Going back out again, are you?' I asked.

He raised his eyebrows. 'No, had it with the sea. Almost died too many times. Better odds in the fucking pits.' We locked gazes then, remembering.

'So what then, what else do you do?'

'I can build walls. I can knock heads together. I can fuck like a god.'

'Which one are you best at?'

He grinned. 'What do you think?'

Herakles worked for me a few days a week. He helped about the place with moving things, maintenance. He could build well enough but he was a better foreman when the time came to put a new storeroom on the back of the building. In time he gave up whatever odd jobs he found around Ostia and managed the day-to-day affairs of the office – the servants were terrified of him and were more hardworking for it.

We drank together a lot of the time, always with few words passing between us. We never spoke of the arena but the ghost of it was there beside us – I just liked having someone around who knew what it was like and I think he did too. When he got really drunk he'd pick fights – there was no real rancour, it was just his idea of a good time and there were plenty in Ostia's docks who thought the same. Some nights I picked him up off the floor and helped him home to his little flat near the waterfront, sometimes I left him singing sailor's songs with the very people who'd bloodied his nose. It was a miracle he kept all his teeth but there was no darkness inside Herakles, or none that went deeper than his customary glower.

I bought a little house on the outskirts of town where the farmland started and the buildings began to peter away; a modest place with a yard and some chickens. It reminded me of Pythagoras' little villa, from all those years ago, and one of the first things I did was to fill the courtyard by the kitchen with thyme and rosemary and bay, dotted through with flowers so that the evening aroma would waft through the house on the breeze, mixing with the smell of burning candle. I kept to myself – even Herakles didn't come out there much. At home I drank nothing but clear water from my own well, except once a year on the day when I'd emerged from the arena pits for the last time. On that day I needed my own company and unwatered wine, because that was also the night the dreams came.

My first year in Ostia I'd woken in a fever, my skin drenched. I'd seen Sporus, thin and wasted and the black rags hanging off him like crow's wings as he wound his way up a sheer cliff path. The dream was so real I felt like I could smell the filth on him and hear the creak of his bones. At the top of the cliff was a hut surrounded by coarse thorn bushes, a lowly place of dried mud and poorly thatched. An old woman sat outside on a low stool, milking a goat. Something was wrong with her eyes – they were black, no whites at all. Her smile was mocking and her teeth were too large; even though she was tiny she had the menace of a thundercloud. Sporus said something to her – he was angry, demanding something but the words were fuzzed out like I was hearing through water. The old woman laughed and the sight of it crawled up my skin. Sporus had tears on his face but his sunken eyes were so angry. Then I was in my bed and my landlord was hammering on my door because of the screaming.

Every year, without fail. Sometimes the wine knocked me out and I woke with nothing more than a hangover in my bed in my house on my quiet street and I was relieved. It didn't always work, though – sometimes the dream broke through and I was with him as he wound his way up the cliff path. As the years went on he appeared stronger, the flesh coming back to his bones and his clothes weren't rags, but that look on his face got darker and darker every time. I could never hear him but I knew he was looking for something from the old woman, something she mockingly refused him.

Once, about ten years after it started, I saw him pull a dagger and advance on her but a flock of ravens appeared as if from nowhere, battering him with beak and wing until he reeled back to the cliff edge. The knife fell from his fingers and his clothes were torn but the birds dissipated like smoke and the old woman's laughter was a vibration that shook the world – I could have sworn I felt it in my guts well into the morning along with a ball of inexpressible dread. Still, he came back every year, I didn't manage to block him out, and every time he looked stronger and angrier. It's hard to describe to you now, but it's as if his shadow was growing larger. I didn't know if it was my own mind doing this to him or whatever strange bond linked us, but every time I woke from those dreams I wished I could forget him.

True, I'd go long periods without thinking about him. When I did it would be a sweet little pain, the kind that made me want to sit and let myself tear up a little as long as there was no one but the chickens to judge me. It was a little self-indulgent but it was when I remembered all the good things like his laugh and his smell and how he'd made me feel totally loved.

I had some lovers, none lasting more than a night or two. Not all of them were paid for. The fucking was all I needed, a scratch to an occasional itch. A widow who lived in the house down the road paid me a few visits and laughed at my poor jokes, but after a few attempts she must have seen that I had no interest in her beyond sharing an evening meal; we went back to nodding politely when we crossed in the street. I missed her conversation for a while, but in truth I liked the solitude of my little patch of earth. There's always another cloud, a fresh patch of wildflower, a spider spinning a new web in the corner of the veranda.

Herakles had a talent for spotting when I was getting morose and would drag me to a bar when the last person who realised I needed to unwind was me. He was terrible at dice, but that didn't stop him trying to take my money.

'You have any Theran blood in you or does Fortuna just like to piss on me?' he asked once as he handed over his *denarii*.

I used it to buy another jug of wine. 'I doubt it. I'm from the North, I told you.'

'Britannia, you said. Are they all as ugly and cruel to their friends as you?'

'Worse. You got lucky,' I said. 'What was that you said about Therans?'

'Just something I heard when I was on the ships. Never gamble with a man from Thera – they'll throw Venus more times than I've had shits and they'll rob the shoes from your feet.'

I tried to push away what the name of that island brought up by pouring the wine slowly, mixing it with iced water because it was a hot, breezeless summer evening. The ghost of an older fantasy reared its head, of chartering a vessel. I had money now. I could likely afford it. I felt the compulsion to stick my tongue in that rotten tooth.

'So there's something odd about Thera?'

'Don't pull that face, Monarchus. I hate it when you get like that. I'm shit at dice, nothing more. There are some oddballs on Thera that think they're special, that they worship better gods, but the truth is they're just a bunch of goat-fucking farmers who make up stories to look interesting. It's a rock in the sea. Now pass me the dice, I'm going to take you for everything you own.'

I felt the pull rise in me, then subside. I'd never forgotten him, nor laid to rest the desire to see him again, but I had *life* here, comfort, even purpose. Instead of heading for the docks, I stuffed the dice in their sack and passed it to Herakles.

He didn't bring Thera up again and I let it lie.

I never raised a hand in anger to anyone again. There's not much confrontation in the life of a scribe, even one who runs his own office, but the stories were amplified by each telling, it seemed. It got back to me that I'd killed fifty men and a dozen beasts in a single day – exaggeration that had Herakles' stamp on it. I didn't feel the need to quash these tales, not when they kept my business insulated and the clients walking through the door, hoping documents produced within my walls would carry some of the fortunate sheen of my 'glorious career'. If only they knew the baseness of it, how devoid of heroism and romance the killing really was. To the smiles and nervous nods, I gave quiet acknowledgements, and they paid in good order.

When I was walking home one evening I stumbled on a couple of drunk lads having a fight outside a wine shop, one of those where it's more like aggressive hugging than any kind of genuine contest. One of them bumped into me, turned, swore and raised a fist. Before he could utter another word, three of his friends dragged him away, begging my mercy, blaming the drink. The next day, the boy came into my office, sheepish as you like, and *apologised*. All I had to do to maintain this reputation was to occasionally look gruff. It suited me just fine.

I kept the business small but it made a decent amount of capital, staying well away from politics, which in Ostia was easy enough – I paid my taxes and kept up with whoever the local magistrate was, but that was it. When I wasn't working or tending to my home, I'd go to the baths and sometimes the adjoining exercise yard where a semi-formal wrestling club met every third day of the week. It wasn't about aggression as much as strategy and I enjoyed the challenge of working through the positions, gaining and losing advantage, sometimes submitting, other times winning. It was a pleasant bone-weariness I had afterwards that kept me going back every so often. Herakles flat refused to come, so instead I enjoyed the easy camaraderie of the other wrestlers.

I bought a couple of goats. I went to plays sometimes. My food was simple. Twenty years of mundane life, but just the one I liked.

I wasn't young anymore, nor so slender of flank, though the wrestling kept my belly from sagging. My eyes had lasted well enough despite the long years copying by candlelight and I often read in the garden when the sun was up – anything I could get my hands on. I kept my beard and hair neat but didn't spend much time thinking of my appearance – once I passed a polished bronze mirror hanging on the wall outside a shop and was astonished to see my father staring back at me. I have grown into his shoulders, his way of walking even, though I would have put us as far apart as two men could ever be. I wondered, as I saw my reflection, when he'd died, and I felt a little sadness I'd not expected.

One evening I dreamed my terrible dream, but it wasn't on the appointed night. Sporus wound his way up the cliffs again and my shade followed him. He was strong again, his steps full of purpose and his clothes were simple but well made; at first I thought he was as I'd known him at his prime, but then I saw lines around his eyes that showed the years on him. At the top was the hut and the old crone, as withered and wild-looking as she'd been every time. Her confidence was gone and her black eyes were full of fear. He walked up to her and his lips moved. For the very first time, I heard them clear and the sound of his voice made my insides knot. Harsher, older, but the voice of my Sporus. I knew they were speaking a kind of Greek, though I understood them perfectly.

Give it willingly, he said. *Or not. I don't need to care anymore.*

The old woman looked tiny and bony next to him, an old crow. Her voice grated like slate on slate. *It took them all. It will die with me. You cannot wield it any more than they could.* She jerked her head back and I saw the land over her shoulder beyond her filthy hut, which I've never been able to see in any of the other dreams. The islet with the tall cliffs was barren, blasted. Something terrible had scoured this place and the pain of it reverberated, a lingering stench of atrocity.

Sporus was beside her. He said one word, and it was loaded with the weight of a curse:

Rome.

The crone looked resigned then, like a traveller at the end of a long road. He cut her throat and she withered before him as her blood soaked into the scrub grass. His chest moved in a deep sigh.

Crows. Hundreds, maybe thousands blackened the sky. They flew at him like they had that first time but instead of rending him they became black smoke that he took into himself, embracing it, feeding on it. His arms were spread wide and his head thrown back but the look on his face held no fear, only triumph.

I woke.

All that day I had a headache, a real stinker: a migraine that set the lights flashing behind my tight-pressed eyelids. I felt like an elephant was squatting on my head so I retired to my bedroom with a soaked cloth draped over my eyes and tried to ride it out in the dark. The pain would ebb and flow, burrowing into my skull. It was like having a toothache, the really bad kind when you can do nothing but ride the crests and troughs of the agony. I was in there for two days. On the second, as if a switch had been flicked, the headache went, leaving behind a smell of wet earth and dust and burnt-out torches, but I wasn't relieved. I knew beyond rationality that Sporus was coming back to Rome and that his purpose was terrible.

I gathered a few things and pulled some money together, just enough to get me to Rome. The final moments of that last dream repeated in a loop in my head, burrowing. *Rome*, he'd said, like it was a curse. Rome was the centre of the world and Rome was the answer – and it had hurt him. I knew with the certainty of a man who'd had the same nightmare for twenty years that this was happening and that the man I loved – or whatever wore his face – would be there. The smell of dank earth never quite went away, slipping into the background. The

238

world around me went on moving, unperturbed, but for me the air had turned yellow and every shadow was too sharp. I rode an oxcart that afternoon, telling no one where I was going, entering the city in the exact way I'd left it all those years ago.

It didn't seem any different from those hazy few days I'd spent there on my way from slave to private citizen. I'm sure houses had burned down and been rebuilt, that bakers now occupied the former sites of butchers and market stalls had passed from mother to daughter, but to me the fabric of the place was the same – it was dirty, close, loud, pungent, shot through with glimpses of beauty – the gleam of a troupe of dancers, the burnished doors of the temples and as we got closer to the main fora, the sweeping colonnades that went on forever. Togas mixed with tunics and the red cloaks of old soldiers. Children with dirty faces danced across the stones that bridged the roads, paved as much with compacted dung as they were with flagstones. Our oxen lurched us into open air at the top of a hill; beyond, something very large had changed. Something that could not escape anyone's notice.

His statue was still there, the Colossus of Nero, except it had been crowned in gold in the likeness of Helios. The Golden House was no more, every stone of it, every marble floor, every window and every tree of its gardens carried away. The lake, where I'd first encountered true Romans in that absurd boat made of stone (the first time I'd crossed paths with *him*, I remembered with a sudden pang) had been filled and in its place rose a monster of stone arches, columns ranked like a procession of soldiers, the whole circular edifice reaching towards the sky as if it might touch the fingers of Olympians. One of Vespasian's sons wore the honours of First Man of Rome and he'd continued with his family's passion project: the great amphitheatre was well underway, most of its third tier complete. Scaffolding crawled over it like a fastidious creeper plant and the cranes that hauled their cargoes of marble and brick were stark against the bruise-bright sky. You've seen the place now, how it glows at night from the work they've done inside it. Back then it was a looming skeleton of a thing that towered over every structure around. Thousands would die on its sands before it would become a ruin, then a tourist attraction, finally a symbol for unity, but even then I could feel the mass of the thing, the pull of blood and slaughter that warped the world around it. The horrible truth is that I'd never forgotten the feeling of the sand between my toes, the braying of those crowds, the release of primal fury. I still haven't.

I found lodging. I had no appetite and drank water in my room to the light of a single candle. I didn't know what I was doing here, what I would do next, but I knew this was where it would be. I slipped into a dream and it was a dark thing of worming tunnels, pits of unseen foulness, but visible through everything was a beacon drawing me on. In the dream I became obsessed with the negotiation of those tunnels, trying to sketch my route on paper as I went in case I needed to find my way back, but every time I came upon torchlight or moonlight I saw my work was nothing but a mass of spiral charcoal lines across the page. The beacon grew no closer and I returned to my methodical, careful mapping. My mind spun; I knew that if only I could complete the map I'd get to where I wanted to be. I felt the heat of the tunnel walls around me as if I were inside the guts of a living thing that pulsed in time with my own heartbeat. I woke and threw up immediately, scalding the back of my throat. I was hot with fever and the migraine was back. It was mid-morning before I felt well enough to rise and gather my belongings.

I flitted from tavern to tavern like this for five nights, waiting for some sign of what I was to do next. I found myself looking in on the whole thing as if watching someone else's life unfurl. I had a real life in Ostia – money, property, a good and loyal friend in Herakles – but here I was, a vagabond, waiting for a sign. Had I snapped, had some kind of psychotic episode? I wondered how I was able to wonder this, how I could examine my own actions and see how out of kilter they were, even as I was powerless to stop them. I bought a jug of wine and drank it under the eaves of the temple of Ceres. It only brought the migraine back.

On the sixth night I woke from the same dream about tunnels and the pounding of the walls didn't stop even after I'd heaved my guts onto the floor. I felt nervous, like I was about to step out on stage, my heart beating the inside of my chest like a galley drummer. The *boom, boom, boom* reverberated through my head, even though I was fully awake, but this time I was free of the headache. The beat thrummed through me, drawing me out of the door in nothing but the tunic I'd worn to bed, and led me, alleyway to street corner to avenue, towards a fixed point. I dunked my head in a trough, certain I'd just lapsed into a new and more detailed version of the usual fever dream but came up soaked, cold, and very much awake. I could feel the pulse through the soles of my bare feet now. It was in front of me and beneath me. I followed, oblivious to the calls of whores and the braying mockery of gang thugs.

10

From the window of my room, high up in the air of this towering spire, the old city looks like a model under glass. It reminds me of visiting museums as a boy, seeing ancient sites reconstructed in paper and plastic and resin, with little day-in-the-life scenes laid out to make the model come alive. From up here I can look down on the tiny cars and people that scurry, indistinct, around the streets; at night it becomes a latticework of light, major arteries like the *Via del Corso* branching into a million capillaries. The Tiber cleaves it all, and there in the distance is the EuroPar, the brightest light of them all. The map is truly alive if you take the time to watch it, and time is something I have nowadays.

The few of us that survived – not even enough to mount a skeleton staff with Easter gone and the only semblance of authority resting in me and Jarvis – were put here by the Euros so they can guarantee our safety. After I was discharged I insisted on visiting the bombed-out palazzo: I don't know exactly what I expected to find, maybe I just needed to see it for myself. The whole site was cordoned off by police and the remains of the structure enclosed in a hazy force dome, like something from an old film. I could still see the stains on the steps where Charteris had died on me. I didn't feel anything; I let them bring me here, to the new Rome I'd only seen from afar.

We have been given two floors of this tower of steel and glass, and we do what we can to wait out the arrival of His Royal Highness, the Prince of Wales – which is precious little. We are alien individuals of a nation distant in time, not a unified delegation; we are leftovers.

I press my hand against the black oblong on the wall and murmur a command in Latin and the window frosts as if on a winter morning, taking away the view: I was starting to feel the shadows of vertigo, staring down from such a height. Such a vantage could make a man feel like an Olympian but knowing my toes are mere inches from a drop of such an immensity makes parts of my brain that are closer to reptile than mammal scream in protest. The simple act of making the glass opaque, recalling the concierge explaining how it could be dimmed in direct sunlight or used to magnify the view or even act as a large projection screen, and I know that these Euros understood us better than we gave them credit. The technology is as advanced as it is easy to use, both simple and elegant: thank God we'd had none of it in the Residence. It could only have made it more obvious how far we have to come before we hold our heads up as a sister nation and we would always have been at the negotiating table at a disadvantage; they knew we'd be frightened, diminished, even resentful, and that is no way to enter a trade if true advantage is desired for both sides. They'd opted to give us the reassurance of pipes that clanked, showers that used water, visible power lines and the smell of old wood because it is one thing to marvel at the future from a distance, another entirely to be dropped in it.

'You have that look on your face again.' Mariko sits at a small glass table in the middle of the living room. Her tablet device rests in its leather sheath next to the coffee that gives off a gentle vapour; she prefers to read a paper magazine, an ancient *National Geographic* featuring old Osaka. Her gaze is thoughtful, her brows ever so slightly knitted as she leafs through it. She makes a little *hmm* noise in her throat, not looking at me.

'I'm still getting used to this place. The height.'

'You will. I did. I used to live in a tower a few kilometres from here; it was nice for a while but, the old city is...' She hesitates. 'Not as perfect, more beautiful.'

I can smell the old leather of her armchairs and feel the softness of the spines of her library. Such a little place – fine for one, stuffy for two. 'How is Monk?'

'Moved into the apartment downstairs. He's almost finished his story – he even let me read some. Don't worry, I cut a deal with the owner, used official-sounding words. It didn't cost very much.' A little shrug.

'I'll pay for it. I mean, the delegation will. When we... when things are more...' God, I'm a bloody mess. 'Look, you shouldn't put yourself out. He's my problem and you shouldn't get in trouble over it.'

'Nonsense.' She arches an eyebrow. 'That is what an English person would say, yes? I've been reading Mr Wodehouse.'

'I fear he's a little out of date.'

'Oh, I'm not so sure.' Her eyes are luminous. She's mocking me in that way that I wish would never stop.

'Will you move back to the tower after...' I don't know what after looks like – so my voice goes wandering off.

She flips a page of her magazine. 'There's something warm about the little old apartment, I've grown to like it. I think I will keep it, maybe modernise just a little.' She flares her fingers in the direction of the window, in that small gesture commencing a journey through glass and miles of empty air, down into the old streets of Rome, twisting all the way to the little apartment that is full of her books and where the light falls in through the skylights. I think about the mezzanine where she sleeps as I would a secret land: closed off but pulling at me with gossamer threads of her scent. After all that has happened in these last few days, I still feel the burn of her fleeting kiss on my cheek.

Her smile is a little crooked. 'What are you looking at me like that for?'

'I think I'm a little in love with you, Ms Albenge.' The words come falling out and I've no chance to intervene. My cheeks redden.

Her eyes widen a mere fraction, her eyebrows rise a hair, the corners of her mouth crease upwards. A little amused, a little frightened by my candour? A week ago I would have stuttered and fumbled an apology and wilted before Orkney's little jibes, but now I only feel the warmth of her, see the gentle curve of her jaw and the line of her hips against the material of her skirt. Death's near miss has uninhibited me.

She pauses, and for a moment even the newly unfettered Lindon Banks fears the signs have been misleading all along. She stands, gathers her things, prepares to leave.

Oh God, now I've done it.

With her coat in hand, she steps in close enough for me to smell the hint of coffee on her and kisses me, this time on the mouth. It's as fleeting as the first, but the affection and – dare I say it – pity of that other one has been supplanted by something else; a velvet press on my lips, a heat in my chest.

She doesn't take my hand, instead indicates the door with a little nod that makes her hair sway like night.

* * *

The sun is in repose, draping its lace tendrils across the city. Bronzed light soaks the air to saturation and some of it falls through the bank of skylights over Mariko's bed, filling me with its warmth. I can stretch out my fingers and toes on the low, mussed bed and barely touch the edges; the universe is a heady thing of body musk, spice and perfume and I have been lying here, every pore of my skin open and receptive, since the moment we climaxed. The hum of it still hasn't left me.

I feel safe for the first time in ages. The delegation is miles away. No drones, no officials. Just me and her and the afternoon.

The door cracks and she comes back from the bathroom. She's still naked – so am I – and neither of us even knows the shadow of shame. We've come too far for that now, our innermost secrets bared in those first fleeting moments when we bundled, awkward as teenagers, up the narrow stairs to her mezzanine, wrapped in the first true embrace of each other, hands darting about as if this was their only chance to touch. It's not like that now: she flops down beside me with an exhalation and the depression of the mattress rolls us into each other's space like the most powerful of gravities. She puts her hand on my knee and rotates it, like a toy, and she puffs out her cheeks. I catch her eye and the smile is followed in short order by a kiss of companionship, perhaps a little congratulation.

I'm not ashamed of my body, though I thought I would be. She is as lithe undressed as I'd dared imagine but it's no cold perfection: she's more beautiful for her age lines, the tiny stretch marks on her thighs, the little scars with their own stories. For my part, I'm a man from behind a desk who's been away from the steep hills and low valleys for far too long, but I don't give one shit about the way I look, what she sees, because we've joined on a primal level, felt the most natural and consequenceless high nature has to offer, so the playing field is level. I kiss her again, the milky hardness of her teeth against my lips as she smiles, her eyes closed. Our breaths judder; we fall together.

A little later, coffee. Freshly percolated from a silver octagonal vessel, another antique, that she heats on the equally ancient-looking stove. It's morning again, and we both agreed it was time to scrub ourselves of our exertions. We made it as far as the shower before we gave in again but tiredness and a little soreness on both sides led to a temporary white flag, a chance to take on supplies. I'm dressed but she's wrapped in a robe that runs over her body, sometimes moving with her, parting enough as she leans to pour me some more; the temptation of shadows and curves.

'Stop it,' I tell her.

'Stop what?' A little smile.

'You know very well.'

She does, and her eyes say so. We both drink our coffee. I don't know if anything will ever replace the sweet-bitter-roasted burn of the stuff and I decide then and there to take some home with me.

When I go home. When will that be? My God, with everything that's happened and is due to happen, my future is indistinct.

'I have to go soon,' she says. 'I have work to do.' As she says it, her eyes become even more alive.

'Not something to do with our lot then.'

'I've requested a transfer. I'm not impartial, after all.' A grin. Just enough flattery – she knows men are such needy creatures. 'We've received communiqués from the East.'

'As in Russia? Not China, surely?' After its collapse, what little remains of that great nation makes our Scottish problem look like a holiday camp. Scotland may have reverted, but at least you can breathe the air without filters and the streams run with clear water.

'Japan.'

Ah, there it is, of course. It wasn't a light in her eyes, it was a blaze. The land of her father. 'You must be thrilled.'

'I am. I feel like I know so little, just what I learned as a child, from before the war. Imagine if we could reach them, talk to them, establish a dialogue? Papa knew he'd never see it again, but I just might.'

'I hope it goes well.'

'You can stay, if you like, or I can order you a car back to the tower.'

'No, that's fine.' I waggle the little black oblong communicator they gave me. 'I think I've got the hang of this thing. Anyhow, I should stop in on Monk and check he's alright. I am meant to be his keeper, after all.' My tone is light, but I don't feel it. I've heavy news for my old friend. I know he's been lying to me.

96 CE

The Colosseum weighed down the valley, a cannonball on a rubber sheet, and I couldn't keep away from it. It was little trouble to scale the fencing and then I was under its terrible shadow, feeling like I was under the face of a breaking wave and about to be crushed. The foyer was a mess of builders' detritus and piles of brick and I found a large double trapdoor that had been propped open, an access to the holding areas for beasts and quarters for the fighters. I went down, at first steps then ladders, until I was below the arena floor. After a while the torches ran out. I was about to turn back, to ignore this insanity that had brought me to the bowels of the Roman world, when I saw light guttering further down the tunnel and a low, bass murmur.

As I got closer I realised it was someone chanting, the sound reverberating from the walls, lending it an otherworldly quality. I was deep inside the construction now, the lowest levels that had sat untouched for some time, judging by the dust. After some minutes I came to a large circular room with several cage doors adjoined, a kind of holding area for wild beasts. In front of each of the cages was a thick wooden post with iron rings set into it, tethers for chains so the handlers could restrain their charges until it was time to send them to their deaths on the sands above; what was tied to those posts were men, or the bloodied remains of men.

Five in all, ruins of exposed flesh, each had been gelded and most had had their faces cut to ribbons. Blood spattered the ground and soaked into the thin carpet of straw. I could tell from the shade of it – some bright red, other patches almost black – that these men had been killed over different nights. As I watched, one of the wrecks twitched and coughed bubbles of pinkish drool. Not yet passed, this one, but blind and tongueless and shorn of his manhood. A terrible way to die; a worse one to live.

I'd been so transfixed by the barbarity of this display that I only noticed the hooded figure behind the dead as he threw back his hood. Here was the source of that eerie chanting, a man with long dark hair. He kneeled; I saw that he'd been holding someone in front of him by the shoulders. A boy, no older than ten, shaking like a rabbit. The man spoke, and my chest felt like it had been grabbed by the fist of a god and twisted, because I knew that voice even across the ridges and valleys of the years that had passed. It was the voice from my memories and my nightmares. He turned his head and the guttering torchlight fell revealed him there, older but still as beautiful as the last time we'd been together, before our plans were shredded.

Sporus. *My* Sporus.

A low groan echoed from the tunnel wall, a sound of pure longing, and it was from me: an animal's reaction, too fast for the mind to intervene. A knife was in his hand, a shard of brilliance in the light and his cloak swished as he moved towards me, casting the boy on the bloodied floor. I was quick enough to step out of the way but I was frozen by the sight of him; he had me by the shirt, the wicked sickle blade pressed to my throat. I tried to say something, anything – how many times over the years had I rehearsed what I'd say if I saw him again.

I missed you.

Where were you?

I hate you.

I love you.

I said nothing, the blade pressed firmer against my jugular and I felt the sting of parted skin.

'Who are you?' he said. His voice had deepened a little with age but still had the same music to it. Something was stopping him, holding him from cutting my throat, and I dared to hope that he knew who I was. 'Speak,' he said, his voice thick.

'You don't damn well recognise me?'

'Turn around and walk away. This is none of your business.'

I wanted to hold him so much that my fingers itched and I thought I'd let him press the blade into my throat if only it would bring us closer together. The little aromas of him insinuated themselves past the noise of blood and straw and I wanted to bottle them; the dam I'd built, that had lasted through the many years, burst and the river was let loose – all I wanted was him, even if it was the last thing I ever did, but what had gathered up in that reservoir, mixing with the need, was resentment at the long years alone.

'Where the fuck did you go?'

He hesitated. The knife's pressure slackened.

'Did you know I'd survived?' I asked, feeling heat on my cheeks.

'Monarchus? Is that you?'

'Did you give a shit I was out there, living, waiting for you to come back?' The words came out like clubs.

He stepped back, his hand to his mouth. Then he smiled, looking like a man who'd won a bet with himself. 'You've come. You know, I wondered if you might. Just like you came on that first night, though I didn't know it then. The gods made you their messenger. Did they tell you where to find me?'

'I don't know what you mean. What is all of this?' I indicated the dead men. 'Who are they?'

He smiled. He took my hand, ran his fingers over the palm. I wanted to wring his neck, break his spine. I wanted to kiss him.

'You've grown older, boy. Of course I knew you were alive. I've worked so hard on their plan, my special plan. I see so *clearly*, Monarchus.' He touched my face, stepped in, kissed me softly. God, I couldn't do a thing to stop him.

'I saw you,' I said. 'Walking the cliffs.'

He looked surprised for just an instant, then the smile returned. There was something dangerous in his eyes, some fanaticism. 'We are bonded, you and I, don't you see? I prayed for you all those years ago and the gods brought you to me. And here you are again, my harbinger.'

'Why didn't you look for me? I made a life. We could have had a life.'

He stepped away. 'I was broken. I had a task to accomplish, old ways to uncover. Nemesis, Monarchus. I told the day I left you what it had cost me to keep myself from death. I went back to Thera to be near the wellspring, to heal. It took a long time.'

I held him again, unable to stop myself. I was a man drowning and he was my raft. We flowed, water on water, fitting each other's form like we were made to be that way, two halves reunited. Still, there was that pit of unease.

'Who was the old woman?'

He pulled away again. His smile was gone. 'Someone who had what I needed. It's not important now.' The child, forgotten on the reddened floor, whimpered and the warmth fled from me. 'Sporus, what have you done here? What in the name of Dis is that *child* doing here?'

His face was solemn. Priestly. It chilled my marrow.

'You found something terrible on Thera, didn't you? I dreamed it.' My voice was quaking.

'This is my reward to Rome for the kindness it showed me. These,' he moved his knife hand in an arc that took in the corpses, 'are Rome. Mighty Rome of the thousand gods and none. This one, a money lender; this one, a farmer; a seller of slaves; a soldier; a senator.' The last man he indicated was the one who'd still been alive; he didn't look that way anymore. 'And this one is the crown for them all. The scion of the greatest of houses. Blood of Caesar, heir to the purple.' He placed his hands on the boy's shoulders, the gold braid running through the rich fabric catching the torchlight.

He'd killed these men cold, with planning and time and care. There was no heat of survival to these deaths; the cruelty of what had been done to them made me sick. I saw the way his fingers curled around the boy's shoulders like an eagle holding its prey and the ground disappeared from under me. Something had gone bad in him, broken by what had happened to him and made worse by his boundless rage. There was an iron taste in my mouth, the old woman's black-on-black eyes in my mind and one word reverberated around my skull:

Evil.

'Don't look sad, boy,' he said. 'You're owed for what they did to you as well. Was there ever an ounce of kindness, of regard for you as a man? Nothing more than an object from the moment that old vulture made you that way, worth little more than a dog.'

He knew nothing of my life, of work and little acts of kindness. Herakles, my friend (I'd not said farewell, that rankled). Long years, greetings in the street, small gifts from staff on feast days, reciprocated. While he festered in hatred

253

and chased after forbidden things in blasted places I'd built a damn existence. 'You need to stop this. Look at him, he's a child. He doesn't deserve this.'

'They *all* deserve this!' he snapped, cutting me off. The boy flinched against him. 'Every last one of them.'

'Even Nero? What about him?'

He paused. I noticed a little patch of blood in the hollow between his collarbones; I didn't think it was his. The light caught the sweat on him, drawing out the angles of his face. He looked like a predatory cat, all power and deadly purpose. 'They took him too, in the end. The last ruler who saw beyond butchery. They forced his hand.'

'Come, Sporus. Leave the boy alone.'

He ignored me. 'They think they spread knowledge and peace and stability across the world when all they do is lie and cheat and steal, passing the greatness of others off as their own. Even their gods are pale imitations. No, Monarchus, this has to end and I will see it done.'

'Fine.' I had to get him out of there, get the knife in his hand away from the boy. 'Then you've had your revenge. You're right, these men are the pillars of Rome and you've showed them what they're worth. It's enough.'

'What he represents deserves more hurt than all of them.'

My voice broke as I snapped. '*Look* at him, Sporus! Is this what you've become, a killer of children?'

His eyes hardened. Even in the close warmth, I felt a winter wind crawl along my spine.

'I thought you at least would understand. They've spread their sickness far and wide, touching every corner of the world. It breaks me to think of it, Monarchus, and I'm even more sure of what has to be done. What I learned in Thera can unmake a city, an island, a culture. It's a deep and old power and it did terrible things to my people, but it's what these cancerous sons of whores deserve. After I'm done with this, Rome will trouble no one.'

He seemed to grow taller and the air around him vibrated. The migraine returned and it was all I could do to remain standing, a pressure behind my eyes like my head was about to explode. This was what I'd felt each night since I'd returned to Rome – my stomach twisted as I saw that each time I'd felt it, a man had died in agony, their lives giving him power. This was worse, though, an earth-shaking pressure, a final gathering of force and intent and will.

The child struggled in his grasp and Sporus lowered his knife to the boy's neck.

'No,' I said, pleading, hoping a little humanity remained.

The touch of the blade welled crimson. The boy gasped at the small cut. Sporus' head sagged back as if in ecstasy or agony. He raised the knife high.

The anger came like an old friend, a cool wind that blew the cobwebs from my mind, making me sharp even as the vibration in the air increased to a fever pitch, shaking the very stones. My limbs were free again, my legs tensed like a sprinter's. I uncoiled with every ounce of my strength and took him high in the chest with an outstretched arm, tackling him to the ground; the air exploded from him as he hit but he held onto the knife. Before he could recover I straddled him, pinning him at the hips and made a grab for his arm. He tried to snatch it free but I caught it again. I bent his wrist back and twisted; he gasped and the knife fell from his fingers.

The boy was on the ground where he'd crumpled, but he lived. His tunic was richly embroidered, an Aquila that was the twin of my brand, soaked with blood; a child from the Imperial household, the son of someone important. I wondered how long it would take for them to raise the alarm, when they realised he was missing. What might he become if I got him away from here – general, politician? Father? Killer? All possible strands of his life hanging in the balance, the nexus of a great power swirling over our heads. I saw his eyes open and fix on mine.

The world pitched as Sporus threw me off like a wrestler, spinning with me as I went and landing on top. His forearm was against my throat, pressing down like a vice. The world was so thick with vibration and the smell of dead men, the universe permeated with concussion and noise and heat and that iron bar clad in flesh pressing down on my windpipe, choking me bit by bit. The animal in me fought, a thing of reflex struggling to save itself but the man behind was defeated.

I'd stopped nothing; a child would die here.

The man I loved was mad.

Nothing was left.

The darkness at the edge of my vision closed in, a swarm of flies obscuring the light. I looked him in the eyes as he killed me, trying with my last thought to remember him as he'd been on those soft nights so long ago. I saw tears, a little doubt even, but the arm remained.

The smell of damp earth rose like a cloud. For some reason, I thought of Britain, Oxford, our old school, playing fields that swept down to the canal. I could smell the dew and the grass and the towpath mud.

Everything pitched on its axis and I was falling, the ground opening up beneath us.

This is oblivion, I thought.

The last thing I heard was Sporus howling.

* * *

After that, it's a little hazy. I found myself back in Rome, but it wasn't my Rome. Lights – real, electric lights, a half-remembered thing. Gods, the sheer *blaze* of the place. Little things flying around, rolling, crawling – drones like an infestation. People speaking Latin that sounded clipped and wrong, but still Latin. I wandered about; I couldn't find my bearings. I was frightened, Banks, terrified.

I found the bridge with the angels that leads to the *Castel Sant'Angelo*. I just stood there for a while and marvelled at the stones that were, by any measure, ancient – and yet I'd been here before the grandfathers of grandfathers of grandfathers of the stonemasons who'd built it were born. The gulf of time was vertiginous.

I must have been a little dizzy from it. I wasn't paying attention. And then some oik with a girl on his arm, half-pissed and making eyes at her, wandered out of a restaurant and knocked me on my arse.

You know the rest.

11

We go for ice cream, of all things.

'None of this back in the day,' Monk says, surveying the *gelateria*. 'They had iced fruits, a little like sorbet, and for some ghastly reason iced eels, but this, none of it.'

The rows of hump-backed tubs stretch all around the semi-circular counter in three banks; to reach the furthest, the seller activates a mechanical arm from the ceiling that hisses and whines in a decidedly ancient way as it scoops the soft ice cream into smaller tubs, from which the seller crafts edifices on soft wafer cones. Every colour I could imagine, and some I couldn't, and the air is a riot of sugar. I'll have to bring Sara here before she's too old to allow it.

'Try the *zabaione*,' Monk says. 'It's made with egg and probably booze.'

'I'm not sure that appeals.'

'It will, trust me. I'm working my way around. Next up is the peppermint and banana.'

'That sounds awful.'

'I won't know until I've tried it.'

Before long we're out in the sunlight of the Pantheon square, loomed over by the old temple. I've opted for a tub piled high with a mound of creamy beige, while green and yellow rivulets run down Monk's wafer cone onto his hand, which he tries to lick off, spilling some more on the floor in the process. He laughs to himself, a little private sound, and I realise he's having quite the day. 'I suppose we won't know now, given all that's happened.'

'How do you mean?'

'About who tried to bump me off. Not much we can glean, given the...' He mimes an explosion.

'No, I don't suppose we will.' The mystery assailants and their total disappearance still niggles at me but I don't have the time to indulge it – the loss of most of our staff, all of the seniors and the Minister himself is more pressing. Towards the end I'd found it harder to keep my anger at Easter from showing as I became surer of his involvement. That anger has blown away like so much dust now, replaced by something even worse. Who did this to us? Both of us agreed caution should be maintained, though – Monk remains where he is and I'm vague about him to Jarvis, which is not hard, given all that's going on. I've not heard anything else about his family back in Britain – I suppose that will have to wait.

'How's the back? You feeling better?' he asks.

'Much better, thank you. I have to take care how I move but it's a marvel I'm up and about.' Yes, at home I'd be a cripple or dead. Dead like the bald man from Trade whose name I never learned. Like those men Easter was talking to as I left, the new arrivals with wary eyes and tense shoulders. Fragments, still fragments, and indeterminate unease.

'They added the letters after my time, you know,' Monk says, flicking his head in the direction of the pediment where Agrippa's name is writ large. 'It was bare, but there were more figures set around the temple – high relief stuff. Good marble – too good for pagans, no doubt. I'm sure some cardinal put them to good use in his villa.'

'Your time.' Half of me says he's not ready for the confrontation, but it's not the louder half. I'm afraid that humouring will only deepen the delusion. If he's ever to return and make a life for himself he needs to face up to the bad things that have happened to him or he won't heal. I can feel my tablet in my pocket and the file I've preloaded, the full report from the homeless refuge, the one that will make me argue with my friend. I almost reach for it, but I balk at the last instant. 'It's lost none of its beauty,' I say instead. 'Just think of the centuries it's stood.'

'You alright, Banks? Your voice sounds funny.'

'Just tired.'

He looks back at the Pantheon. 'In truth, it makes me dizzy just sitting here, thinking about this spot. There was a road running through here and houses right up to the steps of the temple, almost. And the beauty was hidden pretty well under all the mud and shit.' He raises an eyebrow at me and eats more ice cream. 'Oxen, you see. Big bastards move slow and crap mountains. No wonder the rich shut themselves away behind their walls.'

I make a non-committal sound.

At the other side of the square, a pair of men emerge from a little side street. Their clothes are shabby and their faces dark with dirt, pinched with the look of desperation I'm more used to seeing on the streets of London than this metropolis of the future. Even when poverty is mitigated by state support for everything from housing to food to education, there are always some who slip through the cracks; beggars are few and far between, but they exist. It reminds me of my first meeting with Monk on the darkened side street, when I took him for just such a man. The desperate youth in Carcassonne. The Confederacy is no sterile homogeny of plenty – for all its grandeur, it has the manifold problems of any nation.

The men come closer and their voices are razor-grating, a slur of local Italian. I catch a whiff of them as the wind gusts. One of them, the smaller one in a shirt that might have been yellow once upon a time, burps.

Monk takes my arm. I didn't even hear him stand up. 'Come on,' he says. 'Let's go back to the apartment.'

He looks skittish, so I finish what's on my wooden spoon and drop it and the tub in a waste bin. The vagrants cough a chorus of laughter that has the wind of vinegar about it. My earbud has a little trouble picking up their slurred Italian. As we walk away, one of them calls out something. Monk's pace quickens and I hurry to keep up. There's another peal of drunken laughter, and I realise they're following us down the street. Their voices echo from the walls. *Eh, Monko! Che fai, eh?*

Do these men know him? I have to do this. The refuge's words ring in my head.

Four weeks. Full dissociation. He's off medication, could be unpredictable.

Monk's head is down as he strides away.

We emerge onto another piazza, and then there's a pair of policemen sitting at an outside table, eating. They clock the pair following us and are moving to intercept before either of us can say anything. The vagrants are moved on with a little persuasion, though I find it hard to see what happens to them as Monk is marching away in the direction of the alley on the far side, past the steps of a museum.

I only manage to catch up when he is a few steps from the front door of the apartment block. He's regained some of his composure.

'Can't trust those ones, Banks. That sort littered the old world and nothing has changed in the new. Best to stay well clear.'

I need to do this now.

'I know about the halfway house, Winston.' Calling him by his first name like that feels alien, and it gets his attention. When he looks around, it's the first time since he came back that he looks rattled.

'What the hell are you talking about?'

'Look, I don't want you to be upset. I spoke to someone, a woman who runs a place for men just like those, who've fallen off the rails. She has records of you. She spoke to me about your treatm—'

Monk strides away into the building.

I follow him, struggling to keep up as he takes the stairs two at a time. 'Look, I'm sorry to come out with it like this but I'm worried about you. You've not been well.'

'You have no *fucking* idea!' He reaches the landing, fumbles for his passcard. I manage to catch up to him.

'Please, can we stop and talk about this? You've done nothing wrong, I just want to help.'

He spins with a speed that makes me flinch, but there's none of the violence I was expecting in his eyes. He just looks upset. 'You don't get it, Banks. I'm not lying to you. I've put it all there for you to read. You have to believe me.'

I spread my hands, helpless. 'How can you expect me to?'

The door opens at his touch and slams behind him with finality.

'It sounds like you really "buggered" that up,' says Mariko in English, her back to me as she chops a pepper in the kitchenette. I found her here when I came in from my disastrous attempt at an intervention – apparently living in the old city has made her want to experiment with other antiquated activities, like cooking a meal. As I told her what had happened a floor below, I could see the chaos she'd already wrought on the worktop with vegetable peel and blobs of dough crowding the parts that weren't taken up by a multitude of pans, implements and a cookbook large enough to bludgeon with. She is, apparently, also experimenting with baser vocabulary. 'You need to let him calm down. And be more sensitive, also.'

'What are you making?' I ask. I'm staying out of the way at the little round table. Something in the ungainly pile is starting to burn.

She's back to Latin. 'Ratatouille. It's an old vegetable stew.'

'I know it well. Makes good use of allotment produce.'

She's not heard me running over to whip the pan off the burner where smoke has started to bloom. The fire alarm sounds and she waves it silent. *'Bordel de merde,'* she says under her breath, *'c'est pas possible de vivre comme ça.'*

'Can I help? I could do with the distraction.'

'You think you can do better?' She's irritated, but I know it's with herself: the classic response of the high achiever faced with defeat.

'I've had some practice. I had to cook for myself and Sara when we were on our own.'

She looks a little ashamed at that. She pulls the apron over her head and throws it over the back of a chair, then flops down on the sofa. 'Alright. Do what you must.'

The first thing I do is clear the little worktop, piling the pans on the floor and out of the way. I can tell it's never used from how cluttered it is with archaic equipment – a microwave, a thing for spiralling vegetables, a coffee percolator, a pasta-maker. Even with a half-dozen pans on the floor, more hang on the wall rack beside the cooker hood. The electric burners look familiar enough, which in this city would make them ancient. In the pantry cupboard I find what I need – garlic, chili, olive oil. I have to take a moment to look over the rows of jars and tins – what I could have done with all of this back at home, where the only herbs were what we could grow in our greenhouses and spice was jealously hoarded. Anchovies, capers. Olives as black as sin. Armed with a heavy frying pan and a handful of deep red tomatoes, I cook.

Later, pasta piled high in our wide-brimmed bowls, we dig in. Mariko went from feigned indifference to interest as the smells of the pickled ingredients and garlic hit the hot oil of the pan. The tomatoes stewed down to a rich, deep sauce that stains the linguine red, the black olives peeking out like gems.

'This is really good,' she says, her mouth half-full. 'This is worthy of an Italian kitchen.'

'Thank you, but I can't accept that from a French person.'

She hits my arm. 'I'm serious. Where did you learn this?'

'An ancient cookbook of my mother's. Kept it hidden away. Even foreign grub was frowned upon, after a while. Wouldn't do to be called "decadent", even if it was only over a few tomatoes. I never did get to do it properly, though – couldn't get the olives.' I take a forkful. The salt of the anchovies and the capers is fierce, but then the tomato sweetness balances it and the iron-rich olives elevate it, garlic filling my nostrils. A little hint of heat from the chili. 'It was Sara's favourite. I'd make it for her birthday.'

She cups my elbow and leans over to give me a little peck. 'You miss her.'

'Of course.' I twirl myself another forkful. I spoke to June yesterday, Sara, too. They're alright and Sara sounds much brighter away from that school. They were worried about the bombing – it's been all over the news back there. I reassured them; I left out the worst of it.

'Well, she has good taste. I think that if Monk smells this, he might come and knock on the door.'

When the pasta's gone, there's a little red wine. I sip mine, mulling. 'What am I going to do about him?'

'You just need to talk, be his friend.'

'But what about his treatment? I didn't understand a lot of the jargon, but the refuge were pretty clear that he was delusional and nowhere near fit to be released. What if he hurts himself, or someone?'

'Hmm,' she says, pouring both of us some more wine. 'My father. He was so grateful of his adopted nation, after everything he went through in Japan, the voyage out. Most of the year, he was a dedicated Frenchman – my mother thought he overdid it, but she found it funny. There was one day a year, though, when he was not French.' She toys with the stem of her glass, her gaze fixed on the black ripples of her drink. 'Late March, when winter was really ending, when the trees started to wake up. We'd cook little biscuits in the oven – it drove my mother crazy, the mess we made.'

'I can see that very well,' I say, tilting my head at the catastrophe of the kitchen.

'Shut up, I'm telling you something very wise. We'd spend a week getting ready for this one day, me and my brothers, and the only way we knew it was time was when he'd say: "The air smells right." On the weekend we'd go to this park in the middle of the city with a hill in the middle of it. It was still a little cold for picnics, so you can imagine how people looked at us with our hamper and our chairs. We'd set up under some cherry trees, and they were full of blossom. My father would tell us all about how important the *sakura* was in his homeland – beauty that lasted only a little while before fading. I'm not sure we understood what he meant but we

265

enjoyed playing games in the grass and he and my mother sat in their chairs and drank beer. We'd go back every weekend until the blossoms fell.

'I found out, many years later, that there are no cherry trees in that park. The trees we played under are plum; their blossoms are similar but pink instead of white.'

'Do you think he knew?'

'Without a doubt. But the illusion, or the story he'd made for himself – the ritual around it – made him happy. Maybe Monk needs this fiction of his, at least for a while.' She rises, fetches an unopened bottle of red and hands it to me. 'I think you should go have a drink with your friend and talk about what he wants to. Don't force it.'

I take it. I kiss her. I leave, while I still can.

I find him looking over the river on a bridge not far from the Theatre of Marcellus. It looks mid-twentieth century if I'm any judge, just downstream of the Tiber Island which sits like a barge in a shallow weir. The thing that's holding his attention is another bridge that runs alongside this one – that's to do it justice: only a single, moss-encrusted span remains of this much older structure, ornate and narrow, spattered with generations of bird droppings. It sticks out of the river like a bad tooth and it's lit from below, the evening mist off the Tiber lending it an otherworldly quality.

He notices me and doesn't walk away, and I'm glad. I approach carefully, like he's a cat that might bolt; he keeps on looking at the broken bridge as I stand next to him, resting my palms on the cold concrete of the parapet.

'You found me.'

'Eventually.'

'You're a prick, Banks.'

'I'm sorry for ambushing you. I'm not much good at this.'

'Mm.'

We watch the crowds file over the humped bridges onto the Tiber Island. It's getting colder and I wish I'd brought a spare jacket for him, though being out in just a shirt doesn't seem to trouble him. Eventually, he speaks again.

'That's where we kissed, that night we went out drinking. Well, that's a bridge that replaced the bridge I knew. Even that's just a ruin now.' He looks at me over his shoulder. 'I don't suppose you've got to that part.'

'I have.'

'Finished it, have you?'

'Yes. It's... impressive.'

'I know how it sounds. Like I've lost my fucking mind.'

I choose a little honesty. 'I suppose it does.'

'I think I did. Truthfully, I lost my marbles for a little while. After that... whatever that was he was doing under the Colosseum... and coming back here, to this *now*. I have to confess something to you, Banks. I wasn't entirely honest with you in my story.'

'Oh?' Gentle. Allow him the space.

'I came to in Ostia. I was out in the open, under some cypress trees and I knew I was home from the sight of the old theatre down the hill from me. It wasn't right though, things were... out of place, like the theatre having no marble left on its seats. The walls were pockmarked ruins. I wondered if there'd been a riot or something, then I noticed how damn *old* the trees around me were. There hadn't been any in my day, not in this part of town at least, but these buggers were thick and gnarled with long years under the sun. I picked myself up. Even though it was the dead of night, the air glowed like it had when Rome burned. If that wasn't enough to set me off, the next thing surely did.

'A fucking *car horn.*

'After a lifetime of horses and oxen, here was the unmistakeable hoot of motorised transport and it might as well have been the roaring of a dragon. I stumbled some way through the trees; I saw lights, people. Cars without wheels. Glass tubes carrying trams.

'My legs gave out. I cried. This wasn't my time, nor the time I'd lived in, but it was a time I *could* have known. Ostia – my home and yet not my home, where whatever arcane power that had a grip of my fate had dropped me. Maybe it was just down to attachment, long years of habit and friendship that left a mark on me. It was changed, though, nothing left of what I knew save the ruins behind me, a whole existence eroded away to nothing. I sat there for a while, watching this future move, marvelling at the speed and noise and rhythm of it all.' He pauses, eyes downcast.

'What did you do next?'

'I had nothing but the filthy tunic I wore, streaked with blood and mud, straw clinging to it. My feet were covered in the filth of a different century. I wandered, ignoring the stares of passers-by, as I awoke the memories of televisions, power lines and tower blocks that had been laid to rest in the same bed as fantasy. It was the light – this century is so wasteful of it! Every window blazed with the light of a thousand candles with none of the cost in wax, oil, wicks, wood. It was an arrogance of plenty, and it frightened me. The Ostia I knew had been swallowed by this metropolis and I needed an anchor, something familiar; I reasoned that if anything familiar remained from the time I'd known, it would be in the Eternal City. I set out, following a four-lane highway encased in a tunnel of glass in the same direction the merchants had led their mule trains.

'I wondered if this was the last fever-gasp of a dying brain constructing a paper-thin facsimile of my old life. I must have started acting erratic, because people began to look. Some were good Samaritans and tried to talk to me, others were pissed up and found me hilarious. When I saw men with uniforms and what looked like clubs, I panicked. I know now that their police are trained to de-escalate, but I saw thugs coming to rob me, crack my skull. I ran.

'I cut over a skybridge, bumping into people. On the other side was a bazaar – for a split second I fancied I'd ended up in old Ostia after all, surrounded by the spices and perfumes of a dozen nations. I lost my footing and stumbled into a stall, knocking a rack of jars over. They shattered. I remember the smell of vinegar and a child hiding behind his father's legs. There was a hand on my shoulder and I tried to fight them off; while one of them kept me busy the other slipped behind me and shot me with a dart, something strong that had me hitting the deck in moments.

'It's very fractured after that. They took me to the station, I think, but it was a while before I could answer questions. Later, I found out that I trashed an interview room. I don't remember it, Banks. I don't remember things for a long time; something had tripped in my head.

'How I got to the refuge, I don't know. I was in a fugue state by this point, having to be fed and cleaned. I was aware of the passage of time but like everything was happening in another room of a large house, everything muted. About a month, I've worked out, I was just a walking corpse. Gradually, with peace and quiet and meds I was able to piece myself back together again. Remember those two reprobates from earlier?

Those were my friends, or at least the people I shared a table with at dinner.

'What snapped me out of it was when the doctor told me I was being moved to a psychiatric unit – this place wasn't set up for long-term care of the mentally ill, after all. I wasn't having that, and it was like having a purpose pulled me back together. Over a few days I ditched the pills they were giving me and my sharpness returned. Then I escaped.'

'Just like that? How did you manage it?'

'Have you been there?'

'No,' I admit. 'I just spoke to them.'

'Well, it's hardly a prison. Just a fence surrounding it. It was a place for vagabonds and drunks, the few that still fall through the net. Once I found shoes and some old clothes I was over it and gone before you could say bollocks.

'I snagged my trousers, but I made it. I legged it into the streets. Eventually, I found my way to the river.' He gestures at the water churning around the pillars. 'North of here. The bit about the *Castel Sant'Angelo* was true, as was bumping into your sorry arse. That's where it ends.'

'Thank you for telling me that.'

'Oh, don't get all mushy, Banks. Save it for Mariko.'

'All the same. Quite the tale.'

He looks at me, but there's no anger to it. He looks resolved, more than anything. 'Here,' he says, and he pulls the neck of his shirt down, stretching it over his shoulder. In the glow from the streetlamps, I see the dark shape of an old mark on his skin. It's in the shape of the Roman eagle – the Aquila. 'Scars, Banks. Some of them you can see, some you can't. But it happened, all of it.'

'Will you come back to the apartment?'

'Yes, I think so. Bit cold now. Hang on.' He looks down at

the bag at my feet. 'Did you come all the way out here with a bottle of wine?'

'Mariko said… she gave it to me and thought…' I feel a little foolish.

'She's a fine woman. You should listen to her. Now let's stop fucking about and get some glasses. I'm tired of talking about myself. How about it's your turn now?'

He leads the way, heading back into the city. I walk alongside him. I hope the admission tonight is the start of something, a gradual re-coupling with reality. It'll take time, but I'll see it through.

12

Jarvis has informed me that my services will not be required to greet the Prince on his arrival, so I sit in Monk's apartment and watch it on the television. An armoured train – brought through the newly unbricked tunnel under the Channel, no less – pulls up at the station like a battleship on rails, all gun turrets and sharp edges. The word on the lines was that HRH is taking no chances with security, not after the bombing. Jarvis's conspiracy theory about the Euros trying to off us has either trickled down from above, or – quite possibly – filtered up in his rather verbose reports. You'd think they had us in internment camps from the way he writes, instead of palaces of steel and glass.

Mariko's not here, busy as she is with the Japanese mission. She won't tell me the details of it but she can't stop her face from lighting up. I'm jealous for the entire ten seconds before I call myself to task: what's the point of competing with a country? It's not like she's abandoned me – quite the contrary; we've not spent a night apart (though we keep our distance during the day) – but I'm so giddy from it all that anything is liable to make me pine like a schoolboy in his first flush. I wear the suits she bought me and I've even begun checking how I look before I walk out of the door. That's where, some days, the trouble begins.

I'll see this middle-aged man, hair growing back, straightened out by a good jacket and the confidence of fine leather shoes, face clean-shaven, little bags under the eyes from some late nights, and I catch his eye like a stranger through a window. He's free, devoid of care, but I still feel the nub of what I was inside my chest and I cannot reconcile it with what I see staring back at me. Sara's father; Elanor's husband, these pillars of my being don't belong to him, this man caught in the heady days of a new love affair.

By what right, does he look that way?

What right do I have, to feel this way?

Mariko is a drug that clouds every one of my senses when we're together, but in the darkness of my room back in the tower, alone, the black creepers seek me out. I see Elanor with her hair down and her eyes wet with laughter, clad in white; hear the terrible silences after we argued; feel the white panic of the impotent witness as she suffered, hour after hour in animal torment – that elation of seeing her bloodied, exhausted and triumphant beyond my comprehension holding our baby girl to her. Later, fingers wasted to sticks but still warm on my arm in that threadbare hospital chair, telling me not to worry, reassuring me we'd be alright even as her eyes pleaded with me, the doctors, God.

For every zenith of the present, the past offers a nadir. It claws at my chest. I can't breathe. I've abandoned my Elanor to be a picture in photographs and my fading memories. What damned right do I have to start again without her? The wrecked carcass of a side table that offended no one is a testament to these kinds of moods.

Because of this I've done my best to avoid my own company, choosing a frail thread of hope that perhaps time will pave over the torment. That's why, with Mariko away for the night,

I sleep on Monk's couch. We've switched places, him the host while I'm the vagabond. I've listened to his stories, sometimes till the early hours. What else have I had to do, with the negotiations at a standstill and the arrival of our mercurial, confounding Prince imminent?

He is as intent when he speaks, a Scheherazade at work, though some of it he's set down on paper, refusing the offer of tablets or older keyboards in favour of pen and ink (which were harder to find but not impossible, because this is Rome where all antiques have their rightful place). When he wants to be silent, or is too tired, I read what he's set down in his neat script, all of it in English. The narrative winds through a mad year of four emperors and beyond, weaving a sumptuous web of a life. Only at the end, when he talks of his 'return', does the romance of it turn jagged. I think that underneath this careful fiction he has constructed reality is knocking, a water drip on iron that will, given time, corrode through. He feels it, is irritated by it, but ultimately will need to confront it and I will do my best to cushion the fall. Worrying about him stops me from worrying about myself.

Monk returns from the galley kitchen with a pot of tea and two cups as, on the viewscreen embedded in the large mirror over the mantle, the main doors of the Prince of Wales's citadel-train yawn open. That much plate steel takes a while to move, so Monk fixes the drinks and pulls up a wooden chair, leaving the whole couch to me. The welcoming committee is a trio of grey-suited Confederacy diplomats flanked by a dozen armed guards. The significance of these black-clad, visored men and women is not lost on me – after the bombing our fledgling relations have taken on an altogether more cautious tone on both sides; I don't think I saw a single soldier until I arrived in Rome itself, and yet here they are, watching the iron monstrosity extend its ramp to the empty parade square beside it, weapons held in ceremonial salute and, doubtless, loaded with live rounds.

Monk coughs a little of his coffee up as we watch a troupe of ten horses bearing cuirassed members of the Household Cavalry descend the ramp. Their conical helmets are plumed and their eyes are hidden, one gloved hand on the reins while the other holds a sabre up in salute. The horses stamp and toss their heads but have been bred into discipline, not one of them breaking rank even amid what for them must be a new universe of smells and sounds. They reach the flat expanse of the square and advance on the delegation, forming up around halfway across in a rank with a gap in the middle; against Rome's glass and steel modernity, with the great towers filling the skyline, they seem a tiny, archaic aberration.

'What're we trying to say, eh?' says Monk, shaking his head. 'That we'll trample them under our mighty British hooves? Embarrassing.'

I can't disagree.

'God, I hope they don't bring out the bearskins,' he continues.

As if on cue, files and files of red-jacketed guardsmen come tramping out of the train and take up position in front of the horses, each leg and arm moving in perfect synchrony. Sloped rifles with fixed bayonets on every shoulder and every head crowned with a towering black pile of fur. The file-out takes some time as formations break off into counter-marches and sideways shuffles, managing to re-join the main group without a step missed. When the last man comes to a stop and the last bellow of the last sergeant fades away, the scene that lingers is a diorama, a child's play scene of toy regiments ready for battle in another century when drill and formation and blind obedience ruled the day.

The Euro diplomats do their best to look impressed but I know the little tics, the small downturns of lip and upturns of eyebrow that show bemusement bordering on amusement. It's a confusing, bombastic and forlorn display, a small child shaking a wooden sword at a tank and demanding to be taken seriously.

I've spent enough years in the Civil Service – and have sat through enough of these ornate rituals of heraldry – to know this is just the start of a series of drills that will go on for some time. Even as I raise my cup to my lips the cavalry does a kind of rearward shuffle, making a quarter turn in a herringbone pattern and then separating, each horse filing between the ranks of the infantry. They troop past the Euro delegation and follow the sides of the parade square while the infantry start doing something that involves shouting and stamping and moving their rifles from one shoulder to another in as many moves as possible. Soon, I know, someone will take a long time to hand a large flag to someone else.

My tea is milky and hot and sweet, how I've always liked it. I'd almost forgotten the comfort of it. Mariko is, I think, bemused by what must seem like an anaemic substitute for strong Italian coffee, but for all that I've changed in the last weeks some things are bred deep. I wonder what she's doing now – certainly nothing to do with this display. As the heat descends from my mouth towards my chest I think back to the last dismal afternoon I had to spend watching this kind of display, high up in the unimportant part of the bleachers on Horse Guards Parade. The wind had been cutting, the kind of cold that takes days to shake. A colleague of mine, a man well into his sixties but looking older, sat beside me shaking, his fingers turning blue as they clasped and unclasped on his lap as if trying to claw warmth. I remember him turning and offering me what was meant as a smile but came off as a grimace. Cold days.

Monk is paying no attention to the screen and is reading one of Mariko's *National Geographics*. The cover shows a picture of Yellowstone before the eruption and though the paper has taken on that insect-wing texture from age the corners are still sharp. Mariko is fastidious about this sort of thing. I – though I've yet to reveal this shameful, dark secret – am something of a page corner folder. I've not had the heart to admit it and the sex is too good to ruin.

There it is, that little jab of shame at my flippancy, right above the heart. Once it would have been a little raised eyebrow from Orkney, but he's gone now. Nothing so genteel, this shade that sneaks up on me. Monk saves me from a black turn of mood by responding from behind his magazine.

'Can't believe America just went up like that. Poof, gone.'

'It took a little longer than that,' I say. 'But they lost a lot in a short space of time. People in the north and south fared better.' Thanks to the countries that bordered them, I don't add, in a commendable display of letting past antipathies fall away. Caravans of destitute people winding through the arroyos, breaking through the very border walls many of them had called for with so much enthusiasm. I remember those images, and I remember those three terrifying months of black skies.

'Have you given any more thought to what we talked about?' I ask him.

'Ah, yes. The prodigal return and all that. I have given it a ponder.'

'Good, I'm pleased. Again, I'm so sorry about your father passing without you… well, you know.'

'Thank you.'

'But there is a little money left in trust from his will. The pro forma and process around bringing someone back to life is a little inflexible and archaic, but things can be done, ears tweaked.'

'As much as I'd enjoy seeing you tweaking ears, Banks, that won't be necessary.'

'I don't follow.'

'I've lived in this country, one way or another, my whole adult life. I'm not going back to some backward rock in the North Sea. No offence.'

'None taken, but are you sure? Britain is your home.'

Monk sits up and clasps his hands together. For a moment, there is a kind of mass to him that makes every object in the room bend towards him. 'Lindon,' he says, using my forename for the first time I can remember. 'Any other functionary – the standard Ministry stuffed shirt – I'd press home with the story I've told you. But you knew me when I was a boy. We were good friends.'

'We still are, I hope.'

He sidesteps that. 'You were my only friend. And I think I was a little cruel to you. Loneliness and a little cleverness can do that.'

'Come off it, we were children.'

'We were turning into young men. And you knew me better than anyone. I got you to smoke once, remember?'

I do. I'd liked it.

'And we used to make up stories together,' he continues. 'Stories about what we'd do when we were older. You wanted to climb mountains.'

'I proposed to Elanor on Pen y Fan.' Searing sunbeams between wispy clouds.

'In all the hours we spent together at school, what did I talk about doing? Where did I want to end up?'

'You wanted to come to Europe, to live and study here. Look, I know you're worried about, well… you know… how you'll fit in back home. But in the right circles, if you're discreet, I've heard—'

'Leave out the fact that queers, anyone who's not Arthur and Martha, have to hide like they're a breed of pervert. That's just one part of it: a big part, but just one. I've no place there, Banks, can't you see? This isn't the Rome I recognise – no, don't make that face at me – but this is *my* city, my life. This is home.'

'It's most irregular,' I splutter, unable to argue the toss.

'Being dead is a bit like that.' He sips his coffee. 'You're not so different, you know. You've not put on a tie in a month. Face it, old boy, you're as stuck here as I am.'

I think about the cold streets of London, the stink of dung fires. I think of Sara wearing thick woollen tights under her tweed skirt that barely keeps the cold of the classroom out, driving her to distraction with its itchiness. I think about the way the land buckles around the Massif Central, a curvature of woodland and farmland under a warm sky, viewed from the wide window of a whispering train. All we'd have to leave behind is everything we've ever known.

'You think they'll let you see Mariko after you go back?'

Monk's words are iced water down my back.

After that, we sit silent for a while, the parade unfolding in front of us. There are only eight directions a marching man can go, but my word don't they manage to draw it out. Intersections. Formation splits. Right-angle bends. After a while I just see red blocks blurring in and out of each other and all I can think about is cherry blossoms. Mariko has been gentle with me, knowing how dogged ghosts can be. I should make her dinner again.

There's a blast of trumpets. The parade ground goes still. The diplomats shuffle and from within the train a group of men emerges, a dozen soldiers encircling a group of women and children, headed by a single figure in a black dress jacket cut diagonally with a blue sash. The soldiers are just as gaudy but their rifles are held with purpose and their eyes are watching the crowds. They press close to their charges as if reluctant to allow even the air of Rome to get too close to them. The Prince of Wales, by contrast, wears an easy smile.

He's a man in his early forties but good food and money has lent him the complexion of someone five years younger. He is straight-backed as he walks, an easy rolling gait that screams of unchallenged authority over everything he surveys. He stops and looks around at the crowds gathered on the periphery, then lifts his hand in a brief wave from the wrist.

Monk sucks in a sharp breath beside me. His face goes pale.

I've only been in the Royal Presence once before, some years ago at Easter's appointment to the rank of Minister. We lined up, waited our turn, each bowing when he stood before us. He seemed surly and drawn on that occasion and his bland attempts at conversation were muffled as if he couldn't be bothered to articulate the words. I nodded and said 'sir' at the right times and then he moved on to the next person. Though the uniform is the same, splashed with just as many stars and medals and ribbons, the face above it is healthy and open, at odds with the lowered tone of official dispatches in the last few days.

'It's him,' I hear Monk say.

'Yes, that's His Royal Highness, first in line. He looks well rested.'

'No, Banks, it's *him*.'

'I don't follow.'

Monk doesn't wait to explain, already pulling on his boots and reaching for his jacket. 'I have to go to him, have to… you can help me.'

'Even if security wasn't ratcheted up to the highest possible right now, I'd have trouble getting an audience for myself, let alone one for you. Come on, sit down. You look like you've seen a ghost.'

He stops, and the look on his face hits me like a hammer. 'It's him. Sporus. He's back.'

He's snapped. And just when I thought he was getting better – I'd hoped the completion of his story would somehow soothe him and allow him to wander back to reality but instead he's gone off the deep end.

'Monk,' I say, 'that's His Royal Highness Leopold, Prince of Wales and heir to the throne. He's our *de facto* head of state, not…'

'I haven't got time to debate with you or explain it to you, Banks. He might be wearing another identity, but I know him. That's the man I fell in love with and then tried to kill me under the Colosseum two thousand years ago.'

'You have to stop this. These stories aren't helping you. I'm sorry to have to say it but you're hurting yourself.'

'I'll get to him myself, if you won't help me.' He's already moving towards the door, every motion full of purpose. I know I have to stop him before he does something stupid. The Prince's bodyguard won't ask questions before shooting. Though I don't know how I'll do it, knowing how he can move in moments of violence, remembering the night with the assassins. I get to my feet. One last glance at the television.

Sara.

I'm frozen to the spot.

Sara is there, walking behind the Prince, one of a dozen civilians. They're waving to the crowds and she has a garland of wildflowers in her hair. She's not smiling and my gut gives a lurch of panic.

The door slams behind Monk as he goes but I can't move, fixed to the screen where my daughter, who's meant to be in rural Cornwall with my sister, descends the ramp to the parade ground where an executive limousine is waiting for the Prince, a small minibus tailing it.

My communicator rings. I don't look as I answer – only one person ever calls me on it. 'What is it, Jarvis?'

There's a pause at the other end, then a faint clearing of a throat. The voice that replies is dusty and thin. 'Mr Banks?'

'This is he.'

'You are called to wait upon His Royal Highness this afternoon for a general debriefing. A car will be sent for you. Be prompt, there's a good chap.' The line goes dead. My hands feel bloodless.

13

The citadel-train sits on the wide apron of concrete that encircles the EuroPar. They arranged for heavy lifter-drones – a dozen of them, the size of helicopters – to lift the entire hulking mass from its rails and transport it the two kilometres from the train station into the very heart of Rome. The Prince insisted, and still stung from the bombing that took place under their noses and keen to maintain relations, the Confederacy acceded to this seemingly ridiculous demand. Now the headquarters squats like an angry toad a stone's throw from the arena-turned-parliament encircled by sandbags, guard posts and fences, all of it set up by us. Offers of their security have been quietly rebuffed, the message being: *we only trust ourselves to protect ourselves.*

I can just see Monk, in the state he was in, trying to scale the fence from how he was when he ran away, but so far there's been no sign of him. I imagine that will be part of the conversation I've been summoned here to have – there was a weight of authority behind the dry voice on the telephone that left me in no doubt about the optionality of my response. The razor wire glints in the sun, so at odds with the curves of everything else around here, a patch of brambles in a flowerbed. Would they have tried to capture him, I wonder, or would they just have shot him?

The guard checks my identification with deliberate slowness, holding the papers up so my face is alongside my photograph. I know it's a test, meant to unnerve me, so I fight down the rising panic and the desire to rush inside and find Sara, and stare at the clouds flitting through the sky instead. After what feels like a cycle of the universe he hands me back my papers and waves me inside the compound.

Up close the train is even more imposing. It's painted red, which makes it look like a solid lump of rust. Two carriages, each fifty metres long, festooned with heavy guns, and every window is an armoured slit. The thing is three boxy, armour-plated, jagged-sided levels tall and topped with a forest of radio masts. The Euros insisted the guns be unloaded and the ammunition locked away, but the battalion of soldiers who passed out earlier today have doubtless packed away their finery and are inside in more practical gear, armed for action. The piazza is cracking a little under the weight of the huge wheels and I watch teams of Euro engineers working to reinforce it as I wait at the bottom of the ramp for my papers to be checked a second time.

Jarvis is there, his face missing its usual smugness. Another man flanks him, tall and sporting an iron-grey moustache and the kind of stiff-backed posture that speaks of a lifetime of military service.

'Ah, Mr Banks,' he says, cutting Jarvis off. 'Thank you for being so prompt. Smith is my name. If you'll follow me please.' He turns on his heel and marches off down the corridor. Jarvis gives me a look that hovers somewhere between satisfaction and guilt before I follow. The elder man holds a door open for me and we enter an interrogation room.

No other word for it – two chairs, a table, stark lights and a heavy door. It smells of disinfectant and I wonder for a moment if this might be the last room I ever see. Smith takes one of the chairs and invites me to sit across from him with an outstretched palm. As I sit, he says: 'There's no need to look so alarmed, Mr Banks. Unless you've reason to be, of course.' He doesn't smile as he says this.

'I've recently learned that my daughter is here in Rome. I'm anxious to check on her.'

'Yes, young… Sara, is it? Without the h? She's a guest of His Royal Highness and being treated very well.'

'Why is she here?' He's turning on the pressure gradually, but I'm tired of games. 'I want to see my daughter, please.'

'All in good time, my man.'

'What is your position here, Mr Smith?'

He pauses, running his lower lip along the bottom of his bristly moustache. He doesn't blink. 'So we cut to the quick of it, do we Mr Banks? Alright, no pleasantries then. You are under suspicion of collaboration, either indirect or direct, against His Majesty's trade mission.'

'How—'

'You appear to have an… arrangement with a European functionary that contravenes best practice.'

'That's a personal matter.'

'So you confirm you are having relations with a member of a foreign power?'

'I do.'

He pulls a notepad from his jacket pocket and lays it carefully on the desk in front of him before opening it and writing something down in indecipherable handwriting.

'Your honesty is appreciated, Mr Banks, though it does you little credit.'

'What are the grounds for this suspicion? I'll remind you I barely escaped a bombing in His Majesty's service. I almost died.'

'But you didn't.' A slow blink. 'It's at that event that I'd like to start, if that's alright with you?'

'What has Jarvis been saying to you? Has he been through this rigmarole as well?'

The smile is cold. 'Mr Jarvis is not the subject of this conversation. You are.' He taps twice on the table and the door behind me opens. Two soldiers walk in and take up positions either side of the door. They're not bearing guns but the batons they carry look solid.

'Just to avoid any unpleasantries, Mr Banks. Now, let's go over the sequence of events...'

It's getting on for evening when I emerge from the interrogation room. My eyes feel like they've been dragged through the sand. Smith made me repeat what happened, over and over. He asked me about Mariko. He asked me about Monk. But then, warmed up, he moved on to the real meat of the interview, namely every step I took during the night of the bombing. I told him everything because, for all my built-in guilt, in this I know I've nothing to hide.

Well, that's not entirely true. His questions kept returning to who I'd seen there in the foyer that night and for some reason, that gave me pause. The only ones I'd noticed as out of place were those strange, nervous men talking to Easter. Call it instinct, or perhaps paranoia (I had almost been murdered in my own apartment, after all) but admitting to seeing those new arrivals from back home (soldiers, Charteris had said) seemed like a way to get myself into deeper trouble.

He fixated on tiny, unimportant details like what people were wearing. My mouth grew dry and my back ached from the hard chair, but I knew my only chance of getting out of there without the apes behind me getting involved was to be calm and candid. It seems to have worked – after several hours Smith puts away his notebook and dismisses me.

One of the soldiers follows me out and waves at me to come with him. We walk the length of the carriage then through the heavy iron door that leads to the other. Just inside the door, in a little waiting area scattered with the same basic wooden chairs I'd spent the best part of a day in, is Sara. When she sees me she flies at me, grabbing my neck in a hug so strong that it belies her slight arms.

'Dad, you're alright. I didn't know if they'd let me see you.' She sounds close to tears.

'Don't worry, Mouse, I'm alright. I'm here now. How are you doing?'

'They came to Auntie June's in the middle of the night. They had guns. I had to go with them. Oh God, Dad, they shot one of her dogs just to get her to stop fighting them.'

'I'm so sorry you had to see that. I'm sorry you've been dragged into this.'

'Are you sure you're OK? You got blown up.' She prods my shoulders as if to test they're real.

'I'm fine, all better now. They have good hospitals here.'

'I missed you.'

'You too.' Her hair smells like it did when she was a baby. I can't remember the last time she hugged me like this.

Mariko has brought dinner to my room. From the window I can see the EuroPar in the distance, blazing the darkness away; next to it is the armoured train and Sara with it. They wouldn't let her come with me, and when I tried to stay they put their hands on their sidearms and led me out the door. Damn them.

'Come and have something to eat,' she says. 'You look ready to fall over.'

It's skewers of pork in a peanut sauce and bowls of noodles. She admitted defeat on her cooking, but she saw how I reacted to the kinds of fresh ingredients the city has to offer, so she went one further. Two days ago, she ordered Thai food, which arrived by ground drone; my stunted British palate butted up against a quiet onslaught of ginger and sesame. It was sensational, chili creeping around the back like an assassin. She told me I'd get used to the heat, laughing as I cuffed the tears and the sweat away. I told her I didn't want to get used to it, that I never wanted to find food this good commonplace.

This evening I have a knot in my stomach and can barely eat a morsel, though I know my body is crying out for sustenance. I manage a couple of skewers but there's no joy in it.

'Why does she have to stay on the train?' Mariko asks. Perhaps out of sympathy, she's also barely touched her food.

'I was told that she is there at the Prince's pleasure. There were guards and they had guns.'

'Is she being treated well?'

'Yes, I think so, as far as can be managed on an overgrown train. But she's scared. They came to my sister's place in the night and just took her away. She didn't know where she was going, and she's seen people being taken away before and not come back. God, she must have been terrified.' In an instant, it's just too much anger to deal with and I stand up, pacing around the living area. I don't know what to do with my hands. I want to shatter something, smash something.

How *dare* they do this.

'She'll be alright. You have to stay calm for her.'

'This is my fault. They're using her as a damned hostage because they think I... we...'

'You have nothing to hide. You have done nothing wrong. What was the word they used?'

'Best practice.'

'You've broken no laws. We've stretched the rules, but we've been discreet. If it comes to it, I will give full disclosure. I've already informed my office.'

'Are you in trouble?'

'A little. Nothing too bad. Same as you.'

I try and fail to get the faces of those strange men at the Residence out of my head. Everything around that time is blurred, as if the explosion shook the memories around in my head and I've no way of reassembling the whole jigsaw, but that instant when I made eye contact has become clearer with every day. Straight-backed men wearing practical, unobtrusive suits. The one who looked at me wore a serious expression and the skin around his eyes was taut, as if keeping in some inner strain by pure force of will. As Easter's private secretary, I had access to his diary and was on top of his engagements, but these visitors were unknown to me. They stood out in that sea of frivolity like jagged rocks.

I wish I could take one giant step and be there by Sara's side. I wish I had a tank. Or an army. 'Something feels off.'

'I know, I know.'

'No, I mean besides Sara being held hostage like this. You and me, what we have, that's what they're saying is the reason for it all – that's how they opened the examination. Collaboration with a foreign power, or some such. But when he got going all he wanted to know about was the night of the bombing; he made me go over it again and again and again and he wanted to know everything from what I was drinking to who I spoke with.'

Mariko sat back down and took a drink of water. After a moment, she said, 'It sounds like they're not really worried about the Confederacy gaining information from you. They're more worried that you saw something you were not meant to.'

A voice I recognise as belonging to Charteris floats out of a dark corner of my memory.

Look like soldiers to me, but ours is not to question why.

Sweat, I remember, on their foreheads, even though the evening had been cool enough for a scarf. Something tells me that, had I mentioned those men to Smith this afternoon, I wouldn't be sitting in my room in a tower block, failing to eat perfectly good noodles with Mariko.

'Any sign of your friend Monk?'

'Not since he ran off.'

'I'm sorry, you have enough to worry about.'

'No, it's fine, it's a distraction. He knows his way around, probably went to find a bar or something.' As I say it, I imagine him climbing a fence and being picked out by searchlights. 'You've read his story?'

'What he wrote down, yes.'

'He's convinced his fictional lover is the Prince of Wales. I don't know if it's because he finished the story and now reality is a little too much to bear.'

'You did say that the Prince was different, no?'

I give her a long look, wondering if she's teasing me. I hope not: I'm not in the mood for it, but there's no impish gleam in her eyes.

'You can't be serious.'

'You said so yourself. Unprecedented change of foreign policy. And didn't you say the Prince had, before two years ago, stayed in his palaces and left the running of the state to the government?'

'I did. But that doesn't...'

She holds up a hand. 'I know. But sometimes you can't just

ignore the improbable.' She shrugs, making the light dance on the silk of her shirt. 'Perhaps he heard you mention the shift and built it into his fantasy. Maybe not. Strange things happen sometimes.'

'Not like this.'

She takes another sip of water and I see the rings around her eyes. 'I'm sorry,' I tell her. 'You must be exhausted.'

'They are keeping me busy on the other delegation. There's a lot of ritual to it, a lot of mistrust to cut through. The wars hit them very hard and Japan always had a good instinct for self-preservation. They retreated into their islands and now we have to coax them out.' She rubs her eyes. 'And there are so few of us on the other side to do the work.'

She's become something of an expert in the field of coaxing reluctant island nations out of their shells. It must be draining, for all that she can't stay away from it.

'Enough of my problems, then,' I say.

'I've already said more than I should.'

So we go to bed. We're naked but we just hold onto each other for comfort until sleep comes.

I slept like the dead for around four hours but now I'm up; it's one of those awakenings where you know there's no going back. I could read, perhaps? I don't want to wake Mariko, who needs her rest.

I'm thinking about Sara, and the more I do the further a return to sleep gets. What kind of accommodation can they offer her on that rolling fortress? Part of it is outfitted for the comfort of royalty, but does that comfort extend to His Royal Highness's guests? I hope she's not in some rotten army-grade dormitory; boarding school is bad enough. I hope she has her own room, or at least one with people her own age. Then I think: what if she's just been thrown in with the squaddies, having to lie there and listen to their coarse banter?

I get up. Tossing and turning like this is as bad as putting on the bedside light. In the lounge area I take a quick look out the window at the ever-lit EuroPar (a little part of me worries that if I don't check, it might not be there). My tablet's on the table – I'm so used to consulting it now that I've barely handled paper for weeks; my Latin reading is improving, but I still have to flick on the translation tool after a while, especially with the more esoteric news. I pull up my newsfeed; no mention of the contact with the Japanese, not yet anyway. The Prince's arrival is prominent on several news channels and a dozen gossip sites. The news doesn't tell me anything I want to know, so I scan the latter out of morbid curiosity.

DASHING PRINCE WOWS CROWDS
LIKE LOOKING INTO HISTORY: BRITAIN PUTS ON A SHOW
NICE UNIFORMS, SHAME ABOUT THE FAMINE

(That last one is a little surprising, but I suppose some things will always leak to the press in the end.)

HOW YOU COULD BAG YOURSELF A PRINCE CHARMING

One site picks apart the Prince's adornments one by one, spider lines pointing out the name of this or that commendation. There's a link to a site where, for a tidy sum, replica uniforms can be purchased. Another video article shows an interview with a group of youths from Spain, around seventeen, who've all adopted the Prince's rigid side-parting and hair grease. I can't tell if it's homage or (most likely, given the age of the boys featured) being done ironically. Still, His Royal Highness is the talking point of the Confederacy only hours after the display. Britain may be seen as a backward, crippled failure of a nation but the Prince apparently belies that with his elegant yet manly posture (in a very traditional sense, one of the articles is keen to point out). Some of the gaudier sites use words like *hot* and *gorgeous*.

Something has bothered me since that first moment he appeared on the screen but I've been too busy to give it much thought. I remember very little of him in the media at home as he stayed firmly entrenched in Windsor Castle, Kensington Palace or his estates in Cornwall, with only an occasional trip down the road to visit with his ailing father, who is *de jure* but in no way *de facto* our head of state. It's on these visits – where the due pomp is deployed, because to do otherwise would go against all monarchical tradition – that I spied him a couple of times as the convoy trundled down the Mall. Unlike his official portraits, he was heavy about the jowls and his eyes were ringed. He was a scowler and didn't bother with even the most minimalistic of royal waves, though the crowds that always turned out to these pageants (if you can call re-used bunting and some sad trumpeting such) waved back with fervour and shouted his name. In my younger years, I was one of them.

A far cry from the man that currently holds the tabloid media in the palm of his hand, it would seem. *This* Prince is what official portraits, our domesticated media, would have Britain see. Not the tired-looking, middle-aged man with a paunch straining at his military dress jacket that I saw once on a scaffolding cutting a ribbon to open a new wing of the Ministry of Justice. The fiction has, somehow, become a reality.

Monk must have really got to me: I'm seeing shadows where there are none. Who's to say a man can't go on a diet, go for runs, drink less? Everyone, from the bottom to the top, understands the value of putting your best foot forward and the Prince is doing that.

I close down the tablet and slip back into bed. Two years since whispers began to circulate through the halls of the Ministries that contact with the Confederacy was being considered at the highest level, one year since the rumours were substantiated and then just six months ago, the delegates were picked. Two years is an eyeblink in the heart of the bureaucracy, but more than enough time for a man to change his spots. Just look at me.

14

His Royal Highness has elected to give a speech before the EuroPar. His aides are all of a flutter because of it but the royal word is unequivocal and final. I'm caught as much off-guard by it as the rest of them – never a man of many words, public or private, and now the Prince of Wales wishes to stand up before the assembled dignitaries and officials of the world's remaining superpower and speak at length.

In Latin, no less.

Latin had been a dyed-in-the-wool part of public-school life for generations in Britain, but it was another casualty of our isolation – a dead language was fine, a revitalised, federalist tongue spoken from Berlin to Brasilia was anathema in the eyes of the authorities.

No child, least of all the Prince (who is a few years my junior and would have just missed it), would be exposed to it – no more *Quintus est filius* and *Caecilius est pater*. On top of this, it's easy to read between the official lines that His Royal Highness is not a man of deep academic ambition and it is for this reason that I'm taken aback – on top of his physical transformation there seems to have been an internal one. The Prince has, within the limited scope of a burst of rhetoric, applied himself to something bookish. Here we are, barely a week after the arrival of the suitably fortress-like train (which the Euro engineers have managed to shore up before it subsided through concrete never designed to bear anything of its mass), about to witness His Royal Highness take the rostrum and address the Confederacy in its common tongue. When I told Mariko, she raised an eyebrow at me and mouthed the word 'improbable'.

Whatever suspicion hung over me during my protracted conversation with Smith hasn't resulted in any further action; Sara is still a 'guest', so I know they still want to keep me on a leash. At times I wonder what is at play here, when I have chance to draw breath – was my survival so suspicious as to justify dragging my daughter here under implicit threat? What did they think I'd do, or could do? All of this has done nothing to endear me to a way of life I'd already begun to dread returning to, but there's Sara and her future, her wellbeing. When all of this is over she and I will likely have to return home and that's why I have to be seen to be fitting in, showing willing. I've resumed a measure of my old duties, helping to co-ordinate the Prince's movements. There's a lot to do, despite a coterie of Palace flunkies present, more interested at pecking at each other for territory.

Spending time at the train keeps me close to my Sara and at least feels like I'm watching over her, even though they won't let me stay overnight. At least she has her own room and eats with the other 'guests' in a private dining room. One of them, a Lady Margolis, has appointed herself guardian.

'My dear man, you simply must allow yourself to relax. Sara and I are getting along most famously, you know.'

'It's true, Dad. Viviane used to play hockey against my school.'

'An aeon ago, to be sure. Staying close to the youth can

be such a tonic, can't it?' Her smile is broad and open. She's taller than me and willowy, a creature of arches and spans; she seems kind and gentle and she looks after my daughter when I can't. She refuses any offers of assistance. Still, I count the hours until I can take Sara away from all of this, in whatever form that takes, but in the meantime I must play the game my masters have set me.

When the Prince enters the main auditorium – the grandest room in the building, where the old arena floor would have been and surrounded on all sides by armoured glass, banks of seats marching away from the central dais like ripples – the applause is rapturous and tinged with not a little relief. They were expecting rancour, distrust, blame, withdrawal. Instead they get him in all his finery, chest full of medals jangling as he strides down the aisle. He waves at no one in particular on his way to the rostrum carved from a single piece of obsidian and polished smooth. Two microphones embedded in its top have already been checked by our side for anything untoward or explosive, though I doubt any of our engineers really knew where to begin.

The Prince ascends the three small steps and stands in the beam of a hundred lights and before an audience of tens of millions, in the arena, outside on screens and broadcast across the Confederacy (and who knows, perhaps in the partner territories of India and Mercosur). He looks calm, poised, alert, everything you want in a public speaker on this grandest of stages. This is the closest I've been to him yet – with the support staff in a sort of semi-circular dugout behind the podium – and I have to conclude this is the man I've seen in the past. He's fitter, leaner, cleaner and more enthusiastic than at any other time, but it's him; the more time I spend close to the Royal Presence the quieter the odd little voice in my head gets and the more far-fetched Monk's outburst becomes.

I really should look for him, but I just don't have the time. I'm worried for my friend. He's a strong man but there's a deep wound he carries. This part of his road is hard and he doesn't deserve to walk it alone. When things have calmed, perhaps tomorrow, I'll bring him home.

The speakers come to life all around the room. Nothing so crass as a crackle – more of a gentle but weighty humming sensation. Hands either side of the dark stone, the Prince takes another look around the room as the audience takes its seats.

'*Salve*,' he begins. 'On behalf of his Britannic Majesty of the United Kingdom of Great Britain and Lord of the Commonwealth, my Father, King Edward, ninth of his name, I thank you for welcoming me here today.' His voice is sonorous and measured, the Latin coming more naturally than I would have believed even if it has a whiff of the schoolbook about it. He has trained for this, that much is clear. 'In the spirit of friendship, welcome.

'Ours is a great nation, a nation of the sea and the land. We are proud. We know who we are. But it wasn't always so. There was a time, many years ago – when I was just a boy – that Britain decided we'd lost something of ourselves by looking outwards. We needed the time and the space to commune with what is most precious to us, that is our values and our culture and our history.'

Never mind about food and warmth, comes the thought, slapped away before it can cause so much of a flicker on my face. I've become used to being away from my own kind.

'We have taken stock. We have re-invigorated that which makes us truly British. And now, I'm happy to say...' a little pause, a smile for the watching millions, 'that time of isolation is drawing to a close.'

More applause. The glassed-off viewing galleries that surround the chamber are packed to capacity. Somewhere up there, Sara and her new friend Lady Margolis are watching with the rest of the Prince's guests.

'I would like to take this chance to honour the victims of the senseless tragedy that took place in this city only a short while ago, when many prized staff of His Majesty's government lost their lives in the pursuit of their duties.'

The expressions on the nearest faces can't quite hide their discomfort. Where is this going next, they're wondering.

'And I thank the Confederacy for its swift actions in the aftermath. The perpetrators *will* be brought to justice!' A fist-tap on the rostrum for emphasis. The applause is measured.

'Those brave men and women were the vanguard of our nation. They laid the foundations for a new partnership, a partnership of equals, a prosperous meeting of the ways for the Confederacy and Britain that looks forwards, not towards the past. It is my honour,' a clasped fist pressed just above his heart, where the medal clusters are at their thickest, 'to continue where they left off.' This time, the applause comes more easily. He's letting them off the hook, at least for now.

The Prince gets going in earnest now, spelling out the roadmap for the next two years. Trade deals to be negotiated, lines of communication re-established (diplomatic at first but eventually spreading to the commercial and domestic). Travel restrictions will be relaxed gradually and fishing territories will be set out to mutual advantage. The tapestry of our self-imposed isolation is to be unpicked. Until this moment, hearing him say it, I wasn't always completely certain it was going to happen, but here it is, being announced by the man who gives Britain its orders. For a fleeting moment, I see a house in the French countryside we crossed so speedily on our first journey down, a little farmhouse with vines creeping over the eaves and an old millstone in the garden. A place like that would make a good home for a family.

The side doors to the auditorium slam open and the Prince's personal bodyguards stride in, six of them in an arrowhead formation. Without running, they somehow manage to cross the empty floor in a few heartbeats and then the Prince is off the dais and being led away, the khaki jackets cocooning him from all sides. The chamber is in uproar and I can barely hear Jarvis as he yells in my ear.

'What did you say?'

'In the foyer. They found a package during one of the sweeps. It's all over the radio, why haven't you got an earpiece in?'

'I do, I...'

'Not that bloody Euro crap, one of ours. We're at bikini black, Banks.'

'What on earth are you talking about, Jarvis?'

'Highest sodding alert, that's what. Speech is over. They're bundling him back to the train and we're going too.'

'Did you say a package?'

'A suspicious one. They've cordoned off the area.' As Jarvis says this a woman's calm and resonant voice comes on over the loudspeaker and directs everyone to clear the hall in an orderly manner and congregate at the safe zones outside the building. Staff in yellow jackets direct the flow. The delegates look a mixture of worried, annoyed and confused.

'Come on, Banks. Out the side door.' Jarvis indicates where the other members of the support staff have begun filing out.

'My daughter's up in the gallery.'

'They'll get her out with all the rest. And she's with the Prince's friend. They'll not let her come to any harm.'

Through the double doors and into the outer corridors, the sounds are muted by the thick carpets and padded walls. There's a low pulse sounding, an insistent alarm over the heads of people milling. This is a full evacuation. As we move into an atrium the air is a formless hubbub of a thousand confused conversations. Every glass door under every archway has been sprung open and, directed by the staff, people are disgorging in their hundreds.

'HRH'll be back on the train with a G&T in his hand by now, I should expect,' says Jarvis.

'What did you mean back there, about his friend?'

'Come again?'

We hit the evening air, which is cool and smells a little of bonfires.

'You said Sara was with the Prince's friend. What friend?'

'Lady Margolis, Banks. I was being euphemistically delicate. She spends a lot of time at Windsor. Oh, for God's sake, Banks, you really are a violet – she's been warming his bed for a couple of years now. Why do you think he looks so damn chipper?'

'She's not one of his "guests"?'

'She's in charge of them, but no, not one of them per se. Why do you ask?'

I don't answer. Something bothers me about this, though I'm not sure why. If anything, Lady Margolis will be in a better position to secure Sara's release if she's as close to the Prince as Jarvis is claiming.

'Right, well I suppose you'll be getting back to your castle in the clouds then?' Jarvis had bunked up in the train, never having trusted the apartment he was given in the *Portafoglio* tower.

'After I find Sara.'

'Suit yourself. Hang on—' He sticks a finger in one ear and cups the other over his earpiece. 'Oh, bloody hell!'

'What is it?'

'Wait a moment.' Jarvis listens, then his eyes flash up to meet mine. 'It's him, he's gone for them.'

The crowd around us is a distant swirl. Something feels very wrong.

'That fucking brute you found on the streets. They found him at the security cordon trying to gain access to the train. Probably him that laid the device in the first place, bloody diversion.'

'You're not making any sense. They found Monk?'

'No, he got away. Now a bus moving people from the gallery to safety has gone missing, some of ours, some of theirs. The Euro police think it's him taking hostages.'

'What are our people doing on a bus? The train's just over there?'

'God, I don't bloody know, Banks. In case you haven't noticed, there's a bit of confusion about.'

He's right. The Prince was the priority – now he's secured the rest of us have to look after ourselves and no one seems to be co-ordinating. Jarvis hears something else on the radio, then the look in his eyes makes my blood run cold.

'Oh Banks, I'm so sorry.'

'Don't say it.'

'One of the ones he took. It's your daughter.'

The train is in lockdown. I can't get in to speak to whoever is running the search. After two hours of being told nothing by the police and less by my own side, I seriously considered taking my chances with the guards at the ramp just so I could get inside and *do* something.

Mariko finds me. She's brought a car and convinces me to come back to the apartment with her, her place in the old city.

'I checked with some contacts on the way here. The police are sparing no resources – they're embarrassed and there's the matter of the Co-President's boy. They've lifted the embargo on flying drones in the old city – they'll be scanning every street in Rome until they find her.'

I just nod, not knowing what to say.

'He won't hurt her.' She looks at me, but doesn't go on, worried she'll set me off in some way. I feel numb, like I've had my insides scraped out. I try to reconcile the idea of the man I shared drink and conversation with over the last several weeks, who told me his story (even fought off attackers with me) on the run with my daughter as a hostage. I knew he was going to try and approach the Prince, but this? The facts don't match, and yet that's the story all over the newsfeeds.

The bus was pressed into service at short notice, one of many. A small vehicle for a few of the people watching from the upper floors. With no direction from our people, those of our people who were there got lumped in with the Euro VIPs. Sara was one of them, Lady Margolis also and – the real reason the Euro police is so riled up – the son of the current Co-President of the Confederacy herself. A boy around Sara's age, he'd been standing near them in the viewing gallery. It's the corpse of the boy's bodyguard, found in the middle of a busy road, that's escalated this to the level of sure-fire abduction.

Had they talked, I wonder, looking down at the room where their parents were working, or had they listened intently to the Prince's speech? Did Sara know enough Latin to understand what was being said? She probably had an earbud or a necklace to help her understand. These tiny details seem important to me, for some reason. They're the tightrope I'm walking over the yawning chasm of panic. I think I made a little noise, a groan or something, because Mariko takes my hand in the back of the driverless car that carries us through the backstreets of Rome and squeezes.

'They'll find her, Lindon. You have to trust. Trust they'll do their jobs.'

I nod again, a ventriloquist's dummy, unable or unwilling to make a sound because I think I might throw up if I so much as open my mouth. The car judders a little as the wheels take the cobbles of the streets and I see, out of the corner of my eye, a lit triumphal column resplendent with its frieze pass us in the night.

I'm in Mariko's apartment. I don't remember getting out of the car and climbing the two flights of stairs, though I suppose I must have. She guides me to the sofa and I let her. She hands me a glass of something strong and I take a careful sip. It's whisky and it's good and probably a heady bouquet of complex scents and flavours, but all I care about in this moment is the burn and the kick so I knock it back, feeling the roil of it going down my throat. I don't hear what she's saying to me, the bookcases are so full of carefully ordered volumes. I'll bring Sara here, show her these, when I, when we...

I'm in bed with my clothes on, under the blanket. Mariko holds me as if to stop me from drowning. I've nothing left, no anger (that went on the blameless police officers who had nothing to tell me but tried to keep me calm) and no tears. My little girl is out there somewhere with someone who may or may not be a friend who went mad. At some point, I fall into a fitful sleep where I'm re-living every minute since the end of the speech.

Later, eyes gritty from exhaustion, I get up for water, to piss. I look at Mariko there sleeping, curled around the indentation I made in her mattress. My legs are buzzing like I want to run a mile and the pressure in my chest hasn't abated.

Would he hurt Sara?

Maybe more of that whisky will help. Maybe I'll drink it until good old-fashioned biochemistry comes to my rescue and knocks me unconscious. I tiptoe down the stairs, running my fingers along the darkened walls for balance. In the shadowed kitchenette, I can't find fresh glasses; I think about using a dirty one, but the bottle is where we left it on the counter. What the hell, who cares? I pull the stopper and the razor's edge of peaty booze has only a moment to jump up my nose before I take a large swig. It burns my throat and I feel the flush on my face as I dissolve into a coughing mess.

'Never quite works like the movies, does it? Just necking it from the bottle.'

My whole body tenses. The voice came from behind me, near the large windows that lead out onto the balcony. With infinite care, I turn first my head then the rest of my body, to face the interloper.

Monk is half-hidden in shadow and his stillness is complete – I must have assumed he was a piece of furniture, or my senses have been overloaded; either way, I didn't know I wasn't alone until this moment.

There's no one else with him. Shock becomes rage, a match hitting gas. 'Where is she? What have you done with her? If you've hurt her...'

He holds his hands up. 'Steady there, Banks. No need to come at me like that.'

'You will fucking *tell* me!' I snap.

'Tell you what? What the hell are you talking about?'

Before I can answer Mariko comes clattering down the stairs in her underwear, trailing a silk dressing gown from her shoulders. She goes straight for him with a flurry of punches.

'Mariko, what the hell?' Monk tries to dodge, blocks a few, but a couple slip through and knock him back. He recovers, grabs her arms and picks her up, launching her into the air. She hits the couch and rolls onto the floor, but she recovers fast. I heft the whisky bottle, prepare to swing it at him.

'Wait!' he yells, his palms up. 'What have you been told?'

'You took hostages, faked a bombing at the EuroPar to do it. You took my Sara.'

He looks utterly confused – if he's pretending, it's impressive. 'I've been trying to get near the train, that's true. But I've not found a way; they threatened to shoot me, tried to grab me – some ungodly panic going on at the EuroPar. Were you there? I've not fucking *kidnapped* anyone.' He doesn't take his eyes off Mariko, who's still looking for an opportunity. 'I suppose this is all over the news?'

'It is. Are you saying it's not you?'

He looks me in the eye. 'I don't have your daughter. This is not me.'

'Can I believe that? The last thing I know, you were running out of here, shouting that the Prince was your long-lost lover.'

'No, I didn't.'

'I don't have time for this shit, Monk. Sara is lost in the city, and if you didn't do it, who the hell did?'

'I saw Sporus. I maintain that. But I didn't say anything about the Prince. Sporus was standing behind your peacock.'

Mariko straightens. She tilts her head to one side. 'Who?'

'The woman, tall one. She was standing just behind him when he walked out of the train.'

Oh God, am I even considering this?

Mariko turns to me. 'Have you ever heard of this Lady Margolis before?'

'I've not met her before but she's meant to have been close to the Prince for some time now.'

'How long?' asks Monk.

Jarvis mentioned it. Think. 'About two years.'

Monk holds his hand up. 'About the same time the whole of British foreign policy turned on its head?'

I'm damaged from the night, from the extraordinary pressures that have been placed upon me ever since I came to this city. I *have* to be cracking, bit by bit, because I'm actually seeing a connection. What swings it is Mariko's expression. She looks thoughtful.

'Whatever remains, however improbable. Isn't that what your Conan Doyle wrote?'

15

Mariko is on the phone for a while, speaking in rapid-fire Latin that sweeps into Italian and back again to someone on the other end. After a while, she puts it down and her expression is resigned.

'There's no way we can get near the EuroPar tonight. Teams are sweeping the building. You're a foreign diplomat and I don't have a good enough reason. Also, there's him.'

'I suppose I deserve that,' says Monk.

'So there's nothing we can do?'

'Nothing official.' She takes a breath. 'I have a friend; he teaches engineering at the university and he worked on the EuroPar some years ago. He… we were close once.'

On any other day, that would have bothered me. Not today. 'And?'

'You said we should look in the lower levels?' she asks Monk, then continues without waiting for an answer. 'Venting for the archaeological preserve. If no one has decided to seal that grate in the last five years, it could be a way in.'

It's a chance. A fool's chance, but I'll take it. We're heading for a sewer.

* * *

Romans are dogged in their determination to preserve the antiquity buried under them and that hasn't lapsed with the advent of the Confederacy. Yes, they've taken something that has been a half-collapsed but elegant ruin for over a thousand years and re-made it, clad it in modern materials and wired it like any other building, but therein lies the illusion. The erstwhile Colosseum is still there, ensconced within the walls of the EuroPar in protective plastics. Every stone is cocooned for prosperity after being thoroughly scanned and mapped and re-created in the memories of civil and academic servers. As above, so below: the passageways and cells that housed gladiators and beasts are still there beneath the modern floor of the chamber, preserved under armoured glass. Those passageways are where we'll find what we're looking for, according to Monk.

'It's where he did his ritual before. There's a power to that place, maybe even the one that drew me back. That's where your girl will be.'

He's back in control now, the wildness gone. He's the first into the tunnel mouth, hidden behind an ivy-strewn vented door on the side of a ramp, invisible as anything other than a charmingly unkempt part of the old city.

'This section of sewers has been decommissioned,' Mariko assures me. 'Paulo sent me a map – the vent grate is small but we should fit through.'

The light from the street outside barely makes a dent in the gloom and we're just a few steps in when the darkness takes over everything. I catch the last flash of light in Mariko's eyes, then she's just a shape in the dark. She doesn't need to do this, but she refuses to be left out. I'm glad she's here.

I just want to see my Sara again, and I'll follow even this illogical thread – it's not like there's anything better, so I'll take a little dose of the unlikely. I've acquired my own monomania:

I don't get lurches of fear anymore; my mind rubbed smooth by constant fear actually feels sharper than it has in months. Every crevice of every brick under my fingertips, as we grope the first few metres, feels like teeth. Then red light flares as Mariko activates her torch and we proceed downwards, into the belly of Rome.

A sewer will never stop being a sewer. This tunnel may well be thousands of years old and the ghost of past odours permeates the brick and rock down to its molecules and no amount of time or pressure washes will clear it. I think about how many generations of waste has passed over the now-dry stones I'm currently using as a path.

What the hell am I doing here? reverberates. I'm looking inwards when every police unit is looking out, scouring Rome. I think about the unlikely sense of what Monk says Sporus will do, to hide at the eye of the hurricane, and the slim chance, if he's right, of getting my Sara back. It's enough to keep my feet moving.

After about a mile the tunnel narrows to an oval that brushes the top of my head and forces Monk, who's in the lead, to stoop. We're single file now – Mariko's lamp is part-eclipsed and throws jagged shards of red light. I've a little night vision now and my mind drifts to an article I read years ago about how components of the eye that give us this ability still need a tiny amount of illumination to work – starlight, moonlight, and with those comes vision around the periphery only. Focus and clarity are daytime things; night-time is full of shifting shadows and is where our oldest stories come from, the ones about beasts in the dark, malevolence just out of sight that vanishes with the lighting of a torch. Age and logic have written over the fantasies of childhood but no matter how old I get there's still an unease about true pitch-blackness – fear of it is the response of the scared primate that we all are, deep down. Every grate or fork in the tunnel we pass, a little part of me is sure a clawed hand will snatch at my ankles, pulling me off to some grisly end. I wish I wasn't bringing up the rear, with all that blackness behind me.

I almost clatter into the others as Mariko stops. In the base of the wall is a thigh-high grating.

'You're sure?' Monk asks her and receives a nod in return.

Mariko shows us her wrist-screen, the ghost outline of the sewer system glowing, a single red mark showing our destination. 'This should be it. I've been counting the turnings.'

'You can't be sure, though?'

'This is a download. Too much rock above us for a signal. We'll find out soon enough if we're wrong.'

We take turns to squeeze through the opening, and this time I go first into the tomb-like crawlspace. I strike out into the blackness on my hands and knees. The instincts of ancestors trapped in caves a million years ago, gifted to me by my hindbrain, scream at me to *get out, get out* and I have to breathe hard against the panic, the thought of being wedged down here, the three of us unable to move back or forwards, wasting away as the world forgets about us. I fight to keep my composure and maintain my lizard crawl, hands and knees moving against the gritty concrete surface, stale water in my nostrils. Sara, ahead. Sara and open space.

It feels like miles but may have been only a dozen metres, but the end comes. Another opening, the grate mercifully hinging upwards with a soft creak, and there's air and space – not much more than the sewer we left behind but after that nightmare it feels like the Albert Hall. Even Monk looks flustered as he emerges and flops against the wall in a squat. He's the bigger man and it must have been worse for him.

'This is what those sorry bastards had to deal with in the mines.' He brushes dust out of his hair. 'Poor Pythagoras.'

It's not long before the tunnel we're in widens ever so slightly and the brickwork changes. It's old, thin layers of baked earth but kept behind a layer of transparent plastic. The place, if it's possible for such a thing, *feels* old. We're under the EuroPar now. No, under the Colosseum. The ultra-modern Rome above is a phantom next to the mass of ancient stone that surrounds us. The floor is dusty but clear of debris, the tell-tale of archaeology that has been, catalogued, preserved and moved on. We pass a series of openings, doorways to small rooms and I notice the rusty nubs that remain of hinges set into the stonework. I wonder how many have spent their last days in these cells, seeing hope flee and the certainty of death hove in on them, immutable.

'Not far now,' says Monk. He walks like a man moving through an old home, sure of his direction, though the memories are aged. We walk behind him, the red light of Mariko's torch bobbing, casting pale shadows.

Murmurs ahead. Not the sound of stealth, not a person whispering but someone speaking at normal volume at the end of a long tunnel. I look at Mariko, the question unspoken. She shakes her head; her eyes are hard. No one should be down here, especially with the lockdown in force. Confirmation, maybe.

Without anyone telling us to do so, we hunker down as we move. There's light ahead, a white glare that bounces off the walls, beckoning us forwards. Mariko switches off her light and we slow to a creep. Then it's there, fully formed like the place in Monk's story. The skin on my face feels tighter than a drum.

Like something out of a fever dream, the scene is laid out before me. A circular room like the bottom of a well, with two other passages like ours leading off. The floor is clear except for a series of posts set into the ground; in contrast to the antiquity of their surroundings, they look brand new and the dirt is freshly broken around their bases. There are people there. Six people. The air is close as a sauna and there's a smell on it, metallic and dangerous.

Blood. Oh God, there's blood.

A tall figure with long dark hair faces away from us, a casual knife dangling; it's red and dripping. Others are tied to the posts and two of them, a man and a woman, both grey-haired and dressed in modern formal suits, are dead already, throats slashed, leaning forwards against their bonds with red aprons of blood washing down their fronts. The figure with the knife is standing opposite a third, a man of middle years with a bald head and ring glasses. An affectation in a world of state-offered laser correction, the Confederacy's Minister of International Trade. The last time I saw him he'd been sitting the other side of a table as Easter blustered at him; he'd removed his glasses and made a show of cleaning them, methodically, before replying. Now he is shaking as if freezing, his breath coming in great gulps. He looks across at the two dead people and he dry-heaves.

The figure says something that's muffled by the gasps of the Minister. The bald man shakes his head, his eyes wild. Then there's a sound like curtains ripping and his neck gapes crimson; liquid hits stone, he chokes and grabs at his cut throat, panicked and futile as he tries to push it back together. His fingers slip on the wave of blood that pumps out; his eyes are plate-like, disbelieving. Then he goes still, and as he does so there's a feeling on the air like a cello the size of a mountain has been strummed. The room gets closer, the sense of mass crushing. Next to me, Monk grimaces as if feeling some of that pain.

Sara is there. My world is a tunnel of white, screaming noise.

She's bound to the post and she looks tired and afraid but I can see her gaze darting around and I know what she's thinking, can hear the thoughts in her head as clearly as my own. *Must be a way. Has to be a way out. I'll find something.* Even in this horror she's practical, focused, and my father's chest could burst even as terror grips tight. Between her and the dying man is the Co-President's son; he's no older than fifteen and his mouth is a rictus of terror. He's wet himself and he can do nothing other than shake.

She's so close, a headlong dash away from me. My legs are bunching, preparing to launch myself at her kidnapper because in this moment I'm nothing more than an animal with young under threat from a predator.

'Here we are again.' Monk steps forwards into the light of the room, putting himself between me and the knife. He speaks that smooth, round-vowelled Latin that is so unlike the norm.

Mariko puts her hand on my arm, restraining through suggestion. She's right, though the primate snarls at this interruption: I'd likely be killed in a headlong rush and at the very least another hostage would pay the price.

The man with the knife turns, eyes ringed with dark tint watch him with curiosity, perhaps a hint of a widening. I recognise Margolis, though there is no doubt that the shoulders are thicker and the posture is masculine.

'It really is you, boy. I knew it. The reports used another name, but I knew. The gods keep us together.'

'I'm here.'

'This must seem familiar to you. How long, for you, since we last met? A few weeks, maybe? I've been two years stuck in that mouldering ruin you call home.'

'You don't need to do this again. Just like last time, just

give it up. You're murdering real people to get back at ghosts.'

Margolis-Sporus smiles, a bitter little creasing of the mouth. 'Look at what they've become. I think I hurt them a little last time, though I didn't finish, but they've come back bigger and stronger and worse. Rome wants to swallow the damn world. I swore to break this damned cycle, and in my homeland we keep our oaths.'

Monk's hands are by his side and he stands easy but I see the tension in his calves. He's ready to move.

'You've brought others,' he says. Sara sees me and calls out, crying now.

'Get away from my daughter or I'll kill you,' I manage to choke out.

'You don't want this. The man I know didn't believe in blood for blood. It's not too late. I am *here*, Sporus.' Monk is easing closer. Sporus halts him by raising the knife.

'Five have to die, that is the ritual. I didn't want to bring the girl but there was no one else. I needed the boy.'

'She's no power broker, just someone's daughter. This man's daughter. You deserve revenge more than anyone I know but you cannot have it – the ones who wronged you are dust. These children are not to blame. Please, Sporus, a killer of children has no way back.'

Sporus' face flushes but his voice stays calm. 'It was about revenge, at first. You saw what they did to me.'

'I remember. I could do nothing but remember, all those years I thought you'd disappeared.'

'You saw me cut. You saw me weak, but you never saw the things those men did to me when I was in their power. A piece of freakish flesh to fuck, and not just soldiers or sailors; senators who hired me, rich men with stables full of body slaves. They knew me and they wanted to break me; they remembered when

Nero and I belonged to each other and I looked down on them.

'It was that, for many years. But as I got stronger and closer to what I sought, I saw the bigger problem – Rome is a cancer that spreads and spreads. It will sleep but it will always come back to consume more land, tradition, individuality. I knew the gods had a plan for me then, and that's where I got the strength to attain this dread power. I don't like it – I can feel its darkness burning in me – but I have purpose. This is the *right thing.*'

'It's not the same city. They're not the same people.'

'They will be, in time.' He closes his eyes. 'I wish I didn't have to bear it, boy, but I must do this. You say you dreamed of me – well I dreamed of you too. Of a life we could have had.' He smiles, and just for an instant I can see another face there, a gentle one.

Monk's forehead is sheened. 'I don't understand the strange things you do because they make no damn sense. But I do know slaughtering innocents can't be the right answer. I don't give a shit about destiny or purpose – I care about you. Never stopped. Give it up and we can have that life.'

'I've spent two years in this time. I don't know why I fell earlier than you, but I did. Those few words of English – do you remember teaching them to me? I was barely understood, but it was a start. I've had enough time to get to know the world and it is more broken than I ever thought it would be. The gods would have me put a corner of it right.'

'Hang your damned gods. They're imaginary and yet they still manage to shit on you. Can't we just take a corner for ourselves instead?'

There's a flicker in Sporus' eyes, Monk's words hitting home perhaps. He shakes his head as if clearing it. 'I'm so sorry for it to happen this way, boy. I wish you didn't have to be here, that you'd stayed in Ostia and had your life. This will end tonight and none of us can stop it. So much set in motion, nations moving. That bomb in the Residence set off a wildfire in Britain.'

Straight-backed men, soldiers out of uniform, talking to Easter moments before the end of the world. 'You sent the bombers,' I say. The new skin on my back itches.

He doesn't look at me or acknowledge my words, but I see his eyes as he looks at Monk. This was the pretext for it all, a false flag to bring him here where he could do the most damage.

'That idiot tried to kill you,' he says, and I know he means Easter's cack-handed, disproportionate attempt at retribution. 'It was an opportunity, but it gave me some satisfaction, keeping you safe.'

Monk's shoulders have tensed now. He's ready to spring.

Sporus' hands tighten on the knife and the children freeze in terror.

'Come at me, boy, and I'll fight, but there's no point. Those Navy men, they were so proud of their creation, as if that iron monstrosity was a great feat instead of a sad relic of a dying power. Even the Prince thought it would show the world how great Britain still was, still had innovation to offer, but see how sad and crude it looks. The fuse is already burning and, one way or another, the ground we're on will be scoured.'

Somewhere above us is the train. The details didn't interest me before, but now they're etched on my brain – the heart of an old nuclear submarine re-purposed to drive the tons and tons of metal on. Old tech, temperamental. It wouldn't take much. My hands go cold. I turn to Mariko and flick my eyes to her wrist communicator, begging her to somehow understand. She shakes her head. Too much earth.

Sporus presses the knife to the boy's neck. Sara's eyes are locked on mine. The room is a razor's edge, ruin on either side.

'I love you,' Monk says.

Sporus sighs, his eyes flutter closed. 'We never said that enough, did we?'

Monk moves like a thunderclap. Before Sporus' eyes are open he's closed half the distance. Sporus sees him and he's fast also; the knife twitches.

Monk manages to grab the wrist holding the blade just as it pricks the boy's neck and pulls it away. Sporus punches him twice but Monk traps the knife between their bodies. He hooks a leg, hauls his weight forwards and then they both hit the floor with a shock exhalation.

I run for the children as the two men roll, scrapping like cats.

'Dad!' Sara calls, and I want to hug her but I need to get her free, get her out of here before... oh God, if I'm right the centre of this city will be a crater.

Mariko and I manage to haul the posts out of the ground and slip the chains free. Sara grimaces from cramp in her legs, but she can move. I give her a quick squeeze because I might never get the chance again as Mariko gets the Co-President's boy to press hard on the red line on his neck. The boy is shaking as she pulls him to his feet.

Sporus pins Monk's shoulders. Monk flips his hips and gains the top. Fluid, he slips behind his opponent and holds him in place with his legs. His hands are on Sporus' head, and I see him whisper something in his ear.

A crack, like dry wood.

Sporus slumps.

Monk falls back. There's blood on his chest. He moans, low and deep, like a wind from the hills. I don't think I'll ever forget that mournful sound. The air is thicker than ever and my head is thumping, pressure spiking all around us. Mariko has the children by the tunnel entrance and is waving me over. I see the handle of the knife sticking from Monk's ribs and I don't know how bad it is and he yells at me to get the hell out of here.

'I can carry you. Come on, man!'

'She needs you. You have to try,' he says. 'Thank you, Banks.'

I dart another look – Mariko looks frantic. There is a dry pop and the pressure in the room bursts, a billowing gale from nowhere that rips at my clothes, making me shield my eyes.

When I open them, Monk is... gone. Where he and Sporus lay, there's only blood in the dust.

'Lindon!' It's Mariko. The train. We have to try to warn them. We run, holding the children by the hand, racing up through the excavations, hoping we're going the right way.

'The stone is too thick,' Mariko pants. 'There's no signal.'

'Keep trying.'

Ahead, a concrete ramp; a set of heavy double doors of modern make, light beyond it. I feel a pop in my shoulder as I ram it into them but I keep going; I bend the lock and it bursts, disgorging us onto the present day, carpet and air conditioning. There are armed police all around us, their faces surprised but their weapons raised and commands bark. Mariko screams into her communicator, at the men, trying to make them understand the danger and all I can think to do is drop to the floor, holding Sara close as the noise of helicraft thuds the sky outside. This is hell, milling boots and shouting. I don't know where Mariko is. The Co-President's boy is gone, rushed off by minders.

A roar grows from beyond the glass doors that rattles them in their frames, a monster whine that builds and builds. I finally find Mariko, standing there amid the chaos. I hold Sara to me, who has her mother's hair, hugging her close, feeling her shaking in my arms.

A flash from the end of the world jabs through the glass and turns the world white and the heat presses in and the sound of glass shattering is everywhere.

After

It's white and clear, from the walls to the chairs to the ceiling. Everything is pure white. It's hard, if you squint, to tell whether the space has boundaries at all.

There's a prod at my elbow.

'Dad, stop making weird faces,' Sara chides. 'She'll be here in a minute.'

I squeeze her hand and wonder when she grew up.

I've bought a new suit for today, light grey and with thin lapels, green silk lining. I went to the same shop where she took me the day she kissed me for the first time. It's easier now, something I do because I enjoy it and not out of necessity, and somehow it's no longer a thing of vanity. The shirt is soft and feels good against my skin and the jacket slides over it with ease, as if it isn't there at all. New shoes too, brogues (because once an Englishman, and all that).

The official clears his throat and I hear the side door open. This isn't like the first time – there is no aisle, no rows of stone-faced relatives. No vicar or talk of God, just a simple white room with the odd touch of ribbon and some flowers which we'll take away with us. Sara and I wait before the heavy baroque desk that dominates the room, bathed in light from floor-to-ceiling windows facing south. The sun is rising to its

321

zenith, and at this time of year that means the glow of it seeps into the room in gentle waves. One window is open to let the breeze in and there's a distant sound of traffic and birds. Out there, in the city, the green canopy-clouds of the stone pines are already casting their shadows on hot tarmac.

The door – a great dark wood portal that could hold off an army – swings open and she's there. I know this woman now – enough lazy mornings of mussed hair and sour breath, even some arguments (nothing big, the common friction-resolve cycle of two people inhabiting the same space). I've seen her drop tomato down her chin and not realise straight away. I've seen her dancing when she thought I wasn't watching. I've seen her drunk and sober, unkempt in the evening and beautiful in the morning.

But not this, nothing like this. This is Mariko refined, the distillation of her.

Her bodice is fitted and topped with lace, from her mother, and she carries a small bouquet of wildflowers. In deference to her father the straight skirt that extends to the floor is belted around her torso with a white *obi* sash. Her hair is pinned up in wings. Behind me, I hear Sara draw in a breath.

'She is *far* too good for you, Dad.'

'That she might be, Mouse.'

Mariko stands at my side with a solemnity I know is for show. She gives me a sideways look, then her lips crack in a smile and suddenly we're both laughing like idiots.

The official clears his throat to bring us back to the room. He speaks in Latin.

'Shall we begin?'

* * *

Afterwards, we take an auto-cab through the streets. If Sara's embarrassed by her father kissing his new wife she puts it aside for today, at least. There's still a little tension there: after all it's been just the two of us for years. Mariko understands the boundaries and makes the effort; Sara, I'm pleased to see, reciprocates, and I think it has something to do with this city. Rome is just too big, just too hot, too old for being insular. Any doubts she has (and she will, because her mother is still there for both of us) are being kept for another day. Mariko takes her hand and kisses her cheek. Sara wrinkles her nose but smiles a little. This little thing gives me a little lump in my throat, so I watch the city go by.

My city now. They've fast-tracked my dual citizenship because of what happened that night; the Co-President shook my hand and I was embarrassed because I felt like all I'd done was to go along with things, but she thanked me for my part in returning her son to her. The Ministry back in Britain hasn't put up any objections to my resignation or this unprecedented bi-patrimony, busy as it is with the fallout from the Margolis affair; new delegations are being prepared, diplomacy enduring. Small embassies even, soon.

In a few weeks I'll sit the papers Mariko forwarded me and become a member of the Confederacy with all the rights that entails, Sara receiving them by extension. Then there's only the small matter of finding something to do with the rest of my life. I look at Mariko, pointing out to her new stepdaughter a set of ruins colonised by local cats and remember that we already have the beginnings of a plan.

The auto-cab stops near the *Ponte Sant'Angelo*. Hadrian's tomb squats on the other side with its cake-like crown, which is fitting today, I suppose. The narrow street is just as crammed with bikes as it was that night and I find myself thinking of

Winston Monk, as I often do; I still find it hard to reconcile his extraordinary life with reality and that last moment sticks in my mind: the sudden emptiness where a second ago he'd been, like a light flicking off.

Then that damned train. That titanic release of energies as the reactor blew. Dirty radiation, sheer concussive force in a sphere of pure death. I thank any god that'll listen for two things: that the Euros didn't trust us, and that Sporus – a man out of time – had underestimated them.

'My department head debriefed me today,' Mariko had told me as we recuperated. 'There were forcefield generators under the wheels of the train from the first day. There is no way they would have allowed even a modern, safe fission device near a populated area without precautions.' I remembered those engineers shoring up the wheels and wondered why I hadn't thought about this sooner – I had seen this technology before, after all. If only that thought had hit me when I'd been cowering on the floor with Sara.

The piazza is still scorched and there are trace contaminants in the air, but it's nothing to the devastation that would have been if left unchecked. It's a sad boon that only those on the train and the three poor souls Sporus killed himself were lost. God, it could have been so much worse. As I think it, Sara stoops to help Mariko with her dress.

Monk: gone. My friend, who I'd doubted in those last hours, but without whom I wouldn't have my Sara. All that we found in that charnel house of a chamber was a stain on the floor. It's a mark of the strangeness of this whole affair that a man vanishing before my eyes is not the oddest thing I've seen recently. I don't know how and I doubt I ever will, but all I know is that the air was soaked with power, and then it wasn't and both he and Sporus were no more. The police found the knife and traced it back to Margolis – there was a manhunt that uncovered nothing. Cold comfort for the families of the dead in that unholy ritual and the pain of it still marks us; Sara's bravery astounds me, but I worry what seeing those things has done to her.

I think about my friend now and then and when I do I raise a toast, at least in my head. Foul-mouthed, eloquent; mercurial, assured. Contradictions and absurdities, but a brother. I hope he lived somehow, and wherever he is he has a measure of the peace he deserves.

Enough gloom. I have a bride waiting who shows no inclination of changing out of her dress into something more manageable and instead steps into the vaulted little restaurant where we first had dinner a lifetime ago, leading me by the hand. The old man greets us like friends and ushers us to a curtained-off area at the back where a simple table for three has been set on white linen. Two carafes wait for us, one red, one white. I leave a light kiss on Mariko's lips.

Food follows, until the very notion of courses is lost to the winds. I let Sara have a little wine (though Mariko has to drag it out of me). They've already begun to conspire, which makes me glad and uneasy at the same time.

'We have something to tell you,' I say to Sara as the ice cream comes.

Sara looks at me, then Mariko, then takes some of her dessert and contemplates it before spooning it, upside down, into her mouth. 'Are you having a baby?'

'What? No!'

'I'd be OK with that. It's fine. It's gross, but I get it.'

'No, something else. No babies.'

Mariko takes my hand and cuts in. 'You've been asking what we're going to do after the wedding. Something has come up, an opportunity.'

'I thought you had to get your citizenship.'

'I will,' I answer. 'In a few weeks. But after that, we might take a trip.'

'A long trip?'

'Yes, maybe a couple of years.' Mariko smiles. 'I've been appointed to lead a team to establish an embassy in Osaka.'

Sara pushes the ice cream away. 'That's the other side of the world! Is it even safe?'

'Safe enough. It's a great honour.'

'And what am I supposed to do?'

'Well,' I say, 'they have some wonderful mountains there. And as Mariko will be so busy, I'd have a lot of time to explore. But I'd need someone to come with me, just to be sensible.'

'Always walk uncertain hills with trusted companions.' Mariko snorts at herself. 'I'm sorry, the wine…'

'Are you telling me to come with you? To Japan?'

'Asking. You'll still have your schooling, you'd just be doing it with me. When we're not off doing other things.'

Sara gives me a long look. Then she eats a little more ice cream.

'That could be fun,' she says.

And then...

The bars are packed because of the cruise ship wallowing in the sea-flooded caldera, mingling with the other tourists and doubling the island's population. They'll drink and dance and eat and, likely, fuck when they get back to their overnight hotels or take the long, winding path down to the shore from where Fira clings to the cliffs and hop onto a launch back to their iron monsters. Middle-aged couples flirt like teenagers, getting a second wind from the island's natural energy – this lone dot in the Mediterranean, cut off from the world and its rules. The boys in their twenties wear t-shirts that show off their arms. They preen, laugh too loud and try to impress the girls in short skirts who pretend not to care but still shoot their meaningful glances. This little dance has been going on for millennia and won't stop any time soon. Sometimes, if I watch long enough, I'll see girls look at girls and boys look at boys, the eddy within the same flow that is as powerful, if subtler. It's a tolerant age so there's no furtive exit or clandestine meeting under bridges or in back alleys; couples walk off hand in hand to the hollering and jeering of their mates who are looking for just the same thing.

Gods, it's so much easier these days, no matter what your flavour. I feel like an old bastard. I am an old bastard.

I keep just far enough from the main fray. The bar is called Luca's and it's open to the air, perched on the rooftops of the level below and accessed by a steep flight of whitewashed steps that hug the cliff. I've picked a table that sits out on a promontory, away from the main bar, and I've got the space all to myself. I'm on my third Old Fashioned – they make them strong and quick here, just how I like it. Luca, the owner, knows me and doesn't make a song about it; just gives me my usual table when I turn up and lets me hold my own company for the evening. I pay my bills so we get on just fine. He reminds me of Herakles, but that's probably the drink or wishful thinking.

Either side of me Fira dazzles with its constellation of lights. Below the sea is dark and deep and eternal and the sound of the surf is just about audible when the shouting dies down. They use good scotch here, single malt, and the fire is balanced, just so, with sugar and the bitterness of Angostura. The only thing Father and I ever agreed on, this drink. I sit on my high perch over the waves and I think about friends I left behind.

It's gone one in the morning when I haul myself away from Luca's, away from Fira, leaving the firefly colony to carry on with its revels. I'm alone on the clifftop path that takes me in an undulating route past the infinity pools of exclusive apartments, then up a scrub-dotted hill. I slip on the shingle once or twice and call the land a fucker – though we both know I don't mean it. On the other side of the hill the path plunges down, past a little white Orthodox church which will be open even at this hour, but I leave it alone. I want my bed, as narrow and hard as it is.

Six months since I came here. Just like that, out of thin air – one moment I'm holding him in my hands, murdered, in the catacombs under the arena, then we're both here. My wound looked worse than it was but I had to be careful of my self-applied stitches for a while and infection was always a worry – thank the gods for old bottles of Raki left wrapped in sheets. I healed fast, as I've always done, and there's something about the air on this island.

My Sporus, as he was when we came here. Something he did – his last breath perhaps – brought us back to his home. Santorini, Thera, whatever it's been called down the centuries; it was the home of his people, where he claimed the nexus of his power lay. I don't know. Maybe, as he died, he just thought of home. That's a powerful pull.

Off the main path, which by now is good enough for single file only, branches a twisting goat track. I take it slowly because there's a hell of a drop to the bottom of the cliff and I doubt they'd ever find my body. The track doubles back as it descends and winds towards a little farmhouse. This is where we ended up and this is where I stay. The roof is solid, the windows are mostly intact and no one has come to kick me out, so I'll make my home here for as long as I can. There are baby tomatoes on the vines at the back, soaking up the Mediterranean sun, and these I sell in Fira and Oia to restaurants; it pays enough to keep me in bread and wine and the occasional night at Luca's.

As I open the front door, I turn as I always do and check the mouth of the little cave. It's set into the cliff beyond my little horticultural nook, and that's where I laid him to rest. I check him sometimes, worried he'll start to rot and I'll have to throw him in the sea, but he never does, though he's as cold as the day I killed him.

'You're a bloody fool,' I tell myself for the thousandth time.

All those years waiting, watching, hoping for him to come back. Then the scrub-wash of time, leaving him an old pain that flared on bad days. All of that, only to be the instrument of his removal in the end. Any gods that there might be are laughing at me, the sick fucks. Hope is a bastard that lives in my heart and refuses to die. Maybe it's the orange-tinged scotch, or the endless sea, or the crystalline light that fills the air in this part of the world, but I wait every day for… something.

My bed is cold and rickety but I'm drunk enough so I sleep.

Sun slants in through the cracks in the shutters. Motes dance, oblivious. He holds me, warm and yielding; arms encircle me and I feel him pressing into my back, his breath on my cheek and his hair tickling my ears, but I don't mind. In a moment, the dream will pass and I'll be alone again with my hangover. I'll dig my fingers into the earth of this island, tend to my tomatoes. I'll read and I'll eat bread and butter and I'll smoke while I watch the sea. He's in this land, in this air – it birthed him and can never be rid of him. So I'll stay.

'It's morning, boy. Wake up.'

It's a real shit, my memory, this mind. These little tricks it plays. It sounds just like him and I know I'm one leg still in the dream because I feel the words buffet my skin.

'The gods have it in for me,' I say, aloud.

'Fuck the gods.'

'I wish you were real,' I say because I'm fucking sentimental like that when no one's around to see.

'Wake up, boy,' he says again. 'I'm done sleeping.'

I turn in his arms, face him. The heat of his skin, the air of his breath. His smile is a pale crescent in the half-light. I'm afraid. I'm elated.

A little smile. 'I'm sorry I hurt you, boy. I'm sorry I made you hurt me.'

I can't say a word so I hold him, fierce, wanting to push his essence under my skin where it will stay forever. I hope so damn hard. He's there, in my arms, every fibre of him.

Real. Impossible. Mine.

A word about making things up...

There's some Serious History out there. It has evidence and method and rigour. It doesn't make leaps of imagination and sometimes gets snotty with those who do. But for every fully fleshed-out, three-dimensional figure creaking under all the corroborating evidence, there are a hundred who are just mentioned in passing, often not given a lot of fair treatment. That's where people with active imaginations can have *fun*.

There was a man called Sporus. He crops up in Suetonius and Dio Cassius and they can't even agree if he was a slave or a freedman. The consensus is that he was good-looking, young, and that Nero took him to bed. He may or may not have castrated him, but he certainly married him and called him his Empress. The part about him resembling the wife Nero lost (or murdered) is another common theme. This low-born boy appears to have had some measure of power – that must have pissed a few people off. Before he fades out of the sources, he is linked to two emperors and one prefect with delusions of grandeur: Sporus, it seems, didn't need magic to get ahead.

Other than the castration by Nero and the supernatural elements, Sporus is presented here as fully as the scant sources will allow. My other deviation was to have Nero take his own life: another companion, Epaphroditos, is meant to have helped him.

Facts are important, but humans love a good story and it's in the service of that impulse that I've taken certain liberties. In doing that, I'm in good company – Suetonius had river gods and we're still reading him centuries later.

Smart boy.

Acknowledgements

My deepest thanks go to:

Catherine Cho, my agent and all-round impressive human being;

Cat Camacho and Davi Lancett at Titan for going above and beyond in turning a series of half-baked ideas into an actual book, damn good cake and even better advice;

All the hard-working, cheery folk at Titan Books;

My writing coterie – Tim Aldred and Katie Wakefield for the notes and fine gins;

Ed Hunt and Linda Lyne, who taught me Classics with the passion it deserves;

R. Goscinny and A. Uderzo and the indomitable heroes they created – the wellspring of a lifelong obsession;

My family, for putting up with the rollercoaster with love;

Rome and all who sail in her.

About the author

Patrick Edwards lives in Bristol, U.K. with his family and has never grown out of his fascination with the future. Born in 1982, he spent his childhood in France, India and Indonesia. He studied French at Bristol University, which included a year in a garret studio in Paris writing moody stories and watching films when he really should have been working. In 2014 he decided to take writing seriously and graduated a year later from Bath Spa University's Creative Writing MA. His first novel, *Ruin's Wake*, was published in 2019.

For more fantastic fiction, author events,
exclusive excerpts, competitions, limited editions and more

VISIT OUR WEBSITE
titanbooks.com

LIKE US ON FACEBOOK
facebook.com/titanbooks

FOLLOW US ON TWITTER AND INSTAGRAM
@TitanBooks

EMAIL US
readerfeedback@titanemail.com